Studies in Translation

Studies in Translation

Second Revised and Enlarged Edition

Edited by

Mohit K. Ray

ATLANTIC

PUBLISHERS & DISTRIBUTORS (P) LTD

Published by

ATLANTIC

PUBLISHERS & DISTRIBUTORS (P) LTD

7/22, Ansari Road, Darya Ganj,
New Delhi-110002
Phones : +91-11-40775252, 23273880, 23275880, 23280451
Fax : +91-11-23285873
Web : www.atlanticbooks.com
E-mail : orders@atlanticbooks.com

Branch Office
5, Nallathambi Street, Wallajah Road,
Chennai-600002
Phones : +91-44-64611085, 32413319
E-mail : chennai@atlanticbooks com .

Printed in India at Nice Printing Press, A-33/3A, Site-IV, Industrial Area, Sahibabad, Ghaziabad, U.P.

Preface

It is a pleasure to place in the hands of our readers the revised and enlarged second edition of *Studies in Translation* originally published in 2002.

Over the years, Translation Studies has developed into an independent discipline known as Translatology. It now constitutes an important component of Comparative Literature, Applied Linguistics and Culture Studies, though each department of knowledge looks at the act of translation from the parameters of its own discipline.

Now about conventional attitude to translation. In *A Midsummer Night's Dream* when Quince says, "Bless thee Bottom, bless thee, thou art translated," Bottom sharply reacts: "I see the knavery, this is to make an ass of me." The reaction of Bottom, in a way, sums up the popular attitude to the translator, that the translator is a traitor – *traduttore – traditore* (translator—traitor). Another way of saying this is that every version—and translation is a translated version of a source language text—is a subversion if not perversion. The same view is expressed by Anatole France: *Il y a de belles traductions, peut-être; il n'y en a pas de fidèles* (There are perhaps some good translations, there aren't many faithful ones), and this takes us back to two opposing views about translation: fidelity versus freedom, whether the translations should be as faithful to the original, as literal as possible, or should be free in its attempt to convey the *spirit* of the original and not the *letter*. To this second group the spirit or the sense of the source text is more important than the body of the text. In other words, the translator *must be* traitor to be loyal. He must be a traitor to the *letter* in order to be loyal to the *spirit* of the text, because the soul is more important than the body.

While it is true that translation should be as literal as possible when one is translating a scientific treatise or a legal document, it is really debatable whether in literary translation one can really demand absolute fidelity. Paradoxically, one who can judge the quality of a translation does not really need a translation, and those who need a translation would naturally be interested more in the enjoyment of a literary work than in a dull, though faithful, rendering of the source text. Keats could be ecstatic about his experience of first looking into Chapman's Homer in spite of the fact that he could not read Greek, while Coleridge and Arnold who knew Greek very well admired Chapman's Homer but considered it "unHomeric".

Furthermore, a literary translation, like all acts of writing, can never be a predictable and repeatable exercise. It is as much a craft as it is a creation; as much an art as it is a science, because words are the most difficult things to control, and every writer has the experience of the bewildering willfulness of words which always tend to wander off into obscurity and ambiguity. Incidentally, the word "error" in its Latin root *errare* has the ambiguity of error and freedom. To err is to be free. Fortunately, in this age of emphasis on reader-reception, when the reader has returned with a vengeance as the co-author, the critical climate is eminently congenial to the translator for an exercise of his freedom. Every act of reading is, in a profound sense, an act of translation and literary translation involves an interpretative retranslation of the source text.

Even if we accept the conservative view that recommends strict fidelity of the translation to the source text the fact remains, nevertheless, that on account of linguistic and cultural differences, and not infrequently, difference of historical periods (when one is translating an ancient text), the translation is never equal to the source text; it is always equal to a subtext of the source text. The problem becomes more serious and complicated in case of poetry. Poetry, we know, is notoriously untranslatable. While the semantic content of a poem can be translated into another language, its sonic content can never be transferred.

Every poem has a definite sound pattern and in good poems the sound pattern is integral to the poem. It is not decorative; it is functional. It contributes to and reinforces the *poieisis* of a poem, because a good poem is always an organic whole in which the music and the meaning, the sound and the sense, the images and the metaphors, in fact, all the poetic elements, are inextricably interlinked. To change the sound pattern is to mutilate the poem. Even if we try to replace one sound pattern by a closely similar or parallel sound pattern in the target language, it would be, in the words of Benedetto Croce, a matter of "faithless beauty". Moreover, we can reasonably pose the question whether the poetry of a poem can really be separated from the poem. Can the dance be separated from the dancer? The ontology of a poem defies any dichotomy between form and content, for what is communicated is the poem itself.

Despite these limitations, translation is practiced all over the world. It has a definite practical use. There is, of course, the politics of translation. The most translated text, it is believed, is the Bible, and the history of translation in the West is said to have begun with the *Septuagint*—the first translation of the Hebrew Old Testament into Greek done for the benefit of the Jewish communities in Egypt who could no longer read the original. The Romans translated the Greek masters to improve their own language and literature. The colonizers translated some ideologically selected texts for the advancement of cultural imperialism. On the other hand, the colonized also translated the literature of the colonizers to improve their own literature. After the spread of English education in India in the mid-nineteenth century, the Editor of a leading Bengali periodical, *Sambād Prabhākar*, exhorted the poets and translators to translate English poems into Bengali for revitalizing and enriching Bengali literature. Most colonial literatures developed, in fact, through Western influence received through translation. Needless to say, it is translation that has made the literary heritage of human civilization accessible to every part of the world. It is not possible for anybody to learn all the languages of the world, and, but for translation we would never have got a Seneca or a Shakespeare, a Goethe or a Tagore. We should, however, always bear in mind that what we get in translation is not the real substance but a pale shadow or a faint echo of the original text, which can give only a rough idea of what the source text is like.

Now we come back to the translation of poems. More than three centuries ago, in his translation of Virgil's *The Destruction of Troy* (1658), Sir John Denham insisted that the translator's business was not just to "translate Language into Language, but Poesie into Poesie", and he further warned that:

> Poesie is of so subtle a spirit, that in pouring out of one Language into another, it will evaporate, and if a new spirit be not added in the transfusion, there will remain nothing but a *caput mortum*, there being certain Graces and Happinesses peculiar to every Language, which give life energy to the words.

Imagination must seize upon these "Graces and Happinesses" to make the translation an artifact. Shifting shapes, changing identities and renewed inwardness would, then transform the original poem into a new identity. As poet-translator Denham placed his finger at the right point. A poem is a concrete thing; poetry is abstract. It is created by the esemplastic power of the imagination and cannot be easily captured. Except in very best translation it eludes the grasp and we are left with a corpse in place of an organic whole. As a sensitive poet and a practicing translator Shelley also realized that "it were as wise to cast a violet into a crucible that you might discover the formal principle of its colour and odour as to transfuse from one language to another the creations of a poet."

Since a poem is both a cognitive discourse and an aesthetic object, poets are possibly the best translators of poetry. Since the language of a poem is emotive and ambiguous and often exploits several levels of meaning, only a highly sensitive poet can have access to the *sanctum sanctorum* of a poet and is expected not to translate a poem mechanically. Shelley translated quite a number of Greek, Spanish and German poems into English. In our times Eliot translated poems of St. John Perse into English who in his turn translated poems of Eliot into

French. Many major poets have done extensive translation—Mandelstam, Pasternak, Rilke, Pound, Lowell and Paul Valéry, for example—and their translations have enriched their languages. In Bengal, Buddhadev Bose, an eminent poet, translated the poems of Baudelaire into Bengali, and Sudhindranath Datta, another Bengali poet, translated poems of Valéry and Shakespeare. Tagore's translations of his own poems, from Bengali into English, are more transcreations or reincarnations than translation in the general sense. Tagore admired the translations of Satyendranath Datta, a Bengali poet, and described them as "reincarnations". In Europe, Rilke had a similar perception. In a letter to Lou Andrea Salomé, Rilke mused: "A few times I even set myself the same theme in French and German, which then, to my surprise, developed differently from each language: which would speak strongly against the naturalness of translation. He preferred the word "transubstantiation" to translation. This again reminds us of Shelley's dictum: "The plant must spring again from the seed, or it will bear no flower".

Translation was never considered a serious intellectual activity until the seventeenth century although there were some insightful observations on the business of translation from time to time. It was only from the seventeenth century onwards that the critics and particularly the poet-critics started looking more closely into the nature of the translation of poetry, and it was only since the 1970s that Translation Studies or Translation developed into an independent discipline leading to the establishment of full-fledged departments in various universities.

• • •

This anthology of as many as twenty essays (including the Appendix) addresses different aspects of translation and offers brilliant and illuminating insights into various problems involved in the act of translation.

Suka Joshua reaffirms that the history of translation can be broadly divided into four stages—immediate empirical focus, hermeneutic methodology of approach, structural linguistics and communication theory, and finally a reversion to hermeneutic enquiries into translation. Joshua also evaluates the contribution of J.C. Catford, Etienne Dolet, Eugène A. Nida and Newmark and thinks that a good translator must have an original genius to re-write a text in the target language.

Mallikarjun Patil highlights the importance of, and the difficulties involved in, translation. He also makes an important point that adaptation is "still another mode of translation".

R. Shanti warns that translation is not just an imitation of a text, and insists that it is a "creative process in itself". Shanti examines different definitions of translation and agrees with Rushdie that though much is lost in translation "the gain is always more than the loss".

K. Krishnamurthy examines the different views on translation as an art, a craft and a science and highlights the importance of translation by comparing it to the Promethean fire the light of which has revealed the hidden treasures of the world.

The essay of Umashankar Joshi, the recipient of the Jnanpith Award and former President of Sahitya Akademi, may be considered as what Eliot described as "workshop criticism", a craftsman talking about his craft. The essay originally written in Gujarati and translated into English by Professor Avadhesh Kumar Singh calls attention to the practical problems of translating poetry with special reference to Gujarati as the target language, and makes a distinction between *bhāṣāntar* and *anuvād* to explain the "process of appropriating the text to one's own language".

Starting with the basic premise that translation is "both linguistic and cultural activity and it is concerned with communication," Bijay Kumar Das makes an elaborate and in-depth study with many illustrations of the practical problems involved in the art of translation. In course of his luminous discussion he also points out the problems of translating jokes of different kinds.

K. Ayappa Paniker calls attention to the anxiety of authenticity from which a conscientious translator suffers. He substantiates his views with many examples from Malyalam and in the process also shares with the reader his own experience as a translator.

Harish Trivedi in his brilliant analysis of the postcolonial situation in translation and politics involved in it argues that "colonial or postcolonial is a diachronic marker, and it is at the same time an act of ideological or political faith." Translation is often governed by SL-TL power relationship as is evident from Fitzgerald's translation on the one hand and Tagore's translations of his own writings on the other. For translating Indian literatures into international languages the only international language used is English, and Trivedi holds that "the English language has thus become the clearing house for various Indian literatures in India", and "the big dream cherished by nearly all writers in Indian languages [...] is that one day they will be translated into English and will burst upon the international scene in a blaze of global glory". Trivedi also feels that translations of world literature into the Indian languages is not necessary at all because the target readers are supposed to have already read the works in the original. The ultimate question that we must face is "where to situate our literary culture vis-à-vis the postcolonial global configuration" and interestingly, the so-called postcolonial "is nearly also neocolonial, and especially when it masquerades as decolonization".

Basudeb Chakraborty tries to explain the nature of the translation process on the basis of a comparative study of an SL text and its translation in the TL text. He believes that a good translation shows "a spontaneous and creative process of journey of a theme and a meta theme from one linguistic framework to another". Chakraborty illustrates with diagram how the structural and grammatical aspects of the SL text are taken care of in translation. However, since it is not possible "to find out a substitute" for the syntactic pattern of the SL text for TL text all that the translator can finally do is "to carry the meaning of the SL text to the TL text".

Anjana Tiwari discusses with illustrative references different kinds of translation and comes to the conclusion that in the Indian context "translation is the only process by which we bridge the gap between different dialects, languages and cultures".

Rama Kundu critically analyses translations of two poems—one of Subhas Mukhopadhyay and another of Nirendranath Chakravorty—to illustrate what good translations should be like.

Sunil R. Sawant in his well-researched paper makes a review of the European approaches to translation criticism as evinced in the writings of J.C. Catford, Eugène Nida, Peter Newmark, Juliane House, Mary Snell-Hornby, Hans J.Vermeer, Itamar Evan Zohar, Raymond van den Broeck and Jahagirdar, among others and then lists six categories which "determine the position and function of a TT or a group of TTs in the TL culture". The approach Sawant recommends is chiefly meant for "analyzing and evaluating a number of TTs comprising a subsystem, a tradition in the target culture over a definite period of time".

In another well-researched paper Sunil Sawant makes an insightful historical study of the translation activities in Marathi and evolution in the norms of translation that underwent significant changes in the hands of Candy. Sawant also calls attention to the contributions made by Marathi scholars like Gopal Ganesh Agarkar, Vishnushastri Chiplunkar, and others.

My essay calls attention to the insightful and illuminating observations of Dryden, a practicing translator, on the problems of translation and holds that these observations deserve a more serious critical attention than they have received so far.

Prasenjit Chattopadhyay evaluates Arnold's contribution to translation studies and contends that Arnold was "probably the first man in the era of late nineteenth century to dedicate a substantial body of work to the theories of translation" and shows how Arnold anticipates many modern theories of translation.

Subhas Sarkar critically examines the translations of Tagore, first by Tagore himself and then by others. Sarkar starts with Tagore's own translation of *Gitāñjali* and refers to the inadequacies originally pointed out by Buddhadeb Bose. Sarkar then cites examples from other translations of Tagore to substantiate his view that Tagore as an author-translator often took too much liberty so that the translations became mere revisions and recreations rather than real translations. Furthermore, he was so much hurried by the publisher and was obliged to translate the poems at such wicked speed that the fine resonances of the original poems are sometimes lost in the translations. At times, Sarkar contends, he appeared to be "more a purveyor of his merchandise to customers of other lands" than a serious translator. Comparatively recent translators of Tagore, however, have done a good job. In the translation of Radice, for example, despite his "ignorance of certain nuances of the Bengali language [...] there is a considerable honesty and fidelity to the original in his works".

Niranjan Mohanty, an eminent Indian English poet and critic, does a serious "workshop criticism" in his perceptive observations of the art/science of translation. Based on his experience and expertise he prescribes certain "identifiable parameters", the knowledge of which can enable the translator "to comprehend in greater details the diverse facets of the would-be translated text". In course of his discussion he refers to many translation theories, and seems to subscribe to the view that the best test of a translation is that it should not read like a translation. Incidentally, this is a view that was voiced long ago by no less a person than Matthew Arnold in one of his Oxford Lectures, "On Translating Homer", an essay which constitutes the Appendix to this volume. Mohanty, however, hastens to add that "no fixed paradigm, perhaps, can measure the quality of translation". The author sincerely believes that a translator is "a veritable aesthetic" and that a translator is "no less than a creative writer".

Bijay Kumar Das, in his essay "Limits of Translation" holds that the aim of the translator is to produce a text "which can stand in relation of equivalence to another text" and calls attention to some of the linguistic problems such as phonological, morphological and syntactic, and some cultural problems such as ethnic, historical and sociological, which appear insurmountable. He recommends moderation and believes that "translation done within the limits of translating an original writing becomes successful".

Rama Kundu in "Perspectives on Translation: Down the Centuries" makes a short, succinct and masterly survey of the views on translation propounded down the centuries by great thinkers. The survey, which is as useful as it is fascinating, reveals the myriad faceted nature of translation as an intellectual activity.

Arnold's "On Translating Homer" is included as Appendix to this volume for its remarkable contemporaneity. Arnold examines four major translations of Homer and finds them wanting. He writes: "Homer is rapid in his movement, Homer is plain in his words and style, Homer is simple in his ideas, Homer is noble in his manner. Cowper renders him ill because he is slow in his movement, and elaborate in his style; Pope renders him ill because he is artificial both in his style and in his words; Chapman renders him ill because he is fantastic in his ideas; Mr. Newman renders him ill because he is odd in his words and ignoble in his manner." Arnold goes on to substantiate his views. Though the lecture is primarily "a disdainful reaction against the Teutonized or Saxonized translation by Francis William Newman" (Wimsatt and Brooks) it contains innumerable illuminating comments that Arnold makes on different aspects of translation in course of the lecture.

I thank all the contributors for their scholarly papers. I am grateful to my colleague, Professor Rama Kundu for her assistance in readying this volume. My special thanks go to Dr. K.R. Gupta, Chairman, M/s Atlantic Publishers and Distributors (P) Ltd., New Delhi, for the confidence evinced in me as also for seeing the book through the press.

Mohit K. Ray

Contents

Translation: Its Brief History and Theory

1

SUKA JOSHUA

The history of translation is the history of literary innovation and the theory of translation is as old as the tower of Babel says, Willis Barnstone and he considers the act of translation as the other Babel. There was a time when literary translation was considered as a secondary activity, mechanical rather than creative and not worthy of serious critical attention or general interest to the public. But during the recent decades the literary translation has been drawing great public and academic interest.

History of Translation

The history of translation was divided into four periods by George Steiner. The first period which is characterised by the immediate empirical focus extends from the Roman translators Cicero and Horace to Alexander Fraser Tytler. The second period extends upto Valéry. This period is characterised by hermeneutic methodology of approach. The third period is characterised as a period in which structural linguistics and communication theory were introduced into the study of translation. The fourth period begins in the early 1960's and is characterised by a reversion to hermeneutic inquiries into translation.

Till the early 1960's, until Paul Engle, Director of the Writers' Workshop at the University of Iowa, took the initiative to encourage translators by offering academic credit for literary translations, there was no translation centres or associations of literary translators. Engle's efforts were rewarded and the growth and acceptance of literary translations increased in the seventies. In spite of the progress of translation works, negative assumptions about translations still continued. But the emergence of new theories of translation helped to establish new educational techniques that led to a perfect understanding of translation.

Though translation was considered as a secondary work, serious traces of translation could be seen right from 3000 B.C. The most ancient translated work is that of Rosetta Stone of second century B.C. Then came Livius Andronicus of 240 B.C. who translated Homer's *Odyssey* into Latin. Scholars like Quintilian, Cicero, Horace, Catallus and Younger Pliny gave serious attention to the problems of translation and produced different theories. Of those, Cicero and Horace greatly influenced the later generation of translators. It is they who initiated the distinction between 'word for word' and 'sense for sense' translation, which retains its significance till now.

The process of translation gained form and order through the rendering of the *Bible*. The Hebrew Old Testament was translated into Greek before the Christian era. Translation acquired further significance with the emergence of Christian missionaries. The New Testament was translated into a number of languages. Unlike the earlier Old Testament translators, St. Jerome rendered sense for sense translation of the New Testament. John Wycliffe and William Tyndale are also important Bible translators of the 14th and 16th centuries respectively. Translation was promoted greatly by the Arabs during the eighth, ninth and tenth centuries. They translated many books on algebra, geometry, medicine, music and logic from Sanskrit into Arabic. It was during this period that the works of Aristotle, Plato, Galen and Hippocrates were translated into Arabic.

After the Norman conquest of 1060, till Chaucer, English was only used as a debased language only fit for translations. English literature was revived during the fifteenth century. But it also gave birth to a crowd of important translations. William Caxton, better known as the inventor of the printing press, was also a prolific translator.

The sixteenth century is marked by a serious theory of translation. Etienne Dolet was the first to formulate a theory of translation which advocated sense for sense translation. George Chapman, who translated Homer followed Dolet's theory, and reached the spirit of the original in his translation. Contemporary idiom and style were used to add immediacy. Martin Luther was the most influential figure in the field of translation during the 16th century. He laid the foundation for modern English usage in translation. Translation gained importance in the Renaissance Europe. It was no more considered as cheap imitation or as secondary activity.

The seventeenth century is the great age of French classicism. Translation of the French classics increased greatly in France between 1625 and 1660 and the French writers were in turn enthusiastically translated into English. Sir John Denham in his theory stated that the translator and the original writer are equals differentiated only by the social and temporal contexts. Abraham Cowley in his 'Preface' to *Pindarique Odes* argued for freedom in translation and established imitation as a branch of translation. John Dryden devoted most of his last twenty years to translate the ancient classics and update the modern. His preface to Ovid's *Epistles* served as the starting point for nearly every discussion of translation in the Eighteenth century.

The prevalent impulse of the eighteenth century was to clarify the spirit or sense of the text to the readers. As a result, many translated works were rewritten to fit the contemporary standards of language and taste. Samuel Johnson, George Campbell and Alexander Fraser Tytler were some of the eminent stars of this period. According to them, a translator should have the contemporary reader in mind while translating and should convey the author's spirit and manner in a more natural way.

The field of translation flourished with strange theories during the nineteenth century. Shelley was cynical towards translation and Coleridge tried to distinguish between fancy and imagination. Friedrich Schleiermacher suggested a separate sub-language to be used for translation and Dante Gabriel Rossetti proposed that the translation should show faithfulness to the forms and language of the original.

The Victorian translators gave importance to literalness, archaism and formalism. Unlike Dryden and Pope, Victorians wanted to convey the remoteness of the original in time and place. Matthew Arnold for example, gave a literal translation of Homer into English and was criticized for neglecting the spirit of the original work. The Revised and American Standard Versions of the *Bible* best illustrate the harmful effects of a literalistic Victorian translation.

The development of communication theory, the expansion of the field of structural linguistics and the application of linguistics to the study of translation effected significant changes in the principles and theory of translation during the twentieth century. Good Literature written in any part of the world in any language is now made available to the rest of the world through translation. Tagore translated his *Gitanjali* originally written in Bengali into English which won the Nobel Prize for literature in 1913 and is worth mentioning here. Apart from works of translation, prominent contributions to the study and theory of translation were made by profound scholars like J.C. Catford, Eugene A. Nida and Peter Newmark.

Theories of Translation

J.C. Catford is one of the major contributors to the theory of translation. In his *A Linguistic Theory of Translation* he defines translation as the replacement of source language text material by equivalent target language material. Since translation deals with relation between languages, he considers translation as a branch of comparative linguistics. He introduced the phenomena of 'total translation' and 'restricted translation'. 'Total translation' according to Catford is the replacement of source language phonology and graphology by non-equivalent target language phonology and graphology. 'Restricted translation' is replacement of source language textual material by equivalent target language material.

Catford's theory of translation is a theory of meaning. Like Etienna Dolet, Catford also gave importance to meaning and spirit in translation. Catford's theory is derived from J.R. Firth's definition of meaning. He considers meaning as a property of a language *i.e.*, a source language text has a source language meaning and target language text has a target language meaning.

Catford's theory also points out the difference between translation and transference. In translation, the source language meaning is substituted by target language meanings but in transference the implantation of source language meaning into target language text takes place. There are two translation shifts that Catford talks about. They are level shifts and category shifts. Shifts from one linguistic level to the other, like from grammar to lexis and from lexis to grammar are called level shifts. Category shifts include structure-shifts, class-shifts and unit-shifts.

Catford makes it clear that source language texts are not absolutely translatable or absolutely untranslatable, but they are just more or less translatable. He also discusses about two types of untranslatability *i.e.*, linguistic untranslatability and cultural untranslatability. Lack of formal correspondence between the source language and the target language leads to linguistic untranslatability. This untranslatability can occur because of oligosemy *i.e.*, an item having a particularly restricted range of meaning. In the same way cultural untranslatability occurs when a situational feature relevant for the source language text is absent from the culture of the target language text. For example, the Tamil 'Valaikkappu' is untranslatable in English because English has no corresponding lexical item and the formality or ritual as 'Valaikkappu' does not exist in English culture.

Catford's extensive work on the theory of translation, that discusses various aspects and problems of translation has enlarged the boundary of machine translation. The limitation about Catford's theory is that the factors that influence the process of translation, like the translator, his social and cultural background, his audience, his aim in translating are thoroughly ignored.

Eugene A. Nida, yet another significant theorist, provides a descriptive approach to the translation process. His theory is focused upon the receptor. His approach is sociolinguistic and receptor oriented. So he takes into consideration contextual features besides the textual or linguistic features. He considers the pragmatic or emotive meaning as the most important factor in transferring the message from the source language to the target language. Nida also brings a distinction between language and metalanguage and emphasizes that this distinction is extremely important for the translator.

Nida's approach to translation involves three stages. In the first stage the original text gets reduced into its kernels. In the second language, the meaning of the source language gets transferred to the receptor language on the structural level and in the last stage, the generation of the stylistically and semantically equivalent expression in the receptor language takes place.

Nida is of the view that subjectivity cannot be avoided in translation because the translator becomes a part of the cultural context in which he lives and he cannot help being subjective at times. Nida's theory also talks about two types of equivalences, *i.e.,* formal and dynamic equivalences. A formal equivalence focuses its attention on the message, while dynamic equivalence is oriented towards the receptor response. Nida agrees with Leonard Foster's view that the ultimate purpose of the translation is to make it sound as original as possible.

The major focus of Nida's theory of translation is the receptor and his reaction. He talks about the old focus and new focus in translating. The old focus was the form of the message while the new focus is the response of the receptor. Nida also defines two different systems for translating. One is the direct method in which the source language structure gets transferred to that of the receptor language through a universal linguistic structure. The second system consists of three stages: (1) Analysis, in which the surface structure is analysed in terms of the grammatical relationships and meanings of words and combination of words, (2) Transfer, in which the analysed material is transferred in the mind of the translator from source language to receptor language, and (3) Restructuring, in which the transferred material is restructured in order to make the final message fully acceptable in the receptor language. The single-stage procedure of the first approach is inadequate. The second system though looks complicated is a more complete approach. After the three stages have been completed the translation has to be tested focusing the attention upon the amount of dynamic equivalence *i.e.*, how the receptors or users react to it. A good translation also becomes lengthier than the original because whatever is implicit in the source language text is made explicit with more details in the translations.

Thus Nida has made a significant contribution to the field of translation. But the major limitation in Nida's theory is its exclusive concern with the *Bible* translation. Since the process of translation varies depending on the type of the text, his theory cannot be fully followed while translating other literature.

Peter Newmark can be ranked along with Catford and Nida for his major contribution to the theory of translation. His unique tribute to the theory is his detailed treatment of semantic vs. communicative translation. The semantic translation focuses primarily upon the semantic content of the source text and the communicative translation focuses upon the comprehension and response of receptors. This distinction makes the theory of translation relevant for translating a variety of literature unlike Nida's which is limited only to *Bible* translation.

Newmark's translation theory provides a framework of principles, rules and hints for translating texts and criticizing translations. He insists on treating the basic prepositions of translation in terms of a theory of communication. His theory highlights the theory of meaning. Pierce also emphasized the theory of meaning and according to him, the meaning of a word or a sign differs to different people. Newmark also adopts Buhler's statement of the functions of language. He talks about three functions of language—expressive function which is author-centred, informative function which gives the extralinguistic information content of the text and vocative function which is reader centred.

Apart from these principles, Newmark also talks about three levels of translation. They are referential, textual and subjective levels. They are like the tubes of a jointed telescope with which the translator observes the three functions of language in varying degrees, says H. Lakshmi, in her *Problems of Translation.* In translating a literary text the translation language is 'expressive' and level is 'subjective'. In translating a non-literary text the language is 'informative' and level is 'referential'.

Further, Newmark also expounds two basic translation processes *i.e.*, comprehension and formulation. Comprehension has to do with interpretation and formulation has to do with recreation. The translator has to function smoothly between these processes. The two methods of translation that Newmark advocates are the communicative translation and the semantic translation. In the communicative translation, the translator attempts to produce the same effect on the receptors as was produced by the original on the source language readers. In semantic translation the translator attempts to reproduce the precise contextual meaning of the author. But all translations are to some degree both communicative and semantic. This theory of translation is appropriate to translate any type of text. Thus Newmark's theory is an improvement over Nida's theory.

These profound theories prove that a translator needs much original genius necessary to re-create a text in the target language. The very early principle, 'word for word vs. sense for sense' advocated by Cicero, many centuries ago, can be seen emerging again and again with different degrees of emphasis in different times, concepts of language and communication.

WORKS CITED

1. Barnstone, Willis. *The Poetics of Translation: History, Theory and Practice.* London: Yale University Press, 1993.
2. Bassnett-McGuire, Susan. *Translation Studies.* London: Routledge, 1988.
3. Gentzler, Edwin. *Contemporary Translation Theories.* London: Routledge, 1993.
4. Lakshmi, H. *Problems of Translation.* Hyderabad: Booklinks Corporation, 1993.
5. Nair, Sreedevi K. *Aspects of Translation.* New Delhi: Creative Books, 1996.
6. Nida, Eugene A. and Charles, L. Taber. *The Theory and Practice of Translation.* Leiden: The United Bible Societies, 1974.

Literary Translation: Its Importance, Ways and Difficulties

2

MALLIKARJUN PATIL

No wonder, man cannot master many languages. Contrarily, if he can, absolutely he cannot write or speak in his second language fluently. Albert C. Baugh is right when he tells, "Few people ever master a language not their own, and writings done in an alien speech rarely rise above the level of school exercises. Now and then some genius may transcend these limitations, but, even so his works usually remain an aesthetic curiousity, of little consequence in the literary scheme of things." If the condition of an average man's linguistic potentiality and diversity is so bleak then translation for our understanding of others is most essential. Translation is as necessary as our very breathing to understand global relations in terms of Arts, Science and Commerce. Since learning more languages or writing proficiently in an alien tongue is hardly possible, the work of translation for the rise, promotion and development of literature, art, business, technology, medicine etc. is inevitable. It rightly promotes experiments and discoveries, it enables inter-linguistic communication in a country like India where multi-linguistic culture exists. Translation recreates and intensifies the channel of life and diversifies human activities. It is because of translation only, the world's greatest works like the *Bible*, epics like the *Iliad*, the *Ramayan*, the *Mahabharata* and tales like *Panchatantra*, *Arabian Nights*, the histories of ancient Rome, Indus, Babylonian, Sumerian and Chinese civilizations, etc. are known to the people living in all the spheres of the globe. It is translation that led to the medieval renaissance in Europe, to the spread of education and western culture in the New and Third Worlds. The role of translation in enabling the dissemination of new ideas in the developing countries today as ever before is crucial. Owing to translation poets like Kalidas, Shakespeare, Tagore, Eliot, Yeats *et al.* are known to those who can never read each of these poet's mother tongue. Besides, translation for the sake of teaching in one's mother tongue is also emphasized. Indeed, translation plays a vital role in a country like India where besides hundred vernaculars three language tier system at national level works in bringing out a pan-Indian cultural tradition.

Well, translation is indispensable for the welfare of mankind. However, the eternal question that eludes us an answer is 'can the act of translation be possible?' People wonder, since language is a human behaviour and often emotive, whether one can translate or render the sensibility of others into his language. Of course, according to certain people translation of poetry is nearly impossible but not the translation of prose. Dr. Samuel Johnson, Didero and Nebakov subscribe to this view.

However, translation is possible, desirable and essential. For spreading knowledge, to get fame or pecuniary benefits, translation is done every time, everywhere. This is more true of countries which are multilingual. In his letter to Thomas Carlyle the noted poet Goethe wrote: "Whatever might be people's opinion regarding the inconsistency of translation, for the sake of our worldly business, translation is most indispensable." In spite of the belief that the mysteries of human experience, the shades of sense and sensibilities, ambiguities, language change cannot be rendered from one to another language, human mind has already succeeded in rewording one's mind and heart into another's. Although the use of a word by several writers will not be the same always, sets of meanings in all languages for such words and senses exist and such things can be decoded. Indeed, in this light translation can be undertaken to deliver the goods.

Oxford English Dictionary (260) defines translation as "an action or process of turning from one language to another, while the *New Standard Encyclopedia* (Chicago, 360) tells, "translation is rendering of meaning especially in writing, from one language into another". In his work *Translation and Translations*, J.P. Postgate writes, "Translation in literature is the art of rendering the writing of one language into another language. The art of translation lies not merely in translating the literal sense of one language into another but of translating also the feeling, thought and character of the work, so that the finished translation is equal in quality to the original." 'A translation is at best a dislocation' in Collingwood's phrase, while Wilmowitz believes translation to be 'a metempsychosis'.

The word 'Translation' is derived from the Latin term *translatus*. The prefix 'tran' means passing something, while the stem 'slate' means cover. The generic term translation has several implications such as alteration, change, conversion, interpretation, paraphrase, rendering, rephrasing, rewording, transcription, transformation and transliteration, while the specific meanings of the word are translating, rephrasing, interpretation, rendering, decoding etc.

A brief history of translation can be drawn thus. The discipline of translation first developed in Greek. Romans later borrowed this. In medieval times, due to translation, all the ancient Greek and Roman classics were published in other European languages. In later times translation through bureau or courtly support turned oriental knowledge in occidental and *vice versa*. This naturally spread the knowledge everywhere. Al-Mansur's (the Kalif of Baghdad) Bureau of Translation and Translation Institute at Toledo, Spain and Queen Elizabeth's support to her court people gave a great fillip in the field.

However, owing to printing and paper-back revolution, translating-business flourished everywhere. This is how Plato, Aristotle, Socrates, Aesop, Homer, Dante, Petrarch, Plutarch, Virgil, Tasso, Montaigne, Ibsen are available in English. Chaucer's *Roman de la Rose*, Malory's *Arthur*, Wycliffe and Tyndale's *Bible*, Philoman Holland's Pliny's *Natural History*, Plutarch's *Lives* (1579), Ariosto's *Orlando Furioso* (1519) and Tasso's *Jerusalem Delivered*, Chapman's *Homer*, John Florio's *Montaigne's Essays* (1603) and Cervantes' *Don Quixote* (1602) are exquisite translations. Similar are Dryden's *Ovid* and *Virgil*, Pope's *Iliad* and *Odyssey*, Thomas Gray's Icelandic and Celtic verse, Macpherson's Gaelic legends and Max Muller's Sanskrit classics. Likewise due to scholars' love of the orientalism, works like *Rubaiyat, Arabian Nights, Panchatantra,* Chenes and Russian novels are translated in several other languages today.

Translation should be faithful and idiomatic. Nothing should be added or anything should be omitted. Thus translation is like transferring an employee from one office to another but without any promotion or demotion. A translator should accord in all parts, even length, with its original. Through his dynamic encounter between two tongues he should attempt to pursue closely the syntax, cadences and sound of other languages into his own. The following couplet by Lord Roscommon, Dryden's contemporary, insists upon fidelity of tone:

> Your author always will be the best advise
> Fall when he falls, and when he rises, rise.

But it does not means the process of translation is mechanical, exact and artificial endeavour. There should be a compromise between the original author and the translator. Otherwise the translated work loses its flavour. Therefore Benjamin Jovet observes: "All translation is a compromise the effort to be literal and the effort to be idiomatic." In the task of following the rules of translation, never one should turn a doctrinaire. Indeed, in this regard, the translator should involve not only his mind but also his heart.

A faithful or a good translator is supposed to be fluent in the languages he is involved in. He must be familiar with the structure of the other language and its linguistic diversity. He should understand a sentence usually as a unit of thought and in accordance with the system of his language that thought must be reworded. Always the right meanings of the words for the original should be used to avoid the loss of the sensibility in the transaction. This is more so in the case of idioms, proverbs and imageries. For example, the English proverb 'Every dog has its own day' should be *Attegondu kal sosegondu kal* in Kannada but not 'everyone has a chance'. Likewise the following English sayings should be rendered into Kannada as put into the brackets. 'Empty vessel makes much noise' (*Alp vidya mah garvi*); 'Make hay while the sun shines' (*Gali bittaga turiko*); 'Herculean task' (*Bhagirat Sahas*); 'Wolf in sheep's clothing' (*Gomukha vyagra*) etc. A literal translation of idioms, phrases, proverbs is always harmful. In case of dire necessity new words or new patterns in usage and expressions can be created in a way reading public welcomes it. But such innovation must not be ambiguous or obscure. Besides, the style should be in conformity to the contemporary usage. Refined usages should be used to carry on the rhythms, melody and harmony of the original. The exuberance and magniloquence should not be lost. The imprint of tradition and sound and sense must resound in the translated text. If necessary to make the translated text look original the translator can spice it. In this regard, "a good translator conveys the fine distinctions of meaning, feeling, tone, sound, style and diction of the original. It is especially difficult to capture the quality of a great work of literature in another language. Literary translators continuously try to improve upon translations of the classics and new versions are published fairly often" (*New Standard Encyclopaedia*, Chicago, Vol. 13, 360-61). However, during the translation nothing should be lost or changed in the rendering. So there should be a 'Self-denial'.

Similarly a good translator should be familiar with the subject of translation. Familiar more he should be with the author. So in his *Essay on Criticism*, Alexander Pope says:

> Know well each ancient's proper character:
> His fable, subject, scope in every page;
> Religion, country, genius of the age...
> Thence form your judgement, thence
> your maxims bring,
> And trace the Muses upward to their spring.

Indeed, to preserve the original in the reworded version, the process requires the translator's complete involvement in the life and idiom of one's own age. So much care must be taken. Therefore, 'you must not', Samuel Butler remarks, 'skin him, stuff him and set him up in a case'.

Translator's understanding of the original work should be clear, genuine and complete. It is because of a failure in translation either in terms of language or theme or both, that translators are branded as 'traitors'. Indeed owing to this lacunae only a single work is translated many times. Evidently Homer's epics, Indian epics, or great author's great works, etc. are rendered into the same language many times. To avoid translator becoming a free lancer or an arbiter, in 1540, Etienne Dolet codified the following rules for translators:

(a) The translator should clearly know the author and his work while translating,

(b) He should have known his language and the language of the work to be translated by him,

(c) He must conform to the meaning of a sentence instead to the series of words in the translation,

(d) His aim should be translating in a simple language, and

(e) He should achieve a rhythm that soothes the ear and heart of his readers.

Translation can be done in several ways. Firstly a distinction should be drawn between the oral translation and the written. The former is called interpretation in which one who knows the languages of both the speaker and hearers, interprets the speaker's speech in the language of the hearers. During this he may commit some mistakes but such errors are overlooked unless there is a problem of intelligibility. Oral translation is used specially during public speeches, orations and discourses. In written translation, however, there will be no flexibility or excuses for errors. Here everything should be done quite systematically. The translated text should look like the original of course in a different mettle.

Another classification of translation is machine translation and manual translation. Here machine translation is nothing but computer translation. In this process, the translatable text will be coded and decoded with signs, and rendering will be literal however. But so far machines have not yet succeeded in rendering human sensibility faithfully. So the real work of translation is still to be done by man himself.

More familiar modes of translation are literal translation or metaphrasing, free translation or paraphrasing, adaptation and real translation.

In literal translation or metaphrasing or word to word rendering, the translator has to follow the original closely. He has little scope in recreating anything in the process. So this can be suitable only for technical matters. In his work *The Art of Translation,* T.H. Savorie observes, 'Literal or word for word translation is a primitive type; it is only fit for prosaic matters.' Indeed, it does not make a good reading.

Free translation or paraphrasing is another mode. In this type of translation, the original should be retained. Paraphrasing is a 'restatement of the original passage in other words'. Here language is less important than the matter. The aim of the translator is then less to make an accurate rendering than to make the substance of foreign work thoroughly intelligible to the spirit of the language desired. So the character of the translator thus proceeds as much from the mind of the translator as from the mind of the original writer. In this case the translator may add his own and amplify the original. At times due to glossary and notes, the translated work may become bigger and better than the original. However, paraphrasing is good for rewording difficult or obscure texts in plain language. In it there is no scope for linguistic objectivity.

Adaptation is still another mode of translation. In this kind the original text is abridged. It can be called bawdlirization where for the sake of rendering the text, the translator alters it in accordance with the taste of his readers. This is done when an original text looks cumbersome, obscure, big and difficult for reading it in modern times. This is more so in the case of historical, puritanical and mythological works like Vedas, Upanishads, or ancient chronicles of history. Max Muller is right when in connection with Indian epics, he observes: "Life seems too short to read such a gigantic poem as a whole." Therefore, when he was up against a truly Himalayan task Romesh Chunder Dutt decided to reduce the 48,000 lines of the *Ramayana* and 2,00,000 lines of the *Mahabharata* into 4000 lines each or 8000 lines in all. So seven Kāṇdas of the *Ramayana* and the eighteen Parvas of the *Mahabharata* became alike twelve books. Similarly most of the classic these days are adapted to readable extent. Filming a novel or dramatizing a story also involves adaptation. Besides, in adapting a work of art, the translator can omit much of the cumbersome text or at times add his own to make the resultant look enjoyable. For example, many of the translations made before 1660 in Europe, specially those in prose, were marked by a super-abundance of words, characteristic of much of English writing in the 16th and 17th centuries. So the originals were amplified.

More examples of adaptation should be mentioned here. Dryden's *All for Love* is an adaptation of Shakespeare's *Antony and Cleopatra.*

Similarly the Kannada writer Kuvempu's *Raktaksi* is an adaptation of Shakespeare's *Hamlet,* while B.M. Shri's *Ashwathama* is an adaptation of Sophocles' *Ajax.* Adaptation is quite useful to preserve the cultural heritage of the antique world. But adaptations should do justice to the original, lest they will be adulterations.

Translation can also be an interchanging process. In other words, translation of a prose work into poetry or *vice versa*, or translation of a text from old language into new language can be desirably done. So genre to genre, age to age, medium to medium translation has been done ever since the linguistic art of writing began. Again this kind of translation is undertaken solely with a view to carrying on the knowledge of the olden times to the modern people.

When one translates the literature of ancient times to modernize it in a same language, he is bound to face numerous hurdles regarding language and theme. Since language changes both horizontally and vertically, the translator cannot render it faithfully. This is more true in the case of a language that grows rapidly owing to heavy borrowings, coinages etc. For example, as we know the story of English language, the old King's English, through the ages, because of borrowing, has drastically been altered. Even many of the English words have lost their meanings, while many of the remaining have undergone a change. Coinages and borrowings, in translation, require an extensive glossing. For instance when one translates old English poems like *Beowulf, Widsith, Finn, Maldon,* he finds maximum difficulties in regard to language. Besides, prosody troubles a good deal as in the old English there were on-verse and off-verse lifts as much as time and stress factors. Here is an old English runic poem rendered twice in modern English.

> Fooh by frofur fira gehwylcum;
> sceal eah manna gehywylc miclun hyt a lan
> gif he wile for arihtne domnes hleotan

Its modern translation runs thus:

> Valuables are a joy to every man;
> Yet every man must needs be openhanded with them
> If he is minded to win favour with the Lord.

True the following is another version of the same:

> I am a joy to every man;
> Yet every man must needs be openhanded with me
> If he is minded to win favour with the Lord.

Similar is human experience of translating old Sanskrit into new Sanskrit. So is the case with other languages.

Be it as it may when one undertakes the work of translating literature of one genre into another either in the same language or from one language to another, he is to encounter myriad difficulties. Here the difficulties are of two-fold. If, say, an old English poem is to be translated into a different language, again say in prose, because of linguistic barriers, the work upsets the translator. For example, when *Finn,* an old English poem sung by scops and gleemen, was rendered into prose in English and other European languages, it underwent a considerable metamorphosis. That is why, it is said, poetry cannot be translated. But in Hillaire Belloc's view, poetry can be reclothed into a living prose. Therefore, Matthew Arnold thinks since it has a rhythm, rhyme and metre, poetic exuberance and melody cannot be rendered into another medium.

Medium to medium translation is possible excepting poetry. Since it has uninterpretable emotional shades, poetry is bound to lose its flavour if it is translated into another medium. However, in Arnold's view only the poet can do it successfully. In this regard, one can remember Tagore who himself translated his poems into English under the title *Gitanjali.* For poetry translation, at least, in J.P. Postgate's opinion, one should have poetic sensibility.

Unfortunately the art of translation is a difficult job again for the same reason that one cannot have two mother tongues, or one can hardly learn two or more languages sufficiently to do justice to the original work. Besides, the difficulties of understanding are there ever before. The re-translation of great classics, into the same language is a clear evidence for this. Secondly there are no clear-cut rules and regulations in this regard. Maybe for this reason, Wilmowitz thinks translation is a mathematical problem. Since it is not a prestigious work, people do not value it or undertake it willingly.

However, the art of translation is certainly a very useful work—helpful, enlightening and remunerative. But it is not as prestigious as the creative writings. So in Cardinal Newman's view translation is only translation.

Translation Theory

R. SHANTI

3

Man has varied needs, interests and attractions. His interest and knowledge widen to all fields like literature, music, painting, science, technology, economics, history, philosophy, astrology, geology, mathematics, computer and its various communicative technologies. In the modern world, man is not content with his intense knowledge in a single field. He tries to gain the same depth of knowledge in other fields too. This is mainly due to the dependent nature of human life. Our present life is a mere bundle of knowledge collected by our forefathers crossing the barriers of colour, caste, creed, country and so on. Man's nature is to adapt himself to all that is beautiful, potential, powerful and profitable. This is made possible only through translation. Translation helps in the over-all growth of human life.

Translation is an important mode of literary communication. It is a typical bi-lingual activity. It comprises of various developing fields. Translation is a process of retextualising the essence of the Source Language (SL) text to the reader of the Target Language (TL).

Translation is not merely an imitation of a text. It is a creative process in itself. Though creativity is an essential criteria of translation, it is necessary to follow certain general rules for its proper functioning and efficiency. Some scholars such as Theodore Savory define translation as an 'art'; others, such as Eric Jacobson define it as a 'craft'; and like others such as Eugene Nida define it as a 'science'. Horst Frenz claims that translation 'is neither a creative art nor an imitative art, but stands somewhere between the two'.[1] When scholars differ in their theories one may wonder whether it is possible to have general rules for translation. But for the effective functioning of any field, it is essential to formulate general rules. The general rules may change from time to time according to the development of the situation. In spite of the changing need, there is a need to form general theories for the proper functioning of a field. Hence, taking into consideration the practicality of the nature of translation, there is a need to formulate general theories for translation too.

Great scholars have defined translation differently. J.C. Catford defines it as 'the replacement of textual material in one language (SL) by equivalent textual material in another language (TL)'.[2] Isadore Pinchuck defines translation as a practical method of finding equivalence for the SL in the TL.[3] Dostert defines it as '...that branch of the the applied science of language which is specifically concerned with the problem or the fact of the transference of meaning from one set of patterned symbols into another set of patterned symbols.[4] Eugene A. Nida defines it as, 'translation consists in reproducing in the receptor language the closest natural equivalent of the source language message, first in terms of meaning and secondly in terms of style'.[5]

Theodore Savory proposes a set of twelve axioms on translation that appears self-contradictory. The axioms follow:

1. A translation must give the words of the original.
2. A translation must give the ideas of the original.
3. A translation should read like the original work.
4. A translation should read like translation.
5. A translation should reflect the style of the original.
6. A translation should possess the style of the translation.
7. A translation should read as a contemporary of the original.
8. A translation should read as a contemporary of the translation.
9. A translation may add to or omit from the original.
10. A translation may never add or to omit from the original.

11. A translation of verse should be in verse.
12. A translation of verse should be in prose.[6]

At the outset, these axioms may look contradictory and pose a threat to translators. But a close study reveals that the translator must pay attention to the original text and at the same time focus his attention on the readers. The odd numbered axioms show the importance to be given to the original and the care to be taken in conveying the meaning of the original. The even numbered axioms show that in addition to retaining the original meaning, the focus must be on the TL reader. Hence we understand the importance of the relationship between the source writer and the reader to a translator in his work.

From the different definitions, we infer that translation involves the following items:

(i) two languages *i.e.* SL and TL at a time and the linguistic, lexical terms, life-style, history, culture, geographical position of the land and the atmosphere in the land of the speakers of both the languages;

(ii) the translation of the SL text into the TL;

(iii) the source or meaning of the SL text is primary; the style is secondary. To retain the meaning of the SL text, the stylistic features can be altered. But at any cost, there can be no additions, omissions or conscious alterations in the meaning. But an ideal translation will adhere both to the meaning and the style of the SL text;

(iv) the chief aim of a translation is to find an equivalent in TL for the meaning in the SL text;

(v) while the meaning is close to the content of the SL text, it must also appeal to the flair and feeling of the TL readers.

(vi) above all, it must create the same reception in TL as in the SL system.

The above inferences show that it is important to consider the following in translating a part or a complete text. They are:

(i) the meaning of the SL text,

(ii) the linguistic features,
(iii) the cultural background of both SL and TL readers,
(iv) the similarity in meaning and style,
(v) the distribution of formal and dynamic equivalents and its expected response in the TL.

All books are written with the reader in mind. As Dr. Johnson says in the introduction of his Dictionary the purpose of a book is to be read. For a good translation, the source writer, the translator and the reader are its integral parts. At every point—from the selection of a text, the choice of words, phrases and syntactic structure—the translator has to make a proper decision and express the intended meaning of the SL text exactly and clearly. The translator is already provided with a context and he also knows the reader to whom he is writing. A translator has to decide three things carefully—what (the selection of the SL), where (the content of the SL) and to whom (the readers)—which are very relevant for a good translation.

One of the first writers to formulate a theory of translation was the French Humanist Etienne Dolet in 1540. Dolet published a short outline of the principles of translation entitled "La maniere de bieu traduire d'une langue en aultre" (How to translate well from one language into another) and established the following principles for a translator:

(i) The translator must fully understand the sense and meaning of the original author, although he is at liberty to clarify obscurities.
(ii) The translator should have a perfect knowledge of both SL and TL.
(iii) The translator should avoid word-for-word renderings.
(iv) The translator should use forms of speech in common use.
(v) The translator should choose and order words appropriately to produce the correct tone.[7]

The general principles of translation show that a translator must be a poet too; he must be a master of both SL and TL; he must understand the characteristics and style of the source writer and at the same time must conform to the aesthetic canons of his own age. George Chapman, the great translator of the Homer states that a translator must "attempt to reach the 'spirit' of the original and avoid-overloose translations by basing the translation on a sound scholarly of the versions and glosses".[8] The primary requisite is the complete understanding of the SL text. Translation involves both a scholarly and sensitive appraisal of the SL text and an awareness of the intended place of the translated work in the TL system.

Translation theories are formulated taking into consideration the basic principles of translation. The practice of translation is based on the general theories of translation.

In the twentieth century, the reader of the TL is considered very important. Translations are used for different purposes by different types of readers. The readers of translation can be classified into three different types. The first type is the reader who does not know the alien language but reads the translation of that alien language from a genuine interest in the literature of that language. The second type is the student of that language who learns that language by reading its literature through translation. The third is the reader who knows both SL and the TL.

The translator has to adopt a particular type of translation according to the readers who use translations for different purposes. Translation depends on the requirements of the readers and hence the translator has to select a method of translation accordingly. Thus the concept of reader is important in deciding the type of translation.

For a better translation, the translator has to keep the conventions of the language and follow the general theories of translation. Further, he is restricted by both the subject and the reader. Thc work becomes indeterminate when the SL and TL are unrelated. Hence, the whole process of translating from SL into TL is a complex one as I.A. Richards has observed: Translation 'may probably be the most complex type of event yet produced in the evolution of the cosmos'.[9] The difficulty in translating a work may pose a threat to a person who undertakes translation work. As Randolph Quirk asserts, translation is 'one of the most difficult tasks a writer can take upon himself'.[10] Yet from olden days translation has been done constantly and considerably. The truth, beauty, wisdom and potentiality of a work affect a person to a great extent that he is 'urged' to translate it in other language(s) to introduce the 'classic' thought to his native readers.

The purpose of a study of Translation Theories is, as Andre Lefevere says, 'to produce a comprehensive theory which can also be used as a guideline for the production of translation'.[11]

Translation, a growing inter-disciplinary activity, is a means of revival of learning through greater accessibility of texts. It also creates new lexical terms and certain sub-systems to the terms in the process of finding a better translatability. It also introduces new literary genres, trends and movements in literature.

With the help of translation, man's partial perspective can be widened and the wall of prejudices can be broken. Through translation, more unity can be achieved in a nation and in the world than through political propaganda. This is most applicable to a nation like India where we have 1652 spoken languages, 40 nationalized languages and only 18 officials languages. In such a situation, translation is essential to reveal the core of Indian ethos especially because the concept of Indian literature has been shaped in such a way that without it there can be no contacts and interactions between the communities of various Indian languages.

We all unanimously agree with Salman Rushdie's remark: 'it is generally believed that something is always lost in translation: I cling to the notion—and use, in evidence, the success of Fitzgerald-Khayyam—that something can also be gained'.[12]

In translation, the gain is always more than the loss and we realise the importance of translation as we depend more and more on it. To achieve gain from translations, it is better if translations of Classics in the Indian Languages are prescribed in academic circles so that the present generation can meaningfully grasp the past. It will also be an encouragement to good translators.

REFERENCES

1. Horst Frenz, cited in Susan Bassnett-McGuire's *Translation Studies*, 4.
2. J.C. Catford, *A Linguistic Theory of Translation* (London: OUP, 1965), 20.
3. Isadore Pinchuck, *Scientific and Technical Translation* (London: Andre Deutsch, 1977), 38.
4. Dostert, cited in J.C. Catford's *A Linguistic Theory of Translation*, 35.
5. Eugene, A. Nida and Charles, Taber, *The Theory and Practice of Translation* (Leiden: E.J. Brill, 1969), 12.
6. Theodore Savory, *The Art of Translation* (London: Jonathan Cape Limited, 1957).
7. Etienne Dolet, cited in *Translation Studies*, 54.
8. *Ibid.*, 55.
9. I.A. Richards, 'Towards a Theory of Translating' in *Studies in Chinese Thought* (Chicago: Chicago UP, 1953), 250.
10. Randolph Quirk, *The Linguist and the English Language* (London: Erward Arnold, 1974).
11. Andre Lefevere, 'Translation Studies: The Goal of the Discipline'. *Literature and Translation,* University of Amsterdam, August, 1975: 234-35.
12. Salman Rushdie, *Midnight's Children* (Delhi: Rupa, 1983), 29.

Translation Theory

4

K. KRISHNAMURTHY

That Literature is a reflective picture is more or less true, more or less inspiring for those in active life. Every country has its own literature which mirrors its life. Literature represents the hopes and despairs, the enthusiasm and apathy, the thrill of joy and the state of pain in nation's history. Frankly speaking literature is not of one age but of all ages, not of one country but of all countries. For the creation of any work of art, the environment, the body and the atmosphere are necessary besides the heart and soul. Any writer needs language to express his/her feelings, emotions, ideas, thoughts with his/her own curiosity and intensity of commitment.

Literature consists of prose, poetry, drama, novel, fiction, short story, etc. Each age has its own particular lines of interest and its own particular way of thinking and feeling about things.

The language consists of three aspects. The first is 'substance'; the signs must have some kind of physical existence, whether it is noise or marks. The second is 'form'; the signs must have some kind of consistent and conventional patterning. The third is 'situation'; the signs must take place in the context which gives them meaning.

Translation, like creative literature, is an art. It needs some methods to be successful and artistically viable. Translation involves the process of change into another language retaining the sense which is indeed the basic objective. The main process of translation is the search for the right word in the correct perspective. In a multi-lingual country like India, translation in this sense of the word is of paramount importance for cultural exchange and unity beyond the regional difference of language and culture.

Translation is an operation performed on two languages, the source language and the target language. So it is a unidirectional process. It aims at finding the equivalents of the target language for the source language, thus finding the element of 'translation equivalence' which is the key requirement in the process.

Translation has been variously defined as an art, a craft and a science. It only reflects the personal bias of the theorist who want to translate for their own set purpose. For example, Theodore Savory defines translation as an art. Eric Jacobson defines it as a craft. The Germans see it as a science. Translation is a combination of all these and much more. As one is aware, translation is a young discipline with a heritage of two or three centuries to its credit.

Literary translation as the mode of cultural exchange is of utmost importance, especially in multi-lingual countries. Translation of literary texts has led to both the globalization of culture and the promotion of inter- and intra-cultural bonding. It is only through translation that we have been introduced to the greatest minds of the world like Socrates, Homer, Karl Marx and others. It can be compared to the fire stolen from Heaven by Prometheus the light of which has illuminated the darkest corners of the earth and has brought forth the hidden treasures of the world.

Henry H.H. Remak says, "Comparative literature is the study of literature beyond the confines of one particular country and the study of the relationships between literature on the one hand and other areas of knowledge and belief such as the fine arts, philosophy, history, the social sciences, the sciences, religion, etc. In brief, it is the comparison of one literature with another or others and the comparison of literature with other spheres of human expression" (1974: 1-2).

Thus comparative literature is basically a study of literatures, not of a literature or even of literature.

On the basis of the theory that literary history and literary criticism are not opposed but complementary to each other, comparative literature in its scope may be said to cover four areas. Influence and analogies, movements and trends, genres and forms, and themes, motifs and types. Some would consider translations as a branch but they come under "influence" as they are the best intermediaries between any two literatures.

Influence has always been a key concept of comparative literature studies for the very reason that no author or work originates in a state of vacuum. The growth of literature has been perennially stimulated by ideas borrowed by writers consciously or unconsciously, whether the source of the ideas is foreign or native.

Translation is a part of the common core which involves the whole of linguistic, cultural, socio-linguistic, syntactic, semantic, stylistic and comparative levels. It causes:

1. confrontation of two linguistic systems,
2. confrontation of two stylistic systems,
3. confrontation of two aesthetic systems, and
4. confrontation of two cultural-historical traditions that of the original writer and that of the translator.

Catford defines translation as "the replacement of textual materials on language by equivalent textual materials in another language" (1965: 22). According to Nida translation is a process in which a person who knows both the source language and the receptor language, decodes the message of the source language and encodes it into an appropriate form of receptor language" (1976: 14).

Roman Jakobson in his paper on 'Linguistic Aspect of Translation' talks of 3 kinds of translation. They are:

1. Intra-lingual translation; interpretation of verbal signs by means of other signs of the same language,
2. Inter-lingual translation; interpretation of verbal signs by means of some other language, and

3. Inter-semitic translation or transmutation; interpretation of verbal signs by non-verbal sign systems.

Everything has 3 kinds of meaning denotative, pragmatic and textual. It is the pragmatic meaning which is aimed at in the translation of any two languages. There can be substantial agreement only at the pragmatic level. The target language features are expected to fulfil the same purpose as the original did in the source language. Indian languages have not developed their own equivalents. The Englishmen and the Americans do it for us.

In translation, the question of influence arises. Influence is of two types *i.e.*, direct and indirect. Both direct and indirect influences cause complex problems. A native author may introduce a foreign influence into his literary tradition, an influence which may thereafter proceed from the impact of the native author. Therefore, the influence is not always a fully conscious act.

It is when a language or a country is on the verge of bankruptcy of thoughts, when there is a rotting of intellect and staleness of tradition becomes too much of a burden, the only liberating force appears to be the translation of new thoughts and ideas from other languages. Bharati found Shelley and Walt Whitman illuminating and so brought forth a torrential and cataclysmic effect, of revolutionary flavour and ideas. One could discern the choices of these two poets which are very skilfully translated in his poems.

Translation of articles, poems, essays and other forms from one language into the other is on the increase today. The modern world is scientifically advanced. The new inventions and discoveries have helped man in several ways. The know-how skill, expertise and technicalities have to be understood before any new product is to be used. The information has to be given in the concerned language, if it is to reach the nook and corner of the world.

Secondly, communication technology is fast growing today. News of happenings and events in one part of the world is made known through all the languages very soon. The interpreters and experts do invaluable work for this. Books and short brochures are published in all the major languages for the benefit of the particular area.

Thirdly, translation helps to spread a nation's culture, tradition, art, architecture and other fields of activity. The tourists visiting a number of countries ask a number of questions to get to know the significance of festivals, rituals, etc.

Translation studies should be adopted for the broad purpose that concern itself with the problems raised by the production and description of translations. The present dissertation is an attempt in that direction. Most importantly, it is an attempt to demonstrate that translation studies is indeed a discipline in its own right. Translation is an intrinsic part of the foreign language.

Hilaire Belloc summed up the problem of status in his lecture 'On Translation' way back in 1931, and his words are still perfectly applicable today:

> "The art of translation is a subsidiary art and derivative. On this account it has never been granted the dignity of original work and has suffered too much in the general judgement of letters. This natural underestimation of its values has had the bad practical effect of lowering the standard demanded and in some periods has almost destroyed the art altogether. The corresponding misunderstanding of its character has added to its degradation; neither of its importance nor its difficulty has been grasped." (1931: 1)

In the 18th century there had been a number of studies on the theory and practice of translation in various European languages and the year 1791 had been the year of publication of the first theoretical essay on translation in English. In the early 19th century translation was still regarded as a serious and useful method for helping a writer explore and shape his own native style.

Translation studies cover such a wide fields today. It can be roughly divided into four general areas of interest. Two of them are product-oriented and the emphasis is on the functional aspects of the target language text in relation to the source language text and two of them are process-oriented and the emphasis is on analysing what actually takes place during translation.

The first category involves 'the history of translation' and is a component part of literary history. The type of work involved in this area includes investigation of theories of translation at different times, the critical response to translations, the practical processes of commissioning and publishing translations, the role and function of translations in a given period, the methodological development of translation and by far the most common type of study, analysis of the work of individual translators.

The second category of 'translation in the target language culture', extends the work on single texts of authors and includes work on the influence of a text, author or genre on the absorption of the norms of the translated text into the target language system and on the principles of selection operating within that system.

The third category of 'translation and linguistics' includes studies which place their emphasis on the mutual comparative arrangement of linguistic elements in the source language and the target language texts with regard to the phonemic, morphemic, lexical, syntactic and syntagmatic levels. Into this category come studies of the problems of linguistic equivalence of language, bound meaning, linguistic untranslatability, machine translation, etc. and also studies of the translation problems of non-literary texts.

The fourth category, loosely called 'translation and poetics', includes the whole area of literary translation in theory and practice. The studies may be general or genre-specific including investigation. The studies in categories one and three are more widespread than those in categories two and four. It is important to keep in mind the four general categories even while investigating one specific area of interest.

Evaluation is of paramount significance in literature. As far as translation is concerned evaluation may be viewed as a stumbling block. A perfect evaluation on translation can be done only if the critic has access to both languages.

Translation studies, therefore is exploring new grounds, bridging as it does the gap between the vast areas of stylistics, literary history, linguistics, semiotics and aesthetics. It is a discipline, firmly rooted in practical application. So, translation is a 'BOND' not a 'BARRIER'.

BIBLIOGRAPHY

Bassnett Susan (ed.). *Translation Studies*, New York, Methuen & Co. Ltd., 1996.

Belloc, Hilaire. *On Translation*. Oxford: The Clarendon Press, 1931.

Catford, J.C. (ed.). *A Linguistic Theory of Translation*. London: OUP, 1965.

Jakobson, Roman. 'On Linguistic Aspects of Translation' in R.A. Brower ed.: in *On Translation*. Cambridge Mass.: HUP, 1959.

Remak, Henry H.H. *Comparative Literature of Crossroads*. Diagnosis, Therapy and Prognosis. YCGL, 1974.

Sharma, R.P. (ed.). *I.A. Richard's Theory of Language*. New Delhi: S. Chand & Co. Ltd., 1979.

Problem of Translating Poetry*

UMASHANKAR JOSHI

5

Translation has rightly been called as the eternal profession. Great creative works cannot be had even if they are intended. But every language can enrich itself by translating the best creative works from other language into it. English language has availed itself of good number of great writers. But in spite of that it has further enriched itself through translation. There will hardly be any work of significance which has not been translated by them (Englishmen) in it. In the history of English literature the contribution of the Bible's translation by 47 scholars can be understood by the saying that English language means three parts Bible and one part Shakespeare. The kind of superior energy that Europe invests in translation can further be discerned from the fact that Tagore's *Geetanjali* was translated by Andre Gide in French and in Spanish by its Nobel laureate poet Yemnez.

There are two words *bhashantar* and *anuvad* (translation) with us for approximating a text of an alien language into our own. These two words deserve serious consideration. It will help us in understanding the whole process of approximating the text in one's own native tongue. *Bhāsāntar* literally means 'another language'. It stresses on change in the language of the text and thus it focuses on external reality. *Anuvād* (translation) means unlocking the text by following the source text closely. It draws

---

* Reprinted from *Critical Practice* Vol. 1, No. 2 with permission from Creative Books, New Delhi.

our attention to its inner process—how that *bhashantar* actually took place. Mere change in language of the source text i.e., *bhashantar* is not enough and it should never be aimed. Rather the essence of the source text should be captured in it. Every translation *(anuvad)* will definitely be *bhashantar* but every *bhashantar* need not necessarily be translation.

Translating poetry is more problematic than translating prose. In case of a work of prose *bhashantar* may perhaps be satisfactory. But in poetry mere change of word from source language to target language will not do. A poem contains the best words in the best order and it will not be incongruous to say that metre and style, originated from this choice of words, and their order are essential elements of poetry. At the very outset of switching over from one language to another the style of the source text does attain harmony. But in reality translation of a genuine creative work poses certain questions whether it is prose or poetry. Every creative work is an expression of certain vision realized by a genius but a person who intends to approximate this work in another language is not concerned with the vision contained in it or with its expression. His prime concern is to adjust a word from one to another language. How will the translated text received from such an endeavour remain a creative work? In fact it is not possible to raise the countenance of the creative faculty of genius artist, as it is expressed in source language, in another language. What can at the most be achieved is this that it can strive to be as much close as possible to the source text. The success of a translator intending to approximate a source text from another language to his own and in following source writer's intent will depend on his endeavours to share similarity of qualities and properties of the source creator.

Croce speaks of 'impossibility of translations'. Every expression has its specific individual personality. But how to express its specific individuality, as it is manifested through certain linguistic form, in another shape? If words are replaced by words, then only ugly empty shell can be received as its consequence. The translator has to choose between faithful ugliness or faithless beauty. In spite of that Croce accepts 'family likeness' among different creative writers due to different historical reasons, and in that connection he points to relative possibility of translation. It is futile to test translation as reconstruction of original expression but it is not impossible to achieve expressions close and somewhat similar to source expressions. Croce adds that good translation should compare favourably with the source text, it should have its original value as a creative work and should be capable of standing on its own independently.

Dr. Johnson had also observed in the same vein while reviewing John Dryden's translation of *Aeneid.* He said that 'resemblance'—similarity that Dryden expects from a translator dwells in proper choice of style. And that translator has to be like source writer. To better him should not be the end of a translator. The last words of the above stated sentence may perhaps be concerned with possible betrayal to the source writer which may take place in the process of providing better than the source text through translation. Instead of relying on any lord or aristocrat Alexander Pope chose to translate Homer's *Illiad* for his livelihood. After going through it Bentley had remarked: 'A pretty poem, Mr. Pope, but you must not call it Homer.' According to Gibbon, the historian, Pope's *Illiad* has all qualities excepting fidelity to the source text. To translate poetry and then make it like original text is fraught with multiple problems, as Pope must have experienced. But on the other hand inartistic *bhashantar* or paraphrases achieved by adjusting word for word, are just, as Croce has put it, 'simple commentaries' on the source text. Escaping problems pertaining to both these ends a work of translation should resemble source text and proximate it and in spite of *bhashantar* it should not be its mere phantom but stand on its own as an independent work. The problem of translating poetry, in brief, is that of not going away too far in *bhashantar*, in changing language, and of creating an independent work with illumination of originality in a new language. In this manner Bhalan's Gujarati translation of Mahakavi Ban's *Kādambarī* (though in prose, it is a poetic work according to *Kāvyam gadyam padyam ca* i.e. there may be poetical composition in prose and poetry as well) is a successful translation. In this context translation of Omar Khayyam's *Rubaiyat* by Fitzgerald also comes to our mind instantaneously. The translation of Goldsmith's *The Hermit* by Goverdhanram from English into Gujarati that begins with, "*Jogiraj, oobha raho jari*" also is a highly resemblance oriented translation.

It is worth noting here that the process of creating a text anew on the base of source text is different from translation. When Premanand says in *Dashamskandh:*

> Aa pasa Bhat vanche Sanskrit,
> Aa pase marun Prakrit.
>
> (On this side Bhat reads Sanskrit, on the other side I have my Prakrit).

—then he does not translate but transcreates. Transcreator usually takes material. For example, in *Nalakhyan* he uses material of Vyas's Nalopakhyan but for expressing his unique vision through it. Since transcreator has to be faithful to his own vision so he can take sufficient liberty with the source text whereas a translator cannot do so. In *rūpantar* (adaptation) name and place etc. are changed which can be considered negotiable in translation. In translation there should always be ample scope for concessions such as changing Lucy Gray's name in original to Meethi in translated 'Meethi Mathe Bhat'.

There have been quite a few translations in our Gujarati from oriental languages like Sanskrit, from ancient Indian languages like Bengali and from English. Balashankar translated Hafiz from Persian and Karim Muhammad Master translated a good number of verses of Koran. Dr. Taraporewala's translation of Asho Zarathushtra's legend also deserve to be mentioned here. Some scholars have tried their translatorial skills in translating works by Kalidas, Bhavbhuti, Bhasa and Shoodrak among others and most of them have raised issues pertaining to translation of poetry. Since metres of Sanskrit are in use in Gujarati also so Gujarati translators have found it difficult to resist temptation of *samshloki* (composed of similar or parallel verse in the same metre) translation. Three unfinished translation of Kalidas's *Meghadūtām,* which are always not *samshloki* translations, have been attempted by Navalram, Keshav Harshad Dhruv and Tribhuvan Gauri Shankar Vyas. In comparison to them *samshloki* translations of Kilabhai, Nanalal, Vihari Kavi, Poojalal, etc. are more pleasant. To a good measure it can be witnessed in case of translation of plays also. This should not be derived from this that in future pleasant and well reading *samshloki* translations will not be available in Gujarati.

The problems of *samshloki* translation are obvious. What can be accommodated in four lines of Sanskrit with its property of compound (*samas*) is not possible in our Gujarati in spite of construction of compounds to certain extent in it. Further, it is not easy to accommodate all words of Sanskrit in Gujarati as *tatsam* (original having the same form in Prakrit as in Sanskrit). Translators, struggling to be faithful to source metre and narration, have to sacrifice a lot at times. A translator like Nanalal[1] who does not stick to *laghu* (small vowel in prosody) and *guru* (long vowels in prosody) composition of metre, is in a better state. For instance, one who can accept, that in *shardul* (a metre) four *gurus* (long vowels in prosody) cannot be accommodated closely but one *guru* can be arranged in place of two *laghu* faces no problem, for he finds *samshloki* translation a child's play. In comparison to this, translations by K.H. Dhruv, Balashankar, etc. who wish to preserve metre and translate four lines in six to eight lines are more agreeable. If metre gets twisted in *samshloki* translation, it will not be appropriate. Similarly, if words get twisted, that will appear ugly. In Balashankar's poem 'Saundarya', "Dhara ooper hun padepad sakhi tara vichare gharun" '*dhārā*' is not twisted form for '*dharā*' in the metre but it is a word arranged in the context of above referred '*saundarya dharavati*', and to infer meaning thus in the commentary of 'Klantkavis' Balanandini I had left no stone unturned. But it seems that in his translation of the last line of verse number 26 of Act VIII "*Shane jeeve jagat man shath bhar dhārā*" he can, it seems, use 'dhārā' in place of *dharā*. At times in *Samshloki* translation a few words have to be filtered forcibly. In the same manner on some other occasions a few words are to be added to complete a line, as Balashankar had to add '*shath bhar dhara*'.[2]

In *samshloki* translation insistence to achieve alliteration, when it is not in original Sanskrit, amounts to inviting problems. In above cited example there is a reference where Balashankar tried to do *dhaara* in place of *dhara* in alliteration of *vadharnara.* K.H. Dhruv is always tempted to test his alliterative skills in a line. In translating the reference of theft in *Mrachchhkatikam* he tried to translate Charudutt's utterance '*satyam ch na paribhrashtam* ukit' as '*vat chhevat chhe*' in stylish Gujarati which appears quite ridiculous.

In *samshloki* translation even small details can give rise to questions. For example, at times a few problems arise due to the fact that original onomatopoeic words cannot be used as they are in our own language. In the last line of last shloka Act II of *Uttarramcharit "kuhureshugadgadgodavarivarath"* the hurrying tumultous sound of river is heard continuously but it should be kept in mind that the punch word 'gadgad' (choked with emotion) in that line should not indicate to '*galgalu*' (soft with moisture) in Gujarati.

Various questions of different kinds arise when we give up use of Sanskrit metres as they are in original. Such metre should be chosen as would preserve the atmosphere of the source text. It makes no difference if we replace *soratha* (a metre) with *anushtup* (a metre). When Balashankar's *Shakar Soratha* challenges with long raised voice tha sounds beautiful. When Balwantrai's Dushyant speaks in *soratha,* it reminds us of Kathi prince or King. Later on, he regretted its use, so in second edition of *Shankuntalam* he kept *soratha* away. It is possible to translate a *shloka* in a song but it should be done with properiety and discretion. In Manilal's *Uttarramcharit* 'Priye re! te te kayam visrai...Girithi jhamjham jharno vahi jay' is a good instance of such translation. In translation of Sanskrit dramas Balashankar has used dramatic forms that may be sung. He is bestowed with this common sense. According to Professor

Thakore Manilal misplaced Balashankar's translation rather lackadaisically and after that Balashankar's translation of *Uttarramcharit* has not been recovered. It may not come to us as surprise that the following *lavani* (a love song) "*Priye re te te kayam visrai*" may have been influenced by Balashankar. That Manilal was not possessed with the faculty of beautiful song composition should not be inferred from this.

Regarding choice of Gujarati words in Sanskrit translation, sufficient propriety and justification should be observed.[3] Naturally a work will not appear Gujarati if a person changes just *vibhakti* (inflection or variation of nouns or case) or *pratyay* (terminations). But the other kind of mistake often committed is use of native words at unsuitable places just to make its translated version appear Gujarati. Unfortunately, a person gifted with good knowledge of translation like Keshav H. Dhruv does not hesitate to use heavy *tatsam* (similarity of form in Prakrit and Sanskrit) and extremely local native words. In "*thathvath karto'to vats Saumitra, tene*" he has used the word 'thathvath' as synonymous of '*saparya*'. The translation of subsequent verse '*jalptorkramen/ Aviditgatyama*' etc. as "*gupchup gaganta akrame apani te/ Rajni ja rajini shee veetati sambhare ke*" will hardly help him in earning accolades.

His fondness for local words and alliteration as well is fully expressed in hollow terms in "*dhaniyani dhani ni ye dhani*" of *Vikramovarshiya*. Language used in translation should be in accordance with creation of characters and atmosphere of the source text. The words of daily conversation should definitely be used but they should appear appropriate to the characters. Keshav H. Dhruv's translations of Prakrit verses in rustic Gujarati are doubly ridiculous because the rural language used in them is artificial. In *Mrachchhkatikam's* translation (2.2) "Dhori rana rahe hantau chan hun aa varan" the use of *aa varan* in the sense of *atyare* is in its old bookish sense rather than its current use. The source *maggnivdide (margnipatitah)* has been translated as '*dhori rana rahe*'. In place of '*Dhori rahe*' or '*raj marg*' he has shown importance of the path by putting it as *dhori rana rahe* i.e. the king's route. And he indicated this twice. But it cannot be considered proper when he changes '*rajana*' into '*rana*' and tries to render *rajmarg* into rustic Gujarati as *rana*. Even the name 'Mruchchhkatic' is rendered in children's speech as *Mati ni Gayee* in brackets in rustic Gujarati. Here is an example how subtleties of scholarship gets trapped in unnecessary trivialities and allows itself to be ridiculed (because the title of the play in original is not in children's language). The most successful example of using native words in translation is in Keshav H. Dhruv's translation of Shantipath of Ishavasya Upanishad. He could have translated *poornamidam* by retaining the word *poorn* as *poorn chhe aa,* but he has preserved the entire meaning with great flavour through good experimentation in Gujarati: *Bharyu chhe aa, bharyu chhe aa*; *bharyu mathi bharyu chhale;/ Bharyanu bharyu e letan bharyu shesh bharyu rahe!*

A translator from Sanskrit needs very sharp understanding and commonsense, on a good number of occasions, of selecting a text, a good translatable text from its different versions. Keshav Harshad Dhruv has this sense in a good measure. At times he goes beyond scientificness and takes recourse to his imagination. It was proved by thus indicated text by Dhruv regarding *Mudrarakshas* and further has been proved by the manuscript which was recovered later on. All readers of Kalidas will always remain indebted to Prof. Balwantrai K. Thakore for his judgement regarding different versions of the text of his plays.[4]

From ancient Indian languages a few translations of Ravindranath's works from Bengali are attempted. Prose translations of *Vidayabhishap and Chitrangada* by Shree Mahadevbhai Desai and Shree Narharibhai Parikh preserve the entire flavour and charm of the source texts. Nagindas Parikh's translation of some songs of *Geetanjali* in the form of *bhajan* are extremely enjoyable. In *Raveendraveena* Meghani's typical style presents Dhaka's Muslin in a new attractive form as Sorath's *lobadi* (shawl or fine upper woolen garments worn by girl).

There are only a few translations of English works in Gujarati, and God knows when shall we have translations of

French, German, Spanish, Russian and Italian poetry directly and not through English?

Some sincere attempts should be made to translate Shakespeare's plays and other works from English to Gujarati with much attention and interest. The main obstacle in it is of poetic transport. Prof. Thakore has aptly remarked in this regard: "It should not be beyond our comprehension if our poets looked at Shakespeare with a sense of "*Door thi karoon vandana*" (I worship him from distance). How will that vigour, that flow, that spring, that change, that flutter, that fierce pungence wedded to naturalness, that freshness in dialogues, that straightforwardness and depth of heartsearching, that love of nature in description, that lustre, that clash of sentiments, that dissection of fibres of heart etc. be brought in our poetic composition marching with graceful rhythmic gait, dancing with ringing sound of anklets of alliteration or moving like a decorated sheelephant on left and right." But fortunately a few endeavours to tackle such needs and create poetic transport have begun. Keshav H. Dhruv has achieved it in his powerful translation of Mark Antony's speech in traditional *vanveli* (a poetic form):

...manas te manas ja rahyan nathi
Maf karo, bhai, kari gha lagela bolabe chhe
Ne mara antarno oobharo rokato nathi.
E kaink shame tyan sudhi raho, saboor karo.

...Lohi na pravahe relchhel chawk man ja
Pompey in pratima pase e padya, gazab thayo!
Bhaio, gazab thayo! Hune sathe padyo, tame.
Padya; sarv shaheri padya; and dusht drohiyo no
Duniyan man danko vagyo.

Mane

Paur pratye bolwani raza apnara pan
Sari rite sanye chhe. She thi je mara man nathi
Shakti, na thi jukti, nathi chhata, nathi thath, nathi
Shabd nu bhandol, nathi buddhi prabhov, ke hun
Shrota ne ushkeri shakun.

How a traditional verse can help in achieving intended end becomes evident from this example. Balwantrai Thakore is helpless to accept its ability of blossoming fluency of speech: "May be that this is not *vanveli* verse on the crucible of poetics, but after viewing fluency of speech it begins to shine in the hands of a skilful artisan in such places." However, he does not mention the reason and test of poetics which prevents him from calling *vanveli* a metrical form. There is nothing that goes against it. *Kavit* has been in use in Hindi since the Medieval ages, and *Payar* used in Bengali plays and epics belongs to the family of *Kavit.* Hansaben Mehta translated Shakespeare's *Hamlet* and *The Merchant of Venice* in '*anushtup*' (a metre). Let us see a few lines from Hamlet's famous soliloquy 'To be not be':

Mratyu ni ghor ninda man
Swapno kevank avashe, thambhavato vichar ne,
E khayal bale dukho jindagi man khame sahu.
Sha saru sankhva vaki kalna katu chabakha;
Julmi sitmo satta na garvina tuchchhkarne
Premchhitkar ni peeda, fayadana vilamb ne,
Tumakhi adhikarini, je apman dhairya thi
Gunvan sahe vati kuptra jan hath thi
Jo e sau trasno anta ani sake sahej e
Ek gha thi katarna?

Here, *sampads* (a further unit of equal length) of *anushtup* (a metre) have been extensively used but a good actor can recite these parts effectively. Another notable point in this regard is: The number of words in *anushtup* and *kavit vanveli* is the same. Hence, there are good chances of reciting these *vanveli* translations with grace and style of *vanveli.*

In translation of European poetic creations various Indian metrical verses like *vanveli, anushtup, prathvi, mishropjati, paramparit, jhoolna lavani Harigeet, rekkhta, khet katao* etc. can be used in a work. A few of them can be used simultaneously at times.

It is hoped that Sanskrit and European plays will be translated with the view of staging them. When translations of long narrative poems will be needed for recitation and performance in classrooms of schools and college, by *vyas peeth* or radio, then the turn, graceful movement and style of language used in translation will descend naturally, and translation will gain a kind of freshness. However, it is not necessary that a poem should always be translated in verse. It should be translated in prose with discretion and taste. But this must be remembered that translation of a poem in prose will always not be easier than its translation in verse. In poetry its determined style of prose is not determined, a fine sense of style shapes the whole material and moves ahead. As style of prose is not determined, a fine sense of style is seriously needed for this purpose.

Some immortal poetic works have attracted minds of people so much that they should be translated in every age by different generations and a classic like *Meghdoot* and *Geeta* etc. should be translated in every decade.[5] The changing moods and modes of language will definitely enrich and renew their translations.

NOTES

1. It does not seem that in, *Shakuntalam* (5.1) Nanalal was aware of length and scale of *Hanspadika aparwkatra* (a metre).
2. In his brief introduction to the translation of *Iliad* I.A. Richards considers problems of translator while examining the question of translation. With the help of prevalent mechanical terms he says that a translator comprehends and then solves source sound codes and communicates them through target codes. In this process he has to keep in mind that other unnecessary sounds do not disturb us. As a translator he himself had to wrestle with these sounds, says he.
3. It is said about Kishorlal Mashroowala's translation of *Geeta* that Gandhiji did not appreciate excessive use of Gujarati word *Chhe* (is) in Mashroowala's translation from the viewpoint of lucidity of language. It is an ingenius instance of Gandhiji's literary insight. Kishorlalbhai himself notes in his introduction, "I know that this translation does not appear pleasant to a few ears."
4. I do not think that it is a suitable place to discuss problems that I confronted while translating from Sanskrit to Gujarati. I should let go

discussion of problems of translation on the base of different translations of a couple of *shlokas* by different translator or by examining different drafts and subsequent changes effected by me. Prof. Thakore's handwritten drafts of translation of *Geeta* still await such sort of study.

5. Keeping *The Bible's* collective translation in view late Kishorlalbhai mentioned it to me that some institutions like Gujarat Sahitya Sabha or Sahitya Parishad should get an authorized version of *Geeta* prepared in Gujarati. We should have good standard Gujarati translation rather than his own translation. If his translation is considered as the base, then that too will be good.

(Translated from Gujarati into English by Avadhesh Kumar Singh)

Problems of Translation

BIJAY KUMAR DAS

6

Translation in the first place, is a transference of meaning from the Source Language to the Target Language. But what matters is not a translation of words from SL to TL, for exact equivalence of words of the former is hard to get in the latter. Translation is both linguistic and cultural activity and it is concerned with communication of meaning. It is not merely lexical equivalent of words of one language to that of another, (say, TL equivalent of SL words) but much more. Since each word is charged with memory, associations, and literary echoes, it is difficult to find full equivalence of a SL word in another word in TL. That is why, total or full translation is a myth.

What then, are the problems of translation? Ages ago Cicero summed up the translator's dilemma in the following words:

> "If I tender word for word, the result will sound uncouth and if compelled by necessity I alter anything in the order or wording, I shall seem to have departed from the function of a translator." (TS 43)

A translator, in the first place, should possess an inwardness with both the languages—the source language (SL), from which the translation is to be made, and the target language (TL) to which the translation is to be done. He should have a mastery ovcr both languages and the words should "obey his call". Above all, he should have the "feel" of the language. Secondly, in case of literature translation, literal translation should be avoided at all costs because it fails to carry the transposition of culture. The translator should not only give the lexical equivalent of words but keep in mind the socio-cultural matrix. Language is never a mechanical sound system, for each word is charged with memory, associations and literary allusions. Meenakshi Mukherjee makes an apt observation on this subject:

(i) According to her, "the act of translation is voluntary", that is the material has been chosen by the translator himself and the prime mover is a compelling desire to recreate.

(ii) The translator is a writer in the language in which he is translating that is, his handling of the language is not merely competent but creative (73, 74). Since language is to some extent culture oriented, translators face the problem of translating certain culture-based words into another language with a different culture. For instance, Lord Krishna's "Rasa Krida" is difficult to translate into English. Similarly, the translation of "Love Play" for "Lila" seems to me inadequate and something is missing in such a translation. For example, a word like "abhimana" has no equivalent word in English and "Pique" is a poor translation of that great word which has a lot of associations in Indian context. Moreover, Indian languages (particularly, Sanskrit) are rich in erotic vocabulary, but English language with all its richness and luxury is very poor in erotic vocabulary. Thus, the transcription of *Vatsyayan's Kamasutra* into English fails to carry the "feel" of original writing with it. Moreover, words like "uncle", "aunt", "brother-in-law", "cousin" have a lot of equivalent words in Indian languages. How can one translate these culture-based words and "swear words" without taking the context and the "whole" into consideration?

The translator has to make a balance between maintaining close fidelity to the original and utter freedom from it. Sri Aurobindo is in favour of taking liberty with the original. He states that "a translator is not necessarily bound to the original he chooses; he can make his own poem out of it, if he likes, and that is what is generally done" (Kumar: 65). Translation is neither "transliteration" nor "transcreation" and it has to guard against the danger of word for word literal translation as well as taking too much liberty. In the name of creation in the light of recent literary criticism which holds indeterminacy of meaning as its central concept, the art of translation has become increasingly difficult. If each word is a sign and each sign has a signifier and a signified and again a signified is also a signifier then which meaning should one take in translation? Should one take the signification (linguistic code) of a word or its value into consideration for translation?

The problems of translation are greatly enhanced by linguistic indeterminacy which is the result of perpetual change. Next to it is the uncertainty of knowing the meaning of the "text" accurately. In literature translation the "text" is vital for it is the "text" that has to be rendered in another language. The indeterminacy of the text is a crucial concept in contemporary literary criticism. Ronald Barthes rightly observes "as a limiting case, an ideal text that is infinitely plural and contrasts it with the classical text (*i.e.* text classique), which is characterized by a limited or parsimonious plurality of sense (235). The author-text-reader triangle has undergone several changes in recent times. At one end stands the texts created by the author and at the other stands the reader who experiences it. The text controls the reader's response while the reader lends his own complexion to the text. Rajnath is right when he says that "out of the interaction between the text and the reader comes into existence the literary construct" (12). Wolfgang Iser maintains that any description of interaction between the two (the text and the reader) must therefore incorporate both the structure of effects (the text) and that of response (the reader) (21). Thus there are two "texts" now—one, the author's and another the reader's. Text is not what the author thought it to be but what the reader sees in it. Hence, the reader or the critic is the co-author and criticism is not an interpretation of the "text" but an extension of it. In such a state, what is the role of a translator and what will happen to translation? In addition to this there is the problem of the use of language in literature. If literary language is metaphorical, then which meaning should a translator take in translation, literal or metaphorical? "In a translation process", says A.K. Srivastava, "It is the metaphoric *metier* that provokes the problem of ambiguity even when assuming that the "core" meaning arrived at by the translation represents the temper and tone of the original faithfully" (19).

What happens in translation? In the process a new category of 'recording' takes place after 'de-coding' the SL text. Both linguistics and cultural factors shape the acts of 'de-coding' and 'en-coding'. The decoding of the message and meaning of the SL text into the encoding of message and meaning in the TL text, is what we understand by translation in our time. It is well nigh impossible to get an exact equivalent of the messages of the SL text in the target language. The indeterminacy of words and the elusive nature of language have made the task of the translator difficult. Even then the 'meaning' (*i.e.*, the overall meaning) of the SL text can be rendered into the target language. Let us turn to the translator who bears the burnt of translation.

The translator faces many problems while rendering a text from the source language to the target language. His task is more difficult than a creative writer for the latter thinks and writes in one language while the former has to make a tight-rope walking between two languages. In this chapter an attempt has been made to outline the problems faced by translations in general and the difficulties involved in the process of translation—particularly of jokes, humorous statements, poetry, drama and fiction. Culture and culture-words create a good deal of problems in translation.

Language is largely culture oriented and therefore, translators face the problem of translating certain culture based words into another language with a different culture. Colloquial expressions, culture-words, slangs, proverbs are difficult to translate for there is no one to one correspondence between one culture and another or one language and another. Equivalence of words in two or more languages is hard to come by. Hence, the difficulty arises in finding equivalent swear words in another language. Socio-cultural matrix plays a vital role in checking the nuances of the words in both languages—SL and TL. Here are a few culture-words that pose a good deal, problem in translation: 'Abhiman' (Pique), Krishna 'Lila', 'Dharma', 'Rasakrida' (love-play) and a host of others (mentioned earlier) make the life of the translator miserable.

The influence of LI (language one, *i.e.*, mother-tongue) on the use of English by Indian readers creates sentences like 'I am feeling cold', instead of 'I feel cold', 'I am loving her' instead of 'I love her', 'I am liking you', instead of 'I like you' etc. which are un-English in feature. 'To translate is to change into another language, retaining as much of the sense as one can' (vii), says A.H. Smith. But retaining the sense alone is not enough. We have to maintain the semantic compatibility along with grammaticality.

Let's take the question of literal translation, R.S. Pathak gives an interesting account of such a type of translation in the following words:

> Literal translation has its advantages and limitations which need to be weighed carefully for each cultural element and lexical item. If we translate screwdriver as 'penchkus' for example, it is fully acceptable. But what about I'm all eyes? 'Block' in American English means 'a rectangular section of a city or town bounded on each side by consecutive streets' or 'a segment of a street bounded by successive cross streets'. I do not think there is any exact equivalent for block in Hindi which can be helpful in translating a sentence like "We used to live on the same block." Words like sacred, secular, communal convey different shades of meaning to different people. Different races have different notions of 'incest' and therefore, the word will have no uniform meaning for them. The term gentleman cannot be rendered faithfully in Hindi; even 'sambhrant', borrowed from Sanskrit, does not really serve the purpose nor does the Bengali 'bhadralog'. The problem becomes all the more obvious in technical and semi-technical writings. It is not correct to translate, for example, terms like 'pradakshina path', 'vedika' and 'toran' as 'circumambulatory path', 'railing' and 'gateways' respectively, as has been done in a very recent edition of *The Hindustan Times*, for the real sense

> of the original terms evaporates as soon as they are given in English as above. Terms from Indian Poetics like 'rasa', 'vakrokti' are just untranslatable into English. This is also true of scores of words from the spheres of philosophy, grammar and Indian system of medicine.

Nothing would be gained if pig iron and silver fish are rendered in Hindi as 'sookarayask' and 'rajat matsya' respectively. A word-forward translation of the phrase heat and cold will be 'garmi aur sardi' or 'sardi garmi'. A Herculean task, in all propriety, should be rendered as 'Bhagirath prayatna' rather than 'Herculeus ka Karya'. Translating stadium as 'Prashal' shows inventiveness, but such cases are rare. Raghuvir circulated quite a few expressions which have failed to find any acceptance. Some of these words are: 'kanthlangote' (necktie), 'dhumraddhavaldandika' (cigarette), 'louhpathgamini' (train) and so on. 'preshmudrank' for postal stamp, and 'Netrak' for spectacles also belong to the same category. A common expression 'too too mein mein' communicate far too much than its translated version you youing me meing suggested by P. Lal and N. Napony. A literal translation of some typical expressions would be ridiculous (59-100).

Homonymns of Indian languages (*i.e.*, the same form in several Indian languages) create problems for the translators. For example 'darun' in Bengali means 'big' but it is used as an objective to Oriya words 'darun dukh' ('great sorrow') or 'darun aghat' ('great shock'). I am inclined to quote R.S. Pathak again who gives a whole list of such homonymns in the following passage:

> The problem gets compounded because the same form gives different meanings in different languages. For example 'uphar' in Marathi signifies 'refreshment', but it means in Hindi 'a present', and 'uttejit' means 'inspired' in Marathi and 'angry or a agitated' in Hindi, 'Shiksha' in Hindi is 'teaching or education' and in Marathi 'punishment', 'Razinama' is used in Marathi in the sense of 'resignation', but in Hindi it means 'agreement'. Similarly, the word 'ashuddh' means in Hindi 'incorrect' or 'impure'; in Kashmiri it means 'very precious' (thing)

and also 'medicine' or 'cure'. 'Jal', in Hindi is 'water' but 'zal' in Kashmiri is 'urine'. 'Manhoos' in Kashmiri means 'un-social, shy, gloomy' and in Hindi 'ominous' or 'inauspicious'. Such 'false friends' and deceptive cognates will only make the translator's task further complicated. Polysemy and oligosemy, like lexical gaps, also obstruct successful translatability. Moreover, the translator should be able to differentiate between the denotative, connotative and idiomatic meanings of words. Then, words come to acquire certain associations in languages. According to Bertrand Russell, "no one can understand the word 'cheese' unless he has a non-linguistic acquaintance with cheese" (18). Some words gain in due course semitonic function like nodding or shaking of the head or pointing. Roman Jakobson rightly points out that "we distinguish three ways of interpreting a verbal sign; it may be translated into other signs of the same language, into another language, or into another, non-verbal system of symbols". Because of their undertones of connotative meanings translation of some words becomes still more problematic. A couple of examples will make it clear. Dove in Bengali is not a symbol of peace; it is equivalent of a cunning, unprincipled person who drives people out of their homes. The word 'dushra' in Bengali is the highest abuse and conveys far more than what it does in Hindi and other cognate languages. 'Reja' has two meanings in Orissa alone; in and around Sambalpur it means a 'woman worker', but in other dialects of Oriya it stands for 'change or loose coins'.

Certain food items of India and words of common use in everyday conversation based on culture cannot be translated accurately into a foreign tongue. For example 'the Indian' delicacies like *halva*, *puri*, *kheer*, *jalevi* thus cannot be sensibly translated into (Italian) spaghetti, maccheroni, minestrone and pizzas. The English soft drinks means something different in our country. In Serbo-Croatian it is bezalkoholna piea, literally 'without-alcohol drinks'. In West African English, however, we have not drinks, 'alcoholic drinks'. Other culture-bound expressions from the same language are: chewing stick (twig used for cleaning teeth), cover shoulder (a blouse), knocking fee (money paid by a man to a woman's family for initiating negotiations about marriage), outdooring (the first appearance of a baby in public), sleeping cloth (cloth on which one sleeps at night), small room (toilet) and tight friend (close friend)", rightly says R.S. Pathak (100-01). Thus, literal translation and translation based on culture words are beset with pitfalls.

Cultural words create problems, as the impact of them gets lost in the process of translation. For example, the simple word 'you' in English has three corresponding words in most of the Indian languages including Oriya. In Oriya it means, 'Tu', 'Tame' and 'Apana' depending upon the relationship with the person to whom the speaker addresses. English words like 'cousin', 'uncle', 'aunt' have a number of corresponding words in Indian languages and therefore, translation of these words into Indian languages becomes ambiguous. Take for instance a sentence like, "My uncle came yesterday" which when rendered into Oriya may mean either my father's brother or brother-in-law or my mother's brother or brother-in-law came (even, an explanation like paternal uncle or maternal uncle will not do). In Oriya we have a term 'Samudi' that explains the relationship between two persons whose son and daughter get married and become husband and wife respectively. In English we have no equivalent words for these Oriya words 'Samudi' or for that matter his wife 'Samuduni'. How to translate these words? That's a Herculean task.

English is SVO (subject, verb, object) language but most of the Indian languages including Oriya are SOV (subject, object, verb) languages. And moreover when we use simple present tense in English, in Indian languages we use present progressive tense. Take for example the Oriya sentences like "Mun Sabu Januchi" (I am knowing everything), 'Sabu Sunuchi' (am hearing), 'bujhuchi' (am understanding) produce ungrammaticalities if translated 'word for word' into English. The Oriya users of English is confused by tense and aspect. "I have seen him last week" is incorrect in English but if translated word for word into Oriya becomes correct grammatically.

The translation of literature poses a good deal of problems for the translator. Literature translation involves not only the transference of meaning but a host of associations charged with the meaning which need to be translated from SL text into TL text. Since the basic loss of meaning is one a continuum between under translation and over translation, it is imperative on our part to divide literature translation genrewise. First, I take up the problems of poetry translation.

Once Robert Frost said, 'Poetry is that which is lost in translation'. If a good deal of poetry is lost, enough is retained in translation. No doubt, poetry translation poses formidable challenge to the translator. The most difficult thing in poetry translation is to find equivalent words of literary echoes in target language. For example, how to find out equivalent words of Eliot's use of Spenser's line 'Sweet Thames...'? And again the barrier to meaning is not simply cultural, even those sharing the same language may not get the allusions correctly. Does the English-knowing readers recognize Eliot's allusion to 'Prothalamion' in *The Wasteland*?

Secondly, the problem of language in poetry is not easy to overcome. Ornamental words (rhetoric) based on lyricism are almost impossible to translate. I am inclined to agree with Jayanta Mahapatra, the well-known Indian English poet and translator when he draws our attention to the difficulty of Poetry translation in the following words:

> "It is generally believed that a verse translation is itself poetry, but whether it really is poetry or not is a questionable matter. Any poem will not move fluently into translation, my own experience reveals the many hazards and difficulties encountered in the process. My main concern being from Oriya into English, I shall discuss some of these. For example, it is almost impossible to translate poets like Upendra Bhanja or Gangadhar Mehere. In Oriya literature the problem is of language, basically—and this fact is especially noticeable with these earlier poets, poets who used language with such powers of magic and devotion that resulted in instilling in readers' minds a divine and perhaps mystic presence.

Neither Upendra Bhanja nor Gangadhar Mehere used free verse, and their poems literally sag with the weight of ornamentation and alliterative sounds. Lyrical poetry such as they wrote was full of words having too many referential allusions, and was more or less ritualistic, with an incantatory tone. For that matter, I would feel uncomfortable when I heard such a poem being recited aloud, as though I were undergoing a mystic sort of experience. Even the later poets of the Oriya language, like Radhanath Ray, resorted to strict, musical verse forms—something that fed the poetry with a feeling of mysteriousness. Oriya diction is slow and formal, the sounds of words seem to dig into the mind and meander in the deeper layers of the imagination. Let us consider the first four lines of the poem 'Chilika' by Radhanath Ray:

Utkata-kamala bilasa-dirghika
Marala malini nilambu Chilika
Utkalara thui charu alankara
Utkala bhubane shobhara bhandara

How very clever, how concise is the construction of this verse form! And with what perfection has the poet woven the sounds of each line! How very much does each line convey, with its sensual, archaic flavour! Into the four words of each line is compressed the deep passion of the poet; and how does one translate a compact verse form of this type into a foreign medium such as English ? To me, a good translation into English seems almost impossible to make. For the verse resembles a many-petalled flower, each petal having its own word-significance, its individual auditory echoes. To render gems like these into English would be futile exercise, which would only harm the poetry in the original Oriya, like an act of desecration one can't pardon." (27-28)

In a poem sounds, rhythm, words, images, symbols, etc. are not only present together, but they also act on one another. That is why, reading poetry is itself an act of creative interpretation. Re-dering a poem into another language, becomes an act of 'creative transposition', as Jakobson would make us believe. The translator is a guide and a reader and therefore his act of reading (perusal) becomes co-terminous with his reading (meaning) of it. What Hugh Kenner says is that "As the poet begins by seeing, so the translator by reading; but his reading must be a kind of seeing" (10).

The greatest problem when translating a text (*i.e.*, a poem) from a distant past is not that the poet and his contemporaries are dead but "the significance of the poem in its context is dead" (83), says McGuire and rightly so. It is often argued that translation is not interpretation. The job of the translator is to reproduce what the author says not what he means. McGuire refutes such a claim with illustration in the following way:

> "It has often been argued, in accordance with Long fellow, that translation and interpretation are two separate activities, and that it is the duty of the translator to translate what is there and not to 'interpret' it. The fallacy of such an argument is obvious—since every reading is an interpretation, the activities cannot be separated. James Holmes has devised the following useful diagram to show the interrelationship between translation and critical interpretation."

The verse translation rests on the axis point where types of interpretation intersect with types of imitation and derivation.

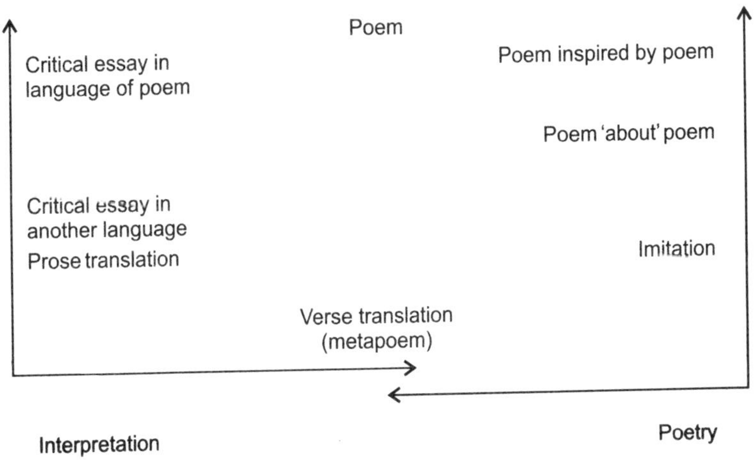

Moreover, a translator will continue to produce 'new' versions of a given text, not so much to reach an ideal 'percent translation' but because each previous version, being context bound, represents a reading accessible to the time in which it is produced, and moreover is individualistic. William Morris' versions of Homer or of Beowulf are both idiosyncratic in that they spring from Morris' own system of priorities and commitment to archaic form and language, and they are Victorian in that they exemplify a set of canons distinctive to one period in time. The great difference between a text and a meta text is that the one is fixed in time and place, and other is variable. There is only one Divina Commedia but there are innumerable readings and in theory innumerable translations" (100-01).

Great poetry taps the mythic reserves of human experience and it also creates myths which provide a meta-language for the social and cultural meanings. The new meanings a work of art creates, are fore-grounded in the traditional meanings and therefore, in a work of art there is always a tension between the two sets of meanings. That adds to the problems of the translator. Take for instance, Keats' "Ode to a Nightingale". The poem is imbued with cultural meanings. Keats' idea of nightingale has something to do with the western core and somehow it becomes a universal symbol. As K. Chellappan has rightly pointed out that 'this basic symbol is evolved in relation to other symbols in the poem, which again are generated in the context of the poem, though they also have traditional links. If the ultimate meaning of the poem depends on all these facts, and if some of the components like Ruth or Hippocrene belong to the particular milieu, what do we do with them? Equivalents in the target culture may not do, because they bring a whole world of associations" (167).

Translation of poetry is the most difficult mode of translation. This is because it abounds in figures of speech such as similes, metaphors, irony, paradox etc. and unprecedented phonological, syntactic and semantic patterns such as rhyming alliteration, versification, morphological parallelism, syntactic parallelism and above all syntagmatic and paradigmatic relations between words. The translator of poetry should remember that he is to 'translate' a piece of poetry, not to 're-write' or 'produce an interpretation' of it.

The translator of poetry must take into account both the linguistic and non-linguistic aspects of a poem and try to re-create the poem in the target language. The linguistic aspect deals with sound pattern of words, rhymes and rhythms while the non-linguistic aspect is concerned with ideas, images, symbols based on culture of the SL poem. Some translators plead for prose rendering of a poem while others argue in favour of 'verse for verse' translation. This brings to our mind the difference between the poetry of earlier ages which was written in metre and rhyme, and the modern poetry in free-verse. It is easier to translate prose-poems (or poems written in free verse) into another language. But traditional poetry with its rhyme, metre and sound poses great problem for the translators. The translator should have the 'feel' of the poem; otherwise it will not be possible to translate it into TL. It should be borne in mind that even when adequate translation of poetry is not possible, there is no need for the translator to raise his hand in despair and say that poetry is not translatable. In spite of all the difficulties, translation of poetry is done for the benefit of the readers in the target language. Changing Robert Frost's dictum, we will say that poetry is that which is survived in translation. Translation of dramatic texts pose another kind of problem. Dialogues in dialects of a language that is far removed from the target language are very difficult to translate. Apart from language, the thought-content of a dramatic text couched in one culture poses serious problems for the translator. For example, it is difficult to translate Shakespeare and his contemporaries into any Indian language because of the linguistic and cultural differences. For example, how does one translate the magical words of Shakespeare, 'Ripeness is all', or 'Forget and Forgive' or 'Thou art soul in bliss/I'm bound upon wheel of Fire' or 'Fair is Foul and Foul is fair' or 'The rest is silence' etc. into our languages which are so vastly different from English language?

Furthermore, a dramatic text exhibits its full meaning only in its performance. As Anne Ubersfeld says that "The task of the director, therefore, is to 'translate into another language' a text of which he has a prime duty to remain 'faithful'. This position is based on the concept of semantic equivalence between the written text and its performance, only the 'mode of expression' in Hjelmslevian sense of the term will be altered, the form and content of the expression will remain identical when transferred from a system of test-signs to a system of performance signs" (TS 121).

The problem of performability is further complicated by the changing concepts of performance. Let us take the case of Shakespearean dramatic texts. In his time young boys were acting as heroines and Shakespeare introduced the technique of disguise according to which the heroine went in search of the hero into the forest. Nowadays can a director think of such a technique in theatre? On the other hand, modern Absurd dramatists and dramatists of Angry Young Man Movement pose another kind of problem for the translator. The dialogues, and performance create special problems for the translator and the director. How does one translate the dialogues of Lucky and Pozzo or Estragon and Vladimir of Beckett's *Waiting for Godot* into Indian languages?

Thus, the dialogues, performance, including stage-craft create problems for the translator. The colloquial and conversational language, intonation and accent including dialogue-delivery make the translation of dramatic texts difficult.

The translation of prose texts including novels pose another kind of problem. Hilaire Belloc outlined six general rules for the translator of prose texts:

(1) The translator should not 'plod on', word by word or sentence by sentence, but should 'always "block out" his work'. By 'block out', Belloc means that the translator should consider the work as an integral unit and translate in sections, asking himself 'before each what the whole sense is he has to render'.

(2) The translator should render idiom by idiom 'and idioms of their nature demand translation into another form from that of the original'. Belloc cites the case of the Greek exclamation 'By the Dog!', which, if rendered literally, becomes merely coming in English, and suggests that the phrase 'By God!' is a much closer translation. Likewise, he points out that the French historic present must be translated into the English narrative tense, which is past, and the French system of defining a proposition by putting it into the form of a rhetorical question cannot be transposed into English where the same system does not apply.

(3) The translator must render 'intention by intention', bearing in mind that 'the intention of a phrase in one language may be less emphatic than the form of the phrase, or it may be more emphatic'. By 'intention', Belloc seems to be talking about the weight a given expression may have in a particular context in the SL that would be disproportionate if translated literally into the TL. He quotes several examples where the weighting of the phrase in the SL is clearly much stronger or much weaker than the literal TL translation, and points out that in the translation of 'intention', it is often necessary to add words not in the original 'to conform to the idiom of one's own tongue'.

(4) Belloc warns against les faux aims, those words or structures that may appear to correspond in both SL and TL but actually do not, *e.g.* demander—to ask, translated wrongly as to demand.

(5) The translator is advised to 'transmute boldly' and Belloc suggests that the essence of translating is 'the resurrection of an alien thing in a native body'.

(6) The translator should never embellish.

Belloc's points are significant for they emphasize both themes and techniques. He attributes moral responsibility to the translator but at the same time gives him the liberty to change the text to suit the needs of the TL text reader. McGuire makes a pertinent comment on this point:

> Belloc's first point, in which he discusses the need for the translator problem for the prose translator: the difficulty of determining translation units. It must be clear at the outset that the text, understood to be in a dialectical relationship with other texts and located within a specific historical context, is the prime unit. But whereas the poet translator can more easily break the prime text down into translatable units, *e.g.* lines, verses, stanzas, the prose translator has a more complex task. Certainly, many novels are broken down into chapters or sections, but as Barthes has shown with his methodology of five reading codes (see S/Z, discussed by T. Hawkes, *Structuralism and Semiotics*, London, 1977) the structuring of a prose text is by no means as linear as the chapter divisions might indicate. Yet if the translator takes each sentence or paragraph as a minimum unit and translates it without relating it to the overall work, he runs the risk of ending up with a TL text like those quoted above, where the paraphrasable content of the passages has been translated at the cost of everything else.

The way round this dilemma must once again be sought through considering the function both of the text and of the devices within the text itself. If the translators of Silone had considered the function of the tone they would have understood why the careful rhetorical patterning of the opening paragraph needed closer examination. Likewise, if the translator of Mann had considered the function of the description of both the young man and the journey, she would have understood the reasons for Mann's choice of language. Every prime text is made up of a series of interlocking systems, each of which has a determinable function in relation to the whole, and it is the task of the translator to apprehend these functions (*TS* 117-18).

Having outlined the problems of different types of literary texts, I should turn to the problems of translating jokes and problems of specialized translations. It is said that humour is universal but joke is local. Unless one knows the exact nature or origin of the joke it would not be possible for him to translate it into another language. A research on jokes based on group studies conducted by M. Radhika and Udaynarayan Singh classifies jokes into the following 13 types:

(i) Ethnic jokes include jokes on people who are stingy, unclean, dumb, or about those who show blind obedience, language distortion, or are cunning, etc. These are usually associated with a particular sect or a group.

(ii) Political jokes expose political situations, state pressions, national traits, defamation of political figures, etc. Since politics affects the whole nation, these are usually immensely popular jokes.

(iii) Sexual jokes include jokes on adultery, obscenity, sexual ignorance, sexual prowess, etc.

(iv) Religious jokes cover jokes that deal with religious subjects including priests, nuns and gods as the butts.

(v) Economy jokes relate to shortage, poverty etc. of a particular group of community or nation. Since any kind of deviance can provide one with a potential source of humour, economic deprivation cannot be avoided.

(vi) Stupid or Aging jokes cover jokes on aging, idiocy, irrationality, etc.

(vii) Clever repartees are actually witty, wacky and deliberate insults. One instance should suffice: John (handling a chocolate): Here, honey, sweets to the sweet. Mary: Oh, Thank you. Won't you have some of these nuts.

(viii) Anti-social jokes are jokes on drinking, stealing, terrorism, etc.

(ix) Uniform jokes are about the military, flying and sailing crews, waiters, police, etc.

(x) Academic jokes relate to all academic institutions, and especially to student-student and student-teacher interactions.

(xi) Professional jokes cover all professions such as lawyers, doctors, businessmen, bureaucrats, clerks, and others.

(xii) Family jokes deal with all members of a family—grand-parents, parents and children, grand-children or other relatives.

(xiii) Linguistic jokes, *i.e.*, spoonerisms, misprints, ghostwriting, daffy definition, puns, parodies, mistakes etc., may come under this category (63).

The problematic jokes are very difficult to translate. They are based on homonymy, polysemy and with double meaning due to literal and figurative interpretations. There are no definite rules or established norms to interpret and translate texts—much less to evaluate it.

Research shows that all jokes are translatable. But he does not try for a Sabun saree. The following observations are made to find out how humour can cripple a human mind:

(1) All jokes are translatable. But the translation of only some kind of jokes produce humorous effect similar to the one produced by the SL joke,

(2) The method of translation adopted was neither very free nor very faithful. The translators aiming for dynamic equivalence,

(3) No two translations of the same joke were alike,

(4) The devices adopted for the translation of the body of jokes is similar to that of non-humorous texts. The punch line is to be translated in such a way that humour is retained as in the source text,

(5) When metaphors or idioms were present in the body of text, the sense was translated,

(6) Jokes based on double meanings due to literal and figurative meanings, polysemy, homonymy and misprints were problematic. The translation of such types of jokes were attempted by adopting the devices of transcription and paraphrasing,

(7) The type of audience and the context within a joke is to be told or situated are both very important for translating jokes,

(8) The evaluations of SL jokes on the basis of 'funniness' and the evaluations of their translations on the basis of their translation techniques were similar, which shows that the translations were evaluated on the basis of the humorous content in the SL joke. In other words, the degree of funniness of the SL joke coloured the evaluation of the translation in TL. This fact was further corroborated when the TL (Telugu) texts were circulated around to elicit reaction/evaluation of these jokes (without showing them as translation) as if they were the originals. The results in both cases only confirmed the hypothesis that evaluation of retelling of jokes (in an other tongue) depends on the fun or humour they generate or retain rather than on the faithfulness to the SL text or such other measurement criterion. (Radhika 91-92)

The problems of translation are many-fold but two major problems that baffle the translators are linguistic and cultural. Again, of all types of translation, the most elusive one is that of the translation of poetry. Two of our distinguished scholar-critics Sri Aurobindo and K.R.S. Iyengar have cautioned us while translating poetry into a second language. Iyengar says:

> "Poetry by its very nature is untranslatable. Ideas can be translated from language to language, but poetry is the idea touched with the magic of phrase and incantatory music. Competent translator can, however, play the good broker between the Poet and the reader, and surpassing the mere prose of statement can give intimations of the poet's sovereign utterance. Good translation can create trust and it can stimulate interest." (Srinivas 52)

Sri Aurobindo is of the opinion that there are two ways of translating poetry: "one to keep it strictly to the manner and turn of the original, (and) the other is to take its spirit, sense and imagery and produce them freely so as to suit the new language". To Aurobindo the second method of translating poetry is preferable. But this is a more difficult path, as is evident from the following admission from Krishna Srinivas, himself an able translator (432). He preferred the second method to the first.

T.S. Eliot on the other hand takes Gilbert Murray to task for the English translation of Medea and complains about the translator's stretching "the Greek brevity to fit the loose frame of William Morris" and blurring "the Greek lyric to the fluid haze of Swinburne" (71-77). And Matthew Arnold found fault with all the three translators of Homer's *Iliad*. He wrote in "On Translating Homer":

> Homer is rapid in his movement. Homer is plain in his words and style. Homer is simple in his ideas. Homer is noble in his manner. Cowper renders him ill because he is slow in his movement, and elaborate in his style; Pope renders him ill because he is fantastic in his ideas; Mr. Newman renders him ill because he is odd in his words and ignoble in his manner. (250)

Translation of metaphors pose a special kind of problem and the translator's burden is how to translate metaphors without affecting the SL discourse. Cultural factors cause difficulties in the translation of metaphors. For instance 'owl' in Oriya symbolizes 'ill fortune' whereas it is the symbol of wisdom in English, 'Bull' is the symbol of endurance in English whereas it is the symbol of rudeness in Persian.

In spite of all the problems that threaten the authenticity of translation and undermine its position, the desire to translate on the part of scholars and translators has shown an upward trend. Translation in the midst of all the problems, continues to be rendered, is something one should rejoice. Ironically enough, it is the problems that make the art of translation challenging and finally fascinating.

WORKS CITED

Arnold, Matthew. *Essays Literary and Critical.* London, 1950.

Barthes, Roland. "Sign, Sense and Roland", *Literary Criticism: Idea and Act.* Barkely: University of California Press, 1974.

Belloc, Holaire. *In Translation.* Oxford: The Clarendon Press, 1931.

Chellappan, K. "The Paradox of Transacreation". *Literature in Translation,* Eds. Pramod Talgeri and S.B. Verma. Bombay: Popular Prakashan, 1988.

Eliot, T.S. *The Sacred Wood.* London: Methuen, 1920.

Iser, Wolfgang. *The Act of Reading.* Baltimore: John Hopkins University Press, 1980.

Kenner, Hugh. "Introduction", *The Translations of Ezra Pound.* London: Faber and Faber, 1953.

Mahapatra, Jayanta. "Translating from the Oriya: An Approach." *Cygnus* 2 : 2, 1981.

McGuire Susan Bassnett. *Translation Studies.* New York: Routledge, 1991.

Mukherjee, Meenakshi. "Transposition of Culture". *Cygnus* 2 : 2, 1981.

Pathak, R.S. "Untranslatability: Myth or Reality?" *Critical Practices* 2 : 1, June 1994.

Radhika, M. and Udaynarayan Singh. "Translation of Jokes: Problems of Specialized Translation". *Critical Practice* 1 : 2, 1994.

Rajnath. "The Text and the Reader: Critique of Reader Response Criticism", *Journal of Literary Criticism,* 3 : 1, 1986.

Russell, Bertrand. "Logical Positivism", *Revue Internationale de Philosophie* 4, 1950.

Smith, A.H. (ed.). *Aspects of Translation.* London: Becker and Warburg, 1958.

Sri Aurobindo. *The Future Poetry.* Pondicherry: Sri Aurobindo Birth Centenary Publication, nd.

Srinivas, Krishna (Quoted). *On Translating Poetry. Creative Forum* 1 : 1, 1988.

Srivastava, A.K. "On Translating Literature". *The Literary Criterion.* 22 : 2, 1987.

The Anxiety of Authenticity: Reflections on Literary Translation*

7

K. AYAPPA PANIKER

1. Translation should be Faithful

It was while directing a 22-day literary translation workshop for eight languages at Trivandrum a few years ago that I had to bear witness to the anxiety of authenticity keenly felt by several practising translators. Overwhelmed by the reputation of the original author and the popularity of the text, most of the translators wanted to be extremely faithful to the original text—some gave up the attempt at translation for fear of being unfaithful. This made me write a limerick in Malayalam:

> Oru kilavanuntayirunnu Malappurattayaloru charitryabhaktan,
> citavare bharyaye kanyakayakkivacchoduvilayalum mariche

which has been "faithfully" translated into English as

> There was an old man in Malappuram
> who wanted his wife to remain chaste.
> He kept her a virgin
> till she's taken to the grave
> Then he too followed her.

There may not be many such people in other places, which explains why the art of translation continues to be practised with little anxiety about faithfulness to the original.

---

* Reprinted from *Critical Practice* Vol. 1, No. 2 with permission from Creative Books, New Delhi.

2. Indian Perspectives: Medieval Example

Talking about Indian perspectives on the translation of literature, it may be said that till the 19th century Indian "translators" were not affected unduly by this anxiety of being true to the original in letter and spirit. All through the Middle Ages, throughout the length and breadth of India, Sanskrit classics like the epics and puranas continued to be retold, adapted, subverted, and "translated" without worrying about the exactness and accuracy of formal equivalence. When Kamban wrote Ramayanam in Tamil, he took all the freedom he needed to make his version of Valmiki's Ramayana, a Tamil classic. He keeps close to the structure of Dravidian epic; he edits, cuts, condenses, elaborates, interprets, modifies etc. to suit his own tastes as well as those of his immediate readers. The features of the target language and the tastes of the target readers at the time of translation are among the factors that promoted this free style translation. The 12th century Malayalam version Ramacharitam, like Tulsidas's Ramacharitamanas or Krittivas Ramayana, is almost a new creation with shift of emphasis and occasionally substantial modification of episodes. Even Adhyatmaramayana in Sanskrit is different in significant ways from Valmiki Ramayana. There are many versions of folk Ramayana like the Malayalam work *Sitadu:kham* which is almost a "feminist" version of the patriarchal text favoured by the elite. The impression one gets from all these multiple versions is that, not only was literal adherence to the original not insisted on, but that deviation was liberally tolerated, even encouraged and preferred. Even in the medieval Malayalam renderings of texts like Bhagavadgita, Arthasastra and Brahmanda Purana, this creative freedom was cherished and maintained. There is scope here for propounding the theory of translation as appropriation through linguistic manipulation. The Aryan or Sanskrit texts were localized in the South, even Dravidianized. The Bhakti Movement which gained momentum with the works of the Alwars and the spread of Bhagavatam was a process of de-sanskritization rather than of sanskritization. The non-Vedic gods entered the pantheon and old rituals, even tribal customs, were accepted and absorbed. Some of the textual variants in the medieval translation seem to illustrate this. The politics of medieval Indian translations could perhaps be understood and interpreted in terms of the visible absence of the anxiety of authenticity on the part of these "translators." If the local/regional versions of Ramayana and Mahabharata became the classics of the regional literatures, the reason is not far to seek. These adapted translations were well received by the public in each region. There was nothing "alien" about them. This has not happened to modern translations from either modern Indian languages or non-Indian languages.

3. The Western Impact

Perhaps it was with the beginning of the attempts to translate the Bible into Indian languages that this question of authenticity became a bugbear. Accuracy became an obsession and literary flavour got only a second or third place. Theories of translation too came to be based on the experience of translating the Bible into non-European languages. Until the reformation, the translation of the Bible into modern European languages was considered a sacrilege. The Malayalam translator of the Quran also refers to a similar disinclination to translate religious scriptures into heathen languages. It is true that since the reformation and with the spread of colonialism the translation of the Bible has promoted the study of the theories of translation. It is nevertheless true that if the purists had their way we would never have enjoyed the works of Tolstoy or Dostoevsky or classics like *The Arabian Nights* or the *Tale of Genji.*

4. Translation and the Globalization of Culture

The 19th century favoured the globalization of culture and as part of the process translation came to acquire a good deal of importance. A few decades after the works of Kalidasa were translated into European languages, they came to be translated into modern Indian languages—about the same time as the works of Shakespeare began to be translated into Indian languages. The growing familiarity of Indian readers with the works of European authors is clearly indicated by the history of translations. English texts led the way; French, German and Russian followed; translations from Asian languages are even now very rare; Latin American works get translated because they are written in European languages. African English writings get precedence over writings in African languages. Contemporary Arabic and Persian literature is still to gain access to the Indian readership. The reception of translated literature is an index to the broadening of literary taste.

5. Malayalam: A Case Study

In Malayalam we still do not have the complete works of Shakespeare in a readable version, let alone a stage-worthy version. Kunhikuttan Tampuran, at the turn of the present century, performed a remarkable feat by translating with utmost faithfulness the whole of Mahabharata, 100,000 stanzas, in a matter of 2½ years. He also translated Shakespeare's *Hamlet* into Malayalam without knowing a word of English. It is not an acting version, but is felt by many to be one of the best translations of a Shakespearian text we have till date. Those who know English well may not care to translate, because they can read the original; they are also held back by the anxiety of authenticity. Those who are familiar with the theatre may not know English well, they are also held back by their own proficiency in the mother tongue.

6. The Role of English in Literary Translation

The spread of English education promoted the industry of translation, because thousands of people became bilinguals through their schooling. English was the school language for many; their home language continued to be the mother-tongue—except for the English-medium-educated urban upper and middle class. The prestige of English is still high; only last year in Kerala a boy's head was shaved because he spoke a Malayalam word in the class! This inverted chauvinism may be fairly ubiquitous—although it may not get reported, if the press people sympathize with it.

7. Translation and the Press

The press in India is a great translation mill, doing overtime work all through the year. Many words, normally difficult to translate, get translated in no time at the editor's desk at the dead of night. Scholars might take ages to produce an exact but imbecile equivalent. The Indian language newspapers have done yeoman service to the cause of translation. Their contribution is recognized and accepted by and large by the community in course of time. Their split-second instant translations often achieve a miraculous success, while some of the laboured efforts of great literary men end up as miserable failures. Nalappad Narayana Menon translated Victor Hugo's *Les Miserables* and he translated the phrase "born with a silver spoon in the mouth" literally into Malayalam as "Vāyil vellikarantiyumyi janichu." This is awkward and the expression provokes only laughter. It has not gained currency in Malayalam. In the same way, V.K. Narayana Menon coined the phrase "O my pot of gold" literally translating the Malayalam phrase "ente ponnumkudam". Both the Menons are gifted scholars and their translations are well received—but still there are certain expressions and coinages used by them which are not unexceptional. "Vellikaranti" in Malayalam and "pot of gold" in English are memorable examples of these.

8. Malayalam *Vs.* Other Languages

When I was editing the book *The Making of Indian Literature* which is based on the reports of four workshops on literary translation—one national and three regional—I found that the experiences and observations of practising translators were more meaningful and valuable than the views of theoreticians including linguists. The gynaecologists could deliver other people's babies; when their turn came, they needed the help of others. We have in India excellent translators who may not be able to theorize or explain how translation is to be done. The best translation into English of any Malayalam work till date is that of *Indulekha* done by Dumergue, who was Collector of Malabar: it came out in 1890 within a year of the first publication of the original in Malayalam. Dumergue has no reputation as a writer in English. I don't know if he translated anything else. *Indulekha* is a difficult work to translate—the local colour, especially the Keralite brand of humour, is very difficult to translate into a Germanic language like English. One of the best recent translations from an Indian language into Malayalam is Tara Shankar Bannerjee's *Arogyaniketanam*: it is the work of a Bengali and a Malayali in ideal collaboration. Translations from western language or other Indian languages into Malayalam are far more successful than those from Malayalam into English. I have myself translated in both directions: the six-hundred-page anthology of Malayalam literature which I helped to bring out from Michigan State University (*JSAL,* 1980-81) leaves much to be desired. But it remains the biggest attempt till date at projecting our literature into a world language.

9. A Personal Note

Forgive me if I take time off to talk about some of the insights I got from my own experience as a translator. I have found that the methodology of translation is dependent on the nature of the work to be translated. When I translated Mayakovsky's poems (including the epic poem on Lenin) I consulted several English versions—Stalinist as well as non-Stalinist—and referred continuously to the original Russian. I also had to read a number of books on the original author. The reference to Trotsky was missing in some editions (English and Russian); the lines like "I will bomb Kremlin, if you build a mausoleum for Lenin; don't make a god of him; he was a simple man" could not be found in some versions. One had to reconstruct the text in the pre-Gorbachev era in order to get the sense of the original. While trying to translate Jibanananda Das, I had to go beyond the English renderings, which appeared to be too free—more like the translator than the original poet—and consult the Hindi and Bengali versions. In my translation of *The Waste Land* I had to avoid imposing my poetic style on Eliot. Some translators use their own style all through—whichever poet they are translating. When I turned to Guru Nanak's poems, I knew this was sacred literature—some passages were holy mantras. The tone and the undertone were as important as, if not more important than, the verbal structure. I had to refer to several English versions along with Devanagari transliterations of the original. I also listened to the recorded versions, as these were not merely literary but also musical compositions. The rhythm was also an important carrier of the meaning.

10. Malayalam and Indian English

Translating from Indian English into Malayalam also throws up special problems. Raja Rao's *The Cat and Shakespeare* was translated by me into Malayalam. Unlike his other novels, this is located in Trivandrum; the characters are normal speakers of Malayalam. Raja Rao writes in English, so he has to invent a form of English which would sound natural when these men and women speak English. Ramakrishna Pai, the central character, is a saraswath Brahmin of Konkani origin; but living in Trivandrum. When people of his group speak Malayalam, there is a certain quality which other Malayalam-speakers easily notice. Ramakrishna Pai in the novel speaks an inter-dialect which, although English, has the characteristic features of Konkani Malayalam. Raja Rao has succeeded in capturing this tone in English. My effort was therefore to render this tone in the Malayalam version also. This inter-dialect was already there in Malayalam, but Raja Rao had to invent it in English. *The Cat and Shakespeare* in this sense was a Malayalam novel written in English; the translation of it into Malayalam was like bringing it back into its original form! And it had to be done without any possible racist overtones.

11. The Translation of Older Texts

The problem of translating ancient and medieval Indian literature into modern English has two dimensions: one is that of the languages, the other is that of the periods. The linguistic and temporal differences have to be absorbed to make readable translations. Translating them into modern Indian languages too bristles with difficulties; the seemingly archaic elements were not so archaic at the time this literature was written. The oral tradition creates another problem in that there is no single standard version available for many texts. The editors have made their editorial discretion; anyway the very idea of a definitive edition is a problematic. It is unlikely that any definitive edition will survive for long as the only definitive version. A.K. Ramanujan, Arvind Mehrotra and others have successfully attempted at making modern(ist) versions of ancient texts. Not all readers are likely to accept their solutions to the problem. Every age will have to translate ancient classics to satisfy the changing tastes of successive generations. Homer has to be rendered from ancient Greek into modern Greek; he has to be translated again and again into modern English. Chapman's version could thrill Keats; yet there have been umpteen translations since Chapman. And this effort at making fresh translations will continue. There are scholarly translations like Gilbert Murray's versions of Sophocles, but they are not quite readable; they should lifeless. Ramanujan's translations from Sangam literature (*Interior Landscape, Poems of Love and War,* etc.) are eminently readable, they do speak across cultures, but some Tamil scholars have their reservations about their authenticity. It is true that these versions have made ancient Tamil classics accessible to modern European and American readers. They are couched in the language of modernism and hence they are said to misrepresent the originals: this is the complaint of Tamil scholars.

12. Theories of Translation

Should the translations carry any trace of the translator, or for that matter, retain any trace of the original language? Should they read like translations? Do we read translated literature for aesthetic enjoyment or for anthropological information? These questions have come up again and again. If translation is motivated, as in the case of Bible translations across the world, as part of missionary activity, the impression created or the tone assumed is that of flow from a superior cultural (or political) position to an inferior level. How far is this assumption valid? And what is its bearing on the art and science of translation? If we begin with the English version as the source text, then we ignore a large number of problems related to the translation of the Bible into English. Anyway theories of translation based on the experience of translating a single scriptural text for missionary purposes have only a limited value for translating literary works for aesthetic pleasure.

13. English as a Link

Today in India English serves as the main link for inter-Indian literary translations as well as for Indian non-Indian translations. When Indian literature, ancient, medieval or modern, passes through English or for that matter Hindi, before it is translated into another Indian language, the loss is perhaps greater than the gain. But something still survives even in the worst of translations. Between the source and the target fall the shadows of language, time, taste, the personality of the translator and the manner of transmission. If something still survives, one may have to modify Robert Frost's dictum—poetry is what is not lost even in translation. We approach a translation knowing very well that it is a translation. The reader's attitude is shaped by his foreknowledge of what he is going to read. And a translator brings to his reader not just the bare text, but a large part of the cultural scaffolding which helps to make sense of that text. If the translation comes through the agency of an intermediate or link language like English, then the cultural scaffolding becomes a complicated matter. We have several translations of *Rubaiyat* of Omar Khayyam via Fitzgerald; it is doubtful whether a translation in reverse of any of these will give us anything remotely resembling the original Persian work. And yet English is for many years to come to continue as an interpreter or a mediator. The mediation of English between Indian literatures can be progressively eliminated in the foreseeable future. But for foreign literatures English may have to continue to play that role for several decades. This is a kind of two-way mediation.

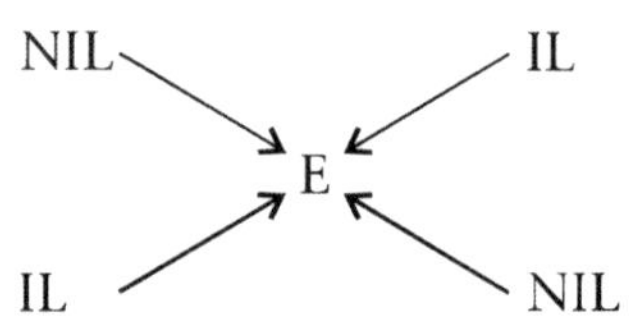

It is perhaps time to think of avoiding the mediation of English for translating from one modern Indian language into another. It is desirable, but not feasible right now. We still have to make do with English.

IL ⟶ English ⟶ IL

As translation in the sense in which we understand it today is a comparatively new or recent phenomenon, the examples of medieval "translation" have only a limited bearing. No translation is perfect in an absolutist sense. The expectations of the readers of the original may be different from those of the readers of the translation. Hence judgments will always vary. It is difficult to assert that a bad translation is better than no translation. A bad translation is certainly harmful, while not having any translation cannot be said to be positively harmful.

A Kind of Conclusion

Of all the arts, literature alone is faced with this problem of translation, because it uses different languages as its medium of expression. In music, painting, dance, sculpture or architecture where the medium of language is not used, there is no question of translation. In literature we have to have translations: multiple translations are themselves an indication of differing tastes and divergent purposes. Tagore by Tagore or by Radice raises the problem of the evaluation of translation. Did Tagore have this problem of the multiplicity of translations in mind when he said in *Gitanjali*:

> Thou hast made me endless;
> such is thy pleasure?

A literary work always carries a subtext along with the surface text. Will the subtext or *dhvanipaath* be automatically carried into the translation of the surface text? If the subtext is not recoverable in the translation, of what use is such an effort? In the 18th century Kathakali text *Kalakeyavanham,* Urvasi is described in such a way as to suggest the qualities of great poetry which the passage is meant to illustrate:

> sulalitha padavinyasa
> ruchiralankarasalini madhura
> mridulapigahanabhava
> suktarivapa so'rvasi vijayam

> Graceful in the movement of her steps
> (set in simple, beautiful words)

> Sweet and adorned with ornaments
> (decked with figures of speech)

Gentle yet magnificent in appearance
(full of soft and profound feelings)

Like poetry Urvasi came to Vijaya (Victory)

Shouldn't the translation do justice to the subtext as well? The reader of the translation cannot be expected to go to the source to get at the subtext, which is what makes the literary work important. Kimon Friar's translation of the Greek epic *The Odyssey: A Modern Sequel* appears to me to carry the subtext all through its 33333 lines. The translator is no more; only the translation survives. But who cares for the translator? He should disappear in the work, shouldn't he? He should not stand between the reader and the original author, why should he? He should achieve the extinction of his personality. He is perhaps most successful when he is least visible, and hence most visible too.

Coda

In Kamala Das's translation of her mother Balamoni Amma's poem "Vibhishana," Rama's request to Sita to "testify her mental purity" is rendered as "Woman, leap into the fire! Prove your chastity!" This reflects the difference in attitude between the mother and the daughter—perhaps the generation gap too. Could we suggest that the translation of a work is like its daughter, born of it, but still different—reflecting such a change in taste and attitude?

The Politics of Postcolonial Translation*

8

HARISH TRIVEDI

To speak of postcolonial translation is at once to beg a crucial question, for it is to assume that there is not only a chronological but a qualitative difference between translations done in the colonial period and those done afterwards. The chronological factor has in this context a doubly problematic bearing. So far as "original" literary works are concerned, the date of composition or publication indicates accurately enough a historical configuration. In the case of translations, however, not one but two sets of historical co-ordinates need to be identified: one for the original text and the other for the translation. The periodization of translations, therefore, as colonial or postcolonial is inevitably a diachronic marker, and it is at the same time an act of ideological or political faith.

Some basic questions of fact which one may need to ask within this framework in order to validate the nomenclature of "postcolonial" may be: (i) whether broadly the same kind of texts continue to be translated in postcolonial times as in the colonial times but as a recognizably distinct political project, (ii) whether quite different kinds of texts now begin to be translated instead or as well, and (iii) whether the balance of payments (or indeed the balance of cultural power) between the

---

* An earlier version of this paper was presented at the biennial conference of the Comparative Literature Association of India, February 1993, Delhi.

Reprinted from *Critical Practice* Vol. 1, No. 2 with permission from Creative Books, New Delhi.

former colony and the metropolis is in any significant way altered in terms of the quantum of translations transacted between them, and in terms of their respective reception and impact.

As has increasingly been recognized, translation involves an interaction not only between two authors, or two author-functions, but also between languages and cultures, an interaction fraught with political implications. The SL-TL power relationship can be highly variable one, as the long history of translation activity amply illustrates. One of the most notorious (and conveniently quotable) instance here perhaps is that of Edward Fitzgerald, who claimed, in the immediate context not of Omar Khayyam but of Attar, that he took such liberties as he pleased with the Persian poets when translating them because they were "not Poets enough" for his taste until he made them so (Bassnett 3). This roughshod, high-and-mighty SL attitude is not merely a matter of personal preference; it may be seen to be at last subliminally a function of the historical fact that it was adopted at the high noon of the British empire (Trivedi 45).

The relationship between all the Indian languages on the one hand and English on the other, either as SL/TL or as TL/SL, represents many of the same factors. As is again well-known, Tagore the English translator treated Tagore the Bengali poet in the most cavalier fashion, now changing, now chopping, now omitting, now adding, and feign altogether ever so solicitous of the orientalist expectations of the English reader, often at the expense of the poor Bengali author, *i.e.* himself, even to the extent of falsifying him (Thompson 264). If this was not an effect of direct imperialism, it was at least a high degree of voluntary assimilation, facilitated by that notably anglophile and anglicized dimension of Tagore's personality.

A tendency on the part of many translators into English, whether foreign or Indian, of works of Indian literature, which is frequent enough to seem to form a significant pattern is their practice of leaving behind substantial chunks of Indian novels when transferring them, sometimes to the tune of as much as one-fourth or even one-third of the whole—as for example in Edward Thompson's translation of *Svarnalata* under the title

The Brothers, in Narayan Menon's translation of *Chemmeen,* or in the translation by T.W. Clarke and Tarapada Mukherjee of *Pather Panchali* (Mukherjee 29). As what often gets deleted or substantially modified in the process is the ending, such suppression probably represents the aesthetic subjugation of an Indian sense of valediction by a Western sense of ending, and is a matter that should especially concern Frank Kermode, author of the highly sophisticated exegetical work *The Sense of an Ending* (which title, aptly for our present purpose, is recalled as *What's the Sense of an Ending?* by a character in David Lodge novel).

A helpful, and even necessary, perspective on colonial and postcolonial translations, therefore, is to study them not as translations of one text or one author at a time, but as part of a larger historical process in which versions of apparently widely different texts still share common features of translatorial practice. The old debate on what is the proper unit of translation —whether it is a word, a phrase, a sentence, a paragraph, a page, or even (the "spirit" of) a complete text has recently found a cogent new formulation, in the suggestion that what gets translated, and what may be sought to be translated, is a whole "culture" into another (Bassnett and Lefevere 4; Snell-Hornby 79-86). This macro project would necessarily entail a greater awareness of the political implications of translation than might a micro project which seeks to practise translation in the smaller New Criticism units of a word or at most a page at a time.

I

The cultural-national project of postcolonial translation in India has two complementary aspects: translations of world literature into the Indian languages (though mainly through English), and translations from the Indian languages into the languages of the world (but mainly into English). Another significant and highly fertile area is that of translations amongst the various Indian languages, an activity systematically sponsored and promoted by organizations such as the Sahitya Akademi and the National Book Trust, by the latter under the happily chosen series titled Adan Pradan. But these intra-Indian translations involve another kind of politics altogether which it is hardly apt to call postcolonial (except perhaps in the case of the relationship of all the rest of the Indian languages *vis-à-vis* the official national language, Hindi), and these will therefore be excluded from the discussion that follows.

Perhaps the single most striking—and politically significant feature of postcolonial translations from foreign languages into the Indian languages has been a resolute and systematic turning away on our part from works of Anglo-American literature. This seems to be a phenomenon common to all Indian languages, and is illustrated by the many volumes of translation edited or personally undertaken by prolific translators such as Manabendra Bandyopadhyay in Bengali or Vishnu Khare in Hindi, and by the Central or the State Sahitya Akademis in various languages.

It is not as if English or American literature is not translated into the Indian languages any more. But even when it is, our attitude towards it has changed perceptibly. Translating Shakespeare, for example, a typically colonial literary activity which had begun in a big way in most of our languages in the last quarter of the nineteenth century, has lately acquired a new justification which is often so nationalist as to be almost an instrument of decolonization. In Hindi for example (as I have shown elsewhere), the most prolific translator of Shakespeare so far, Rangey Raghav, stated that his fifteen translations published in the mid-1950s were motivated rather more by his love of Hindi than by his love of Shakespeare: "A language which does not possess translations of Shakespeare cannot be counted among the more developed language" (qtd. in Trivedi 33).

Some modern Anglo-American authors too have been translated by young and rising Hindi authors on their own appropriatory terms rather than as a tribute to their metropolitan canonical status, as in the case of *The Waste Land* by Vishnu Khare or of *The Portrait of a Lady* by Mohan Rakesh. Anyhow, some other authors whom Rakesh's equally eminent contemporaries chose to translate at the same time were distinctly not Anglo-American: Camus, whose *The Stranger* was translated by Rajendra Yadav, or Brecht, whose *Caucasian Chalk Circle* was translated by Kamaleshwar. In another instructive but not a typical instance, Kedarnath Singh first discovered his poetic talent through translating Paul Eluard in an outpost of the vast Hindi hinterland.

From Anglo-America through Western Europe, the postcolonial Hindi translator moved further afield to explore next Central and Eastern Europe; Czechoslovakia, Yugoslavia, Hungary, Poland, Russia. In the Cold War decades of the 1960s and the 1970s, this was not only to go beyond the Anglo-American literary model and hegemony but virtually to go against it. Such was the sense of excitement and discovery experienced by some of our translators that a direct and fruitful link can be seen between what they translated and what they themselves went on to write creatively, off their own bat. To take only the most eminent examples, Nirmal Varma, the foremost novelist in Hindi today, not only translated early in his career Czech writers of fiction such as Milan Kundera directly into Hindi before they had been translated even into English, but also set his own first novel, unusually, in Czechoslovakia.

Similarly, Raghuvir Sahay, one of the outstanding Hindi poets of our postcolonial half-century, translated not only Shakespeare and Lorca, but also a selection of Hungarian poets, the Polish novelist Jerzi Andrezejewski, and the Yugoslav/Bosnian novelist Ivo Andric. Four of Andric's novels had been published in Hindi in 1969 in translations by various Hindi writers including Sahay, under the common editorship of Ajneya, and Sahay later went on to translate Andric's major epic novel encompassing four centuries of national history, *Na Drini Chupriya,* as *Drina Nadi ka Pul* (1985). In his Introduction, Sahay more than once related the distinct and particular appeal of Andric to something familiar closer at home:

> While Andric's remarkable power of conception brings home to us through his delineation of human characters and their conduct the struggle for opposing values within European history on the one hand, it also alerts the sympathetic Indian reader to the present state of India and to its future, on the other. Such universality is the *dharma* of a great writer. (Andric 4)

> Andric's literary or historical vision of the ups and downs of modern Europe is significant for own society now about to enter the twenty-first century.... In his work, while people accept the new, they do not barter away the old for it. This is the true meaning of knowing one's tradition, and this is also the Indian philosophy of history. (Andric 7)

As in the case of Nirmal Varma, Sahay too went on to let the shadow of his translation fall on his own creative work. His poem "Pul ka Itihas" is a fond ironic testimony of the elective affinity he felt with a work such as Andric's novel, which he had taken on to translate not as apprentice work but relatively late in life, at the peak of his own creative powers. It is a poem so subtly rich in suggestions of reaching out to distant places and then returning home with a wry new recognition of one's own self that it may well stand as an emblem of the translatorial endeavour itself, and may therefore be cited here in full (my translation):

History of a Bridge

I travelled to a country far away.

Changed planes at three airports,
Driving in fine weather
On a road winding through an arduous mountain
Arrived as the sun was setting at a bridge.

Over this bridge four centuries ago had passed
Historic lovers loiterers rebels conquerors.

They were characters now in a twentieth century novel.
On the same bridge, I'd seen in a picture in a book,
Modern armies marching
With ever changing drums and arms.

In the fading daylight I took a photograph.
Returning home by the same rigorous route
I suddenly found there'd been no film in the camera.

Now I retain a picture in my mind
Of my self on that bridge, amidst the bustling traffic,
Standing, holding a camera.

II

The other side of the postcolonial translatorial project, of translating our Indian literatures into the languages of the world, has been on the whole marked by more aspiration and desire than achievement or performance. It has by and large meant translating our literatures into just the one language, English, which though widely international, is not yet fully global. The kind of works which have been translated can be divided into four broad categories: firstly, Indic and indological works from our classical languages; secondly, late ancient and medieval works, largely to do with *bhakti,* such as A.K. Ramanujan translated with notable success and acclaim for two decades following his *Speaking of Siva* (1973); thirdly, works largely fictional, realistically depicting various aspects of modern India, such as novels by Tagore, Premchand, Ananta Murthy, Gopinath Mohanty and Shrilal Shukla; and finally, works by modernist or high-modernist writers such as Lokenath Bhattacharya, Krishna Baldev Vaid, Nirmal Varma and Vilas Sarang. The first two of these categories represent a neo-orientalist or post-orientalist trend; the third conforms broadly to Fredric Jameson's obviously inadequate and slanted description of Third World literary works as national allegories; and the fourth reveals how, contrary to Jameson's thesis, international/universal cosmopolitanism can flourish in the Third World as well, and at the same time, as in the metropolis.

A significant feature of these translations is that a substantially larger number of them are being published now, in the early 1990s, than was the case some ten years or more ago, and that these are being published mostly in India by Indian imprints such as the Oxford University Press India (including the Oxford India Paperbacks), Penguin India, Rupa/HarperCollins/Indus, and Orient Longman/Disha, not to forget the Sahitya Akademi and the National Book Trust, presumably for a largely Indian readership. The English language has thus become the clearing house for various Indian literature of India, just as it was already supposed to serve as the link-language. The success of these translations (and Penguin India alone have published on average about ten titles per year for the last four or five years) would amply prove that—to coin a phrase—English for us is an Indian language first and an international language afterwards. This is further corroborated by the fact that of all the translations (or even original titles) published by Penguin India so far, the parent imprint, Penguin London, has picked up for international distribution barely any copies of hardly any titles.

Such domestication of the English language—or, if one prefers to put it so, such reverse-colonization of it—serves at the same time to thwart the political potential of the project of rendering Indian literature, through translation into English, as part of world literature. The Empire translates back all right, but the metropolitan response seems to be that the Empire itself may lump these translations. The big dream cherished by nearly all writers in the Indian languages, whether great or small, is that one day, after they have won the Sahitya Akademi award and the Jnanapith award and have had art-films made out of their works, the ultimate will happen and they will be translated into English and will burst upon the international scene in a blaze of global glory. It has not happened yet—at least not since lightning struck. Tagore full eighty years ago, in the form of the Nobel prize—but if it can happen to a Marquez and Liosa and a Kundera and an Eco, why (hope springs eternal!) can't it happen to a Karanth or a Varma or a Sarang or a Sahay or a Gangopadhyay? Well, one reason why not, it would seem, is that it is somewhat likelier to happen to a Seth or a Sealy or a Tharoor or a Ghosh.

The bottom-line on the politics of translation in India's literary culture, so far as translation of world literature into the Indian languages is concerned, is that translation is not needed, and can be dispensed with. Even in the rare cases where translators are devotedly rendering works of world literature into an Indian language like Hindi—and two eminent recent examples are *Wole Soyinka ki Kavitayen* (1991) translated by Virendra Kumar Baranwal, and *Nanhi Dibiya: Vasco Popa ke Kavitayen* (1988) translated by Somdatt—they are doing so as an act of personal love, homage, allegiance and affinity, rather than with any realistic hope of effective public transmission and dissemination. If even obviously relevant English classics such as *A Passage to India* or *Kim* have never been translated into a language like Hindi, it can only be because all Hindi speakers who are at all likely to read these books already have—or at least have pretensions to—enough English to be able to read these works in the original.

Even more acute is the case of Indian writers writing in a language such as Hindi but aspiring ultimately to reach beyond to a larger international readership by being translated into English. For such seem recently to have been pre-empted by other Indian writers writing, if one may so put it, directly in English. Right from R.K. Narayan onwards, the Indo-Anglian writer has written with one eye somewhat airily and hopefully aimed at sighting Anglo-America and the other experientially and realistically fixed on India. But recently, since the advent of Rushdie and magic realism, the old debate centring on this dichotomy, about imaginative authenticity and its correlation to the medium one writes in, has well and truly been buried even if it isn't quite dead yet. There is not much local left now, it would seem, for we have all gone global now, even those of us who are culturally disoriented enough hardly to know whether we are coming or we are going.

This aspect of our contemporary cultural situation was highlighted by Gillian Wright in the very first page of her "Translator's Introduction" to a Hindi novel:

> *Raag Darbari* is not widely read in Delhi society and you'd be hard-pressed to find anyone who'd heard of it or its author at the average dinner party. The latest (Indian) English novels, on the other hand, are a favourite subject for discussion. But no novel I have read in English comes close to capturing life in an ordinary north Indian village, whereas the smell of the earth of Uttar Pradesh emanates from every page of Raag Darbari. (Wright v)

This is all true enough, but are there readers anywhere in the wide world, even beyond the irredeemably deracinated circle of dinner party-goers in New Delhi, who would care to smell the earth of Uttar Pradesh?

The ultimate question before us in India therefore is where to situate ourselves and our literary culture *vis-à-vis* the new postcolonial global cultural configuration. Are we going to align ourselves, sooner rather than later, with the great Anglo-American axis, as a nation and a people who read and write only in English? Or do we have the strength of our local earthy smells to hold out against this linguistic and cultural totalization, this increasing monolingual literary authoritarianism? In that case, shall we wait to be translated into English or any other language on our own terms, as do China, Japan, East Europe and Latin America?

Looking back on our past, colonialism seems to have been a simpler if starker historical phenomenon as compared to what we have now. The so-called postcolonial is nearly always also neocolonial, and especially so when it masquerades as decolonization. In a recent, earnestly uniflected metropolitan formulation, "The persistence of Neo-colonialist or imperialist practices in the contemporary world is a very obvious, perhaps the most serious, obstacle to any unproblematic use of the term postcolonial" (Williams and Chrisman 3). It is a most serious obstacle, one may add, also to many of our vitally important cultural practices here on the ground, including the use of our local languages by themselves and in interaction, in translation. The languages of colonialism were many: Spanish, Portuguese, French, Italian, Belgian, Dutch and English. But is the language of postcolonialism going to be just one, English, and for preference, what can in more senses than one be called satellite English? If so, we sha'n't be needing many translations either to or fro; in that monolingual dystopia, all we shall need is capitulation and internalization, whether voluntary or not.

REFERENCES

Bassnett, Susan and Andre Lefevere (eds.). 1990. *Translation, History and Culture,* London. Pinter Publishers.

Bassnett-McGuire, Susan. 1980. *Translation Studies.* New Accents series. London: Methuen.

Mukherjee, Sujit. 1994. *Translation as Discovery and other Essays on Indian Literature in English Translation.* 1981; rpt. Hyderabad: Orient Longman.

Snell-Hornby, Mary. "Linguistic Transcoding or Cultural Transfer?: A criticism of literary Theory in Germany," in Bassnett & Lefevere, 79-86.

Sahay, Raghuvir. 1986. "Prastavana" (Preface) to *Drina Nadi ka Pul* (trans. of *Na Drini Chupriva* by Ivo Andric). New Delhi: Sahitya Akademi.

Sahay, Raghuvir. 1989. "Pul ka Itihas," in *Kuchh Pate Kuchh Chitthiyan*. New Delhi: Rajkamal Prakashan.

Thompson, Edward. 1991. *Rabindranath Tagore: Poet and Dramatist*. 1926; rpt. New Delhi: Oxford India Paperbacks.

Trivedi, Harish. 1993. *Colonial Transactions: English Literature and India*. Calcutta: Papyrus.

Williams, Patrick and Laura Chrisman (eds.). 1993. "Introduction" to *Colonial Discourse and Post-Colonial Theory: A Reader*. Hemel Hempstead: Harvester Wheatsheaf.

Wright, Gillian. 1992. "Translator's Introduction" to *Raag Darbari* (trans. of a novel of the same title by Shrilal Shukla). New Delhi: Penguin Books.

What Translation Really Means

9

BASUDEB CHAKRABORTY

In this article I propose to explain the nature of translation process based on a comparative study of an original text and its translated version. I will also examine a creative translator's problem of transferring a text written in one language into another. The purpose of translation is primarily to carry the theme and the meta-theme of a source language text (SL) into a text written in another language, *i.e.* target language (TL). This journey of the theme and the meta-theme, encoded into one language, to another language, is the kernel of the translation process. We need to remember in this connection that the translation process is no longer considered a mechanistic one. Of course, there are certain translation works—particularly those rendering scientific and technological contents written in one language, which demand relatively mechanical substitution for facts and figures written in a particular language. The process of translation of scientific and technical writings is thus different from that of a creative and literary work. I have not here examined the translation process of scientific and technical writings. Translation is not an attempt of implanting any subject matter or any content written by a creative writer in his mother tongue or a foreign or second language into another language. Had it been so, it will have been then a transplantation of a tree, grown up steadily on a particular soil, into an alien soil and atmosphere. Indeed translation is a creative art. It is not a mechanical transfer of a theme and meta-theme written in one language into another. Perhaps for this reason, there is hardly any set procedure for translation. A good translation can be an artistic creation. In that case it transcends translation; it then becomes a new creation. A good translation shows a spontaneous and creative process of journey of a theme and meta-theme from one linguistic framework to another linguistic framework. Translation of this nature, the aim and objective of which is recreation, is also an artistic marvel.

With a new critical insistence on the inseparability of form and content doubts have been raised in our time about the possibility of translation. Even much much earlier, Shelley who was an admirable translator likened translation to subjecting a violet to chemical analysis. Perhaps he was highlighting the impossibility of exact correspondence between source and target text, and not indeed rejecting translation; he held the view that 'the plant must spring again from the seed, or it will bear no flower.' Some elements in the source text tend to elude being grasped by the target language in the translation. There are others who stress it and draw an attention to the device that may remove hurdles and they are put into target language. The translator who controls the process must be a discerning and honest critic and at the same time a creative writer; he must have the natural ability to locate 'seed' and make it grow. He must have reasonable freedom and should first, to quote Dryden, 'know what is peculiar to the author's style'.

There are divergent opinions about the efficacy and possibility of translation among translation theoreticians. Roger Bacon of 12th century thinks every language is indivisible, unitary, and single. According to him journey from one text to another is impossible. Human societies with different cultures, with different mores of lives, have been growing independently from time immemorial. And one of the expressions of those cultures is the form of their languages. Even at the mentalistic level no human thought can be conceived of without any pre-language or whatever it is called. The pre-language or language at the mentalistic level in which a person belonging to a particular society at a particular point of time thinks is determined by the culture of that community. And the varieties of cultures persisting from the recorded history of men's society resulted in the different forms of surface languages and corresponding forms of pre-language or languages at the mentalistic level. This view is termed 'Monadist.' (It comes from GK. monos meaning—sole, lone, single, indestructible, impenetrable. It is a unit in Greek philosophy constituting the number one or an individual.)

An American linguist Edward Sapir strongly supports this monadist approach. In his article in *Selected Writing in Language Culture and Personality,* he comments:

> No two languages are ever sufficiently similar to be considered as representing the same social reality. The worlds in which different societies live are distinct worlds not merely the same world with different labels attached. (Steiner 87)

If we subscribe to this monadist view any attempt at translation will be futile endeavour. Noam Chomsky on the other hand holds the opinion that the underlying structural commonalities among all human languages—commonalities which he terms Universal Grammar are factors that make translation possible and effective. In his *Syntactic Structure* (1957) Chomsky shows what the Transformational Generative Grammar is and how it is applicable to all human languages.

Let us examine George Steiner's comments on the efficacy and the possibility of translation:

> The one declares that the underlying structure of language is universal and common to all men. Dissimilarities between human tongues are essentially of the surface. Translation is realizable precisely because those deep-seated Universal genetic, historical, social, from which all grammars derive, can be located and recognized as operative in every human idiom, however singular or bizarre its superficial forms.... The contrary view can be termed 'monadist.' The extreme monadist position—we shall find great poets holding it—leads logically to the belief that real translation is a convention of approximate analogies a rough-cast similitude, just tolerable when two relevant Languages or cultures are cognate, but altogether spurious when remote tongues and far-removed sensibilities are in question. (Steiner 73-74)

Difference among languages is the difference of surface structures. "The human child is born with a blue print of language which is called Universal Grammar" (Katamba 6). Indeed Chomsky's Transformational Generative Grammar presents a faithful and objective description of the internal structure of all human languages.

A leading translation theoretician of the present time, Edwin Gentzler's comment on the importance of Chomsky's concept of the 'Universal Grammar' in the context of the translation theories seems relevant:

> Chomsky's deep structure/surface structure model, his transformational rules, although monolinguistically derived, lend themselves to justifying a theory of translation. Whether one accepts Chomsky's beliefs on how the human mind is structured or not, his deep structures, postulated to contain all the necessary syntactic as well as semantic information for a correct transformation into surface structure and interpretation, lend themselves well to the translation practitioner trying to represent an 'underlying message' in a second language. (Gentzler 47)

Without questioning the validity or otherwise of these two sets of intricate opinions about the possibility of translation, I accept the premise that translation is possible; 'the human actually does communicate across linguistic barriers, and this is the pivot of universalism'. After accepting this premise, let us see what goes on in the mind of a practising-translator when he is engaged in the act of translation. Moreover, it will be considered whether a creative piece of writing can at all be translated successfully.

An examination of the process of translatology reveals the following facts: A translator first decodes linguistic symbols, which are the signifiers of SL text. For this he is expected to be intimately familiar with every nuance of any linguistic symbol of the SL text. He should have total skill in the source language. He should not keep aside the formal or categorical aspect of the language of SL text. Every language has certain linguistic features of its syntax, of its inflectional and derivational affixes, of its arbitrary behaviour of the lexical items and so on. A translator while journeying from one SL text to another TL text has to be careful about all these formal aspects of the language he decides to decode first. This decoding is considered the beginning of the translation process. A translator's degree of command over the language of SL text plays a very important role in the translation process.

In this process of decoding the language of the source text, a translator has also to be meticulous about the cultural significance of the text he undertakes to translate. The phrase 'cultural significance' in this context refers to both conceptual and associative meanings of language. Let us give an example of the basic components of a word like *needle* in English. Its conceptual component meanings include 'thin', 'sharp', 'steel', instrument. One may have associations or connections attached to a *needle* which may lead one to think of 'something painful'. This association is not treated as part of the conceptual meaning of *needle*. This is associative meaning.

A translator's awareness of the 'cultural significance' leads him thus to examine the pragmatics of SL text. Pragmatic deals with the 'characterisation of speaker meaning'. Linguistic pragmatics is the analysis of the use of context to make inference about meaning. Interpretation of symbols, imagery, allusion, etc., depends on many occasions upon the analysis of context —the analysis which comes under the purview of pragmatics. Let us give one more example of the study of pragmatics in this context. The utterance, 'Could you drive my Volvo car?' is made by a young girl to a young man. Both of them are found standing in the parking zone of pub. The sentence may generate multiplicity of meanings. One simple meaning may be that the man does not know really the skill of motor driving. Another meaning may be that the man is used to driving an ordinary car, not an expensive foreign car like Volvo. The third meaning may be that the girl wants the man's company or she wants him to be her escort. The fourth meaning may be that the girl is very much conscious about her economic status; she is financially capable of possessing an expensive car like Volvo and she makes the man realise that she is economically superior to him. The examination of the context can determine the exact meaning. This is what exactly pragmatics examines. Pragmatics does not ask 'what does X mean?' but 'what does one mean by X?' Pragmatics is interested in functions, intentions, goals and effects of utterance. A translator's close familiarity with the pragmatics of the SL text—the pragmatics which may be defined as 'cultural significance' of the language is a prerequisite of a journey from one text to another text. Noam Chomsky names it 'Pragmatic Competence'.

The next stage in the process of translation is to encode what is in the mind of the translator about the cultural significance and the structural and grammatical aspect of the SL text. So far as the cultural significance of the linguistic framework of the SL text is concerned, the translator need to be careful about the conceptual as well as the associated meaning of the SL text. At the same time the translator is expected to take utmost care of faithful transference of the structural and grammatical aspects of the language of the SL text into the TL text. The translator transfers the formal and categorical aspect of the linguistic symbols. At the level of phonology the rhapsody of rhythm of one language is very difficult to transfer into another linguistic framework. Even if the transference is made at level of phonology, the comparative evaluation will be subjective, absolutely private. It is because every language has certain and specified way of organizing phonetic symbols of its own, forming a sound cluster—the auditory effect of which is possible in that specific language only. Let me refer to Rabindranath Tagore's *Rakta Karabī* and its translation in English, *Red Oleanders.* At the beginning of the SL text, *Rakta Karabī*, the voice addresses Nandini; as /nandin/; Tagore in this TL text, *Red Oleanders* uses Nandini; the sonority of the auditory effect of /nandin/ cannot be achieved by substituting /nandini/ for/ nandin/. In the source language /nandin /may be the most affectionate and endearing address for /nandini/. One more example of it. During the initial conversation between Nandini and the Voice, Nandini tries to avoid making a distinction between her jubilant state of mind after seeing Ranjan and her state of mind after listening to Raja's voice. Raja insists on her making the distinction between two reactions. Then she says in SL text: /Se naīcer taīl aīlaīdaī, tumi bujhbe naī/. The same speech is transferred to the TL text, *Red Oleanders* by Tagore himself: 'That dance rhythm is different, you won't understand.' Let us examine the constituents of /Se naīcer taīl/ of *Rakta Karabiī* and /That dance rhythm/ of *Red Oleanders*:

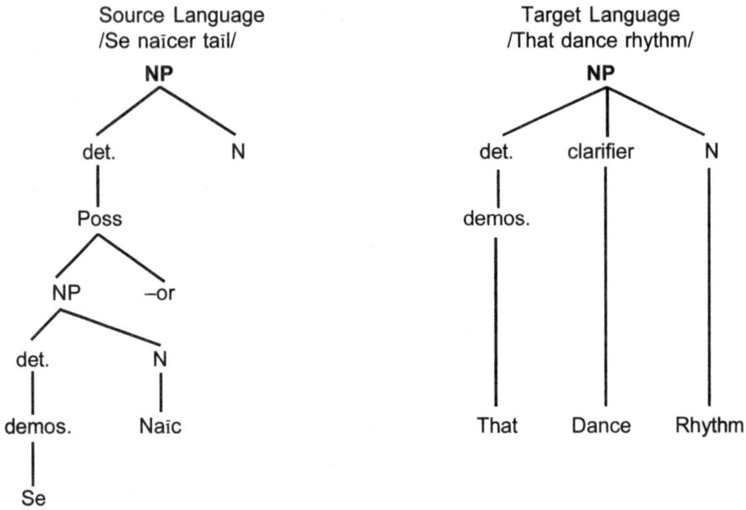

The structural difference between two NPs—/Se naīcer taīl/ and /That dance rhythm/—is conspicuous. The NP in the SL text is constituted by the determiner + noun and again the determiner contains possessive which constituted by NP and possessive. But the corresponding NP in the TL text is constituted by Determiner + Classifier + Noun. So structurally /Se naīcer taīl/ and /That dance rhythm/ are different. One cannot bet the substitution for the other. The translator simply transfers the meaning of the language of SL text into a structurally different linguistic framework of the TL text. Moreover, sonority of the sound in /Se naīcer taīl/, its auditory effect upon the ears of audience, is missing in 'That dance rhythm.'

Problems of translating mythological names seems difficult. The mythological name, Krishna in *Mahabharata* has often been addressed as Kalachand; Krishna, Parthasarathi, Shyam, Dwarkanath, Nandadulal, Debakinandan and many others on various occasions of the SL text. And each of these names of Krishna has its own contextual meaning. The image of Debakinandan has little to do with the image of Parthasarathi. A practising translator usually translates the various names of Krishna as Lord Krishna on all occasions. To an American, for example, the English translation of the *Mahabharata* presents Krishna in all contexts as Lord Krishna.

Raghupati, Raghunath, Raghab, Janakinath, Sitapati—all are known to a person who does not know Indian languages, as Lord Rama. Indeed every name of Lord Rama has its own connotation in each context. Lord Rama does not convey all the shades of meaning conveyed by various names of Rama. Problems again crop up in translating place names, in translating names of seasons like Aasarh, Shravan, Phalgun and so on. The name Varanashi has often translated as Banaras but Varanashi or Kashi has its own meaning which Banaras does not convey. A reader not knowing Indian languages will hardly appreciate the smell associated with name of Varanashi. A comment made by Sukanta Chowdhury is relevant to this context: "Working compromise seems the only feasible solution" (vii). By 'working compromise', Sukanta Chowdhury perhaps means that a translator has to resort to some devices with the help of which he may convey at least the essence of the idea of what he translates into another linguistic framework. On certain occasions a work of translation may be explanatory, interpretative, metaphoric or even symbolic. It is left to the discretion of a translator. A translator enjoys this freedom. Exact substitution and precise transference may not be possible on many occasions. A creator-translator has got this liberty. This freedom makes a translator creative.

At the suprasegmental level, translation of conversation between characters is a problem. English, for example, is an intonation language. It is very difficult to find out suitable substitutions for English intonation, say in Bengali: "Could you bring a glass of water for me?"

Bengali is not an intonational language. What is open to a practising translator in this situation is to invite one or two additional lexical items to convey the request of the English speaker. In English, a sense of politeness or request is very often conveyed through the rising intonation. The translation of this sentence into Bengali poses another problem. The sentence 'Could you bring a glass of water for me?' is a past interrogative in grammatical form. Tense is a matter of form whereas the time reference is a matter of meaning. The sentence is in the past tense but it refers to the present time. Bengali has three tenses. Now to translate it into Bengali a translator is in need of changing the past tense form into the present.

So what is written in SL text is not substituted in the TL text in the matter of form. Here again, neither substitution nor transference of grammatical form in the context of Bengali language is possible. What is possible is to transfer the meaning into a different framework of language.

Thus the way words in sentences of the SL text are arranged may be changed in sentences of the TL text. And the way words are arranged in a sentence governs its style. A translator, before he starts encoding the meaning of a SL text into a TL text, is expected to identify the tone, the colour and the style of SL text. An exact reproduction of all these into TL text may not always be possible. In the circumstances, words, phrases, idioms, symbols which convey more or less the same meaning may be used in the TL text. Here a translator enjoys enormous but reasonable freedom. What matters most here is the translator's bilingual competence. A translator has a good number of strategic options while he starts translating a literary text. These options are:

"(1) to reproduce either the forms (syntax and lexis) or the ideas (the semantic content) of the original;

(2) to retain the style of the original or adopt a different style; to retain or abandon the source language text form;

for example, to translate a poem as a poem or as prose;

(3) to retain the historical stylistic dimension of the original or to render it in contemporary form; to

translate Dante into middle English or into modern English;

(4) to produce a text which reads like an original or one which reads like a translation;

(5) to add or omit words, phrases, clauses...or to attempt to transfer every thing from source to target text." (Beu 68)

At a level of syntax, substitution of one linguistic framework by another is also not possible. Had there been one common syntactic pattern in all human languages, there should have been then one language in the world. Human languages are arbitrary, non-negotiable. And for this reason every human language has its own syntactic pattern. Bengali shows SOV pattern, English SVO, Japanese SOV while the Saudi Arabic language is generally considered to be SVO, with apparent vestiges of an earlier VSO pattern showing up in subordination. Naturally, how can it be possible on the part of a translator to find out a substitution of a syntactic pattern of the SL text for the TL text? At best, what a translator can do is to carry the meaning of the SL text to the TL text.

WORKS CITED

Steiner, George. *After Babel.* Oxford: Oxford University Press, 1975. Cited as Steiner.

Francis, Katamba. *Morphology.* London: Macmillan, 1993. Cited as Katamba.

Gentzler, Edwin. *Contemporary Translation Theories.* London: Routledge, 1993. Cited as Gentzler.

Chowdhury, Sukanta. *Rabindranath Tagore.* New Delhi: Oxford University Press, 2000, p. VII.

Beu, Roger T. *Translation and Translating: Theory and Practice.* London: Longman, 1991. Cited as Beu.

Translation or Transcreation

10

ANJANA TIWARI

"To be a translator, knowing the two languages is not enough. A literary and creative bend of mind is essential."

Translation is a combination of words, (Trans+lation) meaning to take away that is "Anuvad", while Transcreation (Trans+creation) is to transform creatively from one language to another that is "Anurachna". Both are basically linguistic processes which enrich us by providing various literatures and knowledge of different cultures, traditions, politics, philosophies, economics, religion, education, medicine, trade and commerce, tourism, agriculture, telecommunication and a host of other things. That is why translation has become the need of the hour. It is the only medium of exchanging our ideas and to update us in every field. Although everyone feels its essentiality and necessity, still translation has been strangely considered second grade work. As language planners the translators have never quite gained recognition.

There are basically three different translation theories. First, there is the paraphrase method, in which the translator freely rewords the original language to convey in modern English what he takes to be the basic sense of a passage. This method produces an English text that is easy to read and understand, however, it invariably requires the translator to interpret a given passage for the reader. There are different degrees of paraphrase, some reflecting much more interpretation of the meaning of the text than others. Second, there is the dynamic equivalence method. This is a more recent theory of translation developed by Dr. Eugene Nida of the American Bible Society. The object is to produce for the modern reader the closest equivalent meaning of the original text. This does not necessarily require a word-for-word, or literal rendering. Finally, there is the literal or complete equivalence method. It requires the closest possible correspondence between the original language words and their consistent English translation.

Here is an example of each method of translation from Gen 4: 3-4:

> *Paraphrase method*: "Some time later Cain brought some of his farming produce as an offering to the *LORD*, while Abel brought some of the very best of his flock."
>
> *Dynamic equivalence method*: "In the course of time, Cain brought an offering to the LORD from the produce of the soil; and Abel brought the choicest of the firstlings of his flock."
>
> *Literal method*: "And it came about at the end of days that Cain brought an offering to YHVH of the fruit of the ground. And Abel also brought of the firstlings of his flock and of their fat portions."

We may not notice any earth-shaking differences in these particular verses. Indeed, the essential meaning seems to come through in all three examples. However, we believe the literal method is far superior.

One other important translation feature is our attempt to be as consistent as possible with the rendering of original language words. It is true that in any language a single word can have more than one meaning. However, there is no good reason to arbitrarily translate a key original language word with dozens of different English words when a single consistent meaning is perfectly clear and adequate.

The translation, nay, transcreation creates ontological strength and the literary fragrance of original text without making any changes in the stintuation of ideas or information units.

The view that communication is basically a transfer or transportation of fixed messages shows up in many disguises, under several different but related metaphors. One such metaphor is involved in "the bucket theory" of meaning,

> "Words, like little buckets, are assumed to pick up their loads of meaning in one person's mind, carry them across the intervening space, and dump them into the mind of another." (Osgood 1979: 213)

The translation model is a thoroughly misleading and inadequate model as applied to speech communication in face-to-face interaction. It grossly underestimates the complexity of the social interplay between speaker and listener, and of their interaction with the surrounding situation:

> "This model of communication objectifies meaning in a misleading and dehumanizing fashion. It influences us to talk and think about thought as if they had the same kind of external, intersubjective reality as lamps and tables."

Accurately translating a dry piece of text designed to communicate straightforward instructions requires less creative input on the translator's behalf. But there are times when style is just as important as content. In advertising, direct translation can lead to all sorts of problems (a few years ago, the classic 'Come alive with Pepsi', became 'Pepsi brings your ancestors back from the grave' in mainland China!).

Act of translation at its best emerges as an act of transcreation. Transcreation is a cross between straight translation and creative copywriting, using specialist translators to come up with appropriate and relevant counterparts to word plays or other creative concepts while maintaining the sense of the original text. Translations are either too literal and abstract, or written in very formal, incomprehensible English, or are philosophically one-sided—this reader-friendly "transcreation" offers an unbiased philosophical perspective and presents the main theme of the original text in simple, ordinary language easily accessible to today's readers. It enables them to feel that as if it were originally written in their own language—and they can capture the excitement of discovering its relevance to their own lives.

Transcreation uses a simple, clear, and non-pedantic style and language that is accessible to all levels of readers—yet captures the original themes and concepts in all their complexity.

That is why the Bengali writers and poets have become so popular in western world although they are just one branch in India's great literary tradition.

Translation is a tricky business; one of its problems is that the translation sometimes reads like translation. In those instances, they do not communicate the atmospherics, the flavour of dialogue and the rootedness to the soil that every good translation must have. That is when Samanta's translation fails to rise to the level of transcreation. Professor Sukanta Chowdhury, who translated the ostensibly untranslatable when he turned Bengal's greatest nonsense poet Sukumar Ray into English, has this to say in his general editor's preface in the first volume of the recent Oxford Tagore Translations. "Literary translation proceeds by a series of particular, contingent judgements, virtually a species of inspired *ad hocism*. For a start, it soon becomes imperative to break the translator's shibboleth that the same word in the original must always be rendered by the same word in translation."

For example, this is the first line in Samanta's 'The Hungering Stones': "My cousin and I, having completed our travels around the country during the Puja holidays, were returning to Calcutta when we met the babu on the train."

And this is how the same story (more aptly called 'Hungry Stone') kicks off in novelist Amitav Ghosh's hand in the Oxford Tagore Translations: "We met him on the train, my cousin and I, on our way back to Calcutta after a trip around the country during the Puja holidays." That's crisper, less convoluted, more lyrical; qualities one sometimes misses in Samanta's effort.

In Indian context transcreation is the only process by which we bridge the gap between different dialects, languages and cultures. It not only provides its readers the essence of the particular piece of literature but also creates the lust for the reader as the substantial inclusion of real instance of joys and pangs that are necessary corollary to the practice as a creative work of art.

Vande Mataram	
vande mAtaram sujalAM suphalAM malayajas'ltalAM sasyas'yAmalAM mAtaram	Rich with thy hurrying streams, Bright with thy orchard gleams, Cool with thy winds of delight, Dark fields waving, Mother of might, Mother free.
s'ubhrajyotsnApulakitayAminIM phullakusumitadrumadalas'obhinIm suhAsinIM sumadhurabhASiNIM sukhadAM varadAM mAtaram	Glory of moonlight dreams, Over thy branches and lordly streams, Clad in thy blossoming trees, Mother, giver of ease, Laughing low and sweet! Mother, I kiss thy feet, Speaker sweet and low!
saptakoTi-kanTha-kalakala-ninAda-karAle dvisaptakoTibhujairdhruta-khara-karavAle ke bole mA tumi abale bahubaladhAriNIM namAmi tAriNIM ripudalavAriNIM mAtaram vande mAtaram	Mother to thee I bow, Who hath said thou art weak in thy lands, When the swords flash out in twice seventy million hands And seventy million voices roar Thy dreadful name from shore to shore
tumi vidyA tumi dharma tumi hRdi tumi marma tvaM hi prANAh: s'arIre bAhute tumi mA s'akti hRdaye tumi mA bhakti tomaraI pratimA gaDI mandire mandire vande mAtaram	In our hearts that conquers death. Thine the strength that nerves the arm, Thine the beauty, thine the charm. Every image made divine In our temples is but thine. Mother, I bow to thee!
tvaM hi durgAdas'apraharaNadhAriNI kamalA kamaladalavihAriNI vANI vidyAdAyinI namAmi tvAm namAmi kamalAM amalAM atulAM sujalAM suphalAM mAtaram vande mAtaram	Thou art Durga, Lady and Queen, With her hands that strike and her swords of sheen, Thou art Lakshmi lotus-throned, And the Muse a hundred-toned. Pure and perfect without peer, Mother, lend thine ear. Rich with thy hurrying streams, Bright with thy orchard gleams, Mother, I bow to thee!
s'yAmalAMsaralAM susmitAM bhUSitAM dharaNIM bharaNIM mAtaram vande mAtaram	Dark of hue, O candid-fair In thy soul with jewelled hair, And thy glorious smile divine, Loveliest of all earthly lands, Showering wealth from well-stored hands!
Mother, I bow to thee!	Mother, mother mine! Mother sweet, I bow to thee Mother great and free!

Reconstructing the Tower of Babel: Equivalence in Translation: A Rare Case Study

11

RAMA KUNDU

In a seminar on translation studies one may start with Octavio Paz's famous observation:

"Every text is...the translation of another text." (9)

All texts, he claims, are part of a literary system which, again, is descended from and related to other systems, and are thus translations of translation of translations. Paz's observation, of course, foregrounds intertextuality rather than interlingual transference. Anyway, translation as an inter- and intralingual activity has a long history, indeed. According to George Steiner's periodisation of the literature on the theory, practice and history of translation (*After Babel*) into four phases, the first begins with Cicero and Horace, and the fourth period begins in the early 1960s. The global culture of the new millennium only further increases the importance, variety, as also complexity of this literature since there is no other way to meet the burgeoning interest in the literatures of other languages.

A few questions, however, remain to be asked in this connection which specifically relate to *our* situation. The first one is, of course, essentially an old question which has gone on changing its implications in varying continuums; that is, what determines the author-translator relationship?

The central and still hegemonic position of English language in these transcultural activities today (in our country and across the globe) continues to be an unavoidable reality. Not only do we get to know the vast bulk of European literatures through English even the regional literatures in India can be made accessible to other regions of the country only through English translation. In view of this the question of author-translator relationship acquires a special dimension in our situation in Bengal, for example, where Bengali translators have been using English and Bengali as both SL and TL,—the two poles of the transcreative axis.

The socio-political relation governing the users of the SL and the TL had its impact on the colonial days, which could be seen as projection of cultural encounters in the light of colonial and hegemonic imperatives. There was a high tide of transmission of original texts into the vernacular or native language which could be related to the intricate matrix of cultural politics. Nirod C. Chowdhuri has finely brought out this situation in nineteenth century Bengal with exhaustive illustrations in his book, *Ātmaghātī Bāngālī.*

That situation is over. On the one hand, we have our own rich and proud harvest in vernacular; on the other, even a school-going child in Bengal is bilingual these days, and the average educated Bengali can read the original English text, or other languages translated in English. Though we still translate lots of English texts into vernacular, this is done for sheer aesthetic pleasure rather than the need to introduce an English text to the Bengali reader.

But when Bengali is the SL and English is the TL it represents a different case. It remains *our* responsibility to introduce our rich harvest in vernacular to the rest of India and to the world through English translation. (Radices are a hopeless minority!). Here both the author and the translator hail from the SL group; and the latter tries to transfer the SL text into a TL which is, paradoxically, familiar and forbidding at the same time.

When the SL is English and the TL is Bengali, today's translator seems to be rather relaxed; even his postcolonial self-consciousness—often daringly assertive—may operate rather freely without the fear of a watchful headmaster measuring the standard (BBC, the British Coun-ELBS, etc., for example). But in the case of translating our gems into their necklace we cannot forget the question of equivalence and acceptability. At least some constraint/compulsion like that works at the back of our mind; the watchful headmaster—imaginary or real—continues to dominate our consciousness.

Starting from the above premise, the second question is: how far linguistic and cultural phenomena are translatable between *these two* languages at the moment? Thirdly, what is the standard of equivalence that has to be achieved at the multiple layers—linguistic, paradigmatic, stylistic, syntagmatic—or if such complete equivalence is at all possible in the present case? One may recall Sukanta Chowdhury's rather unsavory analogy of two strange dogs sniffing and circling each other (*Translation and Understanding*).

Translation from Bengali to English and *vice versa* involves not only two different sets of language signs or semiotics, but also whole sets of extralinguistic criteria which involve the culture context. As the surgeon, operating on the heart, cannot neglect the body that surrounds it so the translator cannot treat the text in isolation from its empirical-cultural-associational factors/systems.

Let us take for example the following line: "Shall I compare thee to a Summer's day."

If we translate it literally like this—Tomār tulanā se ki grīṣmer dupur—we shall miss a whole gamut of suggestions, and get instead some wrong ones. The lady may appear quite unpleasant and even terrible to the users of the host language, instead of the warm pleasant personality/presence as implied by the same image in the SL.

Again, take the word *mahāprasthān*. How to translate it in English? 'The grand exit' is, of course, literally correct. But it fails to connote the sublime image of the lonely sojourner, the last surviving Pāndava, trudging up the snow-peaked Himalayas, and thus evoke the vast range of suggestions which this word is expected to stir up in an even illiterate Indian listener.

Or, suppose I have to translate the famous prayer of Hopkins:

"Send my roots rain" ('Thou art indeed just Lord')

How should I do it?

āmar śikaḍe bṛṣṭi dāo.

This literal translation would denote to the TL reader only empirical rain, but would fail to convey that religious connotation of divine grace which would have been immediately recognized by the reader in the SL culture.

If we do it like this—āmār śikaḍe eso karunādhārāy. This may be closer to the meaning, but here too we miss the directness and poignancy of the imagistic and phonetic effect of the SL.

Equivalence may appear to be easier in the case of intra-cultural-lingual rewriting, though this too is, by no means, a problem-free zone. In such cases the translator sometimes has to take recourse to archaism in order to reach the spirit of the original. Kaliprasanna Singha's use of heavily Sanskritized Bengali in translating *The Mahabharata* is a classic example.

Again, Sambhu Mitra, in rewriting the *Manasā Maṅgal Kāvya*, a medieval folk-lore, in his play *Chãnd Baniker Pālā* (1978),—which interrogates the spirit of the original and at the same time deconstructively uses it to achieve transmigration of the concealed spirit or tone of defiance in the original, opts for a voice that will have immediate impact on the contemporary readers as being of their own time. Still he tries to reproduce 'period flavour' by means of careful and elaborate use of archaism in verbal structure, wording and imagery.[1]

But this archaic Bengali—though this does not make the text inaccessible to the Bengali reader—practically makes it untranslatable in modern English. One simply would not dare; a reason why Mitra missed his Nobel.

Linguistic untranslatability is apparent when SL sentences involve structures that do not exist in the TL. Also cultural untranslatability surfaces when it involves absence in the TL culture of a relevant situational feature for the SL text. It may also be difficult if not impossible to reconcile the demands of the two disparate geniuses of two different languages.[2]

Today thankfully nobody may be prosecuted for 'mistranslating' as Dolet had been done in 1546 (for mistranslating Plato's *Dialogues*). Rather in view of the various forms of untranslatability which are being increasingly recognised, several solutions have been offered by theorists and practitioners: Jakobson's theory of "creative transposition", Nida's concept of "dynamic equivalence",[3] Moumin's suggestion of "dialectic process",[4] or Tagore's idea of "re-incarnation"[5] are some of the examples.

However, in some rare cases when the translator is gifted with rare sensitivity and fine aesthetic sense, and at the same time has a thorough multilingual-multicultural orientation, then there could be moments of exquisite aesthetic pleasure and instances of excellent, almost complete equivalence. Let me illustrate the point with an example where the SL text is a modern Bengali poem and the TL is English.

The original is a well-known poem by Subhas Mukhopadhyaya,—"*Jete Jete*" (the translation is given in Appendix 2). The very title in the translation offers a delightful surprise. It is not 'When I had been journeying' or 'As I had been going'; it is '*En Route*',—the same cryptic yet open-ended phrase, sending suggestions of an infinite journey; the phrase is even more cryptic with its two syllables replacing the four in the original, and equally eloquent.

At the very onset there is an evocation of the folktale atmosphere through the repeated hyphenations: je-te je-te je-te; it is the endless weary walk, a common narrative device recurring in the '*rūpkathā*'s of Bengal, the tales of *Thākurmār Jhuli*/*Thākurdār Jhuli*, etc. The suggestion of the long weary compulsive journey (not brisk or slow walk) has been finely recaptured in "as I trudged along". The drudgery and endlessness of the journey is also denoted by the sound-trudged along.

Again, the original poem describes the stream as a girl with anklets and wavy blue skirt: "pāye tār ghuṅgur bā̃dhā/parane/ uḍu uḍu dheuer/nīl ghāgra." In the translation we can hear even the jingling sound of the anklet—"anklets jingling at her feet" and the drapery becomes "the blue of the rhythmic ripples". The jingling anklets and the blue rhythmic ripples together evoke the liquid murmur of the quickly flowing river.

In the following lines we have again and again this kind of multiple equivalence, of exquisite transference at the phonetic-linguistic cultural levels; it is perhaps more than equivalence in the sense that it seems, at points, even better than the original. The persona in the poem is supposedly a story-teller who has been shifting from one tale to another in order to capture the attention of his adult listeners. As he tries to gauge the response of his listeners he pauses a little after each tentative fragment. The translator too maintains the same rhythm between speech and silence; the lineation too helps to bring out the halted speech rhythm of the narrator who is constantly watching the listeners' reaction and suitably editing the version. Finally Subhas takes up a paradigm which is typical in the Bengali folktale / fairytale; it is a lonely youth meeting a beautiful girl in a magic palace in the heart of a dense forest. The titillation in the listeners at the mention of a love-lorn beautiful woman is finely captured in the translation, even to the hilt of irony.

> "buḍodhāḍīrā āgrohe uṭhe bose/jigyes korlo: 'tārpar'?"
>
> "All ear, the elders sat up / and asked pruriently — / 'Then?'"

Now follows the climax:

> "tārpar? ki bolbo/sei rākshúsī āmāke khele...."

"Rākshasī" is an embedded figure in our folktale who would often appear in the guise of a beautiful girl. How to translate this culture-specific term in English/? Witch? Ogress? Demoness? Vampire (Egypt)? Lamia (Greece)? None seems adequate; not even *femme fatale*, who is mortal, and not necessarily beautiful. So what could be the exact word or phrase? This is how the translator does it.

> "'Then?'
> What shall I say?
> *La belle dame sans merci*
> ate me up"

The reader is at once thrilled with the pleasure of recognition of the equivalence achieved here. It is only this figure, one feels, which could connote the beautiful, supernatural, destructive feminine spirit mentioned in the original text. Such equivalence is, indeed rare.

Often it so happens that a good translation fails to be a good poem in its own right. Even in cases of autotranslation often we have a different poem, and perhaps not so good as the original after all. That's why Tagore would have his poems read in Bengali rather than in English.[6] Very rarely it so happens that a good translation also becomes a good poem *per se* (See Appendices 1 and 2). Let us first read the Bengali poem then take up the English so that we can follow the process of transcreation in this particular case.

The repetition of voiceless fricatives in the first line suggests a silent slow painful process of cognition. The speaker wakes up to the consciousness of a feeling of vague uneasiness. The translator's choice of "smouldering" instead of 'burning' is significant. The liquid 'l' followed by the plosive—the oppressive presence of 'd' after 'l'—evokes the effect of an acute grinding pain of a prolonged silent suffering.

A pause follows the first clause as in the original. Then comes the first sign of recognition—smell—which is the strongest association of a memory.[7] "I *can* smell" instead of 'I smell" indicates the surprised self-discovery—that 'I *can* recognise', however faintly. This is followed by another pause,—indicating the time needed for identifying the source of the smell—the sad lingering pain of the "smouldering". Thus the second part of the first line is pushed into the second line. The two monosyllables "old love" capture more poignantly than "purāno bhālobāsā" the epiphanic quality and the finality of the slipping flash of recognition.

With memory coming back the heart twists in pain: mucḍe oṭhe jantraṇāy. "Writhing", with its difficult, oppressive, not facile sound, exquisitely captures this wrenching pain. Again, "writhing" also implies a sudden stirring caused by the pang of some spasmodic pain; and thus suggests that the heart which had been sedate so long has now started stirring back to a disturbed consciousness through painful memories.

The pause at the end of the third line holds up a suspense: what is writhing? The suspense is dispelled with the anguished remembrance and recognition in the 4th line—"Old Love". The personification of love prepares us for the subsequent image in the following line: the pain assumes the shape of a distinct image in the poet's mind: "Someone's still waiting by the well." The alliteration echoes the original: ke jeno ājo dā̃ḍie āche kuotalāy, but perhaps in a more evocative way. Again, the literal translation of *Daḍie ache* could be 'is standing'; but the sense of wistful longing, of patient but unexpressed expectation is conveyed better through the eloquent silence and impassivity of "still waiting". As the speaker envisions the image he also extends the claim—"*My* Love". The well-side, possibly the meeting place of the lovers in the "old" times—drawing water being traditionally part of the woman's daily chores—also implies a spot outside the house and under the open sky. Had "Love" been shut out/refused/left unacknowledged in the "old" days? Or had she preferred the freedom of the open space to the confines of the closed room? The image of "Love" "waiting by the well" presages the binaries of the closed room and the open sky which are simultaneously foregrounded and resolved in the second stanza.

The TL text, thus, very sensitively and faithfully, renders the first stanza of the SL one,—its process of slow recognition through sense perceptions, olfactory-tactile-visual, first smell, then pain, then vision, corroborating to the speaker's sensations of waking up to the memory of a wound, the sadness of a separation, or the sadness of the long wait for love not requited, the galling tongue of a slow fire which is not yet dead, but still smouldering within and causing pain.

The sense perception of the first stanza is followed by action and entreaty in the second. In the first stanza the lineation and the repetition every second line underscore the increasing clarity of perception. In the second stanza the same device is used to evoke the rising intensity of the entreaty. The very act of defining his pain seems to have led the speaker to an inspired moment of emotional-imaginative frenzy that gets manifested in the expressions:

> "Śabda kore jānlā-darjā khule diyechi...
> ākāśṭāke gharer madhye ṭene niyechi"
> Śabda kore may be a device of communication: the hope that she may hear even if she does not see.

The translator reenacts the very sound of the act of opening through a series of plosives: "Bang'd open the doors and windows." The silent emotion in St. 1 now finds an outburst; and the mindscope finds an appropriate correlative, both semantic and sonic. The next line,—"sqeez'd the sky into my cloister" is a positive improvement upon the original,—with its remarkable alliteration (of "S" and 'k' sounds) voiced fricative ('z'), closed consonant (cloister), which appropriately bring out the intensity of the mood, as also the compression of the image.

The aspect of interior monologue in St. 1 yields place in St. 2 to the monologic tone; this becomes more apparent in the TL, with the '1' replacing 'something' or 'someone' as subject and repeating its entreaty. The shift of mood from St. 1 to St. 2 is evidenced in the switch from the passivity of smelling-feeling-seeing to the activity of opening out, reaching out, of invoking and imploring "Old Love" for whose reception the stage has been appropriately set now. The small room, with its doors and windows being opened, has now expanded to embrace the sky. 'Opened' and 'squeezed', the two opposites, are paradoxically juxtaposed with better sonic effect of contrast than their equivalent in the SL (*khule* and *ṭene*). The room expands to welcome the sky and the sky concedes to its squeezing embrace. Is this meant to be a correlative for the paradigm of love with its entrenched embedded paradox?

With this the entreaty reaches its climax: "Please come." Then there is a fade/off fall. It is now that the speaker realises that he has forgotten her name.[8] "True" in TL seems to be slightly different from the embarrassed "jodio" in the SL; it is rather a poised acknowledgement of the inaccessibility of "Old Love", which the speaker still paradoxically, nostalgically longs for. So the emphasized entreaty with which the poem ends only negates itself; it seems to hint at near desperation; even as he implores, the prayee knows that the prayer may not be granted. Significantly the addressee, *tumi* in SL disappears in the translation; instead there is only an implied addressee in the last earnest but sad appeal in which hope seems almost like hopelessness. (One may recall Heathcliff's frantic appeal to Catharine in *Wuthering Heights*: "Come in, come in...oh do once more, do come, hear me this time....")

Thus here we have a case of translation which not only achieves equivalence at every level, but also emerges as a fine poem in its own right. This is a case that justifies Octavio Paz's claim that a translation "up to a certain point, is an invention, and as such constitutes a unique text" (9).

NOTES

1. In the preface to *Chā̃nd Baniker Pālā* (1978) the author admits the problem of correctly pronouncing his archaic words and verb forms which are indeed too many. (Preface, *CBP*, Calcutta: M.C. Sarkar & Sons, 1989.)
2. Tagore renders his six lines Bengali original in two lines in English:

   The burning log bursts into flame and cries
   This is my flower, my death.

   But the literal translation of the lines would be much more elaborate:

   The branch of a mango tree tells the branch of an acacia, "Why do you get burnt into cinders in any oven? Ala, alas! how grim is your destiny." The acacia replies: "I am not at all sorry for that. O branch of a mango tree, your success lies in life (your life is meaningful as long as you live), my success lies in turning myself to ashes (my life becomes meaningful only through death). (Translation by M.K. Ray)

   The difference is explained by the different characters of the two languages.
3. "Only creative transposition is possible: either intralingual transposition—from one poetic shape into another, or interlingual transposition—from one language to another, or finally intersemiotic transposition—from one system of signs into another, *e.g.*, from verbal art into music, dance, cinema or painting." (Roman Jakobson, "On Linguistic Aspects of Translation", in R.A. Brower (ed.), *On Translation* (Mass.: Harvard University Press, 1969, pp. 232-39).
4. "...as it (translation) involves the consideration of a language in its entirety, together with its most subjective messages, through an examination of common situations and a multiplication of contacts that

need clarifying, then there is no doubt that communication through translation can never be completely finished, which also demonstrates that it is never wholly impossible either." (George Moumin, *Les problemès théoriques de la traduction.* Paris: Gallimard, 1963, quoted by Bassnett-McGuire 36.)

5. "When poems are changed from one language into another, they acquire a new quality and a new spirit, the ideas get new birth and are reincarnated." [Rabindranath Tagore, 1916 (interview), *Portland Press.* Washington, 23 October]
6. Ray, Mohit K., "Translation as Transcreation and Reincarnation," *Perspectives: Studies in Translatology*, 1995: 2, p. 245.
7. In *Wide Sargasso Sea*, the story of a madwoman remembering her forgotten past, it is the sensation of smell that starts off the process of revival.
8. Rabindranath Tagore's poem 'Swapna' (dream) in *Kalpana* may have been at the back of the poet's mind; there the lovers, meeting across the gulf of ages, have forgotten each other's name.

WORKS CITED

Bassnett-McGuire, S. *Translation Studies.* London & N.Y.: Methuen, 1980.

Chakroborty, Nirendranath. 'Tabu Eso', *Khola Muthi*, Calcutta.

Chowdhury, Sukanta. *Translation and Understanding.* New Delhi: Oxford, 1999.

Nida, Eugene, *Towards a Science of Translating* (Leiden: E.J. Brill, 1964).

Mukhopadhyaya, Subhas. 'Jete Jete', *Subhas Mukhopadhyayaer Srestha Kabita*, Calcutta.

Paz, Octavio. *Traduction: literatura y literalidad* (Barcelona: Tusquets Editor, 1971), trans. Bassnett-McGuire 38.

Ray, Mohit K. "Translation as Transcreation and Reincarnation," *Perspectives: Studies in Translatology*, 1995: 2 (Denmark: University of Copenhagen).

——. 'Still Do Come', *Revaluations*, Vol. 2, No. 3, Winter, 1996.

——. 'En Route', *Revaluations*, Vol. 2, No. 3, Winter, 1996.

APPENDIX 1

Tobu Eso

—Nirendranath Chakroborty

Kothāo kichu puḍche tār gandha pāi,
purāno bhālobāsā.
kothāo kichu mucḍe oṭhe jantranāy,
purāno bhālobāsā.

ke yeno ājo daḍye āche kuotalāy,
āmār bhālobāsā.

śabda kore jānlā-darjā khule diyechi,
akhon tumi eso.
ākāśṭāke gharer madhye ṭene niyechi,
akhon tumi eso.
yodio itimadhye nām bhule giyechi,
tobuo tumi eso.

Revaluations, Vol. 2, No. 3, Winter, 1996

Still Do Come

—*Nirendranath Chakroborty*
Tr. Mohit K. Ray

Something's smouldering somewhere—I can smell:
Old Love.
Something's writhing in pain somewhere:
Old Love.
Someone's still waiting by the well:
My Love.

I've bang'd open the doors and windows:
Please come.
I've squeez'd the sky into my cloister:
Please come.
True, I've forgot your name by now:
Still do come.

APPENDIX 2

Yete Yete

—*Subhas Mukhopadhyay*

Tārpar ye-te ye-te ye-te
ak nadīr saṅge dakhā.

pāe tār ghuṅur bā̃dhā
parane
uḍu-uḍu ḍheuer
nīl ghāgrā.

se nadīr dudike duto mukh.
ek mukhe se āmāke āschi bole
dāḍ korye rekhe
onya mukhe
chuṭte chuṭte cole galo.

ār
yete yete bujhye dilo
āmi omni kore āsi
omni kore yāi.
bujhye dilo
ami thekeo nei,
nā thekeo āchi.

Āmār kā̃dher opor hāt rākhlo
samay
tārpar kāner kāche
phisphis kore bollo—
dekhle!
Kāndoṭā dekhle!
Āmi kintu kakshono
tomāke cheḍe thāki nā.

tār kathā śune
hāter muṭhotā khullām.
kāl rātrer bāsi phulgulo
satyii śukiye kāth hoye āche.

galpoṭār kono māthāmundu nei bole
buḍoḍhaḍider akebarei
bhālo lāglo nā.
ār tāchāḍā
galpotā bānāno.

pāche tārā uṭhe yay
tāi tāḍātāḍi
bhaye bhaye ābār ārambha korlām:
'tārpar ye-te ye-te ye-te...
dekhi baner modhye
ālo-jvālā prakāndo ek śahar.

sekhāne khā̃—khā̃ korche bāḍi
ār śiḍigulo sab
yeno swarge uṭhe gache.
tāri akṭā̃te
dekhi cul elo kore base āche
ak paramāsundarī rājkanyā.'

lokgulor cokh cakcak kore uṭhlo

tāder cokhe cokh rekhe
Āmi bolte lāglām—
'tārpar sei rājkanyā
āmār āṅule āṅul jaḍālo.'
āmi tāke āste āste bollām:

'Tumi āśā,
tumi āmār jīvan.'

sune se bollo:
'atodin tomār janyei
āmi hā kore bose āchi.'
buḍodhādīrā āgrohe uṭhe bose
jigyes korlo: 'tārpar'?

byapārṭā tāder māthāy yāte ḍhoke
tar jonye
dhõāy dhõyākār hoye
miliye yete yete āmi bollām

'tārpar? kī bolbo
sei rākshusī āmāke khele...'

Revaluations, Vol. 2, No. 3, Winter, 1996

En Route

—Subhas Mukhopadhyaya
Tr. Mohit K. Ray

Then
as I trudged along
I met a river
anklets jingling at her feet

and
draped in the blue of the rhythmic ripples.
The river had two faces.
With one face she assured me:
'Just wait; I'm coming:
And with the other face
she ran out of sight.'

And

while retreating
she made me understand
'This is how I come and go.'
She made me understand—
'I am off even when I am here;
I am here even when I am off.'
Time gently touched my shoulders
and mumbled into my ears:
'Just see the cheek!
But I never leave you. Never.'

On hearing her words
I opened my fist.
I found
the stale flowers of the last night
all withered dry and stiff.

Since it is a cock and bull story
the elders did not like it at all.

Moreover, it is a concocted one.

Lest they depart in disgust
I hastily resumed
with genuine trepidation:
'Then
as I went on and on and on
I suddenly came across
a large city
full of lights
and deserted houses

where the stairs have gone up
towards the heaven.

And

I saw a princess of peerless beauty
sitting on one of these
with her hair loose and flowing.'
I saw the eyes of my listeners
glow with desire.
Looking straight into their eyes
I continued:
'Then that princess
interlaced her fingers with mine'
and
I implored softly
'You are Hope
you are my life.'
Answered she—
'All these days
I have been waiting for you
with intense expectation.'
All ear, the elders sat up
and asked pruriently—
'Then?'
In order to hammer the idea into their head
I said
as I started vanishing in the thickening smoke:
'Then?'
What shall I say?
La belle dame sans merci
ate me up.

A Comprehensive Model of Translation Criticism

12

SUNIL R. SAWANT

In India, Translation Studies is still a marginal affair. Translations are not yet treated on an equal footing with original works of art. Even serious translations are reviewed in an amateurish manner. More often, a critic familiar with the source language and the source text invariably presents the profile of the original author and his work followed by one or two commonplace comments on the translation. There is no wonder then that most of the studies dealing with large corpora of translated texts turn out to be simply 'source studies'. In this paper I intend to provide a brief review of European approaches to translation criticism and then evolve a model of translation criticism for the assessment and evaluation of target texts comprising a subsystem within the target culture.

I

The traditional discourse on translation mainly discusses the translation of poetry, the Ancient Greek or Roman Classics, and the Bible. As Mary Snell-Hornby writes: "For 2,000 years, translation theory (some call it 'traditional', others now dismiss it as 'pre-scientific') was primarily concerned with outstanding works of art" (in Bassnett and Lefevere 1990: 79). The target system covers a whole range of target texts: acknowledged translations, free adaptations, abridged versions, etc. Each of them may have a specific function in the target culture. The traditional approach to translation, since it centres on only the Classics, falls short of providing an appropriate framework for the analysis of the totality of target texts in a given culture.

II

The linguistic approaches to translation, which began with the application of insights derived from the activities of the Russian Formalist Circle and the Prague Linguistic Circle, view translation as a linguistic process involving the transfer of a message from a S[OURCE] L[ANGUAGE] to a T[ARGET] L[ANGUAGE] or R[ECEPTOR] L[ANGUAGE], despite the differences in languages.

J.C. Catford, in his well-known book *A Linguistic Theory of Translation* (1965), attempts to describe translation in terms of the scale and category grammar proposed by Halliday et al. (1961, 64) and the contextual view of language proposed by J.R. Firth (1957). He defines translation in terms of equivalence relations. He asserts: "The central problem of translation-practice is that of finding TL translation equivalents. A central task of translation theory is that of defining the nature and conditions of translation equivalence" (1965: 21). In Catford's theory of translation, an extralinguistic domain of objects, persons, emotions, memories, history, etc. (*situation* in Halliday) is posited. Translation Equivalence occurs when an SL and a TL text or item are relatable to (at least some of) the same features of this domain, that is when ST and TT have approximately the same referents. Susan Bassnett finds this reliance on an essentially referential theory of meaning too narrow (1980: 6). One more weakness of Catford is that his model never goes beyond the sentence to incorporate the text as a unit of meaning. Last but not the least, his model is of a very limited use in evaluating translations (Paranjape 1977: 33).

In his essay "Science of Translation" (1969), Eugene Nida differentiates between two types of theories of translation: those based on surface structure and those based on kernel structure. Surface structure theories "think of translating merely in terms of certain more or less complex techniques of comparative linguistics..." (1975: 79). Since the surface structure approach is not much suitable in the case of source and receptor languages having quite different grammatical and semantic structures, Nida adopts a kernel structure approach. Nida argues that "instead of going directly from one set of surface structures to another, the competent translator actually goes through a seemingly roundabout process of analysis, transfer, and restructuring" (79). Nida represents such a set of related procedures in the following diagram:

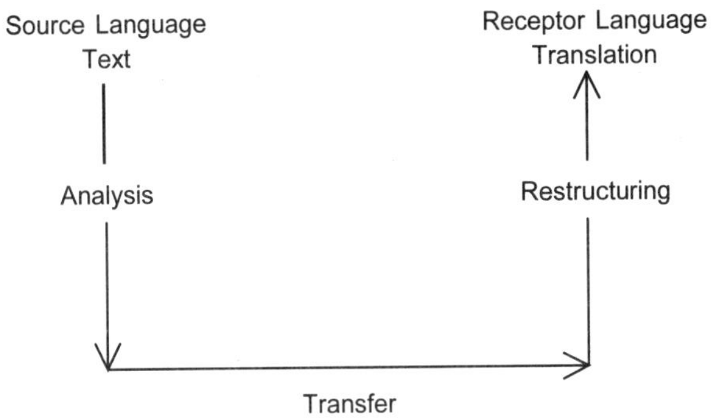

This approach has been dealt with at greater length in the author's later work *The Theory and Practice of Translation* (1974). Besides proposing his own model of the process of translation, Nida introduces his own new category of equivalence called dynamic equivalence. Unlike Catford who establishes equivalence on the basis of the source language and target language words referring to the same thing in the real world, *i.e.*, on the basis of their referential equivalence, he shifts the entire focus in the process of translation towards the potential users of the translation and their reactions to it. The translation has to be tested, not in terms of the extent of verbal correspondence, but in terms of the amount of dynamic equivalence—how the potential receptors of it react to it.

Nida's approach to translation is essentially sociolinguistic with focus on the role of the receptor. He asserts that translation is concerned, not with matching the receptor language message with the source language message, but with extracting the response of the receptors to the RL essentially like that of the original receptors to the SL. For him, the ultimate test of a translation must be based upon three major factors:

(a) the correctness with which the receptors understand the message of the original,

(b) the ease of comprehension, and

(c) the involvement a person experiences as the result of the adequacy of the form of the translation.

Peter Newmark's theory of translation, propounded in his *Approaches to Translation* (1981), is an improvement over Nida's theory of translation. Unlike Nida whose theory is exclusively concerned with the Bible translating, Newmark's takes into account a full range of text-types and their corresponding translation criteria, as well as the major variables involved. Like Nida, Newmark's approach to translation is pragmatic and discourse-oriented. Unlike him, however, he considers a wide diversity of text-types. He also proposes two types of translation: (1) Semantic translation and (2) Communicative translation. The former focuses primarily upon the semantic content of the source text and the latter focuses essentially upon the comprehension and response of receptors. Depending on the text and its function, the mode of translation has to be decided. Newmark's categories of the function of the text—expressive, informative and vocative—as well as his distinction between semantic translation and communicative translation are undoubtedly useful for the analysis of TL texts. Yet his definition of translation as "a craft consisting in the attempt to replace a written message and/or statement in one language by the same message and/or statement in another language" (7) shows that his theory, tied to the issue of transferring message, has not encompassed deviated target texts and socio-cultural dimensions of the target culture.

According to Juliane House, communication models of translation have advanced our theoretical understanding of the process of translation, but they are not very useful for solving the practical problems of describing and assessing translations as finished products. In *A Model for Translation Quality Assessment* (1977), she draws attention to weaknesses in various models of translation quality assessment [especially those of Nida (1964), Nida and Taber (1969), Miller and Beebe-Center (1958), Carroll (1966), Koller (1974), Reiss (1968, 1971, 1973 etc.). She, therefore, makes an attempt to develop her own model for the analysis and comparison of source text and translation text 'in which criteria for judgement are made explicit'.

She defines translation as follows: "Translation is the replacement of a text in the source language by a semantically and pragmatically equivalent text in the target language" (29-30). For her, the concept of 'equivalence' is the fundamental one: an adequate translation should have semantic-pragmatic equivalence. She further posits that the translation text should have a *function* equivalent to that of its source text. She defines textual function as the use of the text in a particular situation. To determine textual function and the ensuing comparison of the source text and the translation text's function, she develops her model on the basis of the system of situational dimensions suggested by Crystal and Davy (1969):

A. Dimensions of Language User :
1. Geographical Origin
2. Social Class
3. Time

B. Dimensions of Language use :
1. Medium [Simple / Complex]
2. Participation [Simple / Complex]
3. Social Role Relationship
4. Social Attitude
5. Province

In her model, the function of a source text is established as a result of an analysis of the text in terms of the above set of extralinguistic, situational constraints. Such analysis yields a particular textual profile for the source text. For House, this textual profile of the source text "is...the norm against which the quality of the translation text is to be measured" (1977: 50). From this, it follows that "the degree to which its textual profile does not match the source text's profile is the degree to which that translation text is inadequate in quality" (50). In evaluating the relative match between ST and TT, she makes a distinction between dimensional mismatches or *covertly erroneous errors,* and non-dimensional mismatches or *overtly erroneous errors*. The final qualitative judgement of TT consists of a listing of both covertly and overtly erroneous errors, and of a statement of the resulting mismatches of each of the two functional components.

House's study of eight German and English textual pairs (STs and TTs) in terms of her model of translation quality assessment leads her to distinguish between two basic types of translation: overt translation and covert translation. The former is made of source culture-linked STs. By making an important modification in her provisional model, she claims that the achievement of functional equivalence, which is possible in cases of overt translation, is impossible in cases of covert translation. Nevertheless, the application of a *cultural filtre* may be needed in translating and evaluating covert translations.

House implements her model of translation quality assessment with a small sample of texts translated from and into English and German, languages which stand on almost equal cultural and linguistic footing. The aim of her model is to test 'the relative match' of the ST and the TT. Her model, therefore, lacks appropriateness in the situation in which the SL and the TL are culturally different from each other and in which TTs may not always aim at functional equivalence with STs as such.

III

Recently, Mary Snell-Hornby has introduced a new German translation theory to the English-speaking world. The four important aspects of this theory are:

(a) Translation is a *cultural* rather than linguistic transfer;

(b) Translation is not a process of transcoding but an act of *communication;*

(c) The *function* of the *target text* (prospective translation) is more important than prescriptions of the source text (retrospective translation); and

(d) The text is *an integral part of the world* and not an isolated specimen of language.

(Snell-Hornby in Bassnett and Lefevere 1990: 81-82)

As she points out, the major theoretical contribution in this new cultural approach to translation has been made by Hans J. Vermeer. The dominating feature of Vermeer's approach is the function of the target text, which may well differ from the original function of the source text. Vermeer differentiates between two types of function of the translated text:

(a) *Functionskonstanz* (unchanged function)

(b) *Funktionsveranderung* (changed function, whereby the text is adapted to meet specified needs in the target culture).

Snell-Hornby finds a new orientation in Vermeer's approach, "something very important, which was largely ignored in both the traditional and the linguistic approach to translation: 'the' translation *per se* does not exist, and neither does the 'perfect translation'" (82).

This functional approach to translation insures against treating the TT as an entity in itself, divorced from the circumstances of its production and reception. A text is produced for specific recipients in a specific context. Translation is no longer the mere transformation of a text from one language to another, but rather the production of a target text that can function within a different context for recipients from a different culture. In Vermeer's functional view of translation, any notion of equivalence between a source text and a target text is subordinate to the *skopos*, or purpose which the target text is intended to fulfil. Adequacy with regard to *skopos* then replaces equivalence as the standard of judging translations.

The functional approach was developed for texts such as user instructions, advertising pamphlets, scientific articles, for professional or for laymen, and so on. Hence Snell-Hornby rccords two drawbacks of this approach. According to her, it focuses only on specialised or general language and on pragmatic rather than literary texts (84).

When Vermeer was proposing a new functional approach to translation in Germany, Itamar Evan-Zohar, a scholar from Tel Aviv, was making a similar attempt to establish a new paradigm for the study of literary translation. Adopting the notion of system from the Russian Formalists, he came to formulate what he termed *polysystem theory*.

According to Evan-Zohar's model, a given national literature can be viewed as a 'polysystem', *i.e.* as a heterogeneous, hierarchized and dynamic 'conglomerate of systems' characterized by internal oppositions and continual shifts. This polysystem is part of a larger socio-cultural polysystem which itself comprises other polysystems besides the literary, such as for example the artistic, the religious or the political.

Evan-Zohar conceives of translated literature as a system in its own right because, he claims, translated works do correlate in at least two ways:

> (a) in the way they are selected by the target literature, the principles of selection never being uncorrelable with the home co-systems...; and
>
> (b) in the way they adopt specific norms, behaviours, and policies which are a result of their relations with the other co-systems. (in Holmes et al., 1978: 118)

Thus, the system of translated literature does not function in isolation. It fully participates in the history of the literary polysystem, as an integral part of it, related with all the other co-systems.

Evan-Zohar's theory of the polysystem further sees 'translated literature as one system among many in the constant struggle for the dominant position'. Evan-Zohar identifies three sets of circumstances in which it can occupy a central position:

> (a) when a polysystem has not yet been crystallized, that is to say, when a literature is "young", in the process of being established;
>
> (b) when a literature is either "pheripheral" or "weak," or both; and
>
> (c) when there are turning points, crises, or literary vacuums in a literature. (121)

Translated literature can play a variety of roles in the target polysystem. Translated literature occupying a central position is mostly innovative and introduces original elements into the polysystem; translated literature constituting a peripheral position, on the other hand, is highly conservative and conforms to already existing norms and models. The former introduces features into the target literature which did not exist there before; whereas the latter becomes a means to preserve traditional taste.

Translated literature may not always depend on central or peripheral relation to the literary polysystem. It is possible that within the sub-system of translated literature one section of translated literature may assume a primary position, another may remain secondary.

Evan-Zohar's work effected a shift away from earlier preoccupation with the nature of *Equivalence* between source and target text and towards a historical and social understanding of the way translated works function collectively, as a sub-system within the target polysystem.

Taking his inspiration from the work of Evan-Zohar, Gideon Toury, another Israeli scholar, has developed a new target-oriented approach to the study of translations. This approach regards translations as facts of the culture which hosts them, assuming that whatever their function and identity, these are constituted within that same culture. In Toury's words:

> Translations are facts of target culture; on occasion facts of a special status, sometimes even constituting identifiable (sub)systems of their own, but of the target culture in any event. (1995: 29)

Instead of viewing translated texts as isolated phenomena, they are rather thought of as manifestations of general translation 'procedures' which are determined by the conditions currently prevalent in the target polysystem. Toury views translation as basically a norm-governed type of behaviour. Being a translator involves fulfilling a function specified by the TL community, rather than simply transferring phrases and sentences from the SL to the TL.

Polysystem theory, as elaborated by Even-Zohar and, by extension Toury's theoretical and methodological model based on the concept of norms, assumes that translations never function in isolation from the dominant and/or peripheral literary and cultural environment. The norms, value scales and models which are prevalent in a given society at a given moment in time shape translation behaviour and influence the position of translated literature. The study of literary translation therefore consists of the study of translation norms, models and traditions in terms of the target culture rather than the source culture.

Raymond van den Broeck, in his article "Second Thoughts on Translation Criticism: A Model of its Analytic Function," asserts the need for a systemic model of translation criticism and reviewing. In order to criticise a single translation, he puts forth a comparative model of translation description and evaluation:

1. A textemic analysis of phonic, lexical, and syntactic components, language varieties, figures of rhetoric, narrative and poetic structures, elements of text convention (text sequences, punctuation, italicizing, etc.), thematic elements, and so on of the ST, leading to the formulation of the Adequate translation, *viz.* the specification of the ST in terms of textemes.
2. A comparison of the TT elements corresponding to these textemes, taking into account the various shifts (or deviations) with respect to the ST.
3. A generalizing description of the differences between the actual TT/ST equivalence and the Adequate Translation, on the basis of the comparison of the textemes. (in Hermans 1985: 58)

Instead of isolated cases, Broeck, however, wants that systems of texts be involved in the comparison. Translation criticism, therefore, should strive 'to detect the translator's norms and options, the constraints under which he works, and the way in which they influence the translational process as well as the ensuing product'. Accordingly, he argues, a model of translation description should take into account the multiple relations:

(a) between the source text and the system of similar and/or other texts originating from the same language, culture and tradition;

(b) between the source and the target systems;

(c) between the target text and its readers;

(d) between the target text and other translations (whether or not in the same target system) of the same source text, and so on. (58-59)

IV

Taking Raymond van den Broeck's systemic model as a point of departure, we here propose a comprehensive model of translation criticism which will help to make a concrete study of any subsystem of translated works in a particular social context from a historical point of view.

Being a reader of the SL text and a producer of the TL text, the translator takes a certain position. In his keynote address given at the seminar on "Novels Translated from Other Indian Languages into Marathi" held at Hyderabad, Dr. Chandrashekhar Jahagirdar has raised the following questions: What was the position of the translator in choosing a particular work of art? What was his intention (1992 : 8)? And he suggests the first category of analysis:

(a) The intention of the translator

According to Susan Bassnett, "The emphasis always in translation is on the reader or listener.... The translator cannot *be* the author of the SL text, but as the author of the TL text has a clear moral responsibility to the TL readers" (1980: 23). Every translator thus has in view a readership with a definite range of knowledge and ability. It may be children of various age groups, neo-literate adults, the average mature reader or even the scholars and the specialists. The strategy used in translation is bound to vary according to the readership envisaged. Dr. Jahagirdar, once again, has raised certain questions: Why did one read a translation? What was exactly the intention of the reader? What kind of contribution did a translation make to the reader's tradition of literature? And the next category of analysis suggested by him is:

(b) Readership

Besides these two categories already suggested by Dr. Jahagirdar, some other aspects of translation culture need to be taken into consideration.

The worth of a translation depends to a large extent upon the public recognition. If the external circumstances of a translator's existence are against him, if there is an absence of interest and sympathy and understanding, his whole production is only too likely to collapse. Thus, the literary attitudes that pervade literary culture at a given point of time determine the value of a translation. Such questions as what was the dominant taste at the time of making a translation? Whose taste—men's, women's, children's—was involved? How was the canon formed? are therefore immensely important. So the next category of analysis is:

(c) Literary taste

The worth of a translation also depends upon whether it fulfils the needs of a literary culture or not. As Andre Lefevere writes, "A literary culture with a high self-image screens out whatever does not fulfil its requirements, or else changes it in such a way as to make it acceptable.... If the potential literary culture does not have all that much of a self-image, it will not dictate any terms at all..." (1985: 236-37). Therefore, the questions need to be raised are: What was the nature of contribution made by a particular translation to literary culture of the TL? What literary needs of the TL community were fulfilled by it? Did it introduce a new mode of perceiving reality in the TL literary order? etc. So the next category of analysis is:

(d) Requirements of literary culture

One of the basic categories of the history of translation, Andre Lefevere argues, is 'authority', "the authority of the person or institution commissioning or later, publishing the translation" (1990 : 15). Further, "authority draws the ideological parameters of the acceptable. It influences the selection of texts for translating, as well as the ways in which texts are translated" (19). The questions important in this regard are:

Who commissioned a particular translation? Was any agency, either from the SL culture or from the TL culture, involved? To what extent such an institution shaped the translational behaviour? So the next category is:

(e) Institutional role

The act of translation is not always guided by the literary needs of a community. Often some 'ideological constraints' are at work. The questions in this regard are: What was added, altered, or omitted to control the message? What sort of a set of beliefs was introduced by a translation? What kind of a situation—social, political, religious, etc.—was responsible for the act of translating? So the next category of analysis needs to be introduced is:

(f) Ideological needs

We, therefore, believe that these six broad categories—(a) The intention of the translator; (b) Readership; (c) Literary taste; (d) Requirements of literary culture; (e) Institutional role; and (f) Ideological needs—determine the position and function of a TT or a group of TTs in the TL culture.

The approach proposed here is not primarily concerned with individual translations or their reception. It is chiefly meant for analysing and evaluating a number of TTs comprising a subsystem, a tradition in the target culture over a definite period of time.

WORKS CITED

Bassnett-McGuire, Susan. 1980. *Translation Studies*. London: Methuen.

—— and Lefevere, Andre (eds.). 1990. *Translation, History and Culture*. London: Pinter Publishers.

Catford, J.C. 1965. *A Linguistic Theory of Translation: An Essay in Applied Linguistics*. London: OUP.

Hermans, Theo (ed.). 1985. *The Manipulation of Literature: Studies in Literary Translation*. London & Sydney: Croom Helm.

Holmes, J.S., Lambert, J. and Lefevere, A. (Eds.). 1978. *Literature and Translation*. The Hague: Mounton.

House, Juliane. 1977. *A Model for Translation Quality Assessment*. Tubingen: TBC Verlag Gunter Narr.

Jahagirdar, Chandrashekhar. 1992. "Keynote Address at the Seminar on Novels Translated from Other Indian Languages into Marathi" in *Panchadhara* (35-1&2).

Lefevere, Andre. 1992. *Translation, Rewriting and the Manipulation of Literary Fame.* London: Routledge.

Newmark, Peter. 1981, *Approaches to Translation.* Oxford: Pergamon.

Nida, Eugene. 1975. *Language, Structure and Translation: Essays by Eugene A. Nida.* Ed. Anwar S. Dil. Stanford: Standford University Press.

—— and Taber, C.R. 1974. *The Theory and Practice of Translation.* Leiden: E.J. Brill.

Paranjape, P.N. 1977. *Explorations in the Theory of Translation Evaluation.* An Unpublished M.Litt. Dissertation submitted to CIEFL, Hyderabad.

Toury, Gideon. 1995. *Descriptive Translation Studies and Beyond.* Amsterdam/ Philadelphia: John Benjamin's Publishing Company.

Nineteenth Century Marathi Literary Polysystem

13

SUNIL R. SAWANT

I

The nineteenth century is known as the age of translation in the history of Marathi Literature. Both Christian missionaries and British officials encouraged the production of numerous translations during this period. Polysystem Theory, as elaborated by Itamar Evan-Zohar (1978), and by extension Toury's theoretical and methodological model based on the concept of norms (1980, 1995) assumes that all translation activity (whether it involves producing, using or commenting on translations) is guided and shaped by such things as the norms, value scales and models which are prevalent in a given society at a given moment of time (Lambert in Baker 1998: 132). This paper records the process of the formation of models, norms and strategies of translation in Marathi.

II

Christian missionaries were the first to develop a model of translation in Marathi. They were primarily concerned with the dissemination of word of God among the natives. The important norm of translation proposed by the missionaries was that the translator should try to observe fidelity to the source text and any deviations from it would have the possibility of changing or distorting the sacred words and meanings. This SL-oriented approach to translation led the missionaries to translate and retranslate the text of the New Testament into Marathi. Strongly critical of the Marathi Bible and the 'Kunkuna' Bible translated by the Serampore missionaries under the supervision of Dr. William Carey, the members of the American Marathi Mission, founded in Mumbai in 1813, undertook the project of retranslating their Bible into Marathi of an altogether different kind. Nevertheless, they followed earlier foreignizing strategy of translation:

> In making the first copy of the New Testament, for the most part, the sense was given to the pundit directly from the original and then he wrote it down in his own words. A very small part only was written by us; and then we endeavoured afterwords to procure carefully all idiomatic corrections from pundits, by a full explanation of words and sentences. (in Pinge 1960: 236)

The missionaries were primarily concerned with producing the most literal translation of the Bible into Marathi. So Rev. J. Murray Mitchell of Scottish Mission undertook the work of revising the Marathi Bible prepared by the American missionaries. This was a single-handed enterprise, without the aid of Brahmin pundits. And the result was:

> I found this work exceedingly laborious. First, to get the exact sense—neither more nor less—and secondly, to convey that exact sense exactly—neither more nor less—into the vernacular language was a most difficult, and often an impossible task. Some of the most characteristic expressions resisted all attempts to render them literally. If you ventured to do so, the natives exclaimed with sneer, 'Nonsense!' or more sneeringly still, 'Missionary Marathi'. On the other hand, if you deviated by a hair's breadth from the literal sense, some missionaries were ready to cry out, 'You are paraphrasing, not translating'. (316-17)

More or less, the source language text demanded unwavering faithfulness from the target language text. This pressure gave rise to the pressure for fidelity and equivalence. The original had priority over other considerations—including the target audience in the target language culture. Here then was a hierarchy in which the SL text wielded a tyrannical power over the TL text. Equivalence was seen in linguistic and aesthetic terms and lexical semantic and syntactic equivalences were achieved, the translation was deemed successful. Equivalence was seen as a search for 'sameness'. This situation led to the development of a strange, pidginized variety of Marathi language, popularly known as 'Missionary Marathi'.

III

Whereas Christian missionaries aimed at the dissemination of the word of God, early British administrators adopted a policy of disseminating secular and moral knowledge among the natives, Mountstuart Elphinstone, the first Governor of the Bombay Presidency, strongly opposed the mixture of religion with education as was done by missionaries.

Elphinstone's educational policy was based on the 1813 charter of the British Parliament. It clearly stated: "A sum not less than Rs. 1,00,000 should be spent every year for the revival and improvement of Oriental literature, for encouragement of the learned natives of India and for introduction and promotion of the knowledge of the sciences among the inhabitants of the territories of British India" (in Kulkarni 1956: 19). This kind of generous gesture on the part of the British colonial power was perhaps the result of what Britain had learnt from its bitter experience in America: "When the thirteen colonies that later became the United States of America broke away from the British Empire in 1776 the British learned the lesson that iron rule from the imperial capital leads to revolt, war and the risk of humiliation..." (Lapping 1985: 7). Elphinstone chose to practise the politics of moderation (Kumar 1968: 45). He decided to appease the otherwise unhappy brahmans by not interfering with their religious training and by continuing the old pattern of patronage through the distribution of the *dakshina*. He established the Hindu college in Pune exclusively for the students of the Brahmin caste.

Elphinstone, however, favoured modern type of education. He, therefore, chose Bombay 'for introduction and promotion of the knowledge of the sciences'. 'The Native School Book and School Society' came into existence to impart secular education through the medium of the vernacular languages of the Bombay

Presidency. The British policy of promoting the vernaculars led to the development of the pedagogical model of translation in Marathi.

The Government Circular of 8 April 1825 is of historical significance because it gave for the first time certain norms of translation to Marathi translation culture. These are:

> In translating English works, it is necessary particularly to point out that in almost all cases, they must undergo *partial* alterations to adapt them to the habits and manners of the natives.... [In translating], the commonly accepted vernacular dialects must be used to their fullest extent, to the exclusion of an unnecessary display of any learned tongue. Where, however, these dialects are deficient in the means of expressions, words must be supplied from cognate language.... The adoption of words from English must necessarily be admitted in cases, where neither the current nor cognate language furnish them directly or by composition. (Jervis 1825: 4)

Here, the norms of the Society ask the translator to consider the needs of the TL readers and adapt or alter the ST in order to make it interesting and instructive as the situation demands. Captain George Jervis, Sadashiv Kashinath Chhatre, Hari Keshavji Pathare, Balshashtri Jambhekar, Dadoba Pandurang, etc. made their translations keeping these norms in mind. Some of these translations became extremely popular, but their prose was found to be fraught with 'Konkanisms', 'superfluous punctuation marks', 'forced borrowing from English', 'non-standardized expressions' etc.

During Elphinstone's tenure, Bomaby became a centre of new learning and public life. Elphinstone's successors, the Utilitarians, however, did not approve of his liberal policy of promoting the vernaculars. Their deviations from his policy had an adverse effect on the growth of Marathi translation culture.

Firstly, in imparting education Elphinstone had no intention of training persons for government service. He wanted to educate the natives to make them better persons morally and intellectually. Malcolm, who succeeded him in 1827, on the contrary, emphasized the need to train Indians for government offices, especially in the administration of civil justice as well as revenue.

Secondly, Elphinstone had stressed the need to impart education through the vernacular languages and encouraged the study of 'Oriental' languages. Thomas Babington Macaulay, Legal Member of Council, found the vernaculars and the 'Oriental' languages (Sanskrit and Arabic) unsuitable for imparting education. About the former, he stated that "the dialects commonly spoken among the natives of this part of India contain neither Literary nor Scientific information, and are, moreover so poor and rude that until, they are enriched from some other quarter, it will not be easy to translate any valuable work into them" (in Clive and Pinney 1972 [1835]: 240). About the latter, he claimed that "a single shelf of a good European library was worth the whole native Literature and Arabia" (241). James Mill had remarked that India must discard her Indianness in order to become civilized (in Niranjana 1992: 58). Macaulay in a similar vein suggested that Indians become 'anglicised' in order to acquire civilization (58). Lord William Cavendish Bentinck's Resolution of 7th March 1835 made English the language of education in India and decided once for all the course of education in India.

Thirdly, both Elphinstone and Malcolm had stressed the need to impart education to all—the higher castes as well as to the lower castes. Contrary to this liberal policy, Macaulay advocated the 'Downward Filtration' theory of education. According to this, the best policy for the Government in a hierarchal society was to take care of the education of the higher or upper classes possessing leisure, hereditary qualities and inclination for learning and natural influence over the minds of their countrymen (in Shinde 1985: 211).

Fourthly, Elphinstone had given priority to the primary education. In primary schools opened by The Native School Book and School Society, such subjects as History of England and India, Geography, Arithmetic, Algebra, Geometry, Astronomy and Natural Philosophy were all taught by means of Marathi translations. Bentinck, however, adopted the policy of giving financial support only to colleges teaching western knowledge in English.

The Bombay Government continued to foster Vernacularism despite warnings from Calcutta (Nemade 1990: 56). This partial breach of policy continued to promote translation culture though it could not prevent the gross negligence of the vernacular at the hands of English-educated bilinguals.

Now, the centre of translation activity was shifted from Bombay to Pune. The Board of Education instructed Thomas Candy to devote himself exclusively to the work of translation with supervision of translation and personal superintendence of Poona College. Candy's "Hints for the guidance of Translators" comprises the most 'prescriptive' statement on the norms of translation:

> The great thing to be aimed at in translation is to give a faithful, idiomatical and grammatical rendering of the original. The first point is gained when *all the meaning* of the original has been transferred into the new version, and nothing beyond it has been added. The second and third points are gained when the translation is agreeable to the rules of correct composition; and to the customary phraseology, of the second language as the text is to those of the original. The translator, in short, should endeavour to render the *sense* of the text, not merely the words which compose it, and he should use such construction that though the *ideas* he presents may strike as novel, there should be nothing uncouth or barbarous in the phraseology by which he expresses them.
>
> The faithfulness to the ST is essential.
>
> ...he should...avoid all unnecessary departure from the style of the original. Most good writers have each a particular style of his own, which style the translator should endeavour to preserve. If attention to this rule be neglected the most opposite styles will lose all difference in the hands of a loose translator.

Besides these general hints, Candy made a few specific suggestions to Marathi translators.

> Whenever a scientific or technical word occurs which has an exact equivalent in Marathi the equivalent is of course to be used.... When a scientific or technical term occurs which has no equivalent in Marathi, and there is no word in use of the same general meaning which might be appropriated to it and be made its equivalent, the best and simplest way seems to be to transfer the word as it stands from English into Marathi.
>
> With respect to titles and dignities peculiar to Europeans or Christians, the English words should of course be transferred bodily, as Duke, Earl, Baron, Bishop, etc. but where a word is descriptive of an office or duty as well as being a title, as Governor, Judge, Doctor, General, etc., I would suggest that where used merely as a title the English word should be retained, but when there is a particular reference to office or duty there the native equivalent should be used, as *Nyayadhish* for Judge, *Senapati* for General, *Vaidya* for Doctor or physician.
>
> With respect to geographical terms, names of places, a rule somewhat similar to the above should...be maintained.

Although Candy insisted upon exactitude in scientific and technical transferences, he was considerate of the needs and limitations of the native readers. He allowed the use of 'explanations' and 'footnotes' in translations. Since the preoccupation was with the translation of non-literary books, what was expected from the translator was the transfer of the 'ideas' from the SL to the TL. The translator was free 'to adapt' the ST to the TL, but must not change the ideas in the original in translating.

When it came to devise norms for translations of English romances, the Duxina Prize Committee, which worked under Candy's supervision, earlier norms underwent a significant change:

> Translations from English into Marathi, if literal are almost certain to be rejected. The idiom of Marathi is so exceedingly unlike that of English that adaptations are far more desirable than mere translations. Style must be

> carefully attended to.... It must be thoroughly grammatical and idiomatical. The Committee hopes to receive works written not only with purity but with elegance. (D.P.I., Government Department, Vol. 6, 1856: 257)

Here, and in Candy's writings on translation, the term 'adaptation' refers specifically to the idiom of language. Candy especially found fault both with the anglicization of Marathi and with the practice of using 'high Sanskrit words which are unintelligible to the great majority of native readers'. He preferred Marathi books having easy and good style and idiomatical and correct composition. He insisted on uniformity in spelling, grammatical forms and syntax. Uniformity of the usage developed certain norms against which all varieties of language were adjusted to form the standard Marathi.

Candy perfected the pedagogical model of translation. In 1850, he produced *Vachanpathmala* (Vernacular Reader No. 1), a collection of translations made from *Series of Lessons* and *Third Reading Book* by McLuck. In preparing these, he followed a very peculiar method of translation: he would give an English passage for Marathi translation to his students; he would then correct their translations and make his own translation of the passage; in the class, finally, he would compare the original passage, translations made by students and his own translation carefully. Thus many passages from McLuck's book were translated and a textbook was made of them. The intention was that 'they might serve as a help and a guide to translation'. And indeed, Krishna Chiplonkar, a student in the Pathshala, was highly praised by Candy for adapting three English stories as *Sahal Karun Yene, Don Rupayanchi Yogyata* and *Vel Loukar Janyacha Upay*.

Candy, with the help of Translation Exhibitioners, prepared in all seven books of the Marathi series, *Shalantil Mulankarita Pustake* from 1858 to 1861. The strategy followed was not adequacy of translation but acceptability to the TL reader: "The translations from English books that have been made by myself and by the Translation Exhibitioners are not simply translations, but are adaptations of the original pieces. I have a good hope, therefore, that this book will prove very acceptable to the native public" (in Pinge 193), Candy wrote about the Fourth Book of the Marathi Series. Candy was not interested in literary graces. He selected tales that would have moral significance and passages that would increase general knowledge of students. When asked 'to examine the Board of Education's publications previous to passing new editions through the press and to strike off books containing false morality or false science', he diligently revised and sometimes even rewrote earlier translations made by S.K. Chhatre, B.G. Jambhekar, T. Gaisford, etc. Above all, he gave a great impetus to the preparation of textbooks in Marathi.

IV

Candy's 'prescriptive' norms of translation controlled the translational activity of non-literary books on the subjects of Geography, History, Chemistry, Botany, Zoology, etc. predominantly. When the natives began to translate imaginative literature from Sanskrit and English, there underwent a significant change in norms and procedures of translation. Candy, who hitherto advocated 'free and flowing adaptations rather than exact versions' from English into Marathi, was the first to oppose, for example, the act of adapting Shakespeare's *Romeo and Juliet* as *Romketuvijaya.* He argued that faithful translation would have given a correct idea of Shakespeare's play, whereas the adaptation would give only mental entertainment to native readers (Translation Department, Vol. XXVIII, 1869-70: 18).

This dichotomy between 'faithful translation' and 'adaptation' dominated the theoretical discourse on translation in Marathi for a very long time. Two groups of translators and translation critics stood in opposition to each other, especially on the basis of whether a play be 'adapted' or 'faithfully translated'. Although the issue at stake was the translation of drama, the debate had bearing on the entire Marathi translation culture.

Gopal Ganesh Agarkar, the noted social reformist, vigorously justified 'faithful translations':

(a) Translations should not deviate from the original as far as possible.

(b) Changes should not be made in the original content to accommodate the cultural and temporal differences between the SL and the TL.

(c) Instead of combining contradictory cultural elements of thoughts from English and Marathi, it is better to write another play in Marathi by just borrowing the main idea and restructuring it in Marathi.

(d) Translations which combine mixtures of elements chosen from two different cultures are irrelevant. On the other hand, if the English culture is to be brought on the stage, if the readers and spectators are to be exposed to the different values of another culture, they would be immensely useful and popular.

(e) The language of the play should be as 'pure' as possible. It is improper to employ pure and impure languages according to the characters.

(f) It is not true that a play is a photographic presentation of the real world. The description in the plays of human emotions is more accentuated than the real life. (1954 [1883]: 1-29; translated)

Here, Agarkar advocates the initial norm of remaining 'faithful' to the ST. He argues that the translator has moral duty to acquaint the people with a world essentially different from their own and thus help bring about a change in the value system of the society and free it from the prejudices and oppressive customs of its conventional way of life.

Vishnushastri Chiplunkar, too, advocates a similar sort of norm in his essay 'Bhashantar': "To think how the author is to be translated would have composed his book in the TL and to produce TT accordingly is the best method of translation" (1889 : 177; translated). He, however, admits the impossibility of this method. Given this 'impossibility' of translating cultural specificities encoded within the SL, he advocates 'adaptation' as the technique of translation. He argues:

> Translations have been made but how many readers for whom they have been made do enjoy them? Who enjoys the translation of *Othello*? Those who know English

> enjoy it but how much a reader who knows Marathi only, despite being a great *rasika,* can enjoy it? I believe that he cannot....
>
> Wherever there are differences in practices, customs, thoughts and beliefs between the nations, translation is an impossibility. Poems, plays and the novels, which contain cultural specificities can hardly be translated, especially when the languages are far removed from each other.... Works of Milton, Shakespeare, Scott are very interesting in English but they can hardly be made so in Marathi. On the contrary, they will be boring and ridiculous. It is, therefore, advisable that their merits, kept in mind while reading them, be adapted in our language. (1889: 215; translated)

This acceptance of 'adaptation' as the proper technique of translation was probably a result of the awareness of the values of individuality and creativity with which the revivalists had been acquainted through education (Narkar 1990: 141).

A number of translation critics of the time, however, unleashed a vigorous attack on the then prevalent practice of adapting texts from English to Marathi. Chiplunkar, who elsewhere defended the TL reader's right to adapt the ST to his needs, strongly criticised Mahajani's adaptation of *Cymbeline* entitled *Tara*: "It is not the duty of the translator to bring about good or bad changes in the original book; he must produce the exact copy of the original in the target language" (1889 : 514; translated). G.C. Wagle disliked discrepancy between Agarkar's theory and practice of translation and suggested: (1) The translator had to remain faithful to the original text; (2) He had to study all the available texts, commentaries, etc. on the original text; and (3) He had to translate it faithfully, without distorting the meaning of the text, without adding anything of his own or deleting portions from the original text (in Narkar 1990: 528). Another voice of protest against the established translation culture came from V.K. Rajwade, a renowned Marathi historian, who, in his own journal called *Bhashanter,* criticised the trend of 'adaptations' and demanded exactness in translating so as to achieve "the enrichment of language, the growth in pride and the awakening of imagination" (1985 [1894]: 3; translated).

Thus, translation critics demanded exactitude and adequacy in translating. Actual practitioners of translation, however, cared for the acceptability of their translations in the TL culture. This situation led to the development of the model based on the process of appropriating English literary texts for puerile entertainment.

Although translation culture lost its earlier central position in the literary polysystem it continued to provide models and norms to original writers to a certain extent. As far as fiction is concerned, the novelist who dominated Marathi translation culture and influenced Marathi literary culture of the time was G.W.M. Reynolds, the novelist whose name hardly figures in any critical history of English literature but who "had written more and solid in far greater numbers than Dickens" and who was "the most popular writer of our time" (in Jog 1973: 419). Moti Bulasa, an eminent Marathi critic of the time, denounced immoral content of these translations in his monthly *Suvicharsamagam* (1998 [1898]: 55). Nevertheless, Reynolds continued to rule the taste of Marathi reading public through G.N. Datar's translations such as *Kalikamurthi*, *Indrabhuvanguha* published by Marathi publisher Damodar Sawalaram Yande.

V

To conclude, translated literature in Marathi occupied a central position till the end of the nineteenth century as all the three important earlier traditions—that of Bhakti, Panditi and Shahiri—had become peripheral under the changed circumstances of the British rule. Neither the tradition of Mahanubhava prose nor that of Bakhar prose could exert any influence on the translators. Missionaries developed their own model of translation for proselytising and British Officials in charge of translation activity developed the pedagogical model of translation to educate the Marathi public. When the Marathi people started translating literary texts from English into Marathi they developed the model of appropriating the colonizer's culture for the colonized. As a result, new norms and strategies came into existence. These controlled the entire working of the Marathi literary polysystem.

WORKS CITED

Agarkar, Gopal Ganesh. 1883. *Vikar Vilasita*. Pune: Venus Prakashan.

Baker, Mona (ed.). 1998. *Routledge Encyclopaedia of Translation Studies*. London: Routledge.

Bulasa, Moti. 1898. *Marathi Vangmayachi Sadhyasththi*, ed. Vidyagauri Tilak and Dr. D.D. Punde. Pune: Snehavardhan.

Chiplunkar, Vishnushastri. 1889. *Nibandhamala*, Vol. I and II. Pune: Aryabhushan Press.

Clive, John and Pinney, Thomas (eds.). 1972. *Thomas Babington Macaulay: Selected Writings*. Chicago and London: The University of Chicago Press.

D.P.I. 1856. Government Department, Vol. VI.

Jervis, George. 1825. *Rewards for Translations, Original Essays, etc.* Bombay: The Bombay Native School Book and School Society.

Jog, R.S. 1973. *Marathi Vangmayach Itihas*, Vol. V, Part I. Pune: Marathi Sahitya Parishad.

Kulkarni, Krishnaji Bhikaji. 1956. *Adhunik Marathi Gaddyachi Utkranti* Mumbai: Marathi Samshodhan Mandal.

Kumar, Ravinder. 1968. *Western India in the Nineteenth Century: A Study in the Social History of Western Maharashtra*. London: Routledge and Kegan Paul.

Lapping, Brian. 1985. *End of Empire*. London: Granada Publishing Limited.

Narkar, Maya. 1990. *A Linguistic Study of the Nineteenth Century Marathi Translations*. An unpublished Ph.D. thesis submitted to the Shivaji University, Kolhapur.

Nemade, Bhalchandra. 1990. *The Influence of English on Marathi: A Sociolinguistic and Stylistic Study*. Panaji: Rajhans.

Niranjana, Tejaswini. 1992. *Siting Translation: History, Poststructuralism and Colonial Context*. Hyderabad: Orient Longman.

Pinge, Srinivas Madhusudhan. 1960. *Europiananchu Marathicha Abhyas Va Seva*. Aurangabad: S.M. Pinge.

Rajwade, V.K. 1894. "Bhashantaracha Upodghat" in *Bhashantar*, 1 January.

Shinde, J.R. 1985. *Dynamics of Cultural Revolution: 19th Century Maharashtra*. Delhi: Ajañta Publications.

Translation Department, Vol. XXVIII. 1869-70.

A Note on Dryden's Views on Translation

14

MOHIT K. RAY

Like many poet-translators, like the great Chaucer before him, Dryden was a practising translator, and it is really amazing that writing in the seventeenth century Dryden discussed problems which we have started taking seriously only now. All his translations are prefaced by insightful essays on the various problems associated with translation. In his preface to *The Life of Lucan* Dryden writes that a translator

> ought to possess himself entirely and perfectly comprehend the genius and sense of his author, the nature of the subject, and the terms of the art of subject treated of. And then he will express himself as justly and with as much life, as if he wrote the original; whereas he who copies word for word loses all the spirit in the tedious transfusion. (Bassnett 149)

The key word is "possession". The translator, Dryden argues, must possess himself of everything the author has to offer, for only then he will create something with as much life as an original. What Dryden then modestly admits that in spite of his sincere efforts he has not been able to translate Virgil satisfactorily. The reasons he assigns tells a lot about the problems of translating an author like Virgil in any modern language:

> Virgil...being so very sparing of his words, and leaving so much to be imagined by the reader, can never be translated as he ought in any modern tongue. To make him copious is to alter his character; and to translate him

> line by line is impossible, because the Latin is naturally a more succinct language than either the Italian, Spanish, French, or even the English (which by reason of its monosyllables, is most compendious of them)...the turn of his verse, the breakings, his propriety, his numbers and his gravity, I have as far imitated as the poverty of our language and the hastiness of my performance would allow. (*Poems* 385)

Dryden then goes on to discuss the special properties of Lucretius and Ovid and shows the same critical insight as is evinced in his discussion of Virgil. The entire *Preface to Sylvae* is interesting in many ways. It shows Dryden's almost New critical exegesis, his comparative method *par excellence*, his interest in the aesthetics of sound in poetry, his workshop criticism and his insights into what is now known as translatology. I shall close this section by referring to one more important passage of Dryden where he provides theoretical categories of translation. He writes:

> All translation, I suppose, may be reduced to these three heads: First that of metaphrase, or turning an author word by word, and line by line, from one language to another. Thus, or near his manner, was Horace his *Art of Poetry* translated by Ben Jonson. The second way is that of paraphrase, or translation with latitude where the author is kept in view by the translator, so as never to be lost, but his words are not so strictly followed as his sense: and that too is admitted to be amplified, but not altered. Such is Mr. Waller's translation of Virgil's fourth *Aeneid.* The third way is that of imitation where the translator (if now he has not lost that name) assumes the liberty, not only to vary from the words and sense, but forsakes both as he sees occasion: and taking only some general hints from the original, to run division on the groundwork, as he pleases. Such is Mr. Cowley's practice in turning two odes of Pinder, and one of Horace, into English. (*Poems* 509)

Dryden then discusses in detail the relative merits and demerits of these three kinds of translation—metaphrase, paraphrase and imitation—which roughly correspond to modern literalism, middle ground and free translation. Lefevere's seven strategies of translation can be seen only as an elaboration of Dryden's three.

What Dryden means by "possession" would be clear from his own practice, for after all, all Dryden's criticism is what Eliot calls "workshop criticism," a craftsman talking about his craft. Dryden writes:

> "...to be a thorough translator he must be a thorough poet. Neither is it enough to give his author's sense in good English in poetical expressions, and in musical number. For, though all these are exceeding difficult to perform there yet remains a harder task: and 'tis secret of which few translators have sufficiently thought...that is the maintaining of the character of an author, which distinguishes him from all others, and make him appear that individual poet whom you would interpret." (*Poems* 383-84)

Dryden then discusses the distinctive features of Virgil and Ovid and narrates how he, as translator, goes about the job:

> I can make the difference more plain by giving you my own method of proceeding, in my translations out of four several poets...Virgil, Theocritus, Lucretius, and Horace. In each of them I considered the genius and distinguishing character of my author. I looked on Virgil, as a succinct and grave majestic writer: one who weighed not only every thought, but every word and syllable: who was still aiming to crowd his sense into as narrow a compass as possibly he could: for which reason he is so very figurative, that he requires (I must almost say) a grammar apart to construe him. His verse is everywhere sounding the very thing in your ears whose sense it bears: yet the numbers are perfectly varied to increase the delight of the reader; so that the sounds are never repeated twice together...though he is smooth where smoothness is required yet he is so far from affecting it, that he seems rather to disdain it; frequently makes use of synaloephas, and concludes his sense in the middle of his verse. He is

> everywhere above conceits of epigrammatic wit and gross hyperboles. He maintains majesty in midst of plainness; he shines but glares not; and is stately without ambition, which is the vice of Lucan. I drew my definition of poetical wit from my particular consideration of him. For propriety of thought and words are only to be found in him; and where they are proper they will be delightful. Pleasure follows necessity, as the effect does the cause; and therefore is not to be put into the definition. This exact propriety of Virgil I particularly regarded as a great part of his character. (*Poems* 384-85)

As a translator Dryden deserves more serious critical attention than he has received so far.

WORKS CITED

Bassnett, Susan. *Comparative Literature.* Oxford: Blackwell, 1993.

Dryden, John. *The Poems of John Dryden.* Ed. John Sergeaunt. London: Oxford UP, 1952. Cited as *Poems*.

Matthew Arnold on Translation

15

PRASENJIT CHATTOPADHYAY

Translation studies which is relevant, actively research oriented, burgeoning field of study today has come to be seen as a discipline in its own right from the late twentieth century. Eminent theorists of translatology Susan Bassnett and Andrè Lefevere rightly note: "Translation has been a major shaping force in the development of world culture, and no study of comparative literature can take place without regard to translation" (*THC* 12).

But the scenario was completely different in Britain from the nineteenth century to late twentieth century. There was a virtual drought of translation activities and theorizing about translations. Barring a few sporadic attempts no one was particularly concerned about translation. In nineteenth century Britain translation was accorded a very low status and even a modicum of respect was not attached to the activity of translation. All these things can be attributed to Britain's steady emergence as a puissant imperial power to be reckoned with, the changes in self-esteem, and an euphoric feeling about the supposed inherent superiority of the English literary system. Itamar Evan-Zohar the avantgarde theorist of modern translation studies tried to explain the reasons behind the extremely low translation related activities in the nineteenth century Britain. Evan-Zohar says that much translation activity takes place when a culture is in a state of transition, in dire need of renewal and expansion. On the contrary when a culture is upon a solid foundation, when it is in an imperialist stage, when it is very conscious about its dominance, translation is neglected, almost relegated to limbo.

This seems to elucidate why the emergent European nations struggle for liberty in the early nineteenth century translated so abundantly and why translation activity steadily declined in the late nineteenth century Britain. Corroborating this point of view in her remarkable critical study on comparative literature Susan Bassnett says: "Certainly by the nineteenth century, the status of a translation was generally considered to be lower than that of an 'original', and theorists of comparative literature, while acknowledging the role played by translation in their work, tended to assert the primacy of reading in original languages" (*CL* 139).

Hillaire Belloc's views in his Taylorian lecture in 1931 was almost a continuation of the prevalent views: "The art of translation is a subsidiary art and derivative. On this account it has never been granted the dignity of original work, and has suffered too much in the general judgement of letters" (*OT* 2).

Matthew Arnold who was much ahead of his time and hailed by many as the founder of the main line of Modern English criticism was probably the first man in his era of late nineteenth century to dedicate a substantial body of work to the theories of translation. But this powerful social and literary critic of nineteenth century had not succumbed to the fascination of translation theories from the very dawn of his career. Initially, he too like his contemporaries, considered translation as a much inferior activity. Mulling over his choice of classical subjects and modes of re-creating it, Arnold made disparaging comments on translation. In the *Preface* to *Merope* (1858) Arnold says: "But a translation is a work not only inferior to the original by the whole difference of talent between the first composer and his translator: it is even inferior to the best which the translator could do under more inspiring circumstances" (*CT* 39).

But interestingly only three years later in 1861 Arnold in a complete *volte-face* concerned himself about the theories of translation, though Arnold professed to give certain practical advice to a translator and not to concern himself with theories: "My one object is to give practical advice to a translator; and I shall not the least concern myself with theories of translation as such" (*CT* 98).

On Translating Homer turns out to be a virtual core book of translation theories in general and Homeric translations in particular.

Apart from *On Translating Homer's* importance as a profound tome of translation theories it also contains precious observations on classical Greek literature and Homer. It earned rich plaudits from such an exacting critic as A.E. Housman.

However in his Oxford lectures, *On Translating Homer* Matthew Arnold's ostensible aim was to dissect the renderings of Homer's *Iliad* by F.H. Newman in unrhymed English meter, and provide certain practical advice to the prospective translators of Homer. But in profounder dimension, in these three lectures and a 'Last Word' appended at the end, Arnold's chief aim was to give some sound instructions about general theories and practices to the translators of future. Here Arnold set some objectives and do's and don'ts for the translators to come.

At the outset Matthew Arnold states that the problem of the most elemental kind is yet to be resolved: "What aim a translator should propose to himself in dealing with his original" (*CT* 97).

In the time of Arnold there were two current conflicting views. One group insisted that the original should be absolutely remoulded into another medium *i.e.* into another language, should be almost newly created. Another group contended that the translator should imitate everything, every detail and peculiarity of the original, and should ever remember that they are translating and not creating a text anew. However at one point, Arnold thinks the contending groups seem unanimous regarding the translators fidelity to the original: "Probably both sides would agree that the translator's 'first duty is to be faithful'" (*CT* 98).

When Arnold dismissed the views that one can evoke the same reaction amid the audience of TL text as evoked by the SL text, he was anticipating in a way the hypothesis of Edward Sapir: "No two languages are ever sufficiently similar to be considered as representing the same social reality. The worlds in which different societies live are distinct worlds not merely the same world with different labels attached" (*CLP* 69).

Arnold speaking in the context of Homeric translation said: "But I advise the translator not to try 'to rear on the basis of the *Iliad*', a poem that shall affect our countrymen as the original may be conceived to have, affected its natural hearers; and for this simple reason, that we cannot possibly tell how the *Iliad* 'affected its natural hearers'" (*CT* 98).

However, Arnold may seem a bit contradictory when he claimed: "It is our translator's business to reproduce the effect of Homer" (*CT* 98).

According to the modern theorists of translation like Peter Newmark, when Arnold stated that the same reaction evoked by the SL text can never be evoked by the TL text, Arnold ruled out any chance of achieving what is known as 'equivalent-effect' in modern parlance. One can really know nothing about Homeric audience now.

Then Arnold turned to the question of proper evaluation of a translated text, the most sensitive point which Susan Bassnett terms as: "One final great stumbling block waiting for the person with an interest in Translation Studies: the question of evaluation" (*TS* 8).

This vexing question is not easy to be solved. Modern translatologists think that this can be achieved by two limited means. First, a view of the closeness of the translation to the SL text can be perceived by a critic having an access to both languages. Arnold simply prefigured this view when he insisted that the proper evaluation of Homeric texts can be made by scholars acquainted with two worlds: "But there are those who can tell him how Homer affects them. These are scholars; who possess, at the same time with knowledge of Greek, adequate poetical taste and feeling. No translation will seem to them of much worth compared with the original; but they alone can say whether the translation produces more or less the same effect upon them as the original" (*CT* 99).

The other view of evaluation consists in the TL text's workability in their own language and culture. But an hauteur is attached with the critics' view that they: "Will define a translation as good or bad from a purely monolingual position occupied by translation *vis-à-vis* another type of *metatext*" (*TS* 9).

Arnold seems to be an avatar of this group of academic critics of translation.

Arnold warns the prospective translators to avoid and discard any: "Special vocabulary for his use in translation" (*CT* 100).

Arcane words and outlandish lingo peculiar to a special class of society should never be used in translation, because this practice makes the readers feel alienated from the text.

Arnold was of the opinion that a perfect translator should try to realize his original text and feel truly the mind of the original author. Arnold thinks that the efficacy of a translator depends upon the attitude, 'the frame of mind' of the translator to the original author. Arnold actually wanted to say that a translator should almost identify himself with the thought content of the original author, his mind and art. The translator should absorb within himself the special traits of the author. To illustrate this point Arnold said that a good translator of Homer should: "Above all be penetrated by a sense of four qualities of his author" (*CT* 102).

These four qualities are Homer's rapidity in movement, plainness alike in words and style, simplicity in ideas and nobility in manners. Then Arnold showed exceedingly well how everyone of the translators of Homer, be he Chapman, Pope, Cowper or Mr. Newman failed to capture a complete Homeric essence in their renderings. Arnold reiterated his emphasis on the point of oneness of the translator with the original author: "that union of the translator with his original, which alone can produce a good translation" (*CT* 103).

According to Susan Bassnett, Matthew Arnold's primary objective was to make the translator involved intimately with the original SL text: "The translator must focus on the SL text primarily, according to Arnold, and must serve that text with complete commitment" (*TS* 69).

Arnold repeatedly asked the translators to depend upon the scholars for right judgement about their work. It is because Arnold emphasized upon the intimate fidelity of the translated texts to the original. The scholar is, Arnold said: "Accustomed to test a translation rigidly by comparison with the original" (*CT* 117).

At this point Arnold introduced the concept of 'general effect' in his writing. He warned the scholars who are to judge the translations that they must judge by the yardstick of 'general effect' evoked by the translated text. The translators too must endeavour to produce the 'general effect' of the original text in their renderings. But he will be the ideal judge: "who demands but one thing in a translation that it shall as nearly as possible reproduce for him the 'general effect' of Homer" (*CT* 118).

Arnold's concept of 'general effect' a *sine qua non* for good translation reminds us of John Dryden who wrote in 1711 in his *Preface* to the *Life of Lucian* thought almost in the same line of Arnold. Dryden thought that a translator: "ought to possess himself entirely and perfectly comprehend the genius and sense of his author, the nature of the subject, and the terms of the art of subject treated of. And then he will express himself as justly, and with as much life, as if he wrote an original; whereas he who copies word for word losses all the spirit in the tedious transfusion" (*CL* 149).

Apart from Dryden's pleas for almost Arnoldian 'general effect' it also has a keen proximity to another argument of Arnold. Though Arnold stressed upon the point of fidelity of the translator to his original text, he at one point asked the translator to sacrifice without 'scruple' the: "verbal fidelity to his original rather than run away risk of producing by literalness an odd and unnatural effect" (*CT* 157-58).

In fact too much honest, close verbal 'word for word' rendering may mar the general effect of the original text instead of enhancing the appeal.

A good translator's language must be unambiguous; his frame of references must be shorn of opacity. When the original text is written the cues and hints in the language are enough for the first reader to comprehend. But TL audience must be presented the matter without any obscurity, otherwise their perceptions would be clouded.

In an alien language and culture many unforeseen problems may crop up if the translated text is not presented with sufficient clarity: "The connection of meaning must be even more distinctly marked in the translation than in the original" (*CT* 165).

We can finally leave the scene by spelling out another counselling of Arnold regarding the prose renderings of poetry. Though Andre Lefevere in his celebrated book *Translating Poetry, Seven Strategies and a Blueprint* thinks that in prose renderings of poetry the SL text suffers the distortion of sense, communicative value and syntax, Arnold considers this method as a safer way for the translators to translate the great works of poetry. The lack of the magical touch of ingeniousness on the part of the translators then would not impede the enjoyment of the essence and flavour of the original text: "There are great works composed of parts so disparate that one translator is not likely to have the requisite gifts for poetically rendering all of them. Such are the works of Shakespeare and Goethe's *Faust*; and these it is best to attempt to render in prose only" (*CT* 167).

The apparent concern of Matthew Arnold's *On Translating Homer* is to determine appropriate methods for a perfect translation of Homer. But in reality it turns out to be a mine of general translation theories, immensely readable and useful for the practitioners of translation theory and praxis. It provides a framework of principles, rules and hints for translating texts and appreciating translations.

WORKS CITED

Arnold, Matthew. *On Classical Tradition. Complete Prose Work*. Ed. R.H. Super. Ann Arbor: University of Michigan Press, 1960. Cited as *CT*.

Bassnett-McGuire, Susan. *Translation Studies*. London: Methuen, 1980. Cited as *TS*.

Bassnett, Susan. *Comparative Literature. A Critical Introduction*. Oxford: Blackwell Publishers, 1993. Cited as *CL*.

Bassnett, Susan and Andre Lefevere. *Translating History and Culture*. London: Pinter, 1990. Cited as *THC*.

Belloc, Hillaire. *On Translation*, Oxford Clarendon Press, 1931. Cited as *OT*.

Sapir, Edward. *Culture, Language and Personality*. Los Angeles: University of California Press, 1956. Cited as *CLP*.

SELECT BIBLIOGRAPHY

Brower, Reuben (ed.). *On Translation*. Cambridge. Mass: Harvard University Press, 1984.

Dryden, John. '*Preface to the Life of Lucian*'. *Of Dramatic Poesy and other Critical Essays*. (ed.) G. Watson. London: Dent, 1962.

Gentzler, E. *Contemporary Translation Theories*. London: Routledge, 1993.

Kelly, L.G. *The True Interpreter: A History of Translation Theory and Practice in the West*. Oxford: Blackwell, 1979.

Lefevere, A. *Translating Poetry: Seven Strategies and a Blueprint*. Amsterdam: Vangorcum, 1977.

Newmark, P. *Approaches to Translation*. Oxford: Pergamon Press, 1984.

Venuti, Lawrence (ed.). *Rethinking Translation: Discourse, Subjectivity, Ideology*. London: Routledge, 1992.

Tagore in Translation: A Case for Revaluation

16

SUBHAS SARKAR

A great deal of misinformation and misinterpretation has arisen out of Tagore's translations of his own works and translations of his poetry and plays by others. This is largely responsible for the decline in Tagore's popularity and fame. It will be my endeavour to assess and analyze some of these problems—problems of judging Tagore in his own translations and the methodology of his translation as well as the problems of translating Tagore.

Tagore's translations from his own poetry—selected poems of *Kheyā, Naibedya, Gītāñjali* and *Gītāñjali*—which came to be published as *Song-Offerings* started as a kind of literary diversion during his days of convalescence in 1912. It at once created several unsettling problems in the critical response to his works abroad. The basic problem was, should the English *Gītāñjali* be treated as a re-creation of his original Bengali poems, or as a collection of Indian English poetry to be set apart from Tagore's own Bengali work? *Song-Offerings* cast an immediate spell on eminent European poets and critics of the time. Among them were ardent admirers like May Sinclair, W.B. Yeats and Ezra Pound.

For a time, Yeats recognized in these translations of Tagore the imprint of a genius greater than all other contemporary poets. Ezra Pound discovered in them 'a new Greece'. Though the spell was short-lived, and Yeats was later highly critical of Tagore's poetry and his English ('Tagore does not know English.[1] Let Tagore cast off English'). Later he included six of Tagore's poems in his *Oxford Book of Modern Verse* (1936), since he considered him to be among the notable translators of the period. It is interesting to note Yeats' early enthusiasm for the lyrics, 'which are in the original...full of subtlety of rhythm, of untranslatable delicacies of colour, of metrical invention... displaying in their thought a world [he had] dreamed of.... The work of a supreme culture, they yet appeared as much the growth of the common soil as the grass and the rushes.'[2] Ezra Pound, who was initially enthusiastic about publishing a number of Tagore's poems in the well-known American journal *Poetry*, wrote in an article accompanying these poems that the publication of these poems was 'an event in the history of English poetry and of world poetry'. But Pound later denounced Tagore's poetry under the wrong impression that "Tagore had taken to writing original poems in English, 'a language for which he had no special talent'. He failed to note that Tagore had almost never composed poetry in any other language but his own."[3]

Ezra Pound made it up in an article written some time later in *New Free Woman* (November 1913) in which he declared, "The intelligent reader will do more than read the prose, he will try to reconstruct some idea of the original, of the long hyper-feminine rhymes, or the rhyme-arrangements like those of the long bars of the Oriental ragini. He will try to fit into this sound-picture the meaning expressed in translation."

It is well-known that with the publication of the English *Gītāñjali* in 1912 Tagore became famous overnight, and received the Nobel Prize for literature in 1913. Tagore's fame as a great poet spread like fire, and his *Song-Offerings* came to be translated into almost all European and Asian languages by eminent poets and litterateurs. Among his translators were Van Eden, Gide and Jimenez, who were great names in their respective countries. Father Pierre Fallon has pointed out that the English *Gītāñjali* has been the most successful of all Tagore translations, read in all European languages; the 'French translation alone passed through some 35 editions'. He had rightly said that 'still Tagore is for the West the author of *Gītāñjali*'.[4] Fallon is not insensitive to the fact that 'The Western *Gītāñjali* loses much of the musical beauty and the evocative power of the original poems', yet he describes it as 'a jewel of English religious poetry'.

What is really interesting about Tagore's translations into English is that they started as a literary diversion and yet catapulted him to world fame, not as a writer of Bengali poetry but as a writer of English poems. Even Buddhadeva Bose, in his *An Acre of Green Grass*, once remarked that 'the English *Gītāñjali* has been rightly praised by the world: it is the quintessence of Rabīndranāth and a miracle of translation'. He even went on record as saying that 'Denuded of the sensuous metrical arrangements of the original and the more than Swinburnian rhymes, they [the poems] are more quiet in the English, more docile, the surrender more utter. The *Song-Offerings* are more of song in the original and more of an offering in the English.' He ever described it 'as more than a great work in English; it is the work of a great English poet'.[5]

But the same illustrious critic of Tagore, in his later book *Kabī Rabīndranīth,* spelt out unfalteringly how Tagore was instrumental in ruining his own image of a great Bengali poet by indulging in reckless, almost callous tampering in translation with his original poems; sometimes taking liberties with the original expressions and images, even at times combining two poems into one, often not only pruning but excising the original into an unhappy compression. The transformation took place not because of his choice of prose as medium but because of the deliberate attempt at simplification and ruthless suppression of native associations or sensibility, lyrical lilts, mythical ambience and verbal effect. Whatever magic the Westerners discovered in Tagore's translations, specially in the English *Gītāñjali,* was largely rooted in Tagore's unparalleled simplicity and oriental mystique which came to be considered as the hallmark of the poetry of piety.

All this happened because Tagore was his own translator—an unusual phenomenon in the history of world literature. By treating the translation of his own works as a creative activity, he may have undermined the responsibility of a translator to be true to the original, thereby causing 'an insult to the original' to quote Edward Thompson, the first serious English critic of

Tagore, who despite all his limitations tried 'to do Tagore a service: base his reputation in the Western world on something more secure than Tagore's own inadequate English translations'.[6] As the years passed, Tagore's own translations might have become more casual, if not irresponsible. This applies to his translations of *Lover's Gift*, *Fruit Gathering*, and even *The Gardener*, as borne out by the absence of some mythical names like Ṛṣyaṣṛṅga in the English rendering of "Patita"; the total loss, in the prose rendering of the dramatic element of the narrative poetry set against a Puranic background as also of the lyrical grace and beauty of a number of poems like 'Jadio sandhyā āsiche manda manthare'. 'Ato cupi cupi keno kathā kao', 'Ogo mā rājār dulāl' etc., spoilt in the *Gardener,* and the poem "Śaṇkha", lost beyond recognition in *Fruit Gathering.*

Buddhadeva Bose has given enough illustrations of the inadequacies of Tagore's translations even in the English *Gītāñjali.* Though there are instances when Tagore seems to have improved upon the original in *Song-Offerings*, in most cases the richness of his imagery, lyrical grace, verbal magic and a subterranean music are missing in the English rendering. In a letter to Edward Thompson in 1921, Tagore confessed that in most of his translations into English there was a sort of counterfeiting and in them, like a coward, he had avoided all the vital problems of translation. He said that he was quite alarmed by the measure of his own counterfeiting. He now wanted to withdraw to his original world of poetic creations in Bengali.

In any good translation the translator has to be true to the original. The temptation to be creative is always there for any good translator of poetry, who is required to exercise great self-discipline in delivering the goods from the Source to the Target Language. An accurate impression of the poet's own texture and rhythms must be given in any successful translation of a poem. But since Tagore was his own translator, such restraint or self-discipline was often sacrificed in favour of the poet's own creativity and freedom to alter. Hence most of his translations from his own poems appear to be a sort of re-creation or near-translation but never a 'literal' translation or 'faithful' rendering of the original.

The poet himself was hardly unaware of this severe limitation of his English translations. In a letter to William Rothenstein a few months before the publication of the English *Gītāñjali,* Tagore wrote:

> I send you some more of my poems rendered into English. They are too simple to bear the strain of translation but I know you will understand them through their faded meanings.[7]

Again, in a letter written to Harriet Moody from Urbana next year. Tagore acknowledges that his English renderings of his original Bengali poems are hardly faithful translations: 'Rathi has begun typing out my poems—I won't call them translations.'[8]

But the success of the *Gītāñjali* translations, which ran into twelve reprints before he won the Nobel Prize, must have lured Tagore into believing that he could indulge in a kind of 'translation' of his own works which would bring most Westerners under the spell of the so-called 'devotional' element in his works, to which they looked for a kind of solace or inspiration. This had a serious repercussion on his own creativity, specially on his scheme of translating his own works into English. This has been clearly brought out in Sujit Mukherjee's book, *Passage to America*:

> Even when he was rendering non-devotional poetry into English, his turn of phrase invariably inclined towards suprahuman connotations. The more substantial side of his poetical work—the landscapes and seascapes of firsthand observation, the social problems and the political dilemma of the time, the poetry of abstract thought, the questions about the nature of poetry—these he avoided altogether or presented in a diluted, unrecognizable form. As with his choice of material, so with his mode of translation he relied more and more on the *Gītāñjali* manner, excising from the original poems words and ideas which could not be treated thus. In their place, he

> either substituted terms which he thought would be familiar to Western understanding or introduced new elements to aid such understanding.[9]

Tagore's next volume of translation, *The Gardener,* suffers from severe lack of depth and substance, since the poet is carried away by the idea of simplicity and clarity, for which he sacrifices whatever was intense or complex in his original poetic texture.

It is true that Tagore was indebted to Yeats and Sturge Moore for some 'revisions' of his original translations in the English *Gītāñjali.* But with the publication of *The Crescent Moon,* Tagore had outgrown these influences or obligations to English men of letters. He had translated it on his own and had not consulted anybody else. But it must be admitted that its translation suffers from an overdose of 'sweetness' and ponderous expressions which fail to take into account a kind of simple, elusive philosophical undertone that runs through the poems of the original Bengali texts in *Śiśu* and *Śiśu Bholānāth.*

A close study of one or two poems of *Gītāñjali* (*Song-Offerings*) would reveal how Tagore's rendering into English often spoilt the immaculate beauty born of the consonance of music and imagery in Tagore's original Bengali text. Think of the harmonious beauty and evocative charm of the sonorous opening lines of the original Bengali poem, 'Āji Srābaṇ ghana gahan mohe/ Gopan taba caraṇ phele/ Nishār mata nirab ohe Sabār dīṭhi erāye ele, and its bland, unimaginative and somewhat prosaic English rendering:

> In the deep shadows of the rainy July,
> With secret steps thou walkest, silent as night
> eluding all watchers.

But the most disappointing part of the translation appears towards the end of the poem. Whereas in the original text there is a note of tenderness and emotional pleading:

> He ekā sakhā, he priyatama.
> Rayeche kholā e ghar mama.
> Samukh diye svapanasama
> Jeyonā more helāy thele.

the English rendering is flat and unpoetical:

> Oh my only friend, my best beloved,
> the gates are open in my house—
> do not pass by like a dream.[10]

It is surprising to see the lyric genius use such dull and out-of-the-way expressions as 'Oh my only friend, my best beloved' to express such tender feelings as *'He ekā sakhā, he priyatama'*. What has really happened is that the poet has taken little heed of the images and music of his original poem. In fact, he has forsaken them to make his poem appear simple and understandable to Western readers.

In another poem, 'Art thou abroad on this stormy right' (a translation of the Bengali poem *Āji jharer rāte tomār abhisār*), towards the end the poet takes liberties with the original and spoils its poetic charm with the patent view of reaching out to the average English or European reader. Let us consider the lines of the original poem and compare them with those of the English version:

> Sudūr kono nadīr pāre
> Gahan kono baner dhāre
> Gabhīr kono andhakāre
> Hatecho tumi pār
> Parānsakha bandhu he āmār.

The music and imagery of the original cast a magic spell on the reader's mind. But in the English rendering, in which the poet takes liberties with the original, much of the effect is spoilt by the poet's deliberate attempt to be explicit rather than suggestive:

> By what dim shore of the ink-black river, by what far edge of the frowning forest, through what mazy depth of gloom art thou threading thy course to come to me, my friend?[11]

The use of such expressions as 'ink-black', 'far edge of the frowning forest' and 'mazy depth of gloom', etc., simply dissipates the emotional integrity of the poem. Here Tagore was hardly a translator; he was more of a purveyor of his merchandise to customers of other lands who took a fancy to his wares.

It was ironical that instead of being assessed as a great master of Bengali literature, he came to be judged internationally for his performance in English, which was never his first love. And what was wrong with his translations was that being his own translator, he took too great liberties with the original (which none else would have dared); so that they were never faithful and literal. Instead of working as a sort of midwife who should deliver the baby intact to the world, he badly maimed it or did some kind of surgery on it, specially when he was translating his plays. Sujit Mukherjee has stated this problem unambiguously: 'Had Tagore translated literally and faithfully, it would have been easier to judge the original work through the translations.'[12] The problem of judging Tagore in translation became all the more acute because Tagore's publisher, The Macmillan Company kept demanding more and more translations from the author so that they could mint more money. As a result, Tagore sometimes obliged them with translations done at hectic speed without proper revision. Once or twice this led to farcical situations, as with the publication of the English rendering of *Rājā* as *The King of the Dark Chamber*. The play was translated by Kṣitīs Chandra Sen, a Bengali student at Cambridge University, in about seven days' time. It was full of grammatical errors and ellipses. But it got into print without Tagore's knowledge, and Macmillan did not even care to announce the name of the translator in their initial publication, thereby tarnishing the image of Tagore. Though a number of illustrious translators and editors (chief among them Kṛshna Kripalani, Edward Thompson, Sister Nivedīta, Marjorie Sykes, Debabrata Mukherjee, Arobinda Bose, Bhabāni Bhattacharya, Amiya Chakrabarti, Sheila Chatterjee, Surendranath Tagore, W.W. Pearson, Taraknāth Sen, Amalendu Bose, Hīren Mukherjee, Śiśir Ghoṣ and Humayun Kabir have rendered Tagore into English, quite often the shadow of Tagore's own translations has haunted them. Most of the translations of Tagore into other Indian languages have also been greatly influenced by Tagore's English renderings.

In recent years some excellent translations of Tagore into English have been attempted by William Radice, Ketaki Kushari

Dyson, P. Lal, Shyamasree Devi and Ananda Lal who must be congratulated for their rational and scientific approach to the translation of Tagore's poetry, plays and short stories since they are almost unaffected by the ills of bardolatry, which have raised the spectre of misinterpretation of Tagore in translation. Although Radice's translation is sometimes handicapped by his ignorance of certain delicate nuances of the Bengali language, specially in the context of intimate household expressions, there is a commendable honesty and fidelity to the original in his works. The time is now ripe for producing an authorized version of Tagore's works in translation by sorting out the various problems of translating his works into English and other languages, specially other Indian languages.

NOTES

1. W.B. Yeats, Letter of 7 May 1935.
2. W.B. Yeats, Introduction to Tagore's *Gītāñjali*, Macmillan Pocket edn., p. ix.
3. See Sujit Mukherjee, *Passage to America* (Calcutta, 1964), 15.
4. Pierre Fallon, "Tagore in the West", in *Rabindranath Tagore A Centenary Volume* (Sahitya Akademi, Delhi, 1961), 316.
5. Buddhadeva Bose, *An Acre of Green Grass* (Calcutta, 1982), 18.
6. William Radice in the Introduction to his translation of Tagore's *Selected Poems* (Harmondsworth, 1987), 8.
7. Tagore's letter to Rothenstein, 7 June 1912, from London: referred to in Mukherjee, 120.
8. Tagore's letter to Harriet Moody, 6 March 1913, found among the Moody papers in the Chicago University Archives: referred to in Mukherjee, 120.
9. Mukherjee, 120.
10. *Gītāñjali, op. cit.,* poem no. 22: 13.
11. *Ibid.,* poem no. 23: 14.
12. Mukherjee, 119.

Demystifying Translation

NIRANJAN MOHANTY

17

Translation, hitherto considered as the product of a low mimesis, has been able to generate a space for itself in the literary circle in India today. The space it occupies is very small in comparison with the space occupied by the rich tradition of regional writings. There is no doubt that this space would get enlarged not merely to justify the necessity of such a body of writing but also to establish a link between one regional writing and the other. A very distinctive shift, in terms of attitude towards translation and translational practices, is slowly emerging. This shift is from bare emotionalism towards a kind of professionalism which sharpens the edge of linguistic competence, besides engendering an objectivity. Consumers of the products of translation are no longer from beyond the seas. They are always from within. From the commercial point of view, there is obviously a large market within the country. To my mind, this market shall automatically create an atmosphere of professionalism in which mediocrity shall find no breathing space, but excellence would appear as the key to successful translation.

Languages in two neighbouring states (for example Orissa and West Bengal, or Orissa and Andhra Pradesh, West Bengal and Assam) bear a tendency to be flexible. The flexibility and fluidity of languages, because of physical contiguity and proximity not only permit an easy flow of words from one linguistic system to another, but also unconsciously initiate the process of translational practices. To be more precise, many devotional poets of 17th and 18th century Orissa (including Salabega) besides writing in Oriya could also write in Bengali. Of course, the script was not Bengali, but the creative medium was Bengali. Such practices create a state of confusion, in the sense that it is really difficult to know whether they translated their poems into Bengali or expressed themselves in Bengali, even without using the script. These poems could be translations as well because the Oriya version of such poems also existed. The veracity of such practices and validity of this body of writing in terms of its acceptance and circulation in the society baffle a literary historian who is interested in mapping the history of translational practices in general and translation in particular. This is perhaps why in India we don't have a history of translation, either of its theoretical development or of its practices. The translation was never believed to be a conscious, mechanical activity. It was always a matter of spontaneous passion, an unselfish and motiveless love. This, therefore, needed no practical or theoretical training. It was taken up very easily, if not seriously, even without a professional attitude and temper. The linguistic borders could easily be crossed, not only because of physical contiguity of the two regions, but also because of a cultural affinity existing between these regions. We needn't regret for having no systematic and scientific record of the translational practices and of the theories involved in such practices. It is interesting even today to note that despite the absence of a recorded history of translation, the translational practices have never experienced set-backs. A scientific or objective orientation of translation as a creative act is desirable. For such an objective orientation, the translator has to bear in mind what Henrik Gottlieb defines as "source text typology" and "transfer typology" (26). The translator can familiarise himself/herself with specific characteristics or nature of the Source Language text to be translated. These are: factuality (falsifiable/non-falsifiable text), function (informative/persuasive/entertaining), provenance (mundane/divine), age of the text (recent/aged/classical), setting (familiar/exotic/magical), linguistic conventions (shared/different), semiotic structure (mono-semiotic or simple/poly-semiotic or complex), receptivity (actor-defined/audience defined), identity of author (known/unknown), audience (private/public).

It would be easy on the part of a translator to know or identify the nature of transfer that he/she is going to initiate through translation. In order to know the nature of transfer, the translator has to identify the types of such transfer. These include, purpose of translation, direction of transfer (into native language or form), directness of transfer (direct/relay translation), preparation (planned/impromptu), balance between semiotic methods (language retained/altered), status of the text in translation (translator credited/not credited), target audience (within a country/outside; children/adult/old; elite/just literate), target language (dominant/repressed), target culture (east/west) etc. Many such identifiable parameters can be prescribed for the translator to enable him to comprehend in greater details the diverse facets of the would-be translated text. Recognising such parameters, the translator can hope to achieve a certain degree of excellence.

'Addition' or 'Deletion'

Should a translator 'add' something to the text he is translating? Should he 'delete'? Should he alter? Such questions often baffle the translators because any decision he/she takes would result in a distortion of his/her fidelity to the SL text. This has been a perennial problem for translation theory. To my mind, the translator's degree of originality and creativity is dependent on this choice, as long as this choice serves or negotiates a very useful purpose. The translator must know the 'what' and 'why' of his choice. Scholars like Juliane House would always advocate against deletion or subtraction. A translated text experiences being a translation only as long as it remains faithful to the overall message of the SL text, or to the vision of the author of the SL text. The translator's creativity must not in any case usurp the creativity of the author of the SL text.

Untranslatability

The inherent strength of every language lies in its resistance to being translated. Yet translational practices proliferate. Language as a system is endowed with this meaningful paradox. On the one hand it is rooted to a society and a culture. On the other hand, because of its richness, sophistication, its users seek to make it known all over. Savory in *The Art of Translation* (1957) and Susan Bassnett-McGuire in *Translation Studies* (1980) and Toury in *In Search of a Theory of Translation* (1980) harp on untranslatability. Wilhelm Von Humboldt (1767-1835) was the first of a line of scholars who have examined the relation between language and thought, claiming that our thought processes and our analysis of the world around us are dependent on our language. The language relativists like Benjamin Lee Whorf and Viggo Hjornager Pedersen attach distinction to language as it can shape and record our attitudes to life and world. The 'depth of intention' and 'direction of intention' are extremely difficult to communicate across language and culture barriers. The depth of intention is the degree to which a speaker feels committed to an utterance. If one claims to be 'dead tired', is he going to die? This is not what the English expression normally means, but a similar combination in other languages might well have to be taken at face value. The "direction of intention" refers to the implications of an utterance. The positive or negative aspects of the world "gay" in the U.S. will not be shared by the Indians. Similarly, often in India instead of grandmother, we use "granny", and when we use it, neither a subversive attitude exists nor a casual attitude. In India we use it with all good, tender intentions and the implication is always intimate. But in the U.S. 'granny' is often used with an offensive connotation or subversive implication. It is from the context that the translator can know the implications involved so that he can create similar implications in the target language.

Because of such complexities in a language, the transfer of meaning from the SL text to the TL text is not total. It was J.C. Catford (in *A Linguistic Theory of Translation*, Oxford, 1965) who demonstrated that whereas *e.g.* a Russian phrase has a Russian meaning, and such meanings are embedded in the specific cultures. To separate them from the context of culture would be illusory. Idiomatic expressions, proverbs often entail this difficulty. It is the translator's creative responsibility to find out a match in the Target Language. For example, the English proverb, "Penny-wise, pound foolish" would have to be translated into say Oriya, as "Sua muhan re bohi jauchi, Pimpudi gata buja hauchi". Here a shift in the use of metaphors has taken place. 'Penny' and 'pound' disappear and new metaphors like 'flow' and 'ant hole' begin to appear so as to communicate the same meaning in the target language. Similarly rituals, festivals, usable items in such rituals can never have their match in another language as these are culture-centric, and can bear meaning in the context of such cultures. Since language is both a repository and transmitter of coordinates of culture, in translation, such coordinates get transferred or shifted to the target culture. Whether such coordinates would be acceptable to the target culture is altogether a different dimension of the problem of translation. But this transfer, however marginal or insignificant, can hardly be ignored by the translator.

Equivalence

In trying to achieve proximity between the Source Language text and Target Language text (*i.e.* identical translation), the scholars of translation began to use a new terminology, *i.e. equivalent* translation. Substitution of 'identical' by 'equivalent' translation leads to demystifying another level of translation. Eugene A. Nida draws a distinction between what he terms 'formal equivalence' and 'dynamic equivalence'. Nida writes:

> Formal equivalence focuses attention on the message itself, in both form and content.... One is concerned that the message in the receptor language should match as closely as possible the different elements in the source language. This means that the message in the receptor culture is constantly compared with the message in the source culture to determine the standards of accuracy and correctness. In contrast, a translation which attempts to produce a dynamic equivalence is based upon the principle of equivalent effect. In such a translation one is concerned that the relationship between receptor and message should be substantially the same as that which existed between the original receptors and the message.

Nida's concept of dynamic equivalence has been accepted as simple equivalence for it is based on the idea of adjusting the message to the audience, and to the linguistic possibilities available in the target language. Popovic, on the other hand, advocates four types of equivalence: Linguistic (where there is homogeneity on the linguistic level of both SL and TL texts), Paradigmatic (where there is equivalence of elements of grammar), Stylistic (where there exists functional equivalence of elements in both original and translation aiming at an identity with an invariant of identical meaning), and Textual (where there exists equivalence of the syntagmatic structuring of the text). To deny the problem of equivalence in translation would be to deny our access to the measures of assessing the quality of translation. Depending on the nature of the text, the creative insight of the translator (for which translation to me is a creative act); the problem of equivalence can be easily sorted out.

Quality in Translation

The most difficult area in translation and translation studies is to define measures which would determine the quality in translation. Fidelity to the SL text has often been considered as a yardstick for measuring quality in translation. The votaries of the manipulative school like Pederson's assert that translation should be described and demonstrated rather than be judged (See Viggo). According to House 'Fidelity' is even inadequate. In literary translation, the translated text must read like as if it were not translated, but originally written in that particular language (*i.e.* TL). J. House discusses two categories of quality assessment: the response-based psycholinguistic studies and source-text-based studies. The former mostly fails to evaluate because they seem to equate elegance of the target language version with quality, without caring for the relation of such a version to the original. The latter allows us to form a profile of the source text and the degree to which the target text measures up to this profile. House also distinguishes between two types of translation: overt and covert. The former category does not cover up difficulties in the original, the latter smoothing the target language reader path for him. No fixed paradigm, perhaps, can measure the quality of translation. It can be both demonstrative and specific. I believe it strongly that the measures which determine the quality of good writing are perhaps the measures to know good piece of translation, in which at least the translator must not take liberties to distance himself from the source text. A good translation makes the reading smooth. A bad translation always makes the reader halt and falter and stumble. A good translation neither surpasses the original, nor does it over-emphasise the original.

Discovering a balance is the insignia of translator's creative role. The translator, therefore, is neither the beggar at the churchgate; nor is he a shadowy presence, nor is he an engineer busy in constructing a bridge between the two languages and two cultures. He is a veritable aesthete. He is no less than a creative writer. As long as we don't recognise this creative role of the translator, translation would always experience a marginalised status.

WORKS CITED

Gottlieb, Henrik. "Typologies of Translation". *An Introduction to Translation Studies*. Ed. Henrick Gottlieb. Copenhagen: University of Copenhagen, 1999. 25-43.

Hjornager, Viggo. *Essays in Translation*. Copenhagen: University of Copenhagen, 1998.

House, Julian. *A Model for Translation Quality Assessment*. Tubingen, 1977.

Nida, E.A. *Towards a Science of Translating*. Leiden: E.J. Brill, 1964.

Popovic, Anton. *A Dictionary for the Analysis of Literary Translation*. Edmonton: University of Alberta, 1976.

The Limits of Translation

18

BIJAY KUMAR DAS

The practice of translation is not without its limitation. The first difficulty lies in the opposition between similarity and difference among words in SL and TL. Translation aims at producing a text which can stand in a relation of equivalence to another text. Since Linguistic codes and cultural contexts are not 'equipollent', to translate a text is to transform it.

The first point that comes to mind is that what should be the length of translation. Should it be longer or shorter than the original? In case of free translation, when translation becomes a paraphrase, it becomes much longer than the original. Moreover, the number of words do not remain the same in both the languages—SL and TL. For instance, only nine words in English 'The quick brown fox jumps over the lazy dog' (Savory Theodore's example) makes use of all the 26 letters of English alphabet. But I do not think any Indian language can use all the letters of its alphabet with the help of nine words—not atleast, Oriya.

The notion that for every word in anyone language there is another word accurately equivalent to it in every other language is no longer tenable. For example, a simple word 'love' in English has a host of equivalent words in Oriya and most of the Indian languages. Similarly, erotic vocabulary is very poor in English, while Indian languages, (particularly Sanskrit) have a rich erotic vocabularly. Julius Caesar's famous words: "Veni, Vidi, Vici" are translated into English as, "I reached the country after long marches, I surveyed the position before undertaking military action, and in this I successfully subjugated the defenders."[1]

Since words are different from language to language, the question arises: when is a translation not a translation? In other words, what are the limits of translation? The limits of translation are many, and therefore, it is necessary to find out when and where translation fails to deliver the good. The first limitation of translation is its failure to convey the jargons of one language through another language. Let us begin with the limits of jargon translation.

Jargons of one language cannot be easily translated into another language. In everyday language and speech we sometimes come across professional language and jargon coming together. Specialists speak in technical language which is very difficult to translate and one is left with no alternative than to transliterate the register of a technical person. As Arthur Koestler rightly points out that 'Needless to say, technical communications addressed to specialists must employ technical language; but even here the overloading with jargon, the tortuous and cramped style, are largely a matter of conforming to fashion' (*The Act of Creation*, 265). And it is difficult to translate such communication into another language.

Alan Duff in course of an article titled, "Professional language or Jargon?" defines international jargon as follows:

> This jargon is characterized by: repetition, redundancy (*i.e.* too many words), mixed metaphor, and above all—by inclarity of thought. It is Lego-language, made up of ready-shaped blocks which can be stuck together to build sentences of readymade meaning, just as the little plastic blocks themselves can without changing their form—be used as doors, windows, aeroplane wings or wigwam flaps.

Critical terms are difficult to translate into another language. For example, terms like 'romanticism', 'classicism', 'structuralism', 'deconstruction', 'objective correlative', 'auditory imagination', 'affective fallacy', etc. cannot be translated into Indian language without footnotes. It is better to transliterate these terms into Indian languages. Thus, one major limitation of translation is that it cannot successfully convey or transform professional jargons, critical terms and idioms from one language to another language.

Faithfulness in translation is indispensible and when it is abandoned, translation turns out to be a virtual paraphrase. When translators have taken freedom to the limit, others have turned it to licence. If unlimited freedom is given to the translator, translation ceases to be translation, it becomes a transcript or an adaptation. Sometimes, translation is based on 'illusory equivalence' (Theodore Savory's Phrase) for it is thought that every word of a language has an equivalent word in another language. In case of cultural expressions, the limitation of translation becomes clear and glaring, cultural idioms are hard to translate and restrict translatability. Theodore Savory hints at the limits of translation in the following words:

> Troubles of a different kind arise from gaps in languages, which cannot be filled by translating because for a word that may be quite familiar in one language there is no equivalent in another. Probably the first example that will occur to many is the failure of French to provide a word for 'home'. 'I shall go home', says the Englishman; and the Frenchman: 'F'irai chez moi'. 'This is my home', says the Englishman on arrival; but the Frenchman can get no nearer than Voild ma maison, or mon logis or ma demeure, all words whose primary significance is that contained in the Englishman's 'house' or 'residence'. So, too, there is no English word for the French menu or for the Latin word augur and no Latin word for the English word 'premier'.[2]

Translation of rhythm and rhyme schemes in poetry into another is almost impossible. In case of poetry, translation is restricted to ideas only, not to the form—for form varies from language to language, the musicality of a poem along with its technical virtuosity cannot be translated. This is a serious limitation of translation.

Humours based on a particular culture and jokes of a particular community or place, are hard to translate and even if they are translated they lose their force, vigour and appeal in the target language. Metaphor, Pun and irony severely limit the degree of translatability. Superstition, folk-belief and myth affect the role of translation. For example, certain numbers which are considered to be inauspicious in one culture becomes normal in another, and that limits the scope of translation.

Languages differ from each other, the way they are structured —phonological, syntactic, lexico-semantic and so on. That is why languages are not all equivalent in expressive power. Take for example, two languages English and Oriya—the former is SVO language and the latter is SOV language. A sentence in English 'I gave you a book' cannot be translated into Oriya as 'Mu dheithili tumaku gotia bahi' for that will create unnaturalness in Oriya and it should be 'Mu tumaku gotia bahi dheithili'. A syntactic possibility in one language does not have equivalence in another language. I am inclined to agree with K.V. Tirumalesh who gave the following example in this context.

As another example, consider the story of Narcissus narrated by Robert Graves in his excellently written book *Greek Myths*. Narcissus is so handsome that whoever looks at him falls in love with him at first sight. But he is also vain and so spurns all offers of love. One day he goes stag-hunting along with his friends. Echo is one of the several young women in love with him and secretly follows him wherever he goes. On that particular day Narcissus gets separated from his companions in the forest. Realizing that he has strayed, he calls: "Is anyone here?" Echo hears him and is only too anxious to respond. But then she is under a terrible curse from Hera. Echo can only repeat what the others may say: she can never say anything new on her own. So the 'conversation' between Narcissus and Echo goes along the following lines:

> "Is anyone here?"
> "Here!"
> "Come!"
> "Come!"
> "Why do you avoid me?"
> "Why do you avoid me?"
> "Let us come together here!"
> "Let us come together here!"

And so Echo gladly rushes from her hiding place to embrace Narcissus. But he rudely shakes her off and says: "I will die before you ever lie with me!" Seizing this wonderful opportunity of making her point, Echo repeats the last part of the sentence and pleads: "Lie with me!" The rest of the story is well-known: Echo was never able to win the love of Narcissus and was ultimately reduced to a feeble voice. The important thing about this example is the ingenuity with which Robert Graves has narrated the story. Since Echo can only repeat what the other person has said, she has to wait for the most opportune moment to make her point. And this is exactly what the story-teller has provided for in the last sentence of the dialogue. The words 'lie with me' exactly summarise what Echo really wants to say to Narcissus. Notice that this is a syntactic possibility that the English language permits. Suppose that you want to translate this into Kannada or any other language in which the subordinate clauses occur on the left of the main clause Echo then will not be able to make her point in this way since she can only repeat either the whole utterance or the last part of it. She has no other choice. Right-branching and left-branching become crucial syntactic differences in such situations.[3]

The ontological and structural considerations point towards the limits of translation. The translator should not only possess an inwardness with both the languages—the SL and the TL, but he should know his subject well. In case of translation of metafiction which is atleast as much about itself as it is 'about' anything else at all, the translator has to be able to understand and interpret this particular type of fiction and its internal resonances. In course of an article K. Balasubramanian and D.R. Mohan Raj underline the limits of translation:

> We must realize, however, the translation is a communication medium, with its own areas of usefulness and its own limitations. The language used in translation, especially of some types of fiction, hardly functions as language *per se*. We are all familiar with discussions regarding the autonomy available to a translator, the dynamism of a translation, its relationship to the original in its time-bound relevance (diachronic and synchronic

> translations of equal value), and so on. Irrespective of the ultimate worth of a translation, it should be recognized that the translator is completely limited in his use of the medium that was available for use in its fullest potential to the author of the original. Not only is creative instinct that gave the original impetus difficult to match in a translation, the translator's task is further complicated by the host of limitations imposed on him by both subject and audience.[4]

Culture-specific words are ethnic, historical and sociological in nature. They restrict the scope of translation and point towards the limits of translation. The pop-slang language used in some fiction are almost untranslatable. Rustic words and slangs, used in fiction enhance the limits of translation. How can one translate the slangs uttered by people belonging to the lower strata of the society in contemporary fiction? How does one translate the sound and rhythm of poetry into another language vastly different from the source language and its culture. How does one translate advertisements from one language into another? The limits of translation will stare in our face when we take up technical subjects and literature for translation into a language which is very much unlike the SL.

Translation of advertisements severely curtail the freedom of translators. Advertisements are concerned with style and therefore, they limit the scope of translatability. Analysis of the language of advertisements reveals that the language-patterns used for accomplishing the advertisers, is fairly limited in its selection and therefore, the scope of deviation is very limited. T.V. advertisements done in English when translated literally into regional languages have jarring effects on the ears. The translator has to maintain readability, and listening ability, memorability and selling ability in the target language. But this cannot be done easily. Translation of advertisements shows the limits of translatability.

To conclude, I should say that there are limits exceeding which in one direction translation ceases to be translation and exceeding in another it becomes mere imitation. In other words, translation done within the limits of translating an original writing becomes successful. The best translation is that which though based on an original writing, never reads like a translation. It gives us the feel of an original writing done in the source language.

REFERENCES

1. Theodore, Savory, *The Art of Translation* (London: Cape, 1957), 156.
2. *Ibid.*, 16.
3. K.V. Tirumalesh, "Translation as Literature Three", *The Literary Criterion*, 15: 3 (1990): 4-5.
4. Kamakshi Balasubramanian and D.R. Mohan Raj, "Contextual Vs Textual Specifics: The Limits of Translation", *Literature in Translation* ed. Pramod Talgeri and S.B. Verma (Bombay: Popular Prakashan, 1988), 36.

Perspectives on Translation: Down the Centuries

19

RAMA KUNDU

In the *Genesis* one may also trace a story of the genesis of multilingualism which perhaps necessitated the practice of translation as a discipline.

> Now the whole earth had one language and few words. And as men migrated from the east, they found a plain in the land of Shiner and settled there....
>
> Then they said, "Come, let us build ourselves a city, and a tower with its top in the heavens, and let us make a name for ourselves, lest we be scattered abroad upon the face of the whole earth."
>
> And the Lord came down to see the city and the tower, which the sons of men had built. And the Lord said, "Behold, they are one people, and they have all one language; and this is only the beginning of what they will do; and nothing that they propose to do will now be impossible for them. Come, let us go down, and there confuse their language, that they may not understand one another's speech."
>
> So the Lord scattered them abroad from there over the face of all the earth, and they left off building the city. Therefore, its name was called Babel, because there the Lord confused the language of all the earth; and from there the Lord scattered them abroad over the face of all the earth. [*Genesis* 11:1-9]

Throughout the history of translation and translation studies the main controversy has veered around the issues of fidelity and freedom.

It was Horace (65—8 B.C.) who had warned so long ago against an overfaithfulness in translation and had encouraged the translator not to be a slavish imitator:

> A theme that is familiar can be made your own property so long as you do not waste your time on a hackneyed treatment; nor should you try to render your original word for word like a slavish translator,.... [*Art of Poetry*]

Horace admonished the translator thus:

> Nor should you try to render your original word for word like an obedient [faithful] Interpres.

Desiderius Erasmus (1466-1536), the Dutch humanist, who published the first Greek New Testament, preferred that the *Bible* should be translated in such a way that it should be widely accessible to the common people:

> I would desire that all women should reade the gospell and Paules epistles and I wold To God they were translated in to the tonges of all men so that they might not only be read and knowne of the scotes and yrishmen but also of the Turks and the Sarracenes.... I wold to God the plowman wold singe a texte of the scripture at his plow-beme. And that the wever at his lowme with this wold drive away the tediousness of tyme. I wold the wayfaringeman with this pastyme wold expelle the weriness of his iorney. And to be shorte I wold that all the communication of the christen shuld be of the scripture for in a manner such are we oure selves as our daylye tales are. [*Novum Instrumentum* 1529]

Erasmus also advocated for a certain degree of freedom for the translator:

> Language consists of two parts, namely words and meaning, which are like the body and the soul. If both of them can be rendered I do not object to word for word translation. If they cannot, it would be preposterous for

> a translator to keep the words and deviate from the meaning. [Preface to his *New Testament*]

George Chapman, the great translator of Homer, stressed the importance of a sensitive understanding of the SL text on the part of the translator in addition to his scholarship:

> The work of a skilful and worthy translator is to observe the sentences, figures and formes of speech proposed in his author, his true sence and height, and to adorne them with figures and formes of oration fitted to the originall in the same tongue to which they are translated: and these things I would gladlie have made the questions of whatsoever my labours have deserved. [Dedication of the *Seven Books* 1598]

Edmund Cary underscores the importance of translation in the sixteenth century France:

> The translation battle raged throughout Dolet's age. The Reformation, after all, was primarily a dispute between translators. Translation became an affair of State and a matter of Religion. The Sorbonne and the king were equally concerned with it. Poets and prose writers debated the matter, Joachim du Bellay's *Defense et Illustration de la Language francaise* is organized around problems relating to translation. [*Les Grands Traducteurs Francais* 1963]

George Steiner highlights the importance of the role played by translation in Renaissance Europe:

> At a time of explosive innovation, and amid a real threat of surfeit and disorder, translation absorbed, shaped, oriented the necessary raw material. It was, in a full sense of the term the matiere premiere of the imagination. Moreover, it established a logic of relation between past and present, and between different tongues and traditions which were splitting apart under stress of nationalism and religious conflict. [*After Babel* 1975]

In the seventeenth century one comes across Sir John Denham's unreserved tribute to the translator of *Peter Fido* which also contains a critique of inferior translations:

Nor ought a Genius less than his that writ,
Attempt Translation...since nothing can beget
A vital spirit, but a vital heat.
That servile path thou nobly dost decline
Of tracing word by word, and line by line.
Those are the labour'd births of slavish brains,
Nor are the effects of Poetry, but pains;
Cheap vulgar arts, whose narrowness affords
No flight for thoughts, but poorly sticks at words.
A new and nobler way thou dost pursue
To make Translations and Translators too.
They but preserve the Ashes, thou the Flame,
True to his sense, but truer to his fame.

["To Sir Richard Fanshaw upon His Translation of *Pastor Fido*" 1648]

Wentworth Dillon, earl of Rosscommon, offers a sensitive response to the issue of the intimate and creative relationship between the original author and his translator:

Then *seek* a Poet who your ways do's bend,
And *chuse* an Author as you *chuse* a Friend:
United by this Sympathetick Bond,
You grow Familiar, Intimate, and Fond;
Your thoughts, *your* Words, *your* Stiles, *your* Souls agree,
No longer his Interpreter, but He.

[*An Essay on Translated Verse* 1684]

Dryden had claimed that as a translator he had steered
Betwixt the two extremes of paraphrase and literal translation.

Dryden had also admitted that as translator he had updated the language of the SL text:

I have endeavoured to make Virgil speak such English as he would himself have spoken, if he had been born in England, and in this present age.

[*Dedication of the Aeneis* 1697]

Alexander Pope's views on the simultaneous impact of the style of the Scripture and the great epics on the translator's art reflect fine critical insight:

> This pure and noble Simplicity is nowhere in such Perfection as in the Scripture and our Author. One may affirm with all respect to the inspired Writings, that the Divine Spirit made use of no other Words, but what were intelligible and common to men at that Time, and in that Part of the World; and as Homer is the Author nearest to those, his Style must of course bear a greater Resemblance to the sacred Books than that of any other Writer. This Consideration (together with what has been observ'd of the Parity of some of his Thoughts) may methinks induce a Translator on the one hand to give into several of those general Phrases and manners of Expression, which have attain'd a Veneration even in our Language from their use in the Old Testament; as on the other, to avoid those which have been appropriated to the Divinity, and in a manner consign'd to Mystery and Religion. [Preface to *The Iliad* 1715]

Christopher Smart observed about the prose translation of the Scripture from the viewpoint of a devotee:

> Impression then, is a talent or gift of Almighty God, by which a Genius is empowered to throw an emphasis upon a word or sentence in such wise, that it cannot escape any reader of sheer good sense, and true critical sagacity. This power will sometimes keep it up thro' the medium of prose translation; especially in Scripture, for in justice to truth and everlasting pre-eminence, we must confess this virtue to be far more powerful and abundant in sacred writings. [Preface to *The Works of Horace* 1767]

William Cowper (1731-1800), however, emphatically underscored the need of 'fidelity' as a thing of primary importance in translation:

> There is indisputably a wide difference between the case of an original writer in rhyme and a translator. In an original work the author is free: if the rhyme be of

> difficult attainment, and he cannot find it in one direction, he is at liberty to seek it another; the matter that will not accommodate to his occasions he may discard, adopting such as will. But in a translation no such option is allowable; the sense of the author is required, and we do not surrender it willingly even to the plea of necessity. Fidelity is indeed the very essence of translation, and the term itself implies it. For which reason, if we suppress the sense of the original, and force into its place our own, we may call our work an *imitation,* if we please, or perhaps a *paraphrase,* but it is no longer the same author only in a different dress, and therefore it is not translation: Should a painter, professing to draw the likeness of a beautiful woman, give her more or fewer features than belong to her, and a general cast of countenance of his own invention, he might be said to have produced a *jeu d'esprit,* a curiosity perhaps in its way, but by no means the lady in question. ["Preface to the First Edition of *The Translation of Homer*" 1791]

One may also recall Goethe's comment in this regard:

> The contradiction[lies] between [translation's] inherent impossibility and its absolute Necessity. [Johann Wolfgang von Goethe (1749-1832)]

Matthew Arnold, while underscoring faithfulness as the translator's first duty, however, tried to define what 'faithfulness' meant in the context:

> The translator's "first duty", says Mr. Newman, "is a historical one, to be faithful". Probably both sides would agree that the translator's "first duty is to be faithful"; but the question at issue between them is, in what faithfulness consists. [*On Translating Homer*]

Matthew Arnold advised the translator to exercise discretion and to trust the scholars who were well-versed in both the languages (of the source and target texts):

> Let not the translator, then, trust to his notions of what the ancient Greeks would have thought of him; he will lose himself in the vague. Let him not trust to what the

> ordinary English reader thinks of him; he will be taking the blind for his guide. Let him not trust to his own judgment of his own work; he may be misled by individual caprices. Let him ask how his work affects those who both know Greek and can appreciate poetry. [*On Translating Homer*]

Henry Wadsworth Longfellow advised even greater restriction on the translator's function. In defending his own translation of Dante's *Divina Comedia* in blank verse Longfellow claimed:

> The only merit my book has is that it is exactly what Dante says, and not what the translator imagines he might have said if he had been an Englishman. In other words, while making it rhythmic, I have also endeavoured to make it as literal as a prose translation.... In translating Dante, something must be relinquished. Shall it be the beautiful rhyme that blossoms all along the line like a honeysuckle on the hedge? It must be, in order to retain something more precious than rhyme, namely, fidelity, truth,—the life of the hedge itself.... The business of a translator is to report what the author says, not to explain what he means; that is the work of the commentator. What an author says and how he says it, that is the problem of the translator.

Dante Gabriel Rossetti had registered the uneasiness of the translator *vis-à-vis* the SL text even as he was engaged in translating Italian poems into English; it seemed to him rather constricting for the translator,—a kind of master-servant relationship, as it were:

> Often would he[the translator] avail himself of any special grace of his own idiom and epoch, if only his will belonged to him; often would some cadence serve him but for his author's structure—some structure but for his author's cadence. [Preface to *Poems and Translations* 1861]

Nietzsche's observation offers an interesting instance of an early awareness of the politics of translation in a particular historical-cultural continuum as he explains the Roman translators' attitude to the Greek texts which they translated with notable freedom:

> When the Romans translated Greek poets into Latin they quickly replaced Greek names with what was contemporary and Roman. They seem to be asking us "should we not be allowed to breathe our souls into this dead body? For it is dead and how ugly are all things dead!"—they did not know the pleasures of the sense of history; what was past and foreign gave them grief and incited them, as Romans, to Roman conquest. Indeed, one conquered, in those days, when translating—not only because history was left out; no allusions to the present were added and, above all, the name of the original poet was rubbed out and replaced by one's own—there was no sense of thieving in this, but rather the best conscience of the imperium Romanum. [Friedrich Nietzsche (1844-1900) "Die frohliche Wissenschaft"]

The problem of the status of translation as literary work has bothered critics all along. As Hillaire Belloc succinctly summed it up:

> The art of translation is a subsidiary art and derivative. On this account it has never been granted the dignity of original work, and has suffered too much in the general judgment of letters. This natural underestimation of its value has had the bad practical effect of lowering the standard demanded, and in some periods has almost destroyed the art altogether. The corresponding misunderstanding of its character has added to its degradation: neither its importance nor its difficulty has been grasped. [*On Translation* 1931]

John Hollander underscores the same problem when he says:

> Every literary document that purports to be a translation from an original in some other language makes a kind of contract to be correct, but it is traditional to regard any such contract, if filled to the letter, with a bit of

> contempt and suspicion. ["Versions, Interpretations, and Performances" 1959]

Roman Jackobson claims that, technically speaking, no poetic art was translatable:

> Only creative transposition is possible: either intralingual transposition—from one poetic shape into another, or interlingual transposition—from one language into another, or finally intersemiotic transposition—from one system of signs to another, *e.g.* from verbal art into music, dance, cinema or painting. ["On Linguisitic Aspects of Translation" 1959]

Jakobson, however, also admits, though a bit ironically:

> Both the practice and the theory of translation abound with intricacies, from time to time attempts are made to sever the Gordian knot by proclaiming the dogma of untranslatability.

One may recall J. Levy's observation in this connection which stresses the toughness of the task of a translator:

> A translation is not a monistic composition, but an interpretation and conglomerate of two structures. On the one hand there are the semantic content and the formal contour of the original, on the other hand the entire system of aesthetic features bound up with the language of the translation. [*Umeni Prekladu* (*The Art of Translation*), 1963]

Georges Mounin, however, upholds the view that translation is ultimately a dialectic process in which a relative success is possible:

> Translation may always start with the clearest situations, the most concrete messages, the most elementary universals. But as it involves the consideration of a language in its entirety, together with its most subjective messages, through an examination of common situations and a multiplication of contacts that need clarifying, then there is no doubt that communication through translation can never be completely finished, which also demonstrates

> that it is never wholly impossible either. [*Les problemes theoriques de la traduction* 1963]

J.C. Catford insists that in translation there could be only substitution of meanings but not transference of meanings from one language into another since linguistically it was not possible.

> In *translation* there is substitution of TL meanings for SL meanings: not transference of TL meanings into the SL. In *transference* there is an implantation of SL meanings into the TL text. These two processes must be clearly differentiated in any theory of translation. [*A Linguistic Theory of Translation* 1965]

On the other hand, Walter Benjamin emphasizes the need of 'literalness' which assures 'fidelity' in the translator's art; he claims that in this process the word is the translator's original element and not the sentence:

> The meaning of fidelity, which is assured by literalness, is that the great longing for the complementarity of languages should make itself felt in the work. Real translation is transparent, it does not hide the original, it does not steal its light, but allows the pure language, as if reinforced through its own medium, to fall on the original work with greater fullness. This lies above all in the power of literalness in the translation of syntax, and even this points to the word, not the sentence, as the translator's original element. ["The Task of the Translator" 1969]

Octavio Paz brings a fresh dimension to translation studies when he claims in his characteristic way that all texts are translations of translation:

> Every text is unique and, at the same time, it is the translation of another text. No text is entirely original because language itself in its essence, is already a translation: firstly, of the non-verbal world and secondly, since every sign and every phrase is the translation of another sign and another phrase. However, this argument can be turned around without losing any of its validity:

> all texts are original because every translation is distinctive. Every translation, up to a certain point, is an invention and as such it constitutes a unique text. [*Traduccion: literatura y literalidad* 1971]

Indeed, translation is no easy task, as it requires on the part of the translator much more than just a working knowledge of two languages. Rather it has been acknowledged by critics as:

> One of the most difficult tasks that a writer can take upon himself. [Randolph Quirk, *The Linguist and the English Language,* 1974]

What Jakobson had described as interlingual transformation in translation was later redefined by A. Ludskanov as semiotic transformation:

> Semiotic transformations(Ts) are the replacements of the signs encoding a message by signs of another code, preserving (so far as possible in the face of entropy) invariant information with respect to a given system of reference. ["A Semiotic Approach to the Theory of Translation" 1975]

According to George Steiner, translation in our times should be placed in a wide frame that would include certain other disciplines as well:

> Classical philology and comparative literature, lexical statistics and ethnography, the sociology of class-speech, formal rhetoric, poetics, and the study of grammar are combined in an attempt to clarify the act of translation and the process of 'life between language'. [*After Babel* 1975]

George Steiner, however, holds a view about translation history to which many may not agree today; he is of the view that in spite of many theorists and critics of translation the actual range of theoretic ideas in this regard remain small:

> List Saint Jerome, Luther, Dryden, Holderlin, Novalis, Schleiermacher, Nietzsche, Ezra Pound, Valery, MacKenna, Franz Rosenzweig, Walter Benjamin, Quine— and you have very nearly the sum total of those who have

> said anything fundamental or new about translation. [*After Babel*]

M.B. Dagut highlights the problem of the untranslatability of metaphors and idioms:

> Since a metaphor in the SL is, by definition, a new piece of performance, a semantic Novelty, it can clearly have no counterpart. Here the translator's bilingual competence —'le sens', as Mallarme put it 'de ce qui est dans la langue et de ce qui n'en est pas'—is of help to him only in the negative sense of telling him that any 'equivalence' in this case cannot be 'found' but will have to be 'created'. The crucial question that arises is thus whether a metaphor can, strictly speaking, be translated as *such*, or whether it can only be 'reproduced' in some way. ["Can Metaphor be Translated?" 1976]

Anton Popovic tries to understand the situation from the translator's angle; according to him, the translator

> is endeavouring to convey the semantic substance of the original in spite of the difference separating the system of the original from that of the translation, in spite of the differences between the two languages and between the two methods of presenting the subject matter. [*A Dictionary for the Analysis of Literary Translation* 1976]

Maimonides upholds the translator's need for freedom from 'slavish' fidelity, stressing that this is *not* the right method:

> Let me promise one canon. Whoever wishes to translate and purports to render each word literally, and at the same time to adhere slavishly to the order of the word and sentences in the original, will meet with much difficulty. This is not the right method. The translator should first try to grasp the sense of the subject thoroughly, and then state the theme with perfect clarity in the other language. This, however, cannot be done without changing the order of the words, putting many words for one word, or *vice versa*, so that the subject be perfectly intelligible in the language into which he translates. [*A Guide for the Perplexed* 1977]

Anne Ubersfeld has drawn the reader's attention to the need to perceive dramatic performance as merely a 'translation':

> The task of the director, therefore, is to 'translate into another language' a text to which he has a prime duty to remain 'faithful'. This position is based on the concept of *semantic equivalence* between the written text and its performance; only the 'mode of expression' in the Hjelmslevian sense of the term will be altered, the form and content of the expression will remain identical when transferred from a system of test-signs to a system of performance-signs. [*Lire le theatre* 1978]

The survey of opinions on translatology may be concluded (for the time being) with a comment of Octavio Paz, which—perceptive and sensitive and profound as it is—takes into account the notion of the 'otherness' of the Universe and history which is at the heart of much postcolonial and postmodern literature and critique today.

> Think of the Chinese translating the Sanskrit texts, or the Jews translating in Alexandria the Hebrew testament and the Romans translating the Greeks. The history of the different civilizations is the history of their translations. Each civilization, each soul, is different, unique. Translation is our way to face this otherness of the universe and history. [Octavio Paz in conversation with Edwin Hong 1985]

WORK CITED

Barnstone, Wills. *The Poetics of Translation.* New Haven and London: Yale University Press, 1993.

Bassnett-McGuire, Susan. *Translation Studies.* London and New York: Methuen, 1980.

Bassnett, Susan and Andre Lefevere [Eds.]. *Translation, History and Culture.* London and New York: Pinter Publishers, 1990.

Brower, Reuben A. [Ed.]. *On Translation.* Cambridge: Harvard University Press, 1959.

Steiner, George. *After Babel: Aspects of Language and Translation.* London: Oxford University Press, 1975.

APPENDIX

On Translating Homer

MATTHEW ARNOLD

I

It has more than once been suggested to me that I should translate Homer. That is a task for which I have neither the time nor the courage; but the suggestion led me to regard yet more closely a poet whom I had already long studied, and for one or two years the works of Homer were seldom out of my hands. The study of classical literature is probably on the decline; but, whatever may be the fate of this study in general, it is certain that, as instruction spreads and the number of readers increases, attention will be more and more directed to the poetry of Homer, not indeed as part of a classical course, but as the most important poetical monument existing. Even within the last ten years two fresh translations of the *Iliad* have appeared in England: one by a man of great ability and genuine learning, Professor Newman; the other by Mr. Wright, the conscientious and painstaking translator of Dante. It may safely be asserted that neither of these works will take rank as the standard translation of Homer; that the task of rendering him will still be attempted by other translators. It may perhaps be possible to render to these some service, to save them some loss of labour, by pointing out rocks on which their predecessors have split, and the right objects on which a translator of Homer should fix his attention.

It is disputed what aim a translator should propose to himself in dealing with his original. Even this preliminary is not yet settled. On one side it is said that the translation ought to be such 'that the reader should, if possible, forget that it is a translation at all, and be lulled into the illusion that he is reading an original work,—something original' (if the translation be in English), 'from an English hand'. The real original is in this case, it is said, 'taken as a basis on which to rear a poem that shall affect our countrymen as the original may be conceived to have affected its natural hearers'. On the other hand, Mr. Newman, who states the foregoing doctrine only to condemn it, declares that he 'aims at precisely the opposite: to retain every peculiarity of the original, so far as he is able, *with the greater care the more foreign it may happen to be*'; so that it may 'never be forgotten that he is imitating, and imitating in a different material'. The translator's 'first duty', says Mr. Newman, 'is a historical one: to be *faithful*'. Probably both sides would agree that the translator's 'first duty is to be faithful'; but the question at issue between them is, in what faithfulness consists.

My one object is to give practical advice to a translator; and I shall not the least concern myself with theories of translation as such. But I advise the translator not to try 'to rear on the basis of the *Iliad*, a poem that shall affect our countrymen as the original may be conceived to have affected its natural hearers'; and for this simple reason, that we cannot possibly tell *how* the *Iliad* 'affected its natural hearers'. It is probably meant merely that he should try to affect Englishmen powerfully, as Homer affected Greeks powerfully; but this direction is not enough, and can give no real guidance. For all great poets affect their hearers powerfully, but the effect of one poet is one thing, that of another poet another thing: it is our translator's business to reproduce the effect of Homer, and the most powerful emotion of the unlearned English reader can never assure him whether he has *re*produced this, or whether he has produced something else. So, again, he may follow Mr. Newman's directions, he may try to be 'faithful', he may 'retain every peculiarity of his original'; but who is to assure him, who is to assure Mr. Newman himself, that, when he has done this, he has done that for which Mr. Newman enjoins this to be done, 'adhered closely to Homer's manner and habit of thought'? Evidently the translator needs some more practical directions than these. No one can tell him how Homer affected the Greeks; but there are those who can tell him how Homer affects *them*. These are scholars; who possess, at the same time with knowledge of Greek, adequate poetical taste and feeling. No translation will seem to them of much worth compared with the original; but they alone can say whether the translation produces more or less the same effect upon them as the original. They are the only competent tribunal in this matter: the Greeks are dead; the unlearned Englishman has not the data for judging; and no man can safely confide in his own single judgment of his own work. Let not the translator, then, trust to his notions of what the ancient Greeks would have thought of him; he will lose himself in the vague. Let him not trust to what the ordinary English reader thinks of him; he will be taking the blind for his guide. Let him not trust to his own judgment of his own work; he may be misled by individual caprices. Let him ask how his work affects those who both know Greek and can appreciate poetry; whether to read it gives the Provost of Eton, or Professor Thompson at Cambridge, or Professor Jowett here in Oxford, at all the same feeling which to read the original gives them. I consider that when Bentley said of Pope's translation, 'It was a pretty poem, but must not be called Homer', the work, in spite of all its power and attractiveness, was judged.

Ὡς ἄν ὁ φρόνιμος ὁρίσειεν,—'as the judicious would determine',—that is a test to which every one professes himself willing to submit his works. Unhappily, in most cases, no two persons agree as to who 'the judicious' are. In the present case, the ambiguity is removed: I suppose the translator at one with me as to the tribunal to which alone he should look for judgment; and he has thus obtained a practical test by which to estimate the real success of his work. How is he to proceed, in order that his work, tried by this test, may be found most successful?

First of all, there are certain negative counsels which I will give him. Homer has occupied men's minds so much, such a literature has arisen about him, that every one who approaches him should resolve strictly to limit himself to that which may directly serve the object for which he approaches him. I advise the translator to have nothing to do with the questions, whether Homer ever existed; whether the poet of the *Iliad* be one or many; whether the *Iliad* be one poem or an *Achilles* and an *Iliad* stuck together; whether the Christian doctrine of the Atonement is shadowed forth in the Homeric mythology; whether the Goddess Latona in any way prefigures the Virgin Mary, and so on. These are questions which have been discussed with learning, with ingenuity, nay, with genius; but they have two inconveniences,—one general for all who approach them, one particular for the translator. The general inconvenience is that there really exist no data for determining them. The particular inconvenience is that their solution by the translator, even were it possible, could be of no benefit to his translation.

I advise him, again, not to trouble himself with constructing a special vocabulary for his use in translation; with excluding a certain class of English words, and with confining himself to another class, in obedience to any theory about the peculiar qualities of Homer's style. Mr. Newman says that 'the entire dialect of Homer being essentially archaic, that of a translator ought to be as much Saxo-Norman as possible, and owe as little as possible to the elements thrown into our language by classical learning'. Mr. Newman is unfortunate in the observance of his own theory; for I continually find in his translation words of Latin origin, which seem to me quite alien to the simplicity of Homer,—'responsive', for instance, which is a favourite word of Mr. Newman, to represent the Homeric ἀμειβόμενος:

> Great Hector of the motley helm thus spake to her *responsive*. But thus *responsively* to him spake god-like Alexander.

And the word 'celestial', again, in the grand address of Zeus to the horses of Achilles,

> You, who are born *celestial*, from Eld and Death exempted!

seems to me in that place exactly to jar upon the feeling too bookish. But, apart from the question of Mr. Newman's fidelity to his own theory, such a theory seems to me both dangerous for a translator and false in itself. Dangerous for a translator; because, wherever one finds such a theory announced (and one finds it pretty often), it is generally followed by an explosion of pedantry; and pedantry is of all things in the world the most un-Homeric. False in itself; because, in fact, we owe to the Latin element in our language most of that very rapidity and clear decisiveness by which it is contradistinguished from the German, and in sympathy with the languages of Greece and Rome: so that to limit an English translator of Homer to words of Saxon origin is to deprive him of one of his special advantages for translating Homer. In Voss's well-known translation of Homer, it is precisely the qualities of his German language itself, something heavy and trailing both in the structure of its sentences and in the words of which it is composed, which prevent his translation, in spite of the hexameters, in spite of the fidelity, from creating in us the impression created by the Greek. Mr. Newman's prescription, if followed, would just strip the English translator of the advantage which he has over Voss.

The frame of mind in which we approach an author influences our correctness of appreciation of him; and Homer should be approached by a translator in the simplest frame of mind possible. Modern sentiment tries to make the ancient not less than the modern world its own; but against modern sentiment in its applications to Homer the translator, if he would feel Homer truly—and unless he feels him truly, how can he render him truly?—cannot be too much on his guard. For example: the writer of an interesting article on English translations of Homer, in the last number of the *National Review*, quotes, I see, with admiration, a criticism of Mr. Ruskin on the use of the epithet φυσίζοος, 'life-giving', in that beautiful passage in the third book of the *Iliad*, which follows Helen's mention of her brothers Castor and Pollux as alive, though they were in truth dead:

> ὣς φάτο τοὺς δ' ἤδη κάτεχεν φυσίζοος αἶα
> ἐν Λακεδαίμονι αὖθι, φίλῃ ἐνπατρίδί γαίῃ[1]

'The poet', says Mr. Ruskin, 'has to speak of the earth in sadness; but he will not let that sadness affect or change his thought of it. No; though Castor and Pollux be dead, yet the earth is our mother still,—fruitful, life-giving.' This is a just specimen of that sort of application of modern sentiment to the ancients, against which a student, who wishes to feel the ancients truly, cannot too resolutely defend himself. It reminds one, as, alas! so much of Mr. Ruskin's writing reminds one, of those words of the most delicate of living critics: 'Comme tout genre de composition a son écueil particulier, *celui du genre romanesque, c'est le faux*.' The reader may feel moved as he reads it; but it is not the less an example of 'le faux' in criticism; it is false. It is not true, as to that particular passage, that Homer called the earth φυσίζοος because, 'though he had to speak of the earth in sadness, he would not let that sadness change or affect his thought of it', but consoled himself by considering that 'the earth is our mother still,—fruitful, life-giving.' It is not true, as a matter of general criticism, that this kind of sentimentality, eminently modern, inspires Homer at all. 'From Homer and Polygnotus I every day learn more clearly', says Goethe, 'that in our life here above ground we have, properly speaking, to enact Hell:'[2]—if the student must absolutely have a keynote to the *Iliad*, let him take this of Goethe, and see what he can do with it; it will not, at any rate, like the tender pantheism of Mr. Ruskin, falsify for him the whole strain of Homer.

These are negative counsels; I come to the positive. When I say, the translator of Homer should above all be penetrated by a sense of four qualities of his author:—that he is eminently rapid; that he is eminently plain and direct, both in the evolution of his thought and in the expression of it, that is, both in his syntax and in his words; that he is eminently plain and direct in the substance of his thought, that is, in his matter and ideas; and, finally that he *is eminently noble*;—I probably seem to be saying what is too general to be of much service to anybody. Yet it is strictly true that, for want of duly penetrating themselves with the first-named quality of Homer, his rapidity, Cowper and Mr. Wright have failed in rendering him; that, for want of duly appreciating the second-named quality, his plainness and directness of style and diction, Pope and Mr. Sotheby have failed in rendering him; that for want of appreciating the third, his plainness and directness of ideas, Chapman has failed in rendering him; while for want of appreciating the fourth, his nobleness, Mr. Newman, who has clearly seen some of the faults of his predecessors, has yet failed more conspicuously than any of them.

Coleridge says, in his strange language, speaking of the union of the human soul with the divine essence, that this takes place

> Whene'er the mist, which stands 'twixt God and thee,
> Defecates to a pure transparency;

and so, too, it may be said of that union of the translator with his original, which alone can produce a good translation, that it takes place when the mist which stands between them—the mist of alien modes of thinking, speaking, and feeling on the translator's part—'defecates to a pure transparency', and disappears. But between Cowper and Homer—(Mr. Wright repeats in the main Cowper's manner, as Mr. Sotheby repeats Pope's manner, and neither Mr. Wright's translation nor Mr. Sotheby's has, I must be forgiven for saying, any proper reason for existing)—between Cowper and Homer there is interposed the mist of Cowper's elaborate Miltonic manner, entirely alien to the flowing rapidity of Homer; between Pope and Homer there is interposed the mist of Pope's literary artificial manner, entirely alien to the plain naturalness of Homer's manner; between Chapman and Homer there is interposed the mist of the fancifulness of the Elizabethan age, entirely alien to the plain directness of Homer's thought and feeling; while between Mr. Newman and Homer is interposed a cloud of more than Egyptian thickness,—namely, a manner, in Mr. Newman's version, eminently ignoble, while Homer's manner is eminently noble.

I do not despair of making all these propositions clear to a student who approaches Homer with a free mind. First, Homer is eminently rapid, and to this rapidity the elaborate movement of Miltonic blank verse is alien. The reputation of Cowper, that most interesting man and excellent poet, does not depend on his translation of Homer; and in his preface to the second edition, he himself tells us that he felt,—he had too much poetical taste not to feel,—on returning to his own version after six or seven years, 'more dissatisfied with it himself than the most difficult to be pleased of all his judges'. And he was dissatisfied with it for the right reason,—that 'it seemed to him deficient *in the grace of ease*'. Yet he seems to have originally misconceived the manner of Homer so much, that it is no wonder he rendered him amiss. 'The similitude of Milton's manner to that of Homer is such,' he says, 'that no person familiar with both can read either without being reminded of the other; and it is in those breaks and pauses to which the numbers of the English poet are so much indebted, both for their dignity and variety, that he chiefly copies the Grecian'. It would be more true to say: 'The unlikeness of Milton's manner to that of Homer is such, that no person familiar with both can read either without being struck with his difference from the other; and it is in his breaks and pauses that the English poet is most unlike the Grecian.'

The inversion and pregnant conciseness of Milton or Dante are, doubtless, most impressive qualities of style; but they are the very opposites of the directness and flowingness of Homer, which he keeps alike in passages of the simplest narrative, and in those of the deepest emotion. Not only, for example, are these lines of Cowper un-Homeric:

> So numerous seemed those fires the banks between
> Of Xanthus, blazing, and the fleet of Greece
> In prospect all of Troy;

where the position of the word 'blazing' gives an entirely un-Homeric movement to this simple passage, describing the fires of the Trojan camp outside of Troy; but the following lines, in that very highly-wrought passage where the horse of Achilles answers his master's reproaches for having left Patroclus on the field of battle, are equally un-Homeric:

> For not through sloth or tardiness on us
> Aught chargeable, have Ilium's sons thine arms
> Stript from Patroclus' shoulders; but a God
> Matchless in battle, offspring of bright-haired
> Latona, him contending in the van
> Slew, for the glory of the chief of Troy.

Here even the first inversion, 'have Ilium's sons thine arms Stript from Patroclus' shoulders', gives the reader a sense of a movement not Homeric; and the second inversion, 'a God him contending in the van Slew', gives this sense ten times stronger. Instead of moving on without check, as in reading the original, the reader twice finds himself, in reading the translation, brought up and checked. Homer moves with the same simplicity and rapidity in the highly-wrought as in the simple passage.

It is in vain that Cowper insists on his fidelity: 'my chief boast is that I have adhered closely to my original':—'the matter found in me, whether the reader like it or not, is found also in Homer; and the matter not found in me, how much soever the reader may admire it, is found only in Mr. Pope.' To suppose that it is *fidelity* to an original to give its matter, unless you at the same time give its manner; or, rather, to suppose that you can really give its matter at all, unless you can give its manner, is just the mistake of our pre-Raphaelite school of painters, who do not understand that the peculiar effect of nature resides in the whole and not in the parts. So the peculiar effect of a poet resides in his manner and movement, not in his words taken separately. It is well-known how conscientiously literal is Cowper in his translation of Homer. It is well-known how extravagantly free is Pope.

> So let it be!
> Portents and prodigies are lost on me:

that is Pope's rendering of the words,

> Ξάνθε, τί μοι θάνατον μαντεύεαι; οὐδέ τί σε χρή.[3]

Xanthus, why prophesiest thou my death to me? Thou needest not at all:

> yet, on the whole, Pope's translation of the *Iliad* is more Homeric than Cowper's, for it is more rapid.

Pope's movement, however, though rapid, is not of the same kind as Homer's ; and here I come to the real objection to rhyme in a translation of Homer. It is commonly said that rhyme is to be abandoned in a translation of Homer, because 'the exigences of rhyme', to quote Mr. Newman, 'positively forbid faithfulness';

because 'a just translation of any ancient poet in rhyme', to quote Cowper, 'is impossible'. This, however, is merely an accidental objection to rhyme. If this were all, it might be supposed that if rhymes were more abundant; Homer could be adequately translated in rhyme. But this is not so; there is a deeper, a substantial objection to rhyme in a translation of Homer. It is, that rhyme inevitably tends to pair lines which in the original are independent, and thus the movement of the poem is changed. In these lines of Chapman, for instance, from Sarpedon's speech to Glaucus, in the twelfth book of the *Iliad*:

> O friend, if keeping back
> Would keep back age from us, and death, and that we might not wrack
> In this life's human sea at all, but that deferring now
> We shunned death ever,—nor would I half this vain valor show,
> Nor glorify a folly so, to wish thee to advance;
> But since we *must* go, though not here, and that besides the chance
> Proposed now, there are infinite fates, etc.

Here the necessity of making the line,

> Nor glorify a folly so, to wish thee to advance,

rhyme with the line which follows it, entirely changes and spoils the movement of the passage.

> οὔτε κεν αὐτὸς ἐνὶ πρώτοισι μαχοίμην,
> οὔτε κε σὲ στέλλοιμι μάχην ἐς κυδιάνειραν.[4]

> Neither would I myself go forth to fight with the foremost,
> Nor would I urge thee on to enter the glorious battle,

says Homer; there he stops, and begins an opposed movement:

> νῦν δ'—ἔμπης γὰρ Κῆρες ἐφεστᾶσιν θανάτοιο—

> But—for a thousand fates of death stand close to us always—

This line, in which Homer wishes to go away with the most marked rapidity from the line before, Chapman is forced, by the necessity of rhyming, intimately to connect with the line before.

But since we *must* go, though not here, and that besides the chance—

The moment the word *chance* strikes our ear, we are irresistibly carried back to *advance* and to the whole previous line, which, according to Homer's own feeling, we ought to have left behind us entirely, and to be moving farther and farther away from.

Rhyme certainly, by intensifying antithesis, can intensify separation, and this is precisely what Pope does; but this balanced rhetorical antithesis, though very effective, is entirely un-Homeric. And this is what I mean by saying that Pope fails to render Homer, because he does not render his plainness and directness of style and diction. Where Homer marks separation by moving away, Pope marks it by antithesis. No passage could show this better than the passage I have just quoted, on which I will pause for a moment.

Robert Wood, whose *Essay on the Genius of Homer* is mentioned by Goethe as one of the books which fell into his hands when his powers were first developing themselves, and strongly interested him, relates of this passage a striking story. He says that in 1762, at the end of the Seven Years' War, being then Under-Secretary of State, he was directed to wait upon the President of the Council, Lord Granville, a few days before he died, with the preliminary articles of the Treaty of Paris. 'I found him', he continues, 'so languid, that I proposed postponing my business for another time'; but he insisted that I should stay, saying, it could not prolong his life to neglect his duty; and repeating the following passage out of Sarpedon's speech, he dwelled with particular emphasis on the third line, which recalled to his mind the distinguishing part he had taken in public affairs:

> ὦ πέπον, εἰ μὲν γὰρ, πόλεμον περὶ τόνδε φυγόντε,
> αἰεὶ δὴ μέλλοιμεν ἀγήρω τ' ἀθανάτω τε
> ἔσσεσθ', οὔτε κεν αὐτὸς ἐνὶ πρώτοισι μαχοίμην,[5]
> οὔτε κε σὲ στέλλοιμι μάχην ἐς κυδιάνειραν
> νῦν δ'—ἔμπης γὰρ Κῆρες ἐφεστᾶσιν θανάτοιο

> μυρίαι, ἃς οὐκ ἔστι φυγεῖν βροτὸν, οὐδ' ὑπαλύξαι—
> ἴομεν.

His Lordship repeated the last word several times with a calm and determinate resignation; and, after a serious pause of some minutes, he desired to hear the Treaty read, to which he listened with great attention, and recovered spirits enough to declare the approbation of a dying statesman (I use his own words) "on the most glorious war, and most honourable peace, this nation ever saw."[6]

I quote this story, first, because it is interesting as exhibiting the English aristocracy at its very height of culture, lofty spirit, and greatness, towards the middle of the last century. I quote it, secondly, because it seems to me to illustrate Goethe's saying which I mentioned, that our life, in Homer's view of it, represents a conflict and a hell; and it brings out, too, what there is tonic and fortifying in this doctrine. I quote it, lastly, because it shows that the passage is just one of those in translating which Pope will be at his best, a passage of strong emotions and oratorical movement, not of simple narrative or description.

Pope translates the passage thus:

> Could all our care elude the gloomy grave
> Which claims no less the fearful than the brave,
> For lust of fame I should not vainly dare
> In fighting fields, nor urge thy soul to war:
> But since, alas! ignoble age must come,
> Disease, and death's inexorable doom;
> The life which others pay, let us bestow,
> And give to fame what we to nature owe.

Nothing could better exhibit Pope's prodigious talent; and nothing, too, could be better in its own way. But, as Bentley said, 'You must not call it Homer.' One feels that Homer's thought has passed through a literary and rhetorical *crucible*, and come out highly intellectualised; come out in a form which strongly impresses us, indeed, but which no longer impresses us in the same way as when it was uttered by Homer. The antithesis of the last two lines:

The life which others pay, let us bestow,
And give to fame what we to nature owe—

is excellent, and is just suited to Pope's heroic couplet; but neither the antithesis itself, nor the couplet which conveys it, is suited to the feeling or to the movement of the Homeric ἴομεν (verse).

A literary and intellectualised language is, however, in its own way well suited to grand matters; and Pope, with a language of this kind and his own admirable talent, comes off well enough as long as he has passion, or oratory, or a great crisis to deal with. Even here, as I have been pointing out, he does not render Homer; but he and his style are in themselves strong. It is when he comes to level passages, passages of narrative or description, that he and his style are sorely tried, and prove themselves weak. A perfectly plain direct style can of course convey the simplest matter as naturally as the grandest; indeed, it must be harder for it, one would say, to convey a grand matter worthily and nobly, than to convey a common matter, as alone such a matter should be conveyed, plainly and simply. But the style of *Rasselas* is incomparably better fitted to describe a sage philosophising than a soldier lighting his camp-fire. The style of Pope is not the style of *Rasselas*; but it is equally a literary style, equally unfitted to describe a simple matter with the plain naturalness of Homer.

Every one knows the passage at the end of the eighth book of the *Iliad*, where the fires of the Trojan encampment are likened to the stars. It is very far from my wish to hold Pope up to ridicule, so I shall not quote the commencement of the passage, which in the original is of great and celebrated beauty, and in translating which Pope has been singularly and notoriously unfortunate. But the latter part of the passage, where Homer leaves the stars, and comes to the Trojan fires, treats of the plainest, most matter-of-fact subject possible, and deals with this, as Homer always deals with every subject, in the plainest and most straightforward style. 'So many in number, between the ships and the streams of Xanthus, shone forth in front of Troy the fires kindled by the Trojans. There were kindled a thousand fires in the plain; and by each one there sat fifty men in the light of the blazing fire. And the horses, munching white barley and rye, and standing by the chariots, waited for the bright-throned Morning.'[7]

In Pope's translation, this plain story becomes the following:

> So many flames before proud Ilion blaze,
> And brighten glimmering Xanthus with their rays;
> The long reflections of the distant fires
> Gleam on the walls, and tremble on the spires.
> A thousand piles the dusky horrors gild,
> And shoot a shady lustre o'er the field.
> Full fifty guards each flaming pile attend,
> Whose umbered arms, by fits, thick flashes send;
> Loud neigh the coursers o'er their heaps of corn,
> And ardent warriors wait the rising morn.

It is for passages of this sort, which, after all, form the bulk of a narrative poem, that Pope's style is so bad. In elevated passages he is powerful, as Homer is powerful, though not in the same way; but in plain narrative, where Homer is still powerful and delightful, Pope, by the inherent fault of his style, is ineffective and out of taste. Wordsworth says somewhere, that wherever Virgil seems to have composed 'with his eye on the object', Dryden fails to render him. Homer invariably composes 'with his eye on the object', whether the object be a moral or a material one: Pope composes with his eye on his style, into which he translates his object, whatever it is. That, therefore, which Homer conveys to us immediately, Pope conveys to us through a medium. He aims at turning Homer's sentiments pointedly and rhetorically; at investing Homer's description with ornament and dignity. A sentiment may be changed by being put into a pointed and oratorical form, yet may still be very effective in that form; but a description, the moment it takes its eyes off that which it is to describe, and begins to think of ornamenting itself, is worthless.

Therefore, I say, the translator of Homer should penetrate himself with a sense of the plainness and directness of Homer's style; of the simplicity with which Homer's thought is evolved and expressed. He has Pope's fate before his eyes, to show him what a divorce may be created even between the most gifted translator and Homer by an artificial evolution of thought and a literary cast of style.

Chapman's style is not artificial and literary like Pope's nor his movement elaborate and self-retarding like the Miltonic movement of Cowper. He is plain-spoken, fresh, vigorous, and, to a certain degree, rapid; and all these are Homeric qualities. I cannot say that I think the movement of his fourteen-syllable line, which has been so much commended, Homeric; but on this point I shall have more to say by and by, when I come to speak of Mr. Newman's metrical exploits. But it is not distinctly anti-Homeric, like the movement of Milton's blank verse; and it has a rapidity of its own. Chapman's diction, too, is generally good, that is, appropriate to Homer; above all, the syntactical character of his style is appropriate. With these merits, what prevents his translation from being a satisfactory version of Homer? Is it merely the want of literal faithfulness to his original, imposed upon him, it is said, by the exigences of rhyme? Has this celebrated version, which has so many advantages, no other and deeper defect than that? Its author is a poet, and a poet, too, of the Elizabethan age; the golden age of English literature as it is called, and on the whole truly called; for, whatever be the defects of Elizabethan literature (and they are great), we have no development of our literature to compare with it for vigour and richness. This age, too, showed what it could do in translating, by producing a master-piece, its version of the Bible.

Chapman's translation has often been praised as eminently Homeric. Keats's fine sonnet in its honour every one knows; but Keats could not read the original, and therefore could not really judge the translation. Coleridge, in praising Chapman's version, says at the same time, 'It will give you small idea of Homer.' But the grave authority of Mr. Hallam pronounces this translation to be 'often exceedingly Homeric'; and its latest editor boldly declares that by what, with a deplorable style, he calls 'his own innative Homeric genius', Chapman 'has thoroughly identified himself with Homer'; and that 'we pardon him even for his digressions, for they are such as we feel Homer himself would have written'.

I confess that I can never read twenty lines of Chapman's version without recurring to Bentley's cry, 'This is not Homer!' and that from a deeper cause than any unfaithfulness occasioned by the fetters of rhyme.

I said that there were four things which eminently distinguished Homer, and with a sense of which Homer's translator should penetrate himself as fully as possible. One of these four things was, the plainness and directness of Homer's ideas. I have just been speaking of the plainness and directness of his style; but the plainness and directness of the contents of his style, of his ideas themselves, is not less remarkable. But as eminently as Homer is plain, so eminently is the Elizabethan literature in general, and Chapman in particular, fanciful. Steeped in humours and fantasticality up to its very lips, the Elizabethan age, newly arrived at the free use of the human faculties after their long-term of bondage, and delighting to exercise them freely, suffers from its own extravagance in this first exercise of them, can hardly bring itself to see an object quietly or to describe it temperately. Happily, in the translation of the Bible, the sacred character of their original inspired the translators with such respect that they did not dare to give the rein to their own fancies in dealing with it. But, in dealing with works of profane literature, in dealing with poetical works above all, which highly stimulated them, one may say that the minds of the Elizabethan translators were *too* active; that they could not forbear importing so much of their own, and this of a most peculiar and Elizabethan character, into their original, that they effaced the character of the original itself.

Take merely the opening pages to Chapman's translation, the introductory verses, and the dedications. You will find:

> An Anagram of the name of our Dread Prince,
> My most gracious and sacred Maecenas,
> Henry, Prince of Wales,
> Our Sunn, Heyr, Peace, Life,—

Henry, son of James the First, to whom the work is dedicated. Then comes an address,

To the sacred Fountain of Princes,
Sole Empress of Beauty and Virtue, Anne, Queen
Of England, etc.

All the Middle Age, with its grotesqueness, its conceits, its irrationality, is still in these opening pages; they by themselves are sufficient to indicate to us what a gulf divides Chapman from the 'clearest-souled' of poets, from Homer; almost as great a gulf as that which divides him from Voltaire. Pope has been sneered at for saying that Chapman writes 'somewhat as one might imagine Homer himself to have written before he arrived at years of discretion'. But the remark is excellent: Homer expresses himself like a man of adult reason, Chapman like a man whose reason has not yet cleared itself. For instance, if Homer had had to say of a poet, that he hoped his merit was now about to be fully established in the opinion of good judges, he was as incapable of saying this as Chapman says it,—'Though truth in her very nakedness sits in so deep a pit, that from Gades to Aurora, and Ganges, few eyes can sound her, I hope yet those few here will so discover and confirm her that, the date being out of her darkness in this morning of our poet, he shall now gird his temples with the sun',—I say, Homer was as incapable of saying this in that manner, as Voltaire himself would have been. Homer, indeed, has actually an affinity with Voltaire in the unrivalled clearness and straightforwardness of his thinking; in the way in which he keeps to one thought at a time, and puts that thought forth in its complete natural plainness, instead of being led away from it by some fancy striking him in connection with it, and being beguiled to wander off with this fancy till his original thought, in its natural reality, knows him no more. What could better show us how gifted a race was this Greek race? The same member of it has not only the power of profoundly touching that natural heart of humanity which it is Voltaire's weakness that he cannot reach, but can also address the understanding with all Voltaire's admirable simplicity and rationality.

My limits will not allow me to do more than shortly illustrate, from Chapman's version of the *Iliad*, what I mean when I speak of this vital difference between Homer and an

Elizabethan poet in the quality of their thought; between the plain simplicity of the thought of the one, and the curious complexity of the thought of the other. As in Pope's case, I carefully abstain from choosing passages for the express purpose of making Chapman appear ridiculous; Chapman, like Pope, merits in himself all respect, though he too, like Pope, fails to render Homer.

In that tonic speech of Sarpedon, of which I have said so much, Homer, you may remember, has:

> εἰ μὲν γὰρ, πόλεμον περὶ τόνδε φυγόντε,
> αἰεὶ δὴ μέλλοιμεν ἀγήρω τ' ἀθανάτω τε
> ἔσσεσθ',—
>
> if indeed, but once *this* battle avoided,
> We were for ever to live without growing old and immortal.

Chapman cannot be satisfied with this, but must add a fancy to it:

> if keeping back
> Would keep back age from us, and death, and *that we might not wrack*
> *In this life's human sea at all*;

and so on. Again, in another passage which I have before quoted, where Zeus says to the horses of Peleus,

> τί σφῶϊ δόμεν Πηλῆϊ ἄνακτι
> θνητῷ; ὑμεῖς δ' ἐστὸν ἀγήρω τ' ἀθανάτω τε.[8]

Why gave we you to royal Peleus, to a mortal? but ye are without old age, and immortal.

Chapman sophisticates this into:

> Why gave we you t' a mortal king, when immortality
> And *incapacity of age so dignifies your states*?

Again; in the speech of Achilles to his horses, where Achilles, according to Homer, says simply, 'Take heed that ye bring your master safe back to the host of the Danaans, in some other sort than the last time, when the battle is ended', Chapman sophisticates this into:

When with blood, for this day's fast observed, revenge shall yield
Our heart satiety, bring us off.

In Hector's famous speech, again, at his parting from Andromache, Homer makes him say: 'Nor does my own heart so bid me' (to keep safe behind the walls), 'since I have learned to be staunch always, and to fight among the foremost of the Trojans, busy on behalf of my father's great glory, and my own'.[9] In Chapman's hands this becomes:

The spirit I first did breathe
Did never teach me that; much less, since the contempt of death
Was settled in me, *and my mind knew what a worthy was,*
Whose office is to lead in fight, and give no danger pass
Without improvement. In this fire must Hector's trial shine:
Here must his country, father, friends, be in him made divine.

You see how ingeniously Homer's plain thought is *tormented*, as the French would say, here. Homer goes on: 'For well I know this in my mind and in my heart, the day will be, when sacred Troy shall perish':

ἔσσεται ἦμαρ, ὅτ' ἄν ποτ' ὀλώλῃ Ἴλιος ἱρή.

Chapman makes this:

And such a *stormy* day shall come, in mind and soul I know,
When sacred Troy *shall shed her towers, for tears of overthrow.*

I might go on for ever, but I could not give you a better illustration than this last, of what I mean by saying that the Elizabethan poet fails to render Homer because he cannot forbear to interpose a play of thought between his object and its expression. Chapman translates his object into Elizabethan, as Pope translates it into the Augustan of Queen Anne; both convey it to us through a medium. Homer, on the other hand, sees his object and conveys it to us immediately.

And yet, in spite of this perfect plainness and directness of Homer's style, in spite of this perfect plainness and directness of his ideas, he is eminently *noble*; he works as entirely in the grand style, he is as grandiose, as Phidias, or Dante, or Michael Angelo. This is what makes his translators despair. 'To give relief', says Cowper, 'to prosaic subjects' (such as dressing, eating, drinking, harnessing, travelling, going to bed), that is to treat such subjects nobly, in the grand style, 'without seeming unseasonably tumid, is extremely difficult'. It *is* difficult, but Homer has done it. Homer is precisely the incomparable poet he is, because he has done it. His translator must not be tumid, must not be artificial, must not be literary; true: but then also he must not be commonplace, must not be ignoble. I have shown you how translators of Homer fail by wanting rapidity, by wanting simplicity of style, by wanting plainness of thought: in a second lecture I will show you how a translator fails by wanting nobility.

II

I must repeat what I said in beginning, that the translator of Homer ought steadily to keep in mind where lies the real test of the success of his translation, what judges he is to try to satisfy. He is to try to satisfy *scholars*, because scholars alone have the means of really judging him. A scholar may be a pedant, it is true, and then his judgment will be worthless; but a scholar may also have poetical feeling, and then he can judge him truly; whereas all the poetical feeling in the world will not enable a man who is not a scholar to judge him truly. For the translator to reproduce Homer, and the scholar alone has the means of knowing that Homer who is to be reproduced. He knows him but imperfectly, for he is separated from him by time, race, and language; but he alone knows him at all. Yet people speak as if there were two real tribunals in this matter,—the scholar's tribunal, and that of the general public. They speak as if the scholar's judgment was one thing, and the general public's judgment another; both with their shortcomings, both with their liability to error; but both to be regarded by the translator. The translator who makes verbal literalness his chief care 'will', says a writer in the *National Review* whom I have already quoted, 'be appreciated by the scholar accustomed to test a translation rigidly by comparison with the original, to look perhaps with excessive care to finish in detail rather than boldness and general effect, and find pardon even for a version that seems bare and bald, so it be scholastic and faithful'. But, if the scholar in judging a translation looks to detail rather than to general effect, he judges it pedantically and ill. The appeal, however, lies not from the pedantic scholar to the general public, which can only like or dislike Chapman's version, or Pope's, or Mr. Newman's, but cannot *judge* them; it lies from the pedantic scholar to the scholar who is not pedantic, who knows that Homer is Homer by his general effect, and not by his single words, and who demands but one thing in a translation,—that it shall, as nearly as possible, reproduce for him the *general effect* of Homer. This, then, remains the one proper aim of the translator: to reproduce on the intelligent scholar, as nearly as possible, the general effect of Homer. Except so far as he reproduces this, he loses his labour, even though he may make a spirited *Iliad* of his own, like Pope, or translate Homer's *Iliad* word for word, like Mr. Newman. If his proper aim were to stimulate in any manner possible the general public, he might be right in following Pope's example; if his proper aim were to help schoolboys to construe Homer, he might be right in following Mr. Newman's. But it is not: his proper aim is, I repeat it yet once more, to reproduce on the intelligent scholar, as nearly as he can, the general effect of Homer.

When, therefore, Cowper says, 'My chief boast is that I have adhered closely to my original'; when Mr. Newman says, 'My aim is to retain every peculiarity of the original, to be *faithful*, exactly as is the case with the draughtsman of the Elgin marbles'; their real judge only replies: 'It may be so: reproduce then upon us, reproduce the effect of Homer, as a good copy reproduces the effect of the Elgin marbles.'

When, again, Mr. Newman tells us that 'by an exhaustive process of argument and experiment' he has found a metre which is at once the metre of 'the modern Greek epic', and a metre 'like in moral genius' to Homer's metre, his judge has still but the same answer for him: 'It may be so: reproduce then on our ear something of the effect produced by the movement of Homer.'

But what is the general effect which Homer produces on Mr. Newman himself? because, when we know this, we shall know whether he and his judges are agreed at the outset, whether we may expect him, if he can reproduce the effect he feels, if his hand does not betray him in the execution, to satisfy his judges and to succeed. If, however, Mr. Newman's impression from Homer is something quite different from that of his judges, then it can hardly be expected that any amount of labour or talent will enable him to reproduce for them *their* Homer.

Mr. Newman does not leave us in doubt as to the general effect which Homer makes upon him. As I have told you what is the general effect which Homer makes upon me,—that of a most rapidly moving poet, that of a poet most plain and direct in his style, that of a poet most plain and direct in his ideas, that of a poet eminently noble,—so Mr. Newman tells us his general impression of Homer. 'Homer's style,' he says, 'is direct, popular, forcible, quaint, flowing, garrulous'. Again: 'Homer rises and sinks with his subject, is prosaic when it is tame, is low when it is mean.'

I lay my finger on four words in these two sentences of Mr. Newman, and I say that the man who could apply those words to Homer can never render Homer truly. The four words are these: *quaint, garrulous, prosaic, low*. Search the English language for a word which does not apply to Homer, and you could not fix on a better than *quaint*, unless perhaps you fixed on one of the other three.

Again; 'to translate Homer suitably,' says Mr. Newman, 'we need a diction sufficiently antiquated to obtain pardon of the reader for its frequent homeliness.' 'I am concerned,' he says again, 'with the artistic problem of attaining a plausible aspect of moderate antiquity, while remaining easily intelligible'. And again, he speaks of 'the more antiquated style suited to this subject'. Quaint! antiquated!—but to whom? Sir Thomas Browne is quaint, and the diction of Chaucer is antiquated: does Mr. Newman suppose that Homer seemed quaint to Sophocles, when he read him, as Sir Thomas Browne seems quaint to us, when we read him? or that Homer's diction seemed antiquated to Sophocles, as Chaucer's diction seems antiquated to us? But we cannot really know, I confess, how Homer seemed to Sophocles: well then, to those who can tell us how he seems to them, to the living scholar, to our only present witness on this matter,—does Homer make on the Provost of Eton, when he reads him, the impression of a poet quaint and antiquated? does he make this impression on Professor Thompson or Professor Jowett? When Shakespeare says, 'The princes *orgulous*', meaning 'the proud princes', we say, 'This is antiquated'; when he says of the Trojan gates, that they:

With massy staples
And corresponsive and fulfilling bolts
Sperr up the sons of Troy,

we say, 'This is both quaint and antiquated.' But does Homer ever compose in a language which produces on the scholar at all the same impression as this language which I have quoted from Shakespeare? Never once. Shakespeare is quaint and antiquated quoted in the lines which I have just quoted; but Shakespeare—need I say it?—can compose, when he likes, when he is at his best, in a language perfectly simple, perfectly intelligible; in a language which, in spite of the two centuries and a half which part its author from us, stops us or surprises us as little as the language of a contemporary. And Homer has not Shakespeare's variations: Homer always composes as Shakespeare composes at his best; Homer is always simple and intelligible, as Shakespeare is often; Homer is never quaint and antiquated, as Shakespeare is sometimes.

When Mr. Newman says that Homer is garrulous, he seems, perhaps, to depart less widely from the common opinion than when he calls him quaint; for is there not Horace's authority for asserting that 'the good Homer sometimes nods', *bonus dormitat Homerus*? and a great many people have come, from the currency of this well-known criticism, to represent Homer to themselves as a diffuse old man, with the full-stocked mind, but also with the occasional slips and weaknesses, of old age. Horace has said better things than his 'bonus dormitat Homerus'; but he never meant by this, as I need not remind any one who knows the passage, that Homer was garrulous, or anything of the kind. Instead, however, of either discussing what Horace meant, or discussing Homer's garrulity as a general question, I prefer to bring to my mind some style which *is* garrulous, and to ask myself, to ask you, whether anything at all of the impression made by that style is ever made by the style of Homer. The mediaeval romancers, for instance, are garrulous; the following, to take out of a thousand instances the first which comes to hand, is in a garrulous manner. It is from the romance of Richard Coeur de Lion.

> Of my tale be not a-wondered!
> The French says he slew an hundred
> (Whereof is made this English saw)
> Or he rested him any thraw.
> Him followed many an English knight
> That eagerly holp him for to fight,—

and so on. Now the manner of that composition I call garrulous; every one will feel it to be garrulous; every one will understand what is meant when it is called garrulous. Then I ask the scholar,—does Homer's manner ever make upon you, I do not say, the same impression of its garrulity as that passage, but does it make, ever for one moment, an impression in the slightest way resembling, in the remotest degree akin to, the impression made by that passage of the mediaeval poet? I have no fear of the answer.

I follow the same method with Mr. Newman's two other epithets, *prosaic* and *low*. 'Homer rises and sinks with his subject', says Mr. Newman; 'is prosaic when it is tame, is low when it is mean'. First I say, Homer is never, in any sense, to be with truth called prosaic; he is never to be called low. He does not rise and sink with his subject; on the contrary, his manner invests his subject, whatever his subject be, with nobleness. Then I look for an author of whom it may with truth be said, that he 'rises and sinks with his subject, is prosaic when it is tame, is low when it is mean'. Defoe is eminently such an author; of

Defoe's manner it may with perfect precision be said, that it follows his matter; his lifelike composition takes its character from the facts which it conveys, not from the nobleness of the composer. In *Moll Flanders* and *Colonel Jack*, Defoe is undoubtedly prosaic when his subject is tame, low when his subject is mean. Does Homer's manner in the *Iliad*, I ask the scholar, ever make upon him an impression at all like the impression made by Defoe's manner in *Moll Flanders* and *Colonel Jack*? Does it not, on the contrary, leave him with an impression of nobleness, even when it deals with Thersites or with Irus?

Well then, Homer is neither quaint, nor garrulous, nor prosaic, nor mean: and Mr. Newman, in seeing him so, sees him differently from those who are to judge Mr. Newman's rendering of him. By pointing out how a wrong conception of Homer affects Mr. Newman's translation, I hope to place in still clearer light those four cardinal truths which I pronounce essential for him who would have a right conception of Homer: that Homer is rapid, that he is plain and direct in word and style, that he is plain and direct in his ideas, and that he is noble.

Mr. Newman says that in fixing on a style for suitably rendering Homer, as he conceives him, he 'alights on the delicate line which separates the *quaint* from the *grotesque*'. 'I ought to be quaint', he says, 'I ought not to be grotesque'. This is a most unfortunate sentence. Mr. Newman is grotesque, which he himself says he ought not to be; and he ought not to be quaint, which he himself says he ought to be.

'No two persons will agree', says Mr. Newman, 'as to where the quaint ends and the grotesque begins'; and perhaps this is true. But, in order to avoid all ambiguity in the use of the two words, it is enough to say, that most persons would call an expression which produced on them a very strong sense of its incongruity, and which violently surprised them, *grotesque*; and an expression, which produced on them a slighter sense of its incongruity, and which more gently surprised them, *quaint*. Using the two words in this manner, I say, that when Mr. Newman translates Helen's words to Hector in the sixth book,

Δᾶερ ἐμεῖο, κυνὸς κακομηχάνου, ὀκρυοέσσης,[10]—

O, brother thou of me, who am a mischief-working vixen,
A numbing horror,—

he is grotesque; that is, he expresses himself in a manner which produces on us a very strong sense of its incongruity, and which violently surprises us. I say, again, that when Mr. Newman translates the common life,

Τὴν δ' ἠμείβετ' ἔπειτα μέγας κορυθαίολος Ἕκτωρ,—

Great Hector of the motley helm then spake to her responsive,—

or the common expression ἐϋκνήμδες Ἀχαιοί, 'dapper-greaved Achaians,' he is quaint; that is, he expresses himself in a manner which produces on us a slighter sense of incongruity, and which more gently surprises us. But violent and gentle surprise are alike far from the scholar's spirit when he reads in Homer κυνὸς κακομηχάνου, or κορυθαίολος Ἕκτωρ, or, ἐϋκνήμδες Ἀχαιοί. These expressions no more seem odd to him than the simplest expressions in English. He is not more checked by any feeling of strangeness, strong or weak, when he reads them, than when he reads in an English book 'the painted savage', or, 'the phlegmatic Dutchman.' Mr. Newman's renderings of them must, therefore, be wrong expressions in a translation of Homer, because they excite in the scholar, their only competent judge, a feeling quite alien to that excited in him by what they profess to render.

Mr. Newman, by expressions of this kind, is false to his original in two ways. He is false to him inasmuch as he is ignoble; for a noble air, and a grotesque air, the air of the address,

Δᾶερ ἐμεῖο, κυνὸς κακομηχάνου, ὀκρυοέσσης,—

and the air of the address,

O, brother thou of me, who am a mischief-working vixen,
A numbing horror,—

are just contrary the one to the other: and he is false to him inasmuch as he is odd; for an odd diction like Mr. Newman's, and a perfectly plain natural diction like Homer's,—'dapper-greaved Achaians' and ἐϋκνήδες Ἀχαιοί,—are also just contrary the one to the other. Where, indeed, Mr. Newman got his diction, with whom he can have lived, what can be his test of antiquity and rarity for words, are questions which I ask myself with bewilderment. He has prefixed to his translation a list of what he calls 'the more antiquated or rarer words' which he has used. In this list appear, on the one hand, such words as *doughty, grisly, lusty, noisome, ravin*, which are familiar, one would think, to all the world; on the other hand such words as *bragly*, meaning, Mr. Newman tells us, 'proudly fine'; *bulkin*, 'a calf'; plump, 'a mass'; and so on. 'I am concerned', says Mr. Newman, 'with the artistic problem of attaining a plausible aspect of moderate antiquity, while remaining easily intelligible'. But it seems to me that *lusty* is not antiquated: and that *bragly* is not a word readily understood. That this word, indeed, and *bulkin*, may have 'a plausible aspect of moderate antiquity', I admit; but that they are 'easily intelligible', I deny.

Mr. Newman's syntax has, I say it with pleasure, a much more Homeric cast than his vocabulary; his syntax, the mode in which his thought is evolved, although not the actual words in which it is expressed, seems to me right in its general character, and the best feature of his version. It is not artificial or rhetorical like Cowper's syntax or Pope's: it is simple, direct, and natural, and so far it is like Homer's. It fails, however, just where, from the inherent fault of Mr. Newman's conception of Homer, one might expect it to fail,—it fails in nobleness. It presents the thought in a way which is something more than unconstrained,—over-familiar; something more than easy,—free and easy. In this respect it is like the movement of Mr. Newman's version, like his rhythm, for this, too, fails, in spite of some good qualities, by not being noble enough; this, while it avoids the faults of being slow and elaborate, falls into a fault in the opposite direction, and is slip-shod. Homer presents his thought naturally; but when Mr. Newman has,

> A thousand fires along the plain, *I say*, that night were burning,—

he presents his thought familiarly, in a style which may be the genuine style of ballad-poetry, but which is not the style of Homer. Homer moves freely; but when Mr. Newman has,

> Infatuate! O that thou wert lord to some other army,—[11]

he gives himself too much freedom; he leaves us too much to do for his rhythm ourselves, instead of giving to us a rhythm like Homer's, easy indeed, but mastering our ear with a fullness of power which is irresistible.

I said that a certain style might be the genuine style of ballad-poetry, but yet not the style of Homer. The analogy of the ballad is ever present to Mr. Newman's thoughts in considering Homer; and perhaps nothing has more caused his faults than this analogy,—this popular, but, it is time to say, this erroneous analogy. 'The moral qualities of Homer's style', says Mr. Newman, 'being like to those of the English ballad, we need a metre of the same genius. Only those metres, which by the very possession of these qualities are liable to degenerate into *doggerel*, are suitable to reproduce the ancient epic.' 'The style of Homer', he says, in a passage which I have before quoted, 'is direct, popular, forcible, quaint, flowing, garrulous: in all these respects it is similar to the old English ballad'. Mr. Newman, I need not say, is by no means alone in this opinion. 'The most really and truly Homeric of all the creations of the English muse is', says Mr. Newman's critic in the *National Review*, 'the ballad-poetry of ancient times; and the association between metre and subject is one that it would be true wisdom to preserve'. 'It is confessed', says Chapman's last editor, Mr. Hooper, 'that the fourteen-syllable verse' (that is, a ballad-verse) 'is peculiarly fitting for Homeric translation'. And the editor of Dr. Maginn's clever and popular *Homeric Ballads* assumes it as one of his author's greatest and most undisputable merits, that he was 'the first who consciously realized to himself the truth that Greek ballads can be really represented in English only by a similar measure'.

This proposition that Homer's poetry is *ballad-poetry*, analogous to the well-known ballad-poetry of the English and other nations, has a certain small portion of truth in it, and at one time probably served a useful purpose, when it was employed to discredit the artificial and literary manner in which Pope and his school rendered Homer. But it has been so extravagantly over-used, the mistake which it was useful in combating has so entirely lost the public favour, that it is now much more important to insist on the large part of error contained in it, than to extol its small part of truth. It is time to say plainly that, whatever the admirers of our old ballads may think, the supreme form of epic poetry, the genuine Homeric mould, is not the form of the Ballad of Lord Bateman. I have myself shown the broad difference between Milton's manner and Homer's; but, after a course of Mr. Newman and Dr. Maginn, I turn round in desperation upon them and upon the balladists who have misled them, and I exclaim: 'Compared with you, Milton is Homer's double; there is, whatever you may think, ten thousand times more of the real strain of Homer in,

> Blind Thamyris, and blind Maeonides,
> And Tiresias, and Phineus, prophets old,—

than in,

> Now Christ thee save, thou proud portèr,
> Now Christ thee save and see,[12]—

or in,

> While the tinker did dine, he had plenty of wine.[13]

For Homer is not only rapid in movement, simple in style, plain in language, natural in thought; he is also, and above all, *noble*. I have advised the translator not to go into the vexed question of Homer's identity. Yet I will just remind him that the grand argument—or rather, not argument, for the matter affords no data for arguing, but the grand source from which conviction, as we read the *Iliad*, keeps pressing in upon us, that there is one poet of the *Iliad*, one Homer—is precisely this nobleness of the poet, this grand manner; we feel that the analogy drawn from other joint compositions does not hold good here, because those works do not bear, like the *Iliad*, the magic stamp of a master; and the moment you have *anything* less than a masterwork, the co-operation or consolidation of several poets becomes possible, for talent is not uncommon; the moment you have *much* less than a masterwork, they become easy, for mediocrity is everywhere. I can imagine fifty Bradies joined with as many Tates to make the New Version of the Psalms. I can imagine several poets having contributed to any one of the old English ballads in Percy's collection. I can imagine several poets, possessing, like Chapman, the Elizabethan vigour and the Elizabethan mannerism, united with Chapman to produce his version of the *Iliad*. I can imagine several poets, with the literary knack of the twelfth century, united to produce the *Nibelungen Lay* in the form in which we have it,—a work which the Germans, in their joy at discovering a national epic of their own, have rated vastly higher than it deserves. And lastly, though Mr. Newman's translation of Homer bears the strong mark of his own idiosyncrasy, yet I can imagine Mr. Newman and a school of adepts trained by him in his art of poetry, jointly producing that work, so that Aristarchus himself should have difficulty in pronouncing which line was the master's, and which a pupil's. But I cannot imagine several poets, or one poet, joined with Dante in the composition of his *Inferno*, though many poets have taken for their subject a descent into Hell. Many artists, again, have represented Moses; but there is only one Moses of Michael Angelo. So the insurmountable obstacle to believing the *Iliad* a consolidated work of several poets is this: that the work of great masters is unique; and the *Iliad* has a great master's genuine stamp, and that stamp is *the grand style*.

Poets who cannot work in the grand style instinctively seek a style in which their comparative inferiority may feel itself at ease, a manner which may be, so to speak, indulgent to their inequalities. The ballad-style offers to an epic poet, quite unable to fill the canvas of Homer, or Dante, or Milton, a canvas which he is capable of filling. The ballad-measure is quite able to give due effect to the vigour and spirit which its employer, when at his very best, may be able to exhibit; and, when he is not at his best, when he is a little trivial, or a little dull, it will not betray him, it will not bring out his weaknesses into broad relief. This is a convenience; but it is a convenience which the ballad-style purchases by resigning all pretensions to the highest, to the grand manner. It is true of its movement, as it is *not* true of

Homer's, that it is 'liable to degenerate into doggerel'. It is true of its 'moral qualities', as it is *not* true of Homer's, that 'quaintness' and 'garrulity' are among them. It is true of its employers, as it is *not* true of Homer, that they 'rise and sink with their subject, are prosaic when it is tame, are low when it is mean'. For this reason the ballad-style and the ballad-measure are eminently *in*appropriate to render Homer. Homer's manner and movement are always both noble and powerful: the ballad-manner and movement are often either jaunty and smart, so not noble; or jog-trot and humdrum, so not powerful.

The *Nibelungen Lay* affords a good illustration of the qualities of the ballad-manner. Based on grand traditions, which had found expression in a grand lyric poetry, the German epic poem of the *Nibelungen Lay*, though it is interesting, and though it has good passages, is itself anything rather than a grand poem. It is a poem of which the composer is, to speak the truth, a very ordinary mortal, and often, therefore, like other ordinary mortals, very prosy. It is in a measure which eminently adapts itself to this commonplace personality of its composer, which has much the movement of the well-known measures of Tate and Brady, and can jog on, for hundreds of lines at a time, with a level ease which reminds one of Sheridan's saying that easy writing may be often such hard reading. But, instead of occupying myself with the *Nibelungen Lay*, I prefer to look at the ballad-style as directly applied to Homer, in Chapman's version and Mr. Newman's, and in the *Homeric Ballads* of Dr. Maginn.

First I take Chapman. I have already shown that Chapman's conceits are un-Homeric, and that his rhyme is un-Homeric; I will now show how his manner and movement are un-Homeric. Chapman's diction, I have said, is generally good; but it must be called good with this reserve, that, though it has Homer's plainness and directness, it often offends him who knows Homer, by wanting Homer's nobleness. In a passage which I have already quoted, the address of Zeus to the horses of Achilles, where Homer has:

> ἆ δειλώ, τί σφῶϊ δόμεν Πηλῆϊ ἄνακτι
> θνητῷ; ὑμεῖς δ' ἐστὸν ἀγήρω τ' ἀθανάτω τε!
> ἦ ἵνα δυστήνοι σιμετ' ἀνδράσιν ἄλγὲ ἔχητον;[14]

Chapman has:

> *'Poor wretched beasts'*, said he,
> 'Why gave we you to a mortal king, when immortality
> And incapacity of age so dignifies your states?
> Was it to haste[15] the miseries poured out on human fates?'

There are many faults in this rendering of Chapman's, but what I particularly wish to notice in it is the expression 'Poor wretched beasts' for ἆ δειλώ. This expression just illustrates the difference between the ballad-manner and Homer's. The ballad-manner—Chapman's manner—is, I say, pitched sensibly lower than Homer's. The ballad-manner requires that an expression shall be plain and natural, and then it asks no more. Homer's manner requires that an expression shall be plain and natural, but it also requires that it shall be noble. Ἆ δειλώ is as plain, as simple as 'Poor wretched beasts'; but it is also noble, which 'Poor wretched beasts' is not. 'Poor wretched beasts' is, in truth, a little over-familiar, but this is no objection to it for the ballad-manner; it is good enough for the old English ballad, good enough for the *Nibelungen Lay*, good enough for Chapman's *Iliad,* good enough for Mr. Newman's *Iliad,* good enough for Dr. Maginn's *Homeric Ballads*; but it is not good enough for Homer.

To feel that Chapman's measure, though natural, is not Homeric; that, though tolerably rapid, it has not Homer's rapidity; that it has a jogging rapidity rather than a flowing rapidity; and a movement familiar rather than nobly easy, one has only, I think, to read half a dozen lines in any part of his version. I prefer to keep as much as possible to passages which I have already noticed, so I will quote the conclusion of the nineteenth book, where Achilles answers his horse Xanthus, who has prophesied his death to him.[16]

> Achilles, far in rage,
> Thus answered him: It fits not thee thus proudly to
> presage

My overthrow. I know myself it is my fate to fall
Thus far from Phthia; yet that fate shall fail to vent her gall
Till mine vent thousands.—These words said, he fell to horrid deeds,
Gave dreadful signal, and forthright made fly his one-hoofed steeds.

For what regards the manner of this passage, the words 'Achilles Thus answered him', and 'I know myself it is my fate to fall Thus far from Phthia,' are in Homer's manner, and all the rest is out of it. But for what regards its movement, who, after being jolted by Chapman through such verse as this,—

These words said, he fell to horrid deeds,
Gave dreadful signal, and forthright made fly his one-hoofed steeds,—

who does not feel the vital difference of the movement of Homer,—

ἦρα, καὶ ἐν πρώτοις ἰάχων ἔχε μώνυχας ἵππους?

To pass from Chapman to Dr. Maginn. His *Homeric Ballads* are vigorous and genuine poems in their own way; they are not one continual falsetto, like the pinchbeck *Roman Ballads* of Lord Macaulay; but just because they are ballads in their manner and movement, just because, to use the words of his applauding editor, Dr. Maginn has 'consciously realized to himself the truth that Greek ballads can be really represented in English only by a similar manner',—just for this very reason they are not at all Homeric, they have not the least in the world the manner of Homer. There is a celebrated incident in the nineteenth book of the *Odyssey*, the recognition by the old nurse Eurycleia of a scar on the leg of her master Ulysses, who has entered his own hall as an unknown wanderer, and whose feet she has been set to wash. 'Then she came near', says Homer, 'and began to wash her master; and straightway she recognized a scar which he had got in former days from the white tusk of a wild boar, when he went to Parnassus unto Autolycus and the sons of Autolycus, his mother's father and brethren'.[17] This, 'really represented' by Dr. Maginn, in 'a measure similar' to Homer's, becomes:

And scarcely had she begun to wash
Ere she was aware of the grisly gash
    Above his knee that lay.
It was a wound from a wild boar's tooth,
    All on Parnassus' slope,
Where he went to hunt in the days of his youth
With his mother's sire,—

and so on. That is the true ballad-manner, no one can deny; 'all on Parnassus' slope' is, I was going to say, the true ballad-slang; but never again shall I be able to read (Homer),

νίζε δ' ἄσσον ἰοῦσα ἄναχθ' ἑόν · αὐτίκα δ' ἔγνω οὐλήν,

without having the detestable dance of Dr. Maginn's:

And scarcely had she begun to wash
Ere she was aware of the grisly gash,—

jigging in my ears, to spoil the effect of Homer, and to torture me. To apply that manner and that rhythm to Homer's incidents, is not to imitate Homer, but to travesty him.

Lastly I come to Mr. Newman. His rhythm, like Chapman's and Dr. Maginn's, is a ballad-rhythm, but with a modification of his own. 'Holding it', he tells us, 'as an axiom, that rhyme must be abandoned', he found, on abandoning it, 'an unpleasant void until he gave a double ending to the verse'. In short, instead of saying:

Good people all with one accord
Give ear unto my *tale*,—

Mr. Newman would say:

Good people all with one accord
Give ear unto my *story*.

A recent American writer[18] gravely observes that for his countrymen this rhythm has a disadvantage in being like the rhythm of the American national air *Yankee Doodle*, and thus provoking ludicrous associations. *Yankee Doodle* is not our national air: for us Mr. Newman's rhythm has not this disadvantage. He himself gives us several plausible reasons why this rhythm of his really ought to be successful: let us examine how far it *is* successful.

Mr. Newman joins to a bad rhythm so bad a diction that it is difficult to distinguish exactly whether in any given passage it is his words or his measure which produces a total impression of such an unpleasant kind. But with a little attention we may analyse our total impression, and find the share which each element has in producing it. To take the passage which I have so often mentioned, Sarpedon's speech to Glaucus. Mr. Newman translates this as follows:

> O gentle friend! if thou and I, from this encounter 'scaping,
> Hereafter might forever be from Eld and Death exempted
> As heavenly gods, not I in sooth would fight among the foremost,
> Nor liefly thee would I advance to man-ennobling battle.
> Now,—sith ten thousand shapes of Death do any-gait pursue us
> Which never mortal may evade, though sly of foot and nimble;—
> Onward! and glory let us earn, or glory yield to some one.—

> Could all our care elude the gloomy grave
> Which claims no less the fearful than the brave—

I am not going to quote Pope's version over again, but I must remark in passing, how much more, with all Pope's radical difference of manner from Homer, it gives us of the real effect of

> εἰ μὲν γὰρ, πόλεμον περὶ τόνδε φυγόντε

than Mr. Newman's lines. And now, why are Mr. Newman's lines faulty? They are faulty, first, because, as a matter of diction, the expressions 'O gentle friend', 'eld', 'in sooth', 'liefly', 'advance', 'man-ennobling', 'sith', 'any-gait', and 'sly of foot', are all bad; some of them worse than others, but all bad: that is, they all of them as here used excite in the scholar, their sole judge,—excite, I will boldly affirm, in Professor

Thompson or Professor Jowett,—a feeling totally different from that excited in them by the words of Homer which these expressions profess to render. The lines are faulty, secondly, because, as a matter of rhythm, any and every line among them has to the ear of the same judges (I affirm it with equal boldness) a movement as unlike Homer's movement in the corresponding line as the single words are unlike Homer's words. Οὔτε κε σὲ στέλλοι μι μάχην ἐς κυδιάνειραν,—'Nor liefly thee would I advance to man-ennobling battle';—for whose ears do those two rhythms produce impressions of, to use Mr. Newman's own words, 'similar moral genius'?

I will by no means make search in Mr. Newman's version for passages likely to raise a laugh; that search, alas! would be far too easy. I will quote but one other passage from him, and that a passage where the diction is comparatively inoffensive, in order that disapproval of the words may not unfairly heighten disapproval of the rhythm. The end of the nineteenth book, the answer of Achilles to his horse Xanthus, Mr. Newman gives thus:

> 'Chestnut! why bodest death to me? from thee this was not needed.
> Myself right surely know also, that 't is my doom to perish,
> From mother and from father dear apart, in Troy; but never
> Pause will I make of war, until the Trojans be glutted.'
> He spake, and yelling, held afront the single-hoofed horses.

Here Mr. Newman calls Xanthus *Chestnut*, indeed, as he calls Balius *Spotted*, and Podarga *Spry-foot*; which is as if a Frenchman were to call Miss Nightingale *Mdlle. Rossignol*, or Mr. Bright *M. Clair*. And several other expressions, too,—'yelling', 'held afront', 'single-hoofed',—leave, to say the very least, much to be desired. Still, for Mr. Newman, the diction of this passage is pure. All the more clearly appears the profound vice of a rhythm, which, with comparatively few faults of words, can leave a sense of such incurable alienation from Homer's manner as, 'Myself right surely know alsó that 't is my doom to perish', compared with the εὖ νυ το οἶδα καὶ αὐτὸς, ὅ μοι μόρος ἐνθάδ' ὀλέσθαι of Homer.

But so deeply seated is the difference between the ballad-manner and Homer's, that even a man of the highest powers, even a man of the greatest vigour of spirit and of true genius,—the Coryphaeus of balladists, Sir Walter Scott,—fails with a manner of this kind to produce an effect at all like the effect of Homer. 'I am not so rash', declares Mr. Newman, 'as to say that if *freedom* be given to rhyme as in Walter Scott's poetry',—Walter Scott, 'by far the most Homeric of our poets', as in another place he calls him,—'a genius may not arise who will translate Homer into the melodies of *Marmion.*' 'The *truly* classical and the *truly* romantic,' says Dr. Maginn, 'are one; the moss-trooping Nestor reappears in the moss-trooping heroes of Percy's *Reliques*'; and a description by Scott, which he quotes, he calls 'graphic, and therefore Homeric'. He forgets our fourth axiom,—that Homer is not *only* graphic; he is also noble, and has the grand style. Human nature under like circumstances is probably in all ages much the same; and so far it may be said that 'the truly classical and the truly romantic are one'; but it is of little use to tell us this, because we know the human nature of other ages only through the representations of them which have come down to us, and the classical and the romantic modes of representation are so far from being 'one', that they remain eternally distinct, and have created for us a separation between the two worlds which they respectively represent. Therefore to call Nestor the 'moss-trooping Nestor' is absurd, because, though Nestor may possibly have been much the same sort of man as many a moss-trooper, he has yet come to us through a mode of representation so unlike that of Percy's *Reliques*, that instead of 'reappearing in the moss-trooping heroes' of these poems, he exists in our imagination as something utterly unlike them, and as belonging to another world. So the Greeks in Shakespeare's *Troilus* and *Cressida* are no longer the Greeks whom we have known in Homer, because they come to us through a mode of representation of the romantic world. But I must not forget Scott.

I suppose that when Scott is in what may be called full ballad swing, no one will hesitate to pronounce his manner neither Homeric nor the grand manner. When he says, for instance:

> I do not rhyme to that dull elf
> Who cannot image to himself,[19]

and so on, any scholar will feel that *this* is not Homer's manner. But let us take Scott's poetry at its best; and when it is at its best, it is undoubtedly very good indeed:

> Tunstall lies dead upon the field,
> His life-blood stains the spotless shield;
> Edmund is down,—my life is reft,—
> The Admiral alone is left.
> Let Stanley charge with spur of fire,—
> With Chester charge, and Lancashire,
> Full upon Scotland's central host,
> Or victory and England's lost.[20]

That is, no doubt, as vigorous as possible, as spirited as possible; it is exceedingly fine poetry. And still I say, it is not in the grand manner, and therefore it is not like Homer's poetry. Now, how shall I make him who doubts this feel that I say true; that these lines of Scott are essentially neither in Homer's style nor in the grand style? I may point out to him that the movement of Scott's lines, while it is rapid, is also at the same time what the French call *saccadé*, its rapidity is 'jerky'; whereas Homer's rapidity is a flowing rapidity. But this is something external and material; it is but the outward and visible sign of an inward and spiritual diversity. I may discuss what, in the abstract, constitutes the grand style; but that sort of general discussion never much helps our judgment of particular instances. I may say that the presence or absence of the grand style can only be spiritually discerned; and this is true, but to plead this looks like evading the difficulty. My best way is to take eminent specimens of the grand style, and to put them side by side with this of Scott. For example, when Homer says:

> ἀλλά, φίλος, θάνε καὶ σύ · τίη ὀλυφύρεαι οὕτως;
> κάτθανε καὶ Πάτροκλος, ὅπερ σέο πολλὸν ἀμείνων.[21]

that is in the grand style. When Virgil says:

> Disce, puer, virtutem ex me verumque laborem,
> Fortunam ex aliis,[22]

that is in the grand style. When Dante says:

> Lascio lo fele, e vo per dolci pomi
> Promessi a me per lo verace Duca;
> Ma fino al centro pria convien ch' io tomi,[23]

that is in the grand style. When Milton says:

> His form had yet not lost
> All her original brightness, nor appeared
> Less than archangel ruined, and the excess
> Of glory obscured,[24]

that, finally, is in the grand style. Now let any one, after repeating to himself these four passages, repeat again the passage of Scott, and he will perceive that there is something in style which the four first have in common, and which the last is without; and this something is precisely the grand manner. It is no disrespect to Scott to say that he does not attain to this manner in his poetry; to say so, is merely to say that he is not among the five or six supreme poets of the world. Among these he is not; but, being a man of far greater powers than the ballad-poets, he has tried to give to their instrument a compass and an elevation which it does not naturally possess, in order to enable him to come nearer to the effect of the instrument used by the great epic poets,—an instrument which he felt he could not truly use,—and in this attempt he has but imperfectly succeeded. The poetic style of Scott is—(it becomes necessary to say so when it is proposed to 'translate Homer into the melodies of *Marmion*')—it is, tried by the highest standards, a bastard epic style; and that is why, out of his own powerful hands, it has had so little success. It is a less natural, and therefore a less good style, than the original ballad-style; while it shares with the ballad-style the inherent incapacity of rising into the grand style, of adequately rendering Homer. Scott is certainly at his best in his battles. Of Homer you could not say this; he is not better in his battles than elsewhere; but even between the battle-pieces of the two there exists all the difference which there is between an able work and a masterpiece.

> Tunstall lies dead upon the field,
> His life-blood stains the spotless shield:
> Edmund is down,—my life is reft,—
> The Admiral alone is left.

—'For not in the hands of Diomede the son of Tydeus rages the spear, to ward off destruction from the Danaans; neither as yet have I heard the voice of the son of Atreus, shouting out of his hated mouth; but the voice of Hector the slayer of men bursts round me, as he cheers on the Trojans; and they with their yellings fill all the plain, overcoming the Achaians in the battle.'—I protest that, to my feeling, Homer's performance, even through that pale and far-off shadow of a prose translation, still has a hundred times more of the grand manner about it, than the original poetry of Scott.

Well, then, the ballad-manner and the ballad-measure, whether in the hands of the old ballad poets, or arranged by Chapman, or arranged by Mr. Newman, or, even, arranged by Sir Walter Scott, cannot worthily render Homer. And for one reason: Homer is plain, so are they; Homer is natural, so are they; Homer is spirited, so are they; but Homer is sustainedly noble, and they are not. Homer and they are both of them natural, and therefore touching and stirring; but the grand style, which is Homer's, is something more than touching and stirring; it can form the character, it is edifying. The old English balladist may stir Sir Philip Sidney's heart like a trumpet, and this is much: but Homer, but the few artists in the grand style, can do more; they can refine the raw natural man, they can transmute him. So it is not without cause that I say, and say again, to the translator of Homer: 'Never for a moment suffer yourself to forget our fourth fundamental proposition, *Homer is noble*.' For it is seen how large a share this nobleness has in producing that general effect of his, which it is the main business of a translator to *re*produce.

I shall have to try your patience yet once more upon this subject, and then my task will be completed. I have shown what the four axioms respecting Homer which I have laid down, exclude, what they bid a translator not to do; I have still to show what they supply, what positive help they can give to the translator in his work. I will even, with their aid, myself try my fortune with some of those passages of Homer which I have already noticed; not indeed with any confidence that I more than others can succeed in adequately rendering Homer, but in the hope of satisfying competent judges, in the hope of making it clear to the future translator, that I at any rate follow a right method, and that, in coming short, I come short from weakness of execution, not from original vice of design. This is why I have so long occupied myself with Mr. Newman's version; that, apart from all faults of execution, his original design was wrong, and that he has done us the good service of declaring that design in its naked wrongness. To bad practice he has prefixed the bad theory which made the practice bad; he has given us a false theory in his preface, and he has exemplified the bad effects of that false theory in his translation. It is because his starting-point is so bad that he runs so badly; and to save others from taking so false a starting-point, may be to save them from running so futile a course.

Mr. Newman, indeed, says in his preface, that if any one dislikes his translation, 'he has his easy remedy; to keep aloof from it'. But (Mr. Newman is a writer of considerable and deserved reputation) he is also a Professor of the University of London, an institution which by its position and by its merits acquires every year greater importance. It would be a very grave thing if the authority of so eminent a Professor led his students to misconceive entirely the chief work of the Greek world; that work which, whatever the other works of classical antiquity have to give us, gives it more abundantly than they all. The eccentricity too, the arbitrariness, of which Mr. Newman's conception of Homer offers so signal an example, are not a peculiar failing of Mr. Newman's own; in varying degrees they are the great defect of English intellect, the great blemish of English literature. Our literature of the eighteenth century, the literature of the school of Dryden, Addison, Pope, Johnson, is a long reaction against this eccentricity, this arbitrariness; that reaction perished by its own faults, and its enemies are left once more masters of the field. It is much more likely that any new English version of Homer will have Mr. Newman's faults than Pope's. Our present literature, which is very far, certainly, from having the spirit and power of Elizabethan genius, yet has in its own way these faults, eccentricity and arbitrariness, quite as much as the Elizabethan literature ever had. They are the cause that, while upon none, perhaps, of the modern literatures has so great a sum of force been expended as upon the English literature, at the present hour this literature, regarded not as an object of mere literary interest but as a living intellectual instrument, ranks only third in European effect and importance among the literatures of Europe; it ranks after the literatures of France and Germany. Of these two literatures, as of the intellect of Europe in general, the main effort, for now many years, has been a *critical* effort; the endeavour, in all branches of knowledge,—theology, philosophy, history, art, science,—to see the object as in itself it really is. But, owing to the presence in English literature of this eccentric and arbitrary spirit, owing to the strong tendency of English writers to bring to the consideration of their object some individual fancy, almost the last thing for which one would come to English literature is just that very thing which now Europe most desires—*criticism*. It is useful to notice any signal manifestation of those faults, which thus limit and impair the action of our literature. And therefore I have pointed out how widely, in translating Homer, a man even of real ability and learning may go astray, unless he brings to the study of this clearest of poets one quality in which our English authors, with all their great gifts, are apt to be somewhat wanting—simple lucidity of mind.

III

Homer is rapid in his movement, Homer is plain in his words and style, Homer is simple in his ideas, Homer is noble in his manner. Cowper renders him ill because he is slow in his movement, and elaborate in his style; Pope renders him ill because he is artificial both in his style and in his words; Chapman renders him ill because he is fantastic in his ideas;

Mr. Newman renders him ill because he is odd in his words and ignoble in his manner. All four translators diverge from their original at other points besides those named; but it is at the points thus named that their divergence is greatest. For instance, Cowper's diction is not as Homer's diction, nor his nobleness as Homer's nobleness; but it is in movement and grammatical style that he is most unlike Homer. Pope's rapidity is not of the same sort as Homer's rapidity, nor are his plainness of ideas and his nobleness as Homer's plainness of ideas and nobleness: but it is in the artificial character of his style and diction that he is most unlike Homer. Chapman's movement, words, style, and manner, are often far enough from resembling Homer's movement, words, style, and manner; but it is the fantasticality of his ideas which puts him farthest from resembling Homer. Mr. Newman's movement, grammatical style, and ideas, are a thousand times in strong contrast with Homer's; still it is by the oddness of his diction and the ignobleness of his manner that he contrasts with Homer the most violently.

Therefore, the translator must not say to himself: 'Cowper is noble, Pope is rapid, Chapman has a good diction, Mr. Newman has a good cast of sentence; I will avoid Cowper's slowness, Pope's artificiality, Chapman's conceits, Mr. Newman's oddity; I will take Cowper's dignified manner, Pope's impetuous movement, Chapman's vocabulary, Mr. Newman's syntax, and so make a perfect translation of Homer.' Undoubtedly in certain points the versions of Chapman, Cowper, Pope, and Mr. Newman, all of them have merit; some of them very high merit, others a lower merit; but even in these points they have, none of them precisely the same kind of merit as Homer, and therefore the new translator, even if he can imitate them in their good points, will still not satisfy his judge, the scholar, who asks him for Homer and Homer's kind of merit, or, at least, for as much of them as it is possible to give.

So the translator really has no good model before him for any part of his work, and has to invent everything for himself. He is to be rapid in movement, plain in speech, simple in thought, and noble; and *how* he is to be either rapid, or plain, or simple, or noble, no one yet has shown him. I shall try to-day to establish some practical suggestions which may help the translator of Homer's poetry to comply with the four grand requirements which we make of him.

His version is to be rapid; and of course, to make a man's poetry rapid, as to make it noble, nothing can serve him so much as to have, in his own nature, rapidity and nobleness. *It is the spirit that quickeneth*; and no one will so well render Homer's swift-flowing movement as he who has himself something of the swift-moving spirit of Homer. Yet even this is not quite enough. Pope certainly had a quick and darting spirit, as he had, also, real nobleness; yet Pope does not render the movement of Homer. To render this the translator must have, besides his natural qualifications, an appropriate metre.

I have sufficiently shown why I think all forms of our ballad-metre unsuited to Homer. It seems to me to be beyond question that, for epic poetry, only three metres can seriously claim to be accounted capable of the grand style. Two of these will at once occur to every one,—the ten-syllable, or so-called *heroic*, couplet, and blank verse. I do not add to these the Spenserian stanza, although Dr. Maginn, whose metrical eccentricities I have already criticized, pronounces this stanza the one right measure for a translation of Homer. It is enough to observe that if Pope's couplet, with the simple system of correspondences that its rhymes introduce, changes the movement of Homer, in which no such correspondences are found, and is therefore a bad measure for a translator of Homer to employ, Spenser's stanza, with its far more intricate system of correspondences, must change Homer's movement far more profoundly, and must therefore be for the translator a far worse measure than the couplet of Pope. Yet I will say, at the same time, that the verse of Spenser is more fluid, slips more easily and quickly along, than the verse of almost any other English poet.

> By this the northern wagoner had set
> His seven-fold team behind the steadfast star
> That was in ocean waves yet never wet,
> But firm is fixt, and sendeth light from far
> To all that in the wide deep wandering are.[25]

One cannot but feel that English verse has not often moved with the fluidity and sweet ease of these lines. It is possible that it may have been this quality of Spenser's poetry which made Dr. Maginn think that the stanza of *The Faery Queen* must be a good measure for rendering Homer. This it is not: Spenser's verse is fluid and rapid, no doubt, but there are more ways than one of being fluid and rapid, and Homer is fluid and rapid in quite another way than Spenser. Spenser's manner is no more Homeric than is the manner of the one modern inheritor of Spenser's beautiful gift,—the poet, who evidently caught from Spenser his sweet and easy-slipping movement, and who has exquisitely employed it; a Spenserian genius, nay, a genius by natural endowment richer probably than even Spenser; that light which shines so unexpected and without fellow in our century, an Elizabethan born too late, the early lost and admirably gifted Keats.

I say then that there are really but three metres,—the ten-syllable couplet, blank verse, and a third metre which I will not yet name, but which is neither the Spenserian stanza nor any form of ballad-verse,—between which, as vehicles for Homer's poetry, the translator has to make his choice. Every one will at once remember a thousand passages in which both the ten-syllable couplet and blank verse prove themselves to have nobleness. Undoubtedly the movement and manner of this:

> Still raise for good the supplicating voice,
> But leave to Heaven the measure and the choice,—

are noble. Undoubtedly, the movement and manner of this:

> High on a throne of royal state, which far
> Outshone the wealth of Ormus and of Ind,—

are noble also. But the first is in a rhymed metre; and the unfitness of a rhymed metre for rendering Homer I have already shown. I will observe, too, that the fine couplet which I have quoted comes out of a satire, a didactic poem; and that it is in didactic poetry that the ten-syllable couplet has most successfully essayed the grand style. In narrative poetry this metre has succeeded best when it essayed a sensibly lower style, the style of Chaucer, for instance; whose narrative manner, though a very good and sound manner, is certainly neither the grand manner nor the manner of Homer.

The rhymed ten-syllable couplet being thus excluded, blank verse offers itself for the translator's use. The first kind of blank verse which naturally occurs to us is the blank verse of Milton, which has been employed, with more or less modification, by Mr. Cary in translating Dante, by Cowper and by Mr. Wright in translating Homer. How noble this metre is in Milton's hands, how completely it shows itself capable of the grand, nay, of the grandest, style, I need not say. To this metre, as used in the *Paradise Lost*, our country owes the glory of having produced one of the only two poetical works in the grand style which are to be found in the modern languages; the *Divine Comedy* of Dante is the other. England and Italy here stand alone; Spain, France, and Germany have produced great poets, but neither Calderon, nor Corneille, nor Schiller, nor even Goethe, has produced a body of poetry in the true grand style, in the sense in which the style of the body of Homer's poetry or Pindar's, or Sophocles's, is grand. But Dante has, and so has Milton; and in this respect Milton possesses a distinction which even Shakespeare, undoubtedly the supreme poetical power in our literature, does not share with him. Not a tragedy of Shakespeare but contains passages in the worst of all styles, the affected style; and the grand style, although it may be harsh, or obscure, or cumbrous, or over-laboured, is never affected. In spite, therefore, of objections which may justly be urged against the plan and treatment of the *Paradise Lost*, in spite of its possessing, certainly, a far less enthralling force of interest to attract and to carry forward the reader than the *Iliad* or the *Divine Comedy*, it fully deserves, it can never lose, its immense reputation; for, like the *Iliad* and the *Divine Comedy*, nay, in some respects to a higher degree than either of them, it is in the grand style.

But the grandeur of Milton is one thing, and the grandeur of Homer is another. Homer's movement, I have said again and again, is a flowing, a rapid movement; Milton's, on the other hand, is a laboured, a self-retarding movement. In each case, the movement, the metrical cast, corresponds with the mode of evolution of the thought, with the syntactical cast, and is indeed determined by it. Milton charges himself so full with thought, imagination, knowledge, that his style will hardly contain them. He is too full-stored to show us in much detail one conception, one piece of knowledge; he just shows it to us in a pregnant allusive way, and then he presses on to another; and all this fullness, this pressure, this condensation, this self-constraint, enters into his movement, and makes it what it is,—noble, but difficult and austere. Homer is quite different; he says a thing, and says it to the end, and then begins another, while Milton is trying to press a thousand things into one. So that whereas, in reading Milton, you never lose the sense of laborious and condensed fullness, in reading Homer you never lose the sense of flowing and abounding ease. With Milton line runs into line, and all is straitly bound together: with Homer line runs off from line, and all hurries away onward. Homer begins, Μῆνιυ ἄειδε, Θεά,—at the second word announcing the proposed action; Milton begins:

> Of man's first disobedience, and the fruit
> Of that forbidden tree, whose mortal taste
> Brought death into the world, and all our woe,
> With loss of Eden, till one greater Man
> Restore us, and regain the blissful seat,
> Sing, heavenly muse.

So chary of a sentence is he, so resolute not to let it escape him till he has crowded into it all he can, that it is not till the thirty-ninth word in the sentence that he will give us the key to it, the word of action, the verb. Milton says:

> O for that warning voice, which he, who saw
> The Apocalypse, heard cry in heaven aloud.

He is not satisfied, unless he can tell us, all in one sentence, and without permitting himself to actually mention the name, that the man who heard the warning voice was the same man who saw the Apocalypse. Homer would have said, 'O for that warning voice, which *John* heard'—and if it had suited him to say that John also saw the Apocalypse, he would have given us that in another sentence. The effect of this allusive and compressed manner of Milton is, I need not say, often very powerful; and it is an effect which other great poets have often sought to obtain much in the same way: Dante is full of it, Horace is full of it; but wherever it exists, it is always an un-Homeric effect. 'The losses of the heavens', says Horace, 'fresh moons speedily repair; we, when we have gone down where the pious *Æneas*, where the rich Tullus and Ancus are,—*pulvis et umbra sumus*'.[26] He never actually says *where* we go to; he only indicates it by saying that it is that place where *Æneas*, Tullus, and Ancus are. But Homer, when he has to speak of going down to the grave, says, definitely, ἐς Ἠλύσιον πεδίον—ἀθάνατοι πέμψουσιν,[27]—'The immortals shall send thee *to the Elysian Plain*'; and it is not till after he has definitely said this, that he adds, that it is there that the abode of departed worthies is placed: ὅθι ξανθὸς 'Ραδάμανθυς—'Where the yellow-haired Rhadamanthus is.' Again; Horace, having to say that punishment sooner or later overtakes crime, says it thus:

> Raro antecedentem scelestum
>   Deseruit pede Poena claudo.[28]

The thought itself of these lines is familiar enough to Homer and Hesiod; but neither Homer nor Hesiod, in expressing it, could possibly have so complicated its expression as Horace complicates it, and purposely complicates it, by his use of the word *deseruit*. I say that this complicated evolution of the thought necessarily complicates the movement and rhythm of a poet; and that the Miltonic blank verse, of course the first model of blank verse which suggests itself to an English translator of Homer, bears the strongest marks of such complication, and is, therefore, entirely unfit to render Homer.

If blank verse is used in translating Homer, it must be a blank verse of which English poetry, naturally swayed much by Milton's treatment of this metre, offers at present hardly any examples. It must not be Cowper's blank verse, who has studied Milton's pregnant manner with such effect, that, having to say of Mr. Throckmorton that he spares his avenue, although it is the fashion with other people to cut down theirs, he says that Benevolus 'reprieves The obsolete prolixity of shade'. It must not be Mr. Tennyson's blank verse.

For all experience is an arch, wherethrough
Gleams that untravelled world, whose distance fades
For ever and for ever, as we gaze.

It is no blame to the thought of those lines, which belongs to another order of ideas than Homer's, but it is true, that Homer would certainly have said of them, 'It is to consider too curiously to consider so.' It is no blame to their rhythm, which belongs to another order of movement than Homer's, but it is true that these three lines by themselves take up nearly as much time as a whole book of the *Iliad*. No; the blank verse used in rendering Homer must be a blank verse of which perhaps the best specimens are to be found in some of the most rapid passages of Shakespeare's plays,—a blank verse which does not dovetail its lines into one another, and which habitually ends its lines with monosyllables. Such a blank verse might no doubt be very rapid in its movement, and might perfectly adapt itself to a thought plainly and directly evolved; and it would be interesting to see it well applied to Homer. But the translator who determines to use it, must not conceal from himself that in order to pour Homer into the mould of this metre, he will have entirely to break him up and melt him down, with the hope of then successfully composing him afresh; and this is a process which is full of risks. It may, no doubt, be the real Homer that issues new from it; it is not certain beforehand that it cannot be the real Homer, as it is certain that from the mould of Pope's couplet of Cowper's Miltonic verse it cannot be the real Homer that will issue; still, the chances of disappointment are great. The result of such an attempt to renovate the old poet may be an Æson; but it may also, and more probably will, be a Pelias.

When I say this, I point to the metre which seems to me to give the translator the best chance of preserving the general effect of Homer,—that third metre which I have not yet expressly named, the hexameter. I know all that is said against the use of hexameters in English poetry; but it comes only to this, that, among us, they have not yet been used on any considerable scale with success. *Solvitur ambulando*: this is an objection which can best be met by *producing* good English hexameters. And there is no reason in the nature of the English language why it should not adapt itself to hexameters as well as the German language does; nay, the English language, from its greater rapidity, is in itself better suited than the German for them. The hexameter, whether alone or with the pentameter, possesses a movement, an expression, which no metre hitherto in common use amongst us possesses, and which I am convinced English poetry, as our mental wants multiply, will not always be content to forego. Applied to Homer, this metre affords to the translator the immense support of keeping him more nearly than any other metre to Homer's movement; and, since a poet's movement makes so large a part of his general effect, and to reproduce this general effect is at once the translator's indispensable business and so difficult for him, it is a great thing to have this part of your model's general effect already given you in your metre, instead of having to get it entirely for yourself.

These are general considerations; but there are also one or two particular considerations which confirm me in the opinion that for translating Homer into English verse the hexameter should be used. The most successful attempt hitherto made at rendering Homer into English, the attempt in which Homer's general effect has been best retained, is an attempt made in the hexameter measure. It is a version of the famous lines in the third book of the *Iliad*, which end with that mention of Castor and Pollux from which Mr. Ruskin extracts the sentimental consolation already noticed by me. The author is the accomplished Provost of Eton, Dr. Hawtrey; and this performance of his must be my excuse for having taken the liberty to single him out for mention, as one of the natural judges of a translation of Homer, along with Professor Thompson and Professor Jowett, whose connection with Greek literature is official. The passage is short;[29] and Dr. Hawtrey's version of it is suffused with a pensive grace which is, perhaps, rather more Virgilian than Homeric; still it is the one version of any part of the *Iliad* which in some degree reproduces for me the original effect of Homer: it is the best, and it is in hexameters.

This is one of the particular considerations that incline me to prefer the hexameter, for translating Homer, to our established metres. There is another. Most of you, probably, have some knowledge of a poem by Mr. Clough, *The Bothie of Toper-na-fuosich*, a long-vacation pastoral, in hexameters. The general merits of that poem I am not going to discuss: it is a serio-comic poem, and, therefore, of essentially different nature from the *Iliad*. Still in two things it is, more than any other English poem which I can call to mind, like the *Iliad*: in the rapidity of its movement, and the plainness and directness of its style. The thought in this poem is often curious and subtle, and that is not Homeric, the diction is often grotesque, and that is not Homeric; still, by its rapidity of movement, and plain and direct manner of presenting the thought however curious in itself, this poem, which being as I say a serio-comic poem, has a right to be grotesque, is grotesque *truly*, not, like Mr. Newman's version of the *Iliad, falsely*. Mr. Clough's odd epithets, 'The grave man nicknamed Adam', 'The hairy Aldrich', and so on, grow vitally and appear naturally in their place; while Mr. Newman's 'dapper-greaved Achaians', and 'motley-helmed Hector', have all the air of being mechanically elaborated and artificially stuck in. Mr. Clough's hexameters are excessively, needlessly rough; still, owing to the native rapidity of this measure, and to the directness of style which so well allies itself with it, his composition produces a sense in the reader which Homer's composition also produces, and which Homer's translator ought to *re*produce,—the sense of having, within short limits of time, a large portion of human life presented to him, instead of a small portion.

Mr. Clough's hexameters are, as I have just said, too rough and irregular; and indeed a good model, on any considerable scale, of this metre, the English translator will nowhere find. He must not follow the model offered by Mr. Longfellow in his pleasing and popular poem of *Evangeline*; for the merit of the manner and movement of *Evangeline*, when they are at their best, is to be tenderly elegant; and their fault, when they are at their worst, is to be lumbering; but Homer's defect is not lumberingness, neither is tender elegance his excellence. The lumbering effect of most English hexameters is caused by their being much too dactylic;[30] the translator must learn to use spondees freely. Mr. Clough has done this, but he has not sufficiently observed another rule which the translator cannot follow too strictly; and that is, to have no lines which will not, as it is familiarly said, *read themselves*. This is of the last importance for rhythms with which the ear of the English public is not thoroughly acquainted. Lord Redesdale, in two papers on the subject of Greek and Roman metres, has some good remarks on the outrageous disregard of quantity in which English verse, trusting to its force of accent, is apt to indulge itself. The predominance of accent in our language is so great, that it would be pedantic not to avail one's self of it; and Lord Redesdale suggests rules which might easily be pushed too far. Still, it is undeniable that in English hexameters we generally force the quantity far too much; we rely on justification by accent with a security which is excessive. But not only do we abuse accent by shortening long syllables and lengthening short ones; we perpetually commit a far worse fault, by requiring the removal of the accent from its natural place to an unnatural one, in order to make our line scan. This is a fault, even when our metre is one which every English reader knows, and when he can see what we want and can correct the rhythm according to our wish; although it is a fault which a great master may sometimes commit knowingly to produce a desired effect, as Milton changes the natural accent on the word *Tirésias* in the line:

> And Tiresias and Phineus, prophets old;

and then it cease to be a fault, and becomes a beauty. But it is a real fault, when Chapman has:

> By him the golden-throned Queen slept, the Queen of
> Deities;

for in this line, to make it scan, you have to take away the accent from the word *Queen*, on which it naturally falls, and to place it on *throned*, which would naturally be unaccented; and yet, after all, you get no peculiar effect or beauty of cadence to reward you. It is a real fault, when Mr. Newman has:

> Infatuate! O that thou wert lord to some other army—

for here again the reader is required, not for any special advantage to himself, but simply to save Mr. Newman trouble, to place the accent on the insignificant word *wert*, where it has no business whatever. But it is still a greater fault, when Spenser has (to take a striking instance):

> Wot ye why his mother with a veil hath covered his face?

for a hexameter; because here not only is the reader causelessly required to make havoc with the natural accentuation of the line in order to get it to run as a hexameter; but also he, in nine cases out of ten, will be utterly at a loss how to perform the process required, and the line will remain a mere monster for him. I repeat, it is advisable to construct *all* verses so that by reading them naturally—that is, according to the sense and legitimate accent,—the reader gets the right rhythm; but, for English hexameters, that they be so constructed is indispensable.

If the hexameter best helps the translator to the Homeric rapidity, what style may best help him to the Homeric plainness and directness? It is the merit of a metre appropriate to your subject, that it in some degree suggests and carries with itself a style appropriate to the subject; the elaborate and self-retarding style, which comes so naturally when your metre is the Miltonic blank verse, does not come naturally with the hexameter; is, indeed, alien to it. On the other hand, the hexameter has a natural dignity which repels both the jaunty style and the jog-trot style, to both of which the ballad-measure so easily lends itself. These are great advantages; and, perhaps, it is nearly enough to say to the translator who uses the hexameter that he cannot too religiously follow, in style, the inspiration of his metre. He will find that a loose and idiomatic grammar—a grammar which follows the essential rather than the formal logic of the thought—allies itself excellently with the hexameter; and that, while this sort of grammar ensures plainness and naturalness, it by no means comes short in nobleness. It is difficult to pronounce, certainly, what is idiomatic in the ancient literature of a language which, though still spoken, has long since entirely adopted, as modern Greek has adopted, modern idioms. Still one may, I think, clearly perceive that Homer's grammatical style is idiomatic,—that it may even be called, not improperly, a loose grammatical style.[31] Examples, however, of what I mean by a loose grammatical style, will be of more use to the translator if taken from English poetry than if taken from

Homer. I call it, then, a loose and idiomatic grammar which Shakespeare uses in the last line of the following three:

> He's here in double trust:
> First, as I am his kinsman and his subject,
> *Strong both against the deed*;—

or in this:

> Wit, *whither wilt*?

What Shakespeare means is perfectly clear, clearer, probably, than if he had said it in a more formal and regular manner; but his grammar is loose and idiomatic, because he leaves out the subject of the verb 'wilt' in the second passage quoted, and because, in the first, a prodigious addition to the sentence has to be, as we used to say in our old Latin grammar days, *understood*, before the word 'both' can be properly parsed. So, again, Chapman's grammar is loose and idiomatic where he says,

> Even share hath he that keeps his tent, and *be to field* doth go,—

because he leaves out, in the second clause, the relative which in formal writing would be required. But Chapman here does not lose dignity by this idiomatic way of expressing himself, any more than Shakespeare loses it by neglecting to confer on 'both' the blessings of a regular government: neither loses dignity, but each gives that impression of a plain, direct, and natural mode of speaking, which Homer, too, gives, and which it is so important, as I say, that Homer's translator should succeed in giving. Cowper calls blank verse 'a style farther removed than rhyme from the vernacular idiom, both in the language itself and in the arrangement of it'; and just in proportion as blank verse is removed from the vernacular idiom, from that idiomatic style which is of all styles the plainest and most natural, blank verse is unsuited to render Homer.

Shakespeare is not only idiomatic in his grammar or style, he is also idiomatic in his words or diction; and here too, his example is valuable for the translator of Homer. The translator must not, indeed, allow himself all the liberty that Shakespeare allows himself; for Shakespeare sometimes uses expressions which pass perfectly well as he uses them, because Shakespeare thinks so fast and so powerfully, that in reading him we are borne over single words as by a mighty current; but, if our mind were less excited,—and who may rely on exciting our mind like Shakespeare?—they would check us. 'To grunt and sweat under a weary load';—that does perfectly well where it comes in Shakespeare; but if the translator of Homer, who will hardly have wound our minds up to the pitch at which these words of Hamlet find them, were to employ, when he has to speak of one of Homer's heroes under the load of calamity, this figure of 'grunting' and 'sweating', we should say, *He Newmanises*, and his diction would offend us. For he is to be noble; and no plea of wishing to be plain and natural can get him excused from being this: only, as he is to be also, like Homer, perfectly simple and free from artificiality, and as the use of idiomatic expressions undoubtedly gives this effect,[32] he should be as idiomatic as he can be without ceasing to be noble. Therefore, the idiomatic language of Shakespeare—such language as, 'prate of his *whereabout*'; '*jump* the life to come'; 'the damnation of his *taking-off*'; 'his *quietus make* with a bare *bodkin*'—should be carefully observed by the translator of Homer, although in every case he will have to decide for himself whether the use, by him, of Shakespeare's liberty, will or will not clash with his indispensable duty of nobleness. He will find one English book and one only, where, as in the *Iliad* itself, perfect plainness of speech is allied with perfect nobleness; and that book is the Bible. No one could see this more clearly than Pope saw it: 'This pure and noble simplicity', he says, 'is nowhere in such perfection as in the Scripture and Homer': yet even with Pope a woman is a 'fair', a father is a 'sire', and an old man a 'reverend sage', and so on through all the phrases of that pseudo-Augustan, and most unbiblical, vocabulary. The Bible, however, is undoubtedly the grand mine of diction for the translator of Homer; and, if he knows how to discriminate truly between what will suit him and what will not, the Bible may afford him also invaluable lessons of style.

I said that Homer, besides being plain in style and diction, was plain in the quality of his thought. It is possible that a thought may be expressed with idiomatic plainness, and yet not be in itself a plain thought. For example, in Mr. Clough's poem, already mentioned, the style and diction is almost always idiomatic and plain, but the thought itself is often of a quality which is not plain; it is *curious*. But the grand instance of the union of idiomatic expression with curious or difficult thought is in Shakespeare's poetry. Such, indeed, is the force and power of Shakespeare's idiomatic expression, that it gives an effect of clearness and vividness even to a thought which is imperfect and incoherent; for instance, when Hamlet says:

> To take arms against a sea of troubles,—

the figure there is undoubtedly most faulty, it by no means runs on four legs; but the thing is said so freely and idiomatically, that it passes. This, however, is not a point to which I now want to call your attention; I want you to remark, in Shakespeare and others, only that which we may directly apply to Homer. I say, then, that in Shakespeare the thought is often, while most idiomatically uttered, nay, while good and sound in itself, yet of a quality which is curious and difficult; and that this quality of thought is something entirely un-Homeric. For example, when Lady Macbeth says:

> Memory, the warder of the brain,
> Shall be a fume, and the receipt of reason
> A limbeck only,—

this figure is a perfectly sound and correct figure, no doubt; Mr. Knight even calls it a 'happy' figure; but it is a *difficult* figure: Homer would not have used it. Again, when Lady Macbeth says:

> When you durst do it, then you were a man;
> And, to be more than what you were, you would
> Be so much more the man,—

the thought in the two last of these lines is, when you seize it, a perfectly clear thought, and a fine thought; but it is a *curious* thought: Homer would not have used it. These are favourable instances of the union of plain style and words with a thought not plain in quality; but take stronger instances of this union,—let the thought be not only not plain in quality, but highly fanciful: and you have the Elizabethan conceits; you have, in spite of idiomatic style and idiomatic diction, everything which is most un-Homeric; you have such atrocities as this of Chapman:

> Fate shall fail to vent her gall
> Till mine vent thousands.

I say, the poets of a nation which has produced such a conceit as that, must purify themselves seven times in the fire before they can hope to render Homer. They must expel their nature with a fork, and keep crying to one another night and day: 'Homer not only moves rapidly, not only speaks idiomatically; he is, also, *free from fancifulness.*'

So essentially characteristic of Homer is his plainness and naturalness of thought, that to the preservation of this in his own version the translator must without scruple sacrifice, where it is necessary, verbal fidelity to his original, rather than run any risk of producing, by literalness, an odd and unnatural effect. The double epithets so constantly occurring in Homer must be dealt with according to this rule; these epithets come quite naturally in Homer's poetry; in English poetry they, in nine cases out of ten, come, when literally rendered, quite unnaturally. I will not now discuss why this is so, I assume it as an indisputable fact that it is so; that Homer's μερόπων ἀνθρώπων comes to the reader as something perfectly natural, while Mr. Newman's 'voice-dividing mortals' comes to him as something perfectly unnatural. Well then, as it is Homer's general effect which we are to reproduce, it is to be false to Homer to be so verbally faithful to him as that we lose this effect: and by the English translator Homer's double epithets must be, in many places, renounced altogether; in all places where they are rendered, rendered by equivalents which come naturally. Instead of rendering Θέτι τανύπεπλε by Mr. Newman's 'Thetis trailing-robed', which brings to one's mind long petticoats sweeping a dirty pavement, the translator must render the Greek by English words which come as naturally to us as Milton's words when he says, 'Let gorgeous Tragedy with sceptred pall come sweeping by.' Instead of rendering μώνυχας ἵππους by Chapman's 'one-hoofed steeds', or Mr. Newman's 'single-hoofed horses', he must speak of horses in a way which surprises us as little as Shakespeare surprises us when he says, 'Gallop apace, you fiery-footed steeds.' Instead of rendering μελιηδέα θυμόν by 'life as honey pleasant', he must characterise life with the simple pathos of Gray's 'warm precincts of the cheerful day'. Instead of converting ποῖόν σε ἔπος φύγεν ἕρκος ὀδόντων; into the portentous remonstrance, 'Betwixt the outwork of thy teeth what word hath slipt?' he must remonstrate in English as straightforward as this of St. Peter, 'Be it far from thee, Lord: this shall not be unto thee'; or as this of the disciples, 'What is this that he saith, a little while? we cannot tell what he saith.' Homer's Greek, in each of the places quoted, reads as naturally as any of those English passages: the expression no more calls away the attention from the sense in the Greek than in the English. But when, in order to render literally in English one of Homer's double epithets, a strange unfamiliar adjective is invented,—such as 'voice-dividing' for μέροψ,—an improper share of the reader's attention is necessarily diverted to this ancillary word, to this word which Homer never intended should receive so much notice; and a total effect quite different from Homer's is thus produced. Therefore, Mr. Newman, though he does not purposely import, like Chapman, conceits of his own into the *Iliad*, does actually import them; for the result of his singular diction is to raise ideas, and odd ideas, not raised by the corresponding diction in Homer; and Chapman himself does no more. Cowper says: 'I have cautiously avoided all terms of new invention, with an abundance of which persons of more ingenuity than judgment have not enriched our language but encumbered it'; and this criticism so exactly hits the diction of Mr. Newman that one is irresistibly led to imagine his present appearance in the flesh to be at least his second.

A translator cannot well have a Homeric rapidity, style, diction, and quality of thought, without at the same time having what is the result of these in Homer,—nobleness. Therefore, I do not attempt to lay down any rules for obtaining this effect of nobleness,—the effect, too, of all others the most impalpable, the most irreducible to rule, and which most depends on the individual personality of the artist. So I proceed at once to give you, in conclusion, one or two passages in which I have tried to follow those principles of Homeric translation which I have laid down. I give them, it must be remembered, not as specimens of perfect translation, but as specimens of an attempt to translate Homer on certain principles; specimens which may very aptly illustrate those principles by falling short as well as by succeeding.

I take first a passage of which I have already spoken, the comparison of the Trojan fires to the stars. The first part of that passage is, I have said, of splendid beauty; and to begin with a lame version of that would be the height of imprudence in me. It is the last and more level part with which I shall concern myself. I have already quoted Cowper's version of this part in order to show you how unlike his stiff and Miltonic manner of telling a plain story is to Homer's easy and rapid manner:

> So numerous seemed those fires the bank between
> Of Xanthus, blazing, and the fleet of Greece,
> In prospect all of Troy—

I need not continue to the end. I have also quoted Pope's version of it, to show you how unlike his ornate and artificial manner is to Homer's plain and natural manner:

> So many flames before proud Ilion blaze,
> And brighten glimmering Xanthus with their rays;
> The long reflections of the distant fires
> Gleam on the walls, and tremble on the spires,—

and much more of the same kind. I want to show you that it is possible, in a plain passage of this sort, to keep Homer's simplicity without being heavy and dull; and to keep his dignity without bringing in pomp and ornament. 'As numerous as are the stars on a clear night', says Homer:

> So shone forth, in front of Troy, by the bed of Xanthus,
> Between that and the ships, the Trojans' numerous fires.
> In the plain there were kindled a thousand fires: by
> each one
> There sat fifty men, in the ruddy light of the fire:
> By their chariots stood the steeds, and champed the
> white barley

While their masters sat by the fire, and waited for
Morning.

Here, in order to keep Homer's effect of perfect plainness and directness, I repeat the word 'fires' as he repeats πυρά, without scruple; although in a more elaborate and literary style of poetry this recurrence of the same word would be a fault to be avoided. I omit the epithet of Morning, and whereas Homer says that the steeds 'waited for Morning', I prefer to attribute this expectation of Morning to the master and not to the horse. Very likely in this particular, as in any other single particular, I may be wrong: what I wish you to remark is my endeavour after absolute plainness of speech, my care to avoid anything which may the least check or surprise the reader, whom Homer does not check or surprise. Homer's lively personal familiarity with war, and with the war-horse as his master's companion, is such that, as it seems to me, his attributing to the one the other's feelings comes to us quite naturally; but, from a poet without this familiarity, the attribution strikes as a little unnatural; and therefore, as everything the least unnatural is un-Homeric, I avoid it.

Again, in the address of Zeus to the horses of Achilles, Cowper has:

Jove saw their grief with pity, and his brows
Shaking, within himself thus, pensive, said.
'Ah hapless pair! wherefore by gift divine
Were ye to Peleus given, a mortal king,
Yourselves immortal and from age exempt?'

There is no want of dignity here, as in the versions of Chapman and Mr. Newman, which I have already quoted: but the whole effect is much too slow. Take Pope:

Nor Jove disdained to cast a pitying look
While thus relenting to the steeds he spoke.
'Unhappy coursers of immortal strain!
Exempt from age and deathless now in vain;
Did we your race on mortal man bestow
Only, alas! to share in mortal woe?'

Here there is no want either of dignity or rapidity, but all is too artificial. 'Nor Jove disdained', for instance, is a very artificial and literary way of rendering Homer's words, and so is, 'coursers of immortal strain'.

> Μυρομένω δ' ἄρα τώ γε ἰδὼν, ἐλέησε Κρονίων.—
>
> And with pity the son of Saturn saw them bewailing,
> And he shook his head, and thus addressed his own bosom:
>
> 'Ah, unhappy pair, to Peleus why did we give you,
> To a mortal? but ye are without old age and immortal.
> Was it that ye, with man, might have your thousands of sorrows?
> For than man, indeed, there breathes no wretcheder creature,
> Of all living things, that on earth are breathing and moving.'

Here I will observe that the use of 'own', in the second line, for the last syllable of a dactyl, and the use of 'To a', in the fourth, for a complete spondee, though they do not, I think, actually spoil the run of the hexameter, are yet undoubtedly instances of that over-reliance on accent, and too free disregard of quantity, which Lord Redesdale visits with just reprehension.[33]

I now take two longer passages in order to try my method more fully; but I still keep to passages which have already come under our notice. I quoted Chapman's version of some passages in the speech of Hector at his parting with Andromache. One astounding conceit will probably still be in your remembrance:

> When sacred Troy *shall shed her tow'rs for tears of overthrow*,—

as a translation of ὅτ' ἄν ποτ' ὀλώῃ Ἴλιος ἱρή. I will quote a few lines which may give you, also, the keynote to the Anglo-Augustan manner of rendering this passage and to the Miltonic manner of rendering it. What Mr. Newman's manner of rendering it would be, you can by this time sufficiently imagine for yourselves. Mr. Wright,—to quote for once from his meritorious version instead of Cowper's whose strong and weak points are those of Mr. Wright also,—Mr. Wright begins his version of this passage thus:

> All these thy anxious cares are also mine,
> Partner beloved; but how could I endure
> The scorn of Trojans and their long-robed wives,
> Should they behold their Hector shrink from war,
> And act the coward's part? Nor doth my soul
> Prompt the base thought.

Ex pede Herculem: you see just what the manner is. Mr. Sotheby, on the other hand (to take a disciple of Pope instead of Pope himself), begins thus:

> 'What moves thee, moves my mind,' brave Hector said,
> 'Yet Troy's upbraiding scorn I deeply dread,
> If, like a slave, where chiefs with chiefs engage,
> The warrior Hector fears the war to wage.
> Not thus my heart inclines.'

From that specimen, too, you can easily derive what, with such a manner, will become of the whole passage. But Homer has neither

> What moves thee, moves my mind,—

nor has he

> All these thy anxious cares are also mine.

> Ἦ καὶ ἐμοὶ τάδε πάντα μέλει, γύναι · ἀλλὰ μάλ' αἰνῶς,—

that is what Homer has, that is his style and movement, if one could but catch it. Andromache, as you know, has been entreating Hector to defend Troy from within the walls, instead of exposing his life, and, with his own life, the safety of all those dearest to him, by fighting in the open plain. Hector replies:

> Woman, I too take thought for this; but then I bethink me
> What the Trojan men and Trojan women might murmur,
> If like a coward I skulked behind, apart from the battle.
> Nor would my own heart let me; my heart, which has bid me be valiant
> Always, and always fighting among the first of the Trojans,

Busy for Priam's fame and my own, in spite of the future.
For that day will come, my soul is assured of its coming,
It will come, when sacred Troy shall go to destruction,
Troy, and warlike Priam too, and the people of Priam.
And yet not that grief, which then will be, of the Trojans,
Moves me so much—not Hecuba's grief, nor Priam my father's,
Nor my brethren's, many and brave, who then will be lying
In the bloody dust, beneath the feet of their foemen—
As thy grief, when, in tears, some brazen-coated Achaian
Shall transport thee away, and the day of thy freedom be ended.
Then, perhaps, thou shalt work at the loom of another, in Argos,
Or bear pails to the well of Messeïs, or Hypereia,
Sorely against thy will, by strong Necessity's order.
And some man may say, as he looks and sees thy tears falling:
See, the wife of Hector, that great pre-eminent captain
Of the horsemen of Troy, in the day they fought for their city.
So some man will say; and then thy grief will redouble
At thy want of a man like me, to save thee from bondage.
But let me be dead, and the earth be mounded above me,
Ere I hear thy cries, and thy captivity told of.

The main question, whether or no this version reproduces for him the movement and general effect of Homer better than other versions[34] of the same passage, I leave for the judgment of the scholar. But the particular points, in which the operation of my own rules is manifested, are as follows: In the second line I leave out the epithet of the Trojan women, ἑλκεσιπέπλους, altogether. In the sixth line I put in five words, 'in spite of the future', which are in the original by implication only, and are not there actually expressed. This I do, because Homer, as I have before said, is so remote from one who reads him in English, that the English translator must be even plainer, if possible, and more unambiguous than Homer himself; the connection of meaning must be even more distinctly marked in the translation than in the original. For in the Greek language itself there is something which brings one nearer to Homer, which gives one a clue to his thought, which makes a hint enough; but in the English language this sense of nearness, this clue, is gone; hints are insufficient, everything must be stated with full distinctness. In the ninth line Homer's epithet for Priam is ἐϋμμελίω,—'armed with good ashen spear', say the dictionaries; 'ashen-speared', translates Mr. Newman, following his own rule to 'retain every peculiarity of his original',—I say, on the other hand, that ἐϋμμελίω (Homer's epithet) has not the effect of a 'peculiarity' in the original, while 'ashen speared' has the effect of a 'peculiarity' in English; and 'warlike' is as marking an equivalent as I dare give for ἐϋμμελίω, for fear of disturbing the balance of expression in Homer's sentence. In the fourteenth line, again, I translate χαλκοχιτώνων by 'brazen-coated.' Mr. Newman, meaning to be perfectly literal, translates it by 'brazen-cloaked', an expression which comes to the reader oddly and unnaturally, while Homer's word comes to him quite naturally; but I venture to go as near to a literal rendering as 'brazen-coated', because a 'coat of brass' is familiar to us all from the Bible, and familiar, too, as distinctly specified in connection with the wearer. Finally, let me further illustrate from the twentieth line the value which I attach, in a question of diction, to the authority of the Bible. The word 'preeminent' occurs in that line; I was a little in doubt whether that was not too bookish an expression to be used in rendering Homer, as I can imagine Mr. Newman to have been a little in doubt whether his 'responsively accosted', for ἀμειβόμενος προσέφη, was not too bookish an expression. Let us both, I say, consult our Bibles: Mr. Newman will nowhere find it in his Bible that David, for instance, '*responsively accosted* Goliath'; but I do find in mine that 'the right hand of the Lord hath the *pre-eminence*'; and forthwith I use 'pre-eminent', without scruple. My Bibliolatry is perhaps excessive; and no doubt a true poetic feeling is the Homeric translator's best guide in the use of words; but where this feeling does not exist, or is at fault, I think he cannot do better than take for a mechanical guide Cruden's

Concordance. To be sure, here as elsewhere, the consulter must know how to consult,—must know how very slight a variation of word or circumstance makes the difference between an authority in his favour, and an authority which gives him no countenance at all; for instance, the 'Great simpleton!' (for μέγα νήπιος) of Mr. Newman, and the 'Thou fool!' of the Bible, are something alike; but 'Thou fool!' is very grand, and 'Great simpleton!' is an atrocity. So, too, Chapman's 'Poor wretched beasts' is pitched many degrees too low; but Shakespeare's 'Poor venomous fool, Be angry and despatch!' is in the grand style.

One more piece of translation and I have done. I will take the passage in which both Chapman and Mr. Newman have already so much excited our astonishment, the passage at the end of the nineteenth book of the *Iliad*, the dialogue between Achilles and his horse Xanthus, after the death of Patroclus. Achilles begins:

> 'Xanthus and Balius both, ye far-famed seed of Podarga!
> See that ye bring your master home to the host of the Argives
> In some other sort than your last, when the battle is ended;
> And not leave him behind, a corpse on the plain, like Patroclus.'
> Then, from beneath the yoke, the fleet horse Xanthus addressed him:
> Sudden he bowed his head, and all his mane, as he bowed it,
> Streamed to the ground by the yoke, escaping from under the collar:
> And he was given a voice by the white-armed Goddess Hera.
> 'Truly, yet this time will we save thee, mighty Achilles!
> But thy day of death is at hand; nor shall *we* be the reason—
> No, but the will of heaven, and Fate's invincible power.
> For by no slow pace or want of swiftness of ours
> Did the Trojans obtain to strip the arms from Patroclus;

But that prince among Gods, the son of the lovely-haired
Leto,
Slew him fighting in front of the fray, and glorified
Hector.
But, for us, we vie in speed with the breath of the West-
Wind,
Which, men say, is the fleetest of winds; 't is thou who
art fated
To lie low in death, by the hand of a God and a Mortal.'
Thus far he; and here his voice was stopped by the Furies.

Then, with a troubled heart, the swift Achilles addressed him:

'Why dost thou prophesy so my death to me,
Xanthus? It needs not.
I of myself know well, that here I am destined to perish,
Far from my father and mother dear: for all that,
I will not
Stay this hand from fight, till the Trojans are utterly
routed.'
So he spake, and drove with a cry his steeds into battle.

Here the only particular remark which I will make is, that in the fourth and eighth line the grammar is what I call a loose and idiomatic grammar. In writing a regular and literary style, one would in the fourth line have to repeat before 'leave' the words 'that ye' from the second line, and to insert the word 'do'; and in the eighth line one would not use such an expression as 'he was given a voice'. But I will make one general remark on the character of my own translations, as I have made so many on that of the translations of others. It is, that over the graver passages there is shed an air somewhat too strenuous and severe, by comparison with that lovely ease and sweetness which Homer, for all his noble and masculine way of thinking, never loses.

Here I stop. I have said so much, because I think that the task of translating Homer into English verse both will be re-attempted, and may be re-attempted successfully. There are great works composed of parts so disparate that one translator is not likely to have the requisite gifts for poetically rendering all of them. Such are the works of Shakespeare, and Goethe's *Faust*; and these *it is best to attempt to render in prose only.* People praise Tieck and Schlegel's version of Shakespeare: I, for my part, would sooner read Shakespeare in the French prose translation, and that is saying a great deal; but in the German poets' hands Shakespeare so often gets, especially where he is humorous, an air of what the French call *niaiserie*! and can anything be more un-Shakespearian than that? Again; Mr. Hayward's prose translation of the first part of *Faust*—so good that it makes one regret Mr. Hayward should have abandoned the line of translation for a kind of literature which is, to say the least, somewhat slight—is not likely to be surpassed by any translation in verse. But poems like the *Iliad*, which, in the main, are in one manner, may hope to find a poetical translator so gifted and so trained as to be able to learn that one manner, and to reproduce it. Only, the poet who would reproduce this must cultivate in himself a Greek virtue by no means common among the moderns in general, and the English in particular,—*Moderation.* For Homer has not only the English vigour, he has the Greek grace; and when one observes the boisterous, rollicking way in which his English admirers—even men of genius, like the late Professor Wilson—love to talk of Homer and his poetry, one cannot help feeling that there is no very deep community of nature between them and the object of their enthusiasm. 'It is very well, my good friends', I always imagine Homer saying to them, if he could hear them: 'you do me a great deal of honour, but somehow or other you praise me too like barbarians'. For Homer's grandeur is not the mixed and turbid grandeur of the great poets of the north, of the authors of *Othello* and *Faust*; it is a perfect, a lovely grandeur. Certainly his poetry has all the energy and power of the poetry of our ruder climates; but it has, besides, the pure lines of an Ionian horizon, the liquid clearness of an Ionian sky.

LAST WORDS

'Multi, qui persequuntur me, et tribulant me: testimoniis non declinavi.'

Buffon, the great French naturalist, imposed on himself the rule of steadily abstaining from all answer to attacks made upon him. 'Je n'ai jamais répondu à aucune critique', he said to one of his friends who, on the occasion of a certain criticism, was eager to take up arms in his behalf; 'je n'ai jamais répondu à aucune critique, et je garderai le même silence sur celle-ci'. On another occasion, when accused of plagiarism, and pressed by his friends to answer, 'Il vaut mieux', he said, 'laisser ces mauvaises gens dans l'incertitude'. Even when reply to an attack was made successfully, he disapproved of it, he regretted that those he esteemed should make it. Montesquieu, more sensitive to criticism than Buffon, had answered, and successfully answered, an attack made upon his great work, the *Esprit des Lois*, by the *Gazetier Janséniste*. This Jansenist Gazetteer was a periodical of those times,—a periodical such as other times, also, have occasionally seen,—very pretentious, very aggressive, and, when the point to be seized was at all a delicate one, very apt to miss it. 'Notwithstanding this example', said Buffon,—who, as well as Montesquieu, had been attacked by the Jansenist Gazetteer,—'notwithstanding this example, I think I may promise my course will be different. I shall not answer a single word'.

And to any one who has noticed the baneful effects of controversy, with all its train of personal rivalries and hatreds, on men of letters or men of science; to any one who has observed how it tends to impair, not only their dignity and repose, but their productive force, their genuine activity; how it always checks the free play of the spirit, and often ends by stopping it altogether; it can hardly seem doubtful, that the rule thus imposed on himself by Buffon was a wise one. His own career, indeed, admirably shows the wisdom of it. That career was as glorious as it was serene; but it owed to its serenity no small part of its glory. The regularity and completeness with which he gradually built up the great work which he had designed, the air of equable majesty which he shed over it, struck powerfully the imagination of his contemporaries, and surrounded Buffon's fame with a peculiar respect and dignity. 'He is', said Frederick the Great of him, 'the man who has best deserved the great celebrity which he has acquired'. And this regularity of production, this equableness of temper, he maintained by his resolute disdain of personal controversy.

Buffon's example seems to me worthy of all imitation, and in my humble way I mean always to follow it. I never have replied, I never will reply, to any literary assailant; in such encounters tempers are lost, the world laughs, and truth is not served. Least of all should I think of using this Chair as a place from which to carry on such a conflict. But when a learned and estimable man thinks he has reason to complain of language used by me in this Chair,—when he attributes to me intentions and feelings towards him which are far from my heart, I owe him some explanation,—and I am bound, too, to make the explanation as public as the words which gave offence. This is the reason why I revert once more to the subject of translating Homer. But being thus brought back to that subject, and not wishing to occupy you solely with an explanation which, after all, is Mr. Newman's affair and mine, not the public's, I shall take the opportunity,—not certainly to enter into any conflict with any one,—but to try to establish our old friend, the coming translator of Homer, yet a little firmer in the positions which I hope we have now secured for him; to protect him against the danger of relaxing, in the confusion of dispute, his attention to those matters which alone I consider important for him; to save him from losing sight, in the dust of the attacks delivered over it, of the real body of Patroclus. He will, probably, when he arrives, requite my solicitude very ill, and be in haste to disown his benefactor: but my interest in him is so sincere that I can disregard his probable ingratitude.

First, however, for the explanation. Mr. Newman has published a reply to the remarks which I made on his translation of the *Iliad*. He seems to think that the respect which at the outset of those remarks I professed for him must have been professed ironically; he says that I use 'forms of attack against him which he does not know how to characterize'; that I 'speak scornfully' of him, treat him with 'gratuitous insult, gratuitous rancour'; that I 'propagate slanders' against him, that I wish to 'damage him with my readers', to 'stimulate my readers to despise' him. He is entirely mistaken. I respect Mr. Newman sincerely; I respect him as one of the few learned men we have, one of the few who love learning for its own sake; this respect for him I had before I read his translation of the *Iliad*, I retained it while I was commenting on that translation, I have not lost it after reading his reply. Any vivacities of expression which may have given him pain I sincerely regret, and can only assure him that I used them without a thought of insult or rancour. When I took the liberty of creating the verb *to Newmanise*, my intentions were no more rancorous than if I had said to *Miltonise*; when I exclaimed, in my astonishment at his vocabulary, 'With whom can Mr. Newman have lived?' I meant merely to convey, in a familiar form of speech, the sense of bewilderment one has at finding a person to whom words one thought all the world knew seem strange, and words one thought entirely strange, intelligible. Yet this simple expression of my bewilderment Mr. Newman construes into an accusation that he is 'often guilty of keeping low company', and says that I shall 'never want a stone to throw at him'. And what is stranger still, one of his friends gravely tells me that Mr. Newman 'lived with the fellows of Balliol'. As if that made Mr. Newman's glossary less inexplicable to me! As if he could have got his glossary from the fellows of Balliol! As if I could believe that the members of that distinguished society—of whose discourse, not so many years afterwards, I myself was an unworthy hearer—were in Mr. Newman's time so far removed from the Attic purity of speech which we all of us admired, that when one of them called a calf a *bulkin*, the rest 'easily understood' him; or, when he wanted to say that a newspaper-article was 'proudly fine', it mattered little whether he said it was that or *bragly*! No; his having lived with the fellows of Balliol does not explain Mr. Newman's glossary to me. I will no longer ask 'with whom he can have lived', since that gives him offence; but I must still declare that where he got his test of rarity or intelligibility for words is a mystery to me.

That, however, does not prevent me from entertaining a very sincere respect for Mr. Newman, and since he doubts it, I am glad to reiterate my expression of it. But the truth of the matter is this: I unfeignedly admire Mr. Newman's ability and learning; but I think in his translation of Homer he has employed that ability and learning quite amiss. I think he has chosen quite the wrong field for turning his ability and learning to account. I think that in England, partly from the want of an Academy, partly from a national habit of intellect to which that want of an Academy is itself due, there exists too little of what I may call a public force of correct literary opinion, possessing within certain limits a clear sense of what is right and wrong, sound and unsound, and sharply recalling men of ability and learning from any flagrant misdirection of these their advantages. I think, even, that in our country a powerful misdirection of this kind is often more likely to subjugate and pervert opinion than to be checked and corrected by it.[35] Hence, a chaos of false tendencies, wasted efforts, impotent conclusions, works which ought never to have been undertaken. Any one who can introduce a little order into this chaos by establishing in any quarter a single sound rule of criticism, a single rule which clearly marks what is right as right, and what is wrong as wrong, does a good deed; and his deed is so much the better the greater force he counteracts of learning and ability applied to thicken the chaos. Of course no one can be sure that he has fixed any such rules; he can only do his best to fix them; but somewhere or other, in the literary opinion of Europe, if not in the literary opinion of one nation, in fifty years, if not in five, there is a final judgment on these matters, and the critic's work will at last stand or fall by its true merits.

Meanwhile, the charge of having in one instance misapplied his powers, of having once followed a false tendency, is no such grievous charge to bring against a man; it does not exclude a great respect for himself personally, or for his powers in the happier manifestation of them. False tendency is, I have said, an evil to which the artist or the man of letters in England is peculiarly prone; but everywhere in our time he is liable to it,— the greatest as well as the humblest. 'The first beginnings of my *Wilhelm Meister*', says Goethe, 'arose out of an obscure sense of the great truth that man will often attempt something for which nature has denied him the proper powers, will undertake and practise something in which he cannot become skilled. An inward feeling warns him to desist' (yes, but there are, unhappily, cases of absolute judicial blindness!), 'nevertheless he cannot get clear in himself about it, and is driven along a false road to a false goal, without knowing how it is with him. To this we may refer everything which goes by the name of false tendency, dilettantism, and so on. A great many men waste in this way the fairest portion of their lives, and fall at last into wonderful delusion.' Yet after all,—Goethe adds,—it sometimes happens that even on this false road a man finds, not indeed that which he sought, but something which is good and useful for him; 'like Saul, the son of Kish, who went forth to look for his father's asses, and found a kingdom'. And thus false tendency as well as true, vain effort as well as fruitful, go together to produce that great movement of life, to present that immense and magic spectacle of human affairs, which from boyhood to old age fascinates the gaze of every man of imagination, and which would be his terror, if it were not at the same time his delight.

So Mr. Newman may see how widespread a danger it is, to which he has, as I think, in setting himself to translate Homer, fallen a prey. He may be well satisfied if he can escape from it by paying it the tribute of a single work only. He may judge how unlikely it is that I should 'despise' him for once falling a prey to it. I know far too well how exposed to it we all are; how exposed to it I myself am. At this very moment, for example, I am fresh from reading Mr. Newman's Reply to my Lectures, a reply full of that erudition in which (as I am so often and so good-naturedly reminded, but indeed I know it without being reminded) Mr. Newman is immeasurably my superior. Well, the demon that pushes us all to our ruin is even now prompting me to follow Mr. Newman into a discussion about the digamma, and I know not what providence holds me back. And some day, I have no doubt, I shall lecture on the language of the Berbers, and give him his entire revenge.

But Mr. Newman does not confine himself to complaints on his own behalf, he complains on Homer's behalf too. He says that my 'statements about Greek literature are against the most notorious and elementary fact'; that I 'do a public wrong to literature by publishing them'; and that the Professors to whom

I appealed in my three Lectures, 'would only lose credit if they sanctioned the use I make of their names'. He does these eminent men the kindness of adding, however, that 'whether they are pleased with this parading of their names in behalf of paradoxical error, he may well doubt,' and that 'until they endorse it themselves, he shall treat my process as a piece of forgery'. He proceeds to discuss my statements at great length, and with an erudition and ingenuity which nobody can admire more than I do. And he ends by saying that my ignorance is great.

Alas! that is very true. Much as Mr. Newman was mistaken when he talked of my rancour, he is entirely right when he talks of my ignorance. And yet, perverse as it seems to say so, I sometimes find myself wishing, when dealing with these matters of poetical criticism, that my ignorance were even greater than it is. To handle these matters properly there is needed a poise so perfect that the least overweight in any direction tends to destroy the balance. Temper destroys it, a crotchet destroys it, even erudition may destroy it. To press to the sense of the thing itself with which one is dealing, not to go off on some collateral issue about the thing, is the hardest matter in the world. The 'thing itself' with which one is here dealing,—the critical perception of poetic truth,—is of all things the most volatile, elusive, and evanescent; by even pressing too impetuously after it, one runs the risk of losing it. The critic of poetry should have the finest tact, the nicest moderation, the most free, flexible, and elastic spirit imaginable; he should be indeed the 'ondoyant et divers', the *undulating and diverse* being of Montaigne. The less he can deal with his object simply and freely, the more things he has to take into account in dealing with it,—the more, in short, he has to encumber himself,—so much the greater force of spirit he needs to retain his elasticity. But one cannot exactly have this greater force by wishing for it; so, for the force of spirit one has, the load put upon it is often heavier than it will well bear. The late Duke of Wellington said of a certain peer that 'it was a great pity his education had been so far too much for his abilities'. In like manner, one often sees erudition out of all proportion to its owner's critical faculty. Little as I know, therefore, I am always apprehensive, in dealing with poetry, lest even that little should prove 'too much for my abilities'.

With this consciousness of my own lack of learning,—nay, with this sort of acquiescence in it, with this belief that for the labourer in the field of poetical criticism learning has its disadvantages,—I am not likely to dispute with Mr. Newman about matters of erudition. All that he says on these matters in his Reply, I read with great interest; in general I agree with him; but only, I am sorry to say, up to a certain point. Like all learned men, accustomed to desire definite rules, he draws his conclusions too absolutely; he wants to include too much under his rules; he does not quite perceive that in poetical criticism the shade, the fine distinction, is everything; and that, when he has once missed this, in all he says he is in truth but beating the air. For instance: because I think Homer noble, he imagines I must think him elegant; and in fact he says in plain words that I do think him so,—that to me Homer seems 'pervadingly elegant'. But he does not. Virgil is elegant,—'pervadingly elegant',—even in passages of the highest emotion:

> O, ubi campi,
> Spercheosque, et virginibus bacchata Lacænis
> Taygeta![36]

Even there Virgil, though of a divine elegance, is still elegant: but Homer is not elegant; the word is quite a wrong one to apply to him, and Mr. Newman is quite right in blaming any one he finds so applying it. Again; arguing against my assertion that Homer is not quaint, he says: 'It is quaint to call waves *wet*, milk *white*, blood *dusky*, horses *single-hoofed*, words *winged*, Vulcan *Lobfoot* (Κυλλοποδίων), a spear *longshadowy*', and so on. I find I know not how many distinctions to draw here. I do not think it quaint to call waves *wet*, or milk *white*, or words *winged*; but I do think it quaint to call horses *single-hoofed*, or Vulcan *Lobfoot*, or a spear *longshadowy*. As to calling blood *dusky*, I do not feel quite sure; I will tell Mr. Newman my opinion when I see the passage in which he calls it so. But then, again, because it is quaint to call Vulcan *Lobfoot*, I cannot admit that it was quaint to call him Κυλλοποδίων; nor that, because it is quaint to call a spear *longshadowy*, it was quaint to call it δολιχόσκιον. Here Mr. Newman's erudition misleads him: he knows the literal value of the Greek so well, that he thinks his literal rendering identical with the Greek, and that the Greek must stand or fall along with his rendering. But the real question is, not whether he has given us, so to speak, full change for the Greek, but *how* he gives us our change: we want it in gold, and he gives it us in copper. Again: 'It is quaint', says Mr. Newman, 'to address a young friends as "O Pippin!"—it is quaint to compare Ajax to an ass whom boys are belabouring'. Here, too, Mr. Newman goes much too fast, and his category of quaintness is too comprehensive. To address a young friend as 'O Pippin!' is, I cordially agree with him, very quaint; although I do not think it was quaint in Sarpedon to address Glaucus as ὦ πέπον: but in comparing, whether in Greek or in English, Ajax to an ass whom boys are belabouring, I do not see that there is of necessity anything quaint at all. Again; because I said that *eld, lief, in sooth*, and other words, are, as Mr. Newman uses them in certain places, bad words, he imagines that I must mean to stamp these words with an absolute reprobation; and because I said that 'my Bibliolatry is excessive', he imagines that I brand all words as ignoble which are not in the Bible. Nothing of the kind: there are no such absolute rules to be laid down in these matters. The Bible vocabulary is to be used as an assistance, not as an authority. Of the words which, placed where Mr. Newman places them, I have called bad words, every one may be excellent in some other place. Take *eld*, for instance: when Shakespeare, reproaching man with the dependence in which his youth is passed, says:

> all thy blessed youth
> Becomes as aged, and doth beg the alms
> Of palsied *eld*,....

it seems to me that *eld* comes in excellently there, in a passage of curious meditation; but when Mr. Newman renders ἀγήρω τ' ἀθανάτω τε by 'from *Eld* and Death exempted', it seems to me he infuses a tinge of quaintness into the transparent simplicity of Homer's expression, and so I call *eld* a bad word in that place.

Once more. Mr. Newman lays it down as a general rule that 'many of Homer's energetic descriptions are expressed in coarse physical words'. He goes on: 'I give one illustration,—Τρῶες προὔτυψαν ἀολλέες. Cowper, misled by the *ignis fatuus* of "stateliness", renders it absurdly:

> The powers of Ilium gave the first assault
> Embattled close;

but it is, strictly, "The Trojans *knocked forward* (or, thumped, butted forward) *in close pack.*" The verb is too coarse for later polished prose, and even the adjective is very strong (*packed together*). I believe, that "forward in pack the Trojans pitched", would not be really unfaithful to the Homeric colour; and I maintain, that "forward in mass the Trojans pitched," would be an irreprovable rendering. He actually gives us all that as if it were a piece of scientific deduction; and as if, at the end, he had arrived at an incontrovertible conclusion. But, in truth, one cannot settle these matters quite in this way. Mr. Newman's general rule may be true or false (I dislike to meddle with general rules), but every part in what follows must stand or fall by itself, and its soundness or unsoundness has nothing at all to do with the truth or falsehood of Mr. Newman's general rule. He first gives, as a strict rendering of the Greek, 'The Trojans knocked forward (or, thumped, butted forward), in close pack.' I need not say that, as a 'strict rendering of the Greek', this is good,—all Mr. Newman's 'strict renderings of the Greek' are sure to be, as such, good; but 'in close pack', for ἀολλέες, seems to me to be what Mr. Newman's renderings are not always,—an excellent *poetical rendering* of the Greek; a thousand times better, certainly, than Cowper's 'embattled close'. Well, but Mr. Newman goes on: 'I believe, that "forward in pack the Trojans pitched", would not be really unfaithful to the Homeric colour.' Here, I say, the Homeric colour is half washed out of Mr. Newman's happy rendering of ἀολλέες; while in 'pitched' for προὔτυψαν, the literal fidelity of the first rendering is gone, while certainly no Homeric colour has come in its place. Finally, Mr. Newman concludes: 'I maintain that "forward in mass the Trojans pitched", would be an irreprovable rendering.' Here, in what Mr. Newman fancies his final moment of triumph,

Homeric colour and literal fidelity have alike abandoned him altogether; the last stage of his translation is much worse than the second, and immeasurably worse than the first.

All this to show that a looser, easier method than Mr. Newman's must be taken, if we are to arrive at any good result in these questions. I now go on to follow Mr. Newman a little further, not at all as wishing to dispute with him, but as seeking (and this is the true fruit we may gather from criticisms upon us) to gain hints from him for the establishment of some useful truth about our subject, even when I think him wrong. I still retain, I confess, my conviction that Homer's characteristic qualities are rapidity of movement, plainness of words and style, simplicity and directness of ideas, and, above all, nobleness, the grand manner. Whenever Mr. Newman drops a word, awakens a train of thought, which leads me to see any of these characteristics more clearly, I am grateful to him; and one or two suggestions of this kind which he affords, are all that now,—having expressed my sorrow that he should have misconceived my feelings towards him, and pointed out what I think the vice of his method of criticism,—I have to notice in his Reply.

Such a suggestion I find in Mr. Newman's remarks on my assertion that the translator of Homer must not adopt a quaint and antiquated style in rendering him, because the impression which Homer makes upon the living scholar is not that of a poet quaint and antiquated, but that of a poet perfectly simple, perfectly intelligible. I added that we cannot, I confess, really know how Homer seemed to Sophocles, but that it is impossible to me to believe that he seemed to him quaint and antiquated. Mr. Newman asserts, on the other hand, that I am absurdly wrong here; that Homer seemed 'out and out' quaint and antiquated to the Athenians; that 'every sentence of him was more or less antiquated to Sophocles, who could no more help feeling at every instant the foreign and antiquated character of the poetry than an Englishman can help feeling the same in reading Burns's poems'. And not only does Mr. Newman say this, but he has managed thoroughly to convince some of his readers of it. 'Homer's Greek', says one of them, 'certainly seemed antiquated to the historical times of Greece. Mr. Newman, taking a far broader historical and philological view than Mr. Arnold, stoutly maintains that it did seem so.' And another says: 'Doubtless Homer's dialect and diction were as hard and obscure to a later Attic Greek as Chaucer to an Englishman of our day.'

Mr. Newman goes on to say, that not only was Homer antiquated relatively to Pericles, but he is antiquated to the living scholar; and, indeed, is in himself 'absolutely antique, being the poet of a barbarian age'. He tells us of his 'inexhaustible quaintnesses', of his 'very eccentric diction'; and he infers, of course, that he is perfectly right in rendering him in a quaint and antiquated style.

Now this question,—whether or no Homer seemed quaint and antiquated to Sophocles,—I call a delightful question to raise. It is not a barren verbal dispute; it is a question 'drenched in matter', to use an expression of Bacon; a question full of flesh and blood, and of which the scrutiny, though I still think we cannot settle it absolutely, may yet give us a directly useful result. To scrutinize it may lead us to see more clearly what sort of a style a modern translator of Homer ought to adopt.

Homer's verses were some of the first words which a young Athenian heard. He heard them from his mother or his nurse before he went to school; and at school, when he went there, he was constantly occupied with them. So much did he hear of them that Socrates proposes, in the interests of morality, to have selections from Homer made, and placed in the hands of mothers and nurses, in his model republic; in order that, of an author with whom they were sure to be so perpetually conversant, the young might learn only those parts which might do them good. His language was as familiar to Sophocles, we may be quite sure, as the language of the Bible is to us.

Nay, more. Homer's language was not, of course, in the time of Sophocles, the spoken or written language of ordinary life, any more than the language of the Bible, any more than the language of poetry, is with us; but for one great species of composition—epic poetry—it was still the current language; it was the language in which every one who made that sort of poetry composed. Every one at Athens who dabbled in epic poetry, not only understood Homer's language,—he possessed it. He possessed it as every one who dabbles in poetry with us, possesses what may be called the poetical vocabulary, as distinguished from the vocabulary of common speech and of modern prose: I mean, such expressions as *perchance* for *perhaps, spake* for *spoke, aye* for *ever, don* for *put on, charméd for charm'd* and thousands of others.

I might go to Burns and Chaucer, and, taking words and passages from them, ask if they afforded any parallel to a language so familiar and so possessed. But this I will not do, for Mr. Newman himself supplies me with what he thinks a fair parallel, in its effect upon us, to the language of Homer in its effect upon Sophocles. He says that such words as *mon, londis, libbard, withouten, muchel*, give us a tolerable but incomplete notion of this parallel; and he finally exhibits the parallel in all its clearness, by this poetical specimen:

Dat mon, quhich hauldeth Kyngis-af
  Londis yn féo, niver
(I tell'e) feereth aught; sith hee
  Doth hauld hys londis yver.

Now, does Mr. Newman really think that Sophocles could, as he says, 'no more help feeling at every instant the foreign and antiquated character of Homer, than an Englishman can help feeling the same in hearing' these lines? Is he quite sure of it? He says he is; he will not allow of any doubt or hesitation in the matter. I had confessed we could not really know how Homer seemed to Sophocles;—'Let Mr. Arnold confess for himself', cries Mr. Newman, 'and not for me, who know perfectly well.' And this is what he knows!

Mr. Newman says, however, that I 'play fallaciously on the words familiar and unfamiliar'; that 'Homer's words may have been familiar to the Athenians (*i.e.* often heard) even when they were either not understood by them or else, being understood, were yet felt and known to be utterly foreign. Let my renderings', he continues, 'be heard, as Pope or even Cowper has been heard, and no one will be "surprised"'.

But the whole question is here. The translator must not assume that to have taken place which has not taken place, although, perhaps, he may wish it to have taken place,—namely, that his diction is become an established possession of the minds of men, and therefore is, in its proper place, familiar to them, will not 'surprise' them. If Homer's language was familiar,—that is, often heard,—then to this language words like *londis* and *libbard*, which are not familiar, offer, for the translator's purpose, no parallel. For some purpose of the philologer they may offer a parallel to it; for the translator's purpose they offer none. The question is not, whether a diction is antiquated for current speech, but whether it is antiquated for that particular purpose for which it is employed. A diction that is antiquated for common speech and common prose, may very well not be antiquated for poetry or certain special kinds of prose. 'Peradventure there shall be ten found there', is not antiquated for Biblical prose, though for conversation or for a newspaper it is antiquated. 'The trumpet spake not to the arméd throng', is not antiquated for poetry, although we should not write in a letter, 'he *spake* to me', or say, 'the British soldier is *arméd* with the Enfield rifle'. But when language is antiquated for that particular purpose for which it is employed,—as numbers of Chaucer's words, for instance, are antiquated for poetry,—such language is a bad representative of language which, like Homer's, was never antiquated for that particular purpose for which it was employed. I imagine that Πηληϊάδεω for Πηλείδου, in Homer, no more sounded antiquated to Sophocles, than *arméd* and *arm'd*, in Milton, sounds antiquated to us; but Mr. Newman's *withouten* and *muchel* do sound to us antiquated, even for poetry, and therefore they do not correspond in their effect upon us with Homer's words in their effect upon Sophocles. When Chaucer, who used such words, is to pass current amongst us, to be familiar to us, as Homer was familiar to the Athenians, he has to be modernized, as Wordsworth and others set to work to modernize him; but an Athenian no more needed to have Homer modernized, than we need to have the Bible modernized, or Wordsworth himself.

Therefore, when Mr. Newman's words *bragly*, *bulkin*, and the rest, are an established possession of our minds, as Homer's words were an established possession of an Athenian's mind, he may use them; but not till then. Chaucer's words, the words of Burns, great poets as these were, are yet not thus an established possession of an Englishman's mind, and therefore they must not be used in rendering Homer into English.

Mr. Newman has been misled just by doing that which his admirer praises him for doing, by taking a 'far broader historical and philological view than' mine. Precisely because he has done this, and has applied the 'philological view' where it was not applicable, but where the 'poetical view' alone was rightly applicable, he has fallen into error.

It is the same with him in his remarks on the difficulty and obscurity of Homer. Homer, I say, is perfectly plain in speech, simple, and intelligible. And I infer from this that his translator, too, ought to be perfectly plain in speech, simple, and intelligible; ought not to say, for instance, in rendering

Οὔτε κε σὲ στέλλς μι μάχην ἐς κυδιάνειραν...

'Nor liefly thee would I advance to man-ennobling battle',—and things of that kind. Mr. Newman hands me a list of some twenty hard words, invokes Buttmann, Mr. Malden, and M. Benfey, and asks me if I think myself wiser than all the world of Greek scholars, and if I am ready to supply the deficiencies of Liddell and Scott's *Lexicon*! But here, again, Mr. Newman errs by not perceiving that the question is one not of scholarship, but of a poetical translation of Homer. This, I say, should be perfectly simple and intelligible. He replies by telling me that ἀδινὸς, εἰλίποδες, and σιγαλόεις are hard words. Well, but what does he infer from that? That the poetical translator, in his rendering of them, is to give us a sense of the difficulties of the scholar, and so is to make his translation obscure? If he does not mean that, how, by bringing forward these hard words, does he touch the question whether an English version of Homer should be plain or not plain? If Homer's poetry, as poetry, is in its general effect on the poetical reader perfectly simple and intelligible, the uncertainty of the scholar about the true meaning of certain words can never change this general effect. Rather will the poetry of Homer make us forget his philology, than his philology make us forget his poetry. It may even be affirmed that every one who reads Homer perpetually for the sake of enjoying his poetry (and no one who does not so read him will ever translate him well), comes at last to form a perfectly clear sense in his own mind for every important word in Homer, such as ἀδινὸς, or ἠλίβατος, whatever the scholar's doubts about the word may be. And this sense is present to his mind with perfect clearness and fullness, whenever the word recurs, although as a scholar he may know that he cannot be sure whether this sense is the right one or not. But poetically he feels clearly about the word, although philologically he may not. The scholar in him may hesitate, like the father in Sheridan's play; but the reader of poetry in him is, like the governor, fixed. The same thing happens to us with our own language. How many words occur in the Bible, for instance, to which thousands of hearers do not feel sure they attach the precise real meaning; but they make out *a* meaning for them out of what materials they have at hand; and the words, heard over and over again, come to convey this meaning with a certainty which poetically is adequate, though not philologically. How many have attached a clear and poetically adequate sense to 'the *beam*' and 'the *mote*', though not precisely the right one! How clearly, again, have readers got a sense from Milton's words, 'grate on their *scrannel* pipes', who yet might have been puzzled to write a commentary on the word *scrannel* for the dictionary! So we get a clear sense from ἀδινὸς as an epithet for grief, after often meeting with it and finding out all we can about it, even though that all be philologically insufficient; so we get a clear sense from εἰλίποδες as an epithet for cows. And this his clear poetical sense about the words, not his philological uncertainties about them, is what the translator has to convey. Words like *bragly* and *bulkin* offer no parallel to these words; because the reader, from his entire want of familiarity with the words *bragly* and *bulkin*, has no clear sense of them poetically.

Perplexed by his knowledge of the philological aspect of Homer's language, encumbered by his own learning,

Mr. Newman, I say, misses the poetical aspect, misses that with which alone we are here concerned. 'Homer *is* odd', he persists, fixing his eyes on his own philological analysis of μῶνυξ, and μέροψ, and Κυλλοποδίων, and not on these words in their synthetic character;—just as Professor Max Muller, going a little farther back, and fixing his attention on the elementary value of the word θυγάτηρ, might say Homer was 'odd' for using that word;—'if the whole Greek nation, by long familiarity, had become inobservant of Homer's oddities,'—of the oddities of this 'noble barbarian', as Mr. Newman elsewhere calls him, this 'noble barbarian' with the 'lively eye of the savage',—'that would be no fault of mine. That would not justify Mr. Arnold's blame of me for rendering the words correctly.' *Correctly*,—ah, but what *is* correctness in this case? This correctness of his is the very rock on which Mr. Newman has split. He is so correct that at last he finds peculiarity everywhere. The true knowledge of Homer becomes at last, in his eyes, a knowledge of Homer's 'peculiarities, pleasant and unpleasant'. Learned men know these 'peculiarities', and Homer is to be translated because the unlearned are impatient to know them too. 'That', he exclaims, 'is just why people want to read an English Homer,—*to know all his oddities, just as learned men do*'. Here I am obliged to shake my head, and to declare that, in spite of all my respect for Mr. Newman, I cannot go these lengths with him. He talks of my 'monomaniac fancy that there is nothing quaint or antique in Homer'. Terrible learning,—I cannot help in my turn exclaiming,—terrible learning, which discovers so much!

Here, then, I take my leave of Mr. Newman, retaining my opinion that his version of Homer is spoiled by his making Homer odd and ignoble; but having, I hope, sufficient love for literature to be able to canvass works without thinking of persons, and to hold this or that production cheap, while retaining a sincere respect, on other grounds, for its author.

In fulfilment of my promise to take this opportunity for giving the translator of Homer a little further advice, I proceed to notice one or two other criticisms which I find, in like manner, *suggestive*; which give us an opportunity, that is, of seeing more clearly, as we look into them, the true principles on which translation of Homer should rest. This is all I seek in criticisms; and, perhaps (as I have already said) it is only as one seeks a positive result of this kind, that one can get any fruit from them. Seeking a negative result from them,—personal altercation and wrangling,—one gets no fruit; seeking a positive result,—the elucidation and establishment of one's ideas,—one may get much. Even bad criticisms may thus be made suggestive and fruitful. I declared, in a former lecture on this subject, my conviction that criticism is not the strong point of our national literature.

Well, even the bad criticisms on our present topic which I meet with, serve to illustrate this conviction for me. And thus one is enabled, even in reading remarks which for Homeric criticism, for their immediate subject, have no value,—which are far too personal in spirit, far too immoderate in temper, and far too heavy-handed in style, for the delicate matter they have to treat,—still to gain light and confirmation for a serious idea, and to follow the Baconian injunction, *semper aliquid addiscere*, always to be adding to one's stock of observation and knowledge. Yes, even when we have to do with writers who,—to quote the words of an exquisite critic, the master of us all in criticism, M. Sainte-Beuve,—remind us, when they handle such subjects as our present, of 'Romans of the fourth or fifth century, coming to hold forth, all at random, in African style, on papers found in the desk of Augustus, Mæcenas, or Pollio,'—even then we may instruct ourselves if we regard ideas and not persons; even then we may enable ourselves to say, with the same critic describing the effect made upon him by D'Argenson's *Memoirs:* 'My taste is revolted, but I learn something;—*Je' suis choqué mais je suis instruit.*'

But let us pass to criticisms which are suggestive directly and not thus indirectly only,—criticisms by examining which we may be brought nearer to what immediately interests us,—the right way of translating Homer.

I said that Homer did not rise and sink with his subject, was never to be called prosaic and low. This gives surprise to many persons, who object that parts of the *Iliad* are certainly pitched lower than others, and who remind me of a number of absolutely level passages in Homer. But I never denied that a *subject* must rise and sink, that it must have its elevated and its level regions; all I deny is, that a poet can be said to rise and sink when all that he, as a poet, can do, is perfectly well done; when he is perfectly sound and good, that is, perfect as a poet, in the level regions of his subject as well as in its elevated regions. Indeed, what distinguishes the greatest masters of poetry from all others is, that they are perfectly sound and poetical in these level regions of their subject,—in these regions which are the great difficulty of all poets but the very greatest, which they never quite know what to do with. A poet may sink in these regions by being falsely grand as well as by being low; he sinks, in short, whenever he does not treat his matter, whatever it is, in a perfectly good and poetic way. But, so long as he treats it in this way, he cannot be said to *sink*, whatever his matter may do. A passage of the simplest narrative is quoted to me from Homer:

> ὤτρυνεν δὲ ἕκαστον ἐποιχόμενος ἐπέεσσιν,
> Μέσθλην τε, Γλαῦκόν τε, Μέδοντά τε, Θερσίλοχόν τε...[37]

and I am asked, whether Homer does not sink *there*; whether he '*can* have intended such lines as those for poetry'? My answer is: Those lines are very good poetry indeed, poetry of the best class, *in that place*. But when Wordsworth, having to narrate a very plain matter, tries *not* to sink in narrating it, tries, in short, to be what is falsely called poetical, he does sink, although he sinks by being pompous, not by being low.

> Onward we drove beneath the Castle; caught,
> While crossing Magdalene Bridge, a glimpse of Cam,
> And at the Hoop alighted, famous inn.

That last line shows excellently how a poet may sink with his subject by resolving not to sink with it. A page or two farther on, the subject rises to grandeur, and then Wordsworth is nobly worthy of it:

> The antechapel, where the statue stood
> Of Newton with his prism and silent face,

The marble index of a mind for ever
Voyaging through strange seas of thought, alone.

But the supreme poet is he who is thoroughly sound and poetical, alike when his subject is grand, and when it is plain: with him the subject may sink, but never the poet. But a Dutch painter does not rise and sink with his subject,—Defoe, in *Moll Flanders*, does not rise and sink with his subject,—in so far as an artist cannot be said to sink who is sound in his treatment of his subject, however plain it is: yet Defoe, yet a Dutch painter, may in one sense be said to sink with their subject, because though sound in their treatment of it, they are not *poetical*,—poetical in the true, not the false sense of the word; because, in fact, they are not in the grand style. Homer can in no sense be said to sink with his subject, because his soundness has something more than literal naturalness about it; because his soundness is the soundness of Homer, of a great epic poet; because, in fact, he in the grand style. So he sheds over the simplest matter he is touches the charm of his grand manner; he makes everything noble. Nothing has raised more questioning among my critics than these words,—*noble, the grand style.* People complain that I do not define these words sufficiently, that I do not tell them enough about them. 'The grand style,—but what *is* the grand style?'—they cry; some with an inclination to believe in it, but puzzled; others mockingly and with incredulity. Alas! the grand style is the last matter in the world for verbal definition to deal with adequately. One may say of it as is said of faith: 'One must feel it in order to know what it is.' But, as of faith, so too one may say of nobleness, of the grand style: 'Woe to those who know it not!' Yet this expression, though indefinable, has a charm; one is the better for considering it; *bonum est, nos hic esse*; nay, one loves to try to explain it, though one knows that one must speak imperfectly. For those, then, who ask the question,—What is the grand style?—with sincerity, I will try to make some answer, inadequate as it must be. For those who ask it mockingly I have no answer, except to repeat to them, with compassionate sorrow, the Gospel words: *Moriemini in peccatis vestris*,—Ye shall die in your sins.

But let me, at any rate, have the pleasure of again giving, before I begin to try and define the grand style, a specimen of what it *is*.

> Standing on earth, not rapt above the pole,
> More safe I sing with mortal voice, unchanged
> To hoarse or mute, though fall'n on evil days,
> On evil days though fall'n, and evil tongues....

There is the grand style in perfection; and any one who has a sense for it, will feel it a thousand times better from repeating those lines than from hearing anything I can say about it.

Let us try, however, what *can* be said, controlling what we say by examples. I think it will be found that the grand style arises in poetry, *when a noble nature, poetically gifted, treats with simplicity or with severity a serious subject.* I think this definition will be found to cover all instances of the grand style in poetry which present themselves. I think it will be found to exclude all poetry which is not in the grand style. And I think it contains no terms which are obscure, which themselves need defining. Even those who do not understand what is meant by calling poetry noble, will understand, I imagine, what is meant by speaking of a noble nature in a man. But the noble or powerful nature—the *bedeutendes Individuum* of Goethe—is not enough. For instance, Mr. Newman has zeal for learning, zeal for thinking, zeal for liberty, and all these things are noble, they ennoble a man; but he has not the poetical gift: there must be the poetical gift, the 'divine faculty', also. And, besides all this, the subject must be a serious one (for it is only by a kind of license that we can speak of the grand style in comedy); and it must be treated *with simplicity or severity*. Here is the great difficulty: the poets of the world have been many; there has been wanting neither abundance of poetical gift nor abundance of noble natures; but a poetical gift so happy, in a noble nature so circumstanced and trained, that the result is a continuous style, perfect in simplicity or perfect in severity, has been extremely rare. One poet has had the gifts of nature and faculty in unequalled fullness, without the circumstances and training which make this sustained perfection of style possible. Of other poets, some have caught this perfect strain now and then, in short pieces or single lines, but have not been able to maintain it through considerable works; others have composed all their productions in a style which, by comparison with the best, one must call secondary.

The best model of the grand style simple is Homer; perhaps the best model of the grand style severe is Milton. But Dante is remarkable for affording admirable examples of both styles; he has the grand style which arises from simplicity, and he has the grand style which arises from severity; and from him I will illustrate them both. In a former lecture I pointed out what that severity of poetical style is, which comes from saying a thing with a kind of intense compression, or in an allusive, brief, almost haughty way, as if the poet's mind was charged with so many and such grave matters, that he would not deign to treat any one of them explicitly. Of this severity the last line of the following stanza of the *Purgatory* is a good example. Dante has been telling Forese that Virgil had guided him through Hell, and he goes on:

> Indi m' han tratto su gli suoi conforti,
> Salendo e rigirando la Montagna
> *Che drizza voi che il mondo fece torti.*[38]

'Thence hath his comforting aid led me up, climbing and circling the Mountain, *which straightens you whom the world made crooked.*' These last words, 'la Montagna *che drizza voi che il mondo fece torti,*'—'the Mountain *which straightens you whom the world made crooked*',—for the Mountain of Purgatory, I call an excellent specimen of the grand style in severity, where the poet's mind is too full charged to suffer him to speak more explicitly. But the very next stanza is a beautiful specimen of the grand style in simplicity, where a noble nature and a poetical gift unite to utter a thing with the most limpid plainness and clearness:

> Tanto dice di farmi sua compagna
> Ch' io sarò là dove fia Beatrice;
> Quivi convien che senza lui rimagna.[39]

'So long', Dante continues, 'so long he (Virgil) saith he will bear me company, until I shall be there where Beatrice is; there it behoves that without him I remain.' But the noble simplicity of that in the Italian no words of mine can render.

Both these styles, the simple and the severe, are truly grand; the severe seems, perhaps, the grandest, so long as we attend most to the great personality, to the noble nature, in the poet its author; the simple seems the grandest when we attend most to the exquisite faculty, to the poetical gift. But the simple is no doubt to be preferred. It is the more *magical*: in the other there is something intellectual, something which gives scope for a play of thought which may exist where the poetical gift is either wanting or present in only inferior degree: the severe is much more imitable, and this a little spoils its charm. A kind of semblance of this style keeps Young going, one may say, through all the nine parts of that most indifferent production, the *Night Thoughts*. But the grand style in simplicity is inimitable:

αἰὼν ἀσφαλὴς
οὐκ ἔγεντ' οὔτ' Αἰακίδᾳ παρὰ Πηλεῖ,
οὔτε παρ' ἀντιθέῳ Κάδμῳ · λέγονται μὰν βροτῶν
ὄλβον ὑπέρτατον οἳ σχεῖν, οἵ τε καὶ χρυσαμπύκων
μελπομενᾶν ἐν ὄρει Μοισᾶν, καὶ ἐν ἑπταπύλοις
ἄϊον Θήβαις...[40]

There is a limpidness in that, a want of salient points to seize and transfer, which makes imitation impossible, except by a genius akin to the genius which produced it.

Greek simplicity and Greek grace are inimitable, but it is said that the *Iliad* may still be ballad-poetry while infinitely superior to all other ballads, and that, in my specimens of English ballad-poetry, I have been unfair. Well, no doubt there are better things in English ballad-poetry than

Now Christ thee save, thou proud portér,....

but the real strength of a chain, they say, is the strength of its weakest link; and what I was trying to show you was, that the English ballad-style is not an instrument of enough compass and force to correspond to the Greek hexameter; that, owing to an inherent weakness in it as an epic style, it easily runs into one of two faults,—either it is prosaic and humdrum, or, trying to avoid that fault, and to make itself lively (*se faire vif*), it becomes pert and jaunty. To show that, the passage about King Adland's porter serves very well. But these degradations are not proper to a true epic instrument, such as the Greek hexameter.

You may say, if you like, when you find Homer's verse, even in describing the plainest matter, neither humdrum nor jaunty, that this is because he is so incomparably better a poet than other balladists, because he is Homer. But take the whole range of Greek epic poetry,—take the later poets, the poets of the last ages of this poetry, many of them most indifferent,—Coluthus, Tryphiodorus, Quintus of Smyrna, Nonnus. Never will you find in this instrument of the hexameter, even in their hands, the vices of the ballad-style in the weak moments of this last: everywhere the hexameter—a noble, a truly epical instrument—rather resists the weakness of its employer than lends itself to it. Quintus of Smyrna is a poet of merit, but certainly not a poet of a high order; with him, too, epic poetry, whether in the character of its prosody or in that of its diction, is no longer the epic poetry of earlier and better times, nor epic poetry as again restored by Nonnus: but even in Quintus of Smyrna, I say, the hexameter is still the hexameter; it is a style which the ballad-style, even in the hands of better poets, cannot rival. And in the hands of inferior poets, the ballad-style sinks to vices of which the hexameter, even in the hands of a Tryphiodorus, never can become guilty.

But a critic, whom it is impossible to read without pleasure, and the disguise of whose initials I am sure I may be allowed to penetrate,—Mr. Spedding,—says that he 'denies altogether that the metrical movement of the English hexameter has any resemblance to that of the Greek'. Of course, in that case, if the two metres in no respect correspond, praise accorded to the Greek hexameter as an epical instrument will not extend to the English. Mr. Spedding seeks to establish his proposition by pointing out that the system of accentuation differs in the English and in the Virgilian hexameter; that in the first, the accent and the long syllable (or what has to do duty as such) coincide, in the second they do not. He says that we cannot be so sure of the accent with which Greek verse should be read as of that with which Latin should; but that the lines of Homer in which the accent and the long syllable coincide, as in the English hexameter, are certainly very rare. He suggests a type of English hexameter in agreement with the Virgilian model, and formed on the supposition that 'quantity is as distinguishable in English as in Latin or Greek by any ear that will attend to it'. Of the truth of this supposition he entertains no doubt. The new hexameter will, Mr. Spedding thinks, at least have the merit of resembling, in its metrical movement, the classical hexameter, which merit the ordinary English hexameter has not. But even with this improved hexameter he is not satisfied; and he goes on, first to suggest other metres for rendering Homer, and finally to suggest that rendering Homer is impossible.

A scholar to whom all who admire Lucretius owe a large debt of gratitude,—Mr. Munro,—has replied to Mr. Spedding. Mr. Munro declares that 'the accent of the old Greeks and Romans resembled our accent only in name, in reality was essentially different'; that 'our English reading of Homer and Virgil has in itself no meaning'; and that 'accent has nothing to do with the Virgilian hexameter'. If this be so; of course the merit which Mr. Spedding attributes to his own hexameter, of really corresponding with the Virgilian hexameter, has no existence. Again; in contradiction to Mr. Spedding's assertion that lines in which (in our reading of them) the accent and the long syllable coincide,[41] as in the ordinary English hexameter, are 'rare even in Homer', Mr. Munro declares that such lines, 'instead of being rare, are among the very commonest types of Homeric rhythm'. Mr. Spedding asserts that 'quantity is as distinguishable in English as in Latin or Greek by any ear that will attend to it'; but Mr. Munro replies, that in English 'neither his ear nor his reason recognizes any real distinction of quantity except that which is produced by accentuated and unaccentuated syllables'. He, therefore, arrives at the conclusion that in constructing English hexameters, 'quantity must be utterly discarded; and longer or shorter unaccentuated syllables can have no meaning, except so far as they may be made to produce sweeter or harsher sounds in the hands of a master'.

It is not for me to interpose between two such combatants; and indeed my way lies, not up highroad where they are contending, but along a bypath. With the absolute truth of their general propositions respecting accent and quantity, I have nothing to do; it is most interesting and instructive to me to hear such propositions discussed, when it is Mr. Munro or Mr. Spedding who discusses them; but I have strictly limited myself in these Lectures to the humble function of giving practical advice to the translator of Homer. He, I still think, must not follow so confidently, as makers of English hexameters have hitherto followed, Mr. Munro's maxim,—*quantity may be utterly discarded.* He must not, like Mr. Longfellow, make *seventeen* a dactyl in spite of all the length of its last syllable, even though he can plead that in counting we lay the accent on the first syllable of this word. He may be far from attaining Mr. Spedding's nicety of ear;—may be unable to feel that 'while *quantity* is a dactyl, *quiddity* is a tribrach', and that '*rapidly* is a word to which we find no parallel in Latin';—but I think he must bring himself to distinguish, with Mr. Spedding, between '*th' o'er*-wearied eyelid', and '*the* wearied eyelid', as being, the one a correct ending for a hexameter, the other an ending with a false quantity in it; instead of finding, with Mr. Munro, that this distinction 'conveys to his mind no intelligible idea.' He must temper his belief in Mr. Munro's dictum,—*quantity must be utterly discarded*,—by mixing with it a belief in this other dictum of the same author,—*two or more consonants take longer time in enunciating than one.*[42]

Criticism is so apt in general to be vague and impalpable, that when it gives us a solid and definite possession, such as is Mr. Spedding's parallel of the Virgilian and the English hexameter with their difference of accentuation distinctly marked, we cannot be too grateful to it. It is in the way in which Mr. Spedding proceeds to press his conclusions from the parallel which he has drawn out, that his criticism seems to me to come a little short. Here even he, I think, shows (if he will allow me to say so) a little of that want of pliancy and suppleness so common among critics, but so dangerous to their criticism; he is a little too absolute in imposing his metrical laws; he too much forgets the excellent maxim of Menander, so applicable to literary criticism:

> Καλὸν οἱ νόμοι σφόδρ' εἰσίν · ὁ δ' ἁρῶν τοὺς νόμους
> λίαν ἀκριβῶς, συκοφάντης φαίνεται·

'Laws are admirable things; but he who keeps his eye too closely fixed upon them, runs the risk of becoming'—let us say, a purist. Mr. Spedding is probably mistaken in supposing that Virgil pronounced his hexameters as Mr. Spedding pronounces them. He is almost certainly mistaken in supposing that Homer pronounced his hexameters as Mr. Spedding pronounces Virgil's. But this, as I have said, is not a question for us to treat; all we are here concerned with is the imitation, by the English hexameter, of the ancient hexameter *in its effect upon us moderns*. Suppose we concede to Mr. Spedding that his parallel proves our accentuation of the English and of the Virgilian hexameter to be different: what are we to conclude from that; how will a criticism—not a formal, but a substantial criticism—deal with such a fact as that? Will it infer, as Mr. Spedding infers, that the English hexameter, therefore, must not pretend to reproduce better than other rhythms the movement of Homer's hexameter for us,—that there can be no correspondence at all between the movement of these two hexameters,—that if we want to have such a correspondence, we must abandon the current English hexameter altogether, and adopt in its place a new hexameter of Mr. Spedding's Anglo-Latin type,—substitute for lines like the

> Clearly the rest I behold of the dark-eyed sons of Achaia....

of Dr. Hawtrey, lines like the

> Procession, complex melodies, pause, quantity, accent,
> After Virgilian precedent and practice, in order....

of Mr. Spedding? To infer this, is to go, as I have complained of Mr. Newman for sometimes going, a great deal too fast. I think prudent criticism must certainly recognize, in the current English hexameter, a fact which cannot so lightly be set aside; it must acknowledge that by this hexameter the English ear, the genius of the English language, have, in their own way, adopted, have *translated* for themselves the Homeric hexameter; and that a rhythm which has thus grown up, which is thus, in a manner, the production of nature, has in its general type something necessary and inevitable, something which admits change only within narrow limits, which precludes change that is sweeping and essential. I think, therefore, the prudent critic will regard Mr. Spedding's proposed revolution as simply impracticable. He will feel that in English poetry the hexameter, if used at all, must be, in the main, the English hexameter now current. He will perceive that its having come into existence as the representative of the Homeric hexameter, proves it to have, for the English ear, a certain correspondence with the Homeric hexameter, although this correspondence may be, from the difference of the Greek and English languages, necessarily incomplete. This incompleteness he will endeavour,[43] as he may find or fancy himself able, gradually somewhat to lessen through minor changes, suggested by the ancient hexameter, but respecting the general constitution of the modern: the notion of making it disappear altogether by the critic's inventing in his closet a new constitution of his own for the English hexameter, he will judge to be a chimerical dream.

When, therefore, Mr. Spedding objects to the English hexameter, that it imperfectly represents the movement of the ancient hexameters, I answer: We must work with the tools we have. The received English type, in its general outlines, is, for England, the necessary given type of this metre; it is by rendering the metrical beat of its pattern, not by rendering the accentual beat of it, that the English language has adapted the Greek hexameter. To render the metrical beat of its pattern is something; by effecting so much as this the English hexameter puts itself in closer relations with its original, it comes nearer to its movement than any other metre which does not even effect so much as this; but Mr. Spedding is dissatisfied with it for not effecting more still, for not rendering the accentual beat too. If he asks me *why* the English hexameter has not tried to render this too, *why* it has confined itself to rendering the metrical beat, *why*, in short, it is itself, and not Mr. Spedding's new hexameter,—

that is a question which I, whose only business is to give practical advice to a translator, am not bound to answer; but I will not decline to answer it nevertheless. I will suggest to Mr. Spedding that, as I have already said, the modern hexameter is merely an attempt to imitate the effect of the ancient hexameter, as read by us moderns; that the great object of its imitation has been the hexameter of Homer; that of this hexameter such lines as those which Mr. Spedding declares to be so rare, even in Homer, but which are in truth so common,—lines in which the quantity and the reader's accent coincide,—are, for the English reader, just from that simplicity (for him) of rhythm which they owe to this very coincidence, the master-type; that so much is this the case, that one may again and again notice an English reader of Homer, in reading lines where his Virgilian accent would not coincide with the quantity, abandoning this accent, and reading the lines (as we say) *by quantity*, reading them as if he were scanning them; while foreigners neglect our Virgilian accent even in reading Virgil, read even Virgil by quantity, making the accents coincide with the long syllables. And no doubt the hexameter of a kindred language, the German, based on this mode of reading the ancient hexameter, has had a powerful influence upon the type of its English fellow. But all this shows how extremely powerful accent is for us moderns, since we find not even Greek and Latin quantity perceptible enough without it. Yet in these languages, where we have been accustomed always to look for it, it is far more perceptible to us Englishmen than in our own language, where we have not been accustomed to look for it. And here is the true reason why Mr. Spedding's hexameter is not and cannot be the current English hexameter, even though it is based on the accentuation which Englishmen give to all Virgil's lines, and to many of Homer's,—that the quantity which in Greek or Latin words we feel, or imagine we feel, even though it be unsupported by accent, we do not feel or imagine we feel in English words when it is thus unsupported. For example, in repeating the Latin line,

Ipsa tibi blandos *fundent* cunabula flores,

an Englishman feels the length of the second syllable of *fundent*, although he lays the accent on the first; but in repeating Mr. Spedding's line,

> Softly cometh slumber closing th' o'erwearied eyelid,

the English ear, full of the accent on the first syllable of *closing*, has really no sense at all of any length in its second. The metrical beat of the line is thus quite destroyed.

So when Mr. Spedding proposes a new Anglo-Virgilian hexameter he proposes in impossibility; when he 'denies altogether that the metrical movement of the English hexameter has *any* resemblance to that of the Greek', he denies too much; when he declares that, 'were every other metre impossible, an attempt to translate Homer into English hexameters might be permitted, *but that such an attempt he himself would never read*', he exhibits, it seems to me, a little of that obduracy and over-vehemence in liking and disliking,—a remnant, I suppose, of our insular ferocity,—to which English criticism is so prone. He ought to be enchanted to meet with a good attempt in any metre, even though he would never have advised it, even though its success be contrary to all his expectations; for it is the critic's first duty—prior even to his duty of stigmatizing what is bad—*to welcome everything that is good*. In welcoming this, he must at all times be ready, like the Christian convert, even to burn what he used to worship, and to worship what he used to burn. Nay, but he need not be thus inconsistent in welcoming it; he may retain all his principles: principles endure, circumstances change; absolute success is one thing, relative success another. Relative success may take place under the most diverse conditions; and it is in appreciating the good in even relative success, it is in taking into account the change of circumstances, that the critic's judgment is tested, that his versatility must display itself. He is to keep his idea of the best, of perfection, and at the same time to be willingly accessible to every second best which offers itself. So I enjoy the ease and beauty of Mr. Spedding's stanza,

> Therewith to all the gods in order due....

I welcome it, in the absence of equally good poetry in another metre,[44] although I still think the stanza unfit to render Homer thoroughly well,—although I still think other metres fit to render him better. So I concede to Mr. Spedding that every form of translation, prose or verse, must more or less break up Homer in order to reproduce him; but then I urge that that form which needs to break him up least is to be preferred. So I concede to him that the test proposed by me for the translator—a competent scholar's judgment whether the translation more or less reproduces for him the effect of the original—is not perfectly satisfactory; but I adopt it as the best we can get, as the only test capable of being really applied; for Mr. Spedding's proposed substitute—the translation's making the same effect, more or less, upon the unlearned which the original makes upon the scholar—is a test which can never really be applied at all. These two impressions—that of the scholar, and that of the unlearned reader—can, practically, never be accurately compared; they are, and must remain, like those lines we read of in Euclid, which, though produced ever so far, can never meet. So, again, I concede that a good verse-translation of Homer, or, indeed, of any poet, is very difficult, and that a good prose-translation is much easier; but then I urge that a verse-translation, while giving the pleasure which Pope's has given, might at the same time render Homer more faithfully than Pope's; and that this being possible, we ought not to cease wishing for a source of pleasure which no prose-translation can ever hope to rival.

Wishing for such a verse-translation of Homer, believing that rhythms have natural tendencies which, within certain limits, inevitably govern them; having little faith, therefore, that rhythms which have manifested tendencies utterly un-Homeric can so change themselves as to become well adapted for rendering Homer,—I have looked about for the rhythm which seems to depart least from the tendencies of Homer's rhythm. Such a rhythm I think may be found in the English hexameter, somewhat modified. I look with hope towards continued attempts at perfecting and employing this rhythm; but my belief in the immediate success of such attempts is far less confident than has been supposed. Between the recognition of this rhythm as ideally the best, and the recommendation of it to the translator for instant practical use, there must come all that consideration of circumstances, all that pliancy in foregoing, under the pressure of certain difficulties, the absolute best, which I have said is so indispensable to the critic. The hexameter is, comparatively, still unfamiliar in England; many people have a great dislike to it. A certain degree of unfamiliarity, a certain degree of dislike, are obstacles with which it is not wise to contend. It is difficult to say at present whether the dislike to this rhythm is so strong and so widespread that it will prevent its ever becoming thoroughly familiar. I think not, but it is too soon to decide. I am inclined to think that the dislike of it is rather among the professional critics than among the general public; I think the reception which Mr. Longfellow's *Evangeline* has met with indicates this. I think that even now, if a version of the *Iliad* in English hexameters were made by a poet who, like Mr. Longfellow, has that indefinable quality which renders him popular,—something *attractive* in his talent, which communicates itself to his verses,—it would have a great success among the general public. Yet a version of Homer in hexameters of the *Evangeline* type would not satisfy the judicious, nor is the definite establishment of this type to be desired; and one would regret that Mr. Longfellow should, even to popularize the hexameter, give the immense labour required for a translation of Homer, when one could not wish his work to stand. Rather it is to be wished that by the efforts of poets like Mr. Longfellow in original poetry, and the efforts of less distinguished poets in the task of translation, the hexameter may gradually be made familiar to the ear of the English public; at the same time that there gradually arises, out of all these efforts, an improved type of this rhythm; a type which some man of genius may sign with the final stamp, and employ in rendering Homer; a hexameter which may be as superior to Voss's as Shakespeare's blank verse is superior to Schiller's. I am inclined to believe that all this travail will actually take place, because I believe that modern poetry is actually in want of such an instrument as the hexameter.

In the meantime, whether this rhythm be destined to success or not, let us steadily keep in mind what originally made us turn to it. We turned to it because we required certain Homeric characteristics in a translation of Homer, and because all other rhythms seemed to find, from different causes, great difficulties in satisfying this our requirement. If the hexameter is impossible, if one of these other rhythms must be used, let us keep this rhythm always in mind of our requirements and of its own faults, let us compel it to get rid of these latter as much as possible. It may be necessary to have recourse to blank verse; but then blank verse must *de-Cowperise* itself, must get rid of the habits of stiff self-retardation which make it say '*Not fewer* shone', for '*So many* shone'. Homer moves swiftly: blank verse *can* move swiftly if it likes, but it must remember that the movement of such lines as

> A thousand fires were burning, and by each...

is just the slow movement which makes us despair of it. Homer moves with noble ease: blank verse must not be suffered to forget that the movement of

> Came they not over from sweet Lacedæmon...

is ungainly. Homer's expression of his thought is simple as light: we know how blank verse affects such locutions as

> While the steeds *mouthed their corn aloof...*

and such modes of expressing one's thought are sophisticated and artificial.

One sees how needful it is to direct incessantly the English translator's attention to the essential characteristics of Homer's poetry, when so accomplished a person as Mr. Spedding, recognizing these characteristics as indeed Homer's, admitting them to be essential, is led by the ingrained habits and tendencies of English blank verse thus repeatedly to lose sight of them in translating even a few lines. One sees this yet more clearly, when Mr. Spedding, taking me to task for saying that the blank verse used for rendering Homer 'must not be Mr. Tennyson's blank verse', declares that in most of Mr. Tennyson's blank verse all Homer's essential characteristics—'rapidity of movement, *plainness of words and style, simplicity and directness of ideas*, and, above all, nobleness of manner—are as conspicuous as in Homer himself'. This shows, it seems to me, how hard it is for English readers of poetry, even the most accomplished, to feel deeply and permanently what Greek plainness of thought and Greek simplicity of expression really are: they admit the importance of these qualities in a general way, but they have no ever-present sense of them; and they easily attribute them to any poetry which has other excellent qualities, and which they very much admire. No doubt there are plainer things in Mr. Tennyson's poetry than the three lines I quoted; in choosing them, as in choosing a specimen of ballad-poetry, I wished to bring out clearly, by a strong instance, the qualities of thought and style to which I was calling attention; but when Mr. Spedding talks of a plainness of thought *like Homer's*, of a plainness of speech *like Homer's*, and says that he finds these constantly in Mr. Tennyson's poetry, I answer that these I do not find there at all. Mr. Tennyson is a most distinguished and charming poet; but the very essential characteristic of his poetry is, it seems to me, an extreme subtlety and curious elaborateness of thought, an extreme subtlety and curious elaborateness of expression. In the best and most characteristic productions of his genius, these characteristics are most prominent. They are marked characteristics, as we have seen, of the Elizabethan poets; they are marked, though not the essential, characteristics of Shakespeare himself. Under the influences of the nineteenth century, under wholly new conditions of thought and culture, they manifest themselves in Mr. Tennyson's poetry in a wholly new way. But they are still there. The essential bent of his poetry is towards such expression as:

> Now lies the Earth all Danaë to the stars;

>   O'er the sun's bright eye
> Drew the vast eyelid of an inky cloud;
> When the cairned mountain was a shadow, sunned
> The world to peace again;

> The fresh young captains flashed their glittering teeth,
> The huge bush-bearded barons heaved and blew;

> He bared the knotted column of his throat,
> The massive square of his heroic breast,
> And arms on which the standing muscle sloped
> As slopes a wild brook o'er a little stone,
> Running too vehemently to break upon it.

And this way of speaking is the least *plain*, the most *un-Homeric*, which can possibly be conceived. Homer presents his thought to you just as it wells from the source of his mind: Mr. Tennyson carefully distils his thought before he will part with it. Hence comes, in the expression of the thought, a heightened and elaborate air. In Homer's poetry it is all natural thoughts in natural words; in Mr. Tennyson's poetry it is all distilled thoughts in distilled words. Exactly this heightening and elaboration may be observed in Mr. Spedding's

> While the steeds *mouthed their corn aloof*,

(an expression which might have been Mr. Tennyson's) on which I have already commented; and to one who is penetrated with a sense of the real simplicity of Homer, this subtle sophistication of the thought is, I think, very perceptible even in such lines as these,—

> And drunk delight of battle with my peers,
> Far on the ringing plains of windy Troy,—

which I have seen quoted as perfectly Homeric. Perfect simplicity can be obtained only by a genius of which perfect simplicity is an essential characteristic.

So true is this, that when a genius essentially subtle, or a genius which, from whatever cause, is in its essence not truly and broadly simple, determines to be perfectly plain, determines not to admit a shade of subtlety or curiosity into its expression, it cannot even then attain real simplicity; it can only attain a semblance of simplicity.[45] French criticism, richer in its vocabulary than ours, has invented a useful word to distinguish this semblance (often very beautiful and valuable) from the real quality. The real quality it calls *simplicité*, the semblance *simplesse*. The one is natural simplicity, the other is artificial simplicity. What is called simplicity in the productions of a genius essentially not simple, is, in truth, *simplesse*. The two are distinguishable from one another the moment they appear in company. For instance, let us take the opening of the narrative in Wordsworth's *Michael*:

> Upon the forest-side in Grasmere Vale
> There dwelt a shepherd, Michael was his name;

An old man, stout of heart, and strong of limb.
His bodily frame had been from youth to age
Of an unusual strength; his mind was keen,
Intense, and frugal, apt for all affairs;
And in his shepherd's calling he was prompt
And watchful more than ordinary men.

Now let us take the opening of the narrative in Mr. Tennyson's *Dora*:

With Farmer Allan at the farm abode
William and Dora. William was his son,
And she his niece. He often looked at them,
And often thought, 'I'll make them man and wife'.

The simplicity of the first of these passages is *simplicité*; that of the second, *simplesse*. Let us take the end of the same two poems; first, of *Michael*:

The cottage which was named the Evening Star
Is gone,—the ploughshare has been through the ground
On which it stood; great changes have been wrought
In all the neighbourhood: yet the oak is left
That grew beside their door: and the remains
Of the unfinished sheepfold may be seen
Beside the boisterous brook of Green-head Ghyll.

And now, of *Dora*:

So those four abode
Within one house together; and as years
Went forward, Mary took another mate:
But Dora lived unmarried till her death.

A heedless critic may call both of these passages simple if he will. Simple, in a certain sense, they both are; but between the simplicity of the two there is all the difference that there is between the simplicity of Homer and the simplicity of Moschus.

But—whether the hexameter establish itself or not, whether a truly simple and rapid blank verse be obtained or not, as the vehicle for a standard English translation of Homer—I feel sure that this vehicle will not be furnished by the ballad-form. On this question about the ballad-character of Homer's poetry, I see that Professor Blackie proposes a compromise: he suggests that those who say Homer's poetry is pure ballad-poetry, and those who deny that it is ballad-poetry at all, should split the difference between them; that it should be agreed that Homer's poems are ballads *a little*, but not so much as some have said. I am very sensible to the courtesy of the terms in which Mr. Blackie invites me to this compromise; but I cannot, I am sorry to say, accept it; I cannot allow that Homer's poetry is ballad-poetry at all. A want of capacity for sustained nobleness seems to me inherent in the ballad-form when employed for epic poetry. The more we examine this proposition, the more certain, I think, will it become to us. Let us but observe how a great poet, having to deliver a narrative very weighty and serious, instinctively shrinks from the ballad-form as from a form not commensurate with his subject-matter, a form too narrow and shallow for it, and seeks for a form which has more amplitude and impressiveness. Every one knows the *Lucy Gray* and the *Ruth* of Wordsworth. Both poems are excellent; but the subject-matter of the narrative of *Ruth* is much more weighty and impressive to the poet's own feeling than that of the narrative of *Lucy Gray*, for which latter, in its unpretending simplicity, the ballad-form is quite adequate. Wordsworth, at the time he composed *Ruth*,—his great time, his *annus mirabilis,* about 1800,—strove to be simple; it was his mission to be simple; he loved the ballad-form, he clung to it, because it was simple. Even in *Ruth* he tried, one may say, to use it; he would have used it if he could: but the gravity of his matter is too much for this somewhat slight form; he is obliged to give to his form more amplitude, more augustness, to shake out its folds.

> The wretched parents all that night
>   Went shouting far and wide;
> But there was neither sound nor sight
>   To serve them for a guide.

That is beautiful, no doubt, and the form is adequate to the subject-matter. But take this, on the other hand:

> I, too, have passed her on the hills,
> Setting her little water-mills

By spouts and fountains wild;
Such small machinery as she turned,
Ere she had wept, ere she had mourned,
A young and happy child.

Who does not perceive how the greater fullness and weight of his matter has here compelled the true and feeling poet to adopt a form of more *volume* than the simple ballad-form?

It is of narrative poetry that I am speaking; the question is about the use of the ballad-form for *this*. I say that for this poetry (when in the grand style, as Homer's is) the ballad-form is entirely inadequate; and that Homer's translator must not adopt it, because it even leads him, by its own weakness, away from the grand style rather than towards it. We must remember that the matter of narrative poetry stands in a different relation to the vehicle which conveys it,—is not so independent of this vehicle, so absorbing and powerful in itself,—as the matter of purely emotional poetry. When there comes in poetry what I may call the *lyrical cry*, this transfigures everything, makes everything grand; the simplest form may be here even an advantage, because the flame of the emotion glows through and through it more easily. To go again for an illustration to Wordsworth;—our great poet, since Milton, by his performance, as Keats, I think, is our great poet by his gift and promise;—in one of his stanzas to the Cuckoo, we have:

And I can listen to thee yet;
Can lie upon the plain
And listen, till I do beget
That golden time again.

Here the lyrical cry, though taking in simple ballad-form, is as grand as the lyrical cry coming in poetry of an ampler form, as grand as the

An innocent life, yet far astray!

of *Ruth*; as the

There is a comfort in the strength of love

of *Michael*. In this way, by the occurrence of this lyrical cry, the ballad-poets themselves rise sometimes, though not so often as one might perhaps have hoped, to the grand style.

O lang, lang may their ladies sit,
Wi' their fans into their hand,
Or ere they see Sir Patrick Spence
Come sailing to the land.

O lang, lang may the ladies stand,
Wi' their gold combs in their hair,
Waiting for their ain dear lords,
For they'll see them nae mair.

But from this impressiveness of the ballad-form, when its subject-matter fills it over and over again,—is, indeed, in itself, all in all,—one must not infer its effectiveness when its subject-matter is not thus overpowering, in the great body of a narrative.

But, after all, Homer is not a better poet than the balladists, because he has taken in the hexameter a better instrument; he took this instrument because he was a *different* poet from them; so different,—not only so much better, but so essentially different,—that he is not to be classed with them at all. Poets receive their distinctive character, not from their subject, but from their application to that subject of the ideas (to quote the *Recluse*):

On man, on nature, and on human life,

which they have acquired for themselves. In the ballad-poets in general, as in men of a rude and early stage of the world, in whom their humanity is not yet variously and fully developed, the stock of these ideas is scanty, and the ideas themselves not very effective or profound. [For] them the narrative itself is the great matter, not the spirit and significance which underlies the narrative. Even in later times of richly developed life and thought, poets appear who have what may be called a *balladist's mind*; in whom a fresh and lively curiosity for the outward spectacle of the world is much more strong than their sense of the inward significance of that spectacle. When they apply ideas to their narrative of human events, you feel that they are, so to speak, travelling out of their own province: in the best of them you feel this perceptibly, but in those of a lower order you feel it very strongly. Even Sir Walter Scott's efforts of this kind,—even, for instance, the

> Breathes there the man with soul so dead,

or the

> O woman! in our hours of ease,—

even these leave, I think, as high poetry, much to be desired; far more than the same poet's descriptions of a hunt or a battle. But Lord Macaulay's

> Then out spake brave Horatius,
> The captain of the gate:
> 'To all the men upon this earth
> Death cometh soon or late',

(and here, since I have been reproached with undervaluing Lord Macaulay's *Lays of Ancient Rome*, let me frankly say that, to my mind, a man's power to detect the ring of false metal in those Lays is a good measure of his fitness of give an opinion about poetical matters at all),—I say, Lord Macaulay's

> To all the men upon this earth
> Death cometh soon or late,

it is hard to read without a cry of pain. But with Homer it is very different. This 'noble barbarian', this 'savage with the lively eye',—whose verse, Mr. Newman thinks, would affect us, if we could hear the living Homer, 'like an elegant and simple melody from an African of the Gold Coast',—is never more at home, never more nobly himself, than in applying profound ideas to his narrative. As a poet he belongs—narrative as is his poetry, and early as is his date—to an incomparably more developed spiritual and intellectual order than the balladists, or than Scott and Macaulay; he is here as much to be distinguished from them, and in the same way, as Milton is to be distinguished from them. He is, indeed, rather to be classed with Milton than with the balladists and Scott; for what he has in common with Milton—the noble and profound application of ideas to life—is the most essential part of poetic greatness. The most essentially grand and characteristic things of Homer are such things as:

> ἔτλην δ', οἷ' οὔ πώ τις ἐπιχθόνιος βροτὸς ἄλλος,
> ἀνδρὸς παιδοφόνοιο ποτὶ στόμα χεῖρ' ὀρέγεσθαι,[46]

or as:

> καὶ σὲ, γέρον, τὸ πρὶν μὲν ἀκούομεν ὄλβιον εἶναι,[47]

or as:

> ὥς γὰρ ἐπεκλώσαντο θεοὶ δειλοῖσι βροτοῖσιν,
> ζώειν ἀχνυμένους · αὐτοὶ δέ τ' ἀκηδέες εἰσίν,[48]

and of these the tone is given, far better than by anything of the balladists, by such things as the

> Io non piangeva; sì dentro impietrai:
> Piangevan elli...[49]

of Dante; or the

> Fall'n Cherub! to be weak is miserable

of Milton.

I suppose I must, before I conclude, say a word or two about my own hexameters; and yet really, on such a topic, I am almost ashamed to trouble you. From those perishable objects I feel, I can truly say, a most Oriental detachment. You yourselves are witnesses how little importance, when I offered them to you, I claimed for them,—how humble a function I designed them to fill. I offered them, not as specimens of a competing translation of Homer, but as illustrations of certain cannons which I had been trying to establish for Homer's poetry. I said that these canons they might very well illustrate by failing as well as by succeeding: if they illustrate them in any manner, I am satisfied. I was thinking of the future translator of Homer, and trying to let him see as clearly as possible what I meant by the combination of characteristics which I assigned to Homer's poetry,—by saying that this poetry was at once rapid in movement, plain in words and style, simple and direct in its ideas, and noble in manner. I do not suppose that my own hexameters are rapid in movement, plain in words and style, simple and direct in their ideas, and noble in manner; but I am in hopes that a translator, reading them with a genuine interest in his subject, and without the slightest grain of personal feeling, may see more clearly, as he reads them, what I mean by saying that Homer's poetry is all these. I am in hopes that he may be able to seize more distinctly, when he has before him my

> So shone forth, in front of Troy, by the bed of the
> Xanthus,

or my

> Ah, unhappy pair, to Peleus why did we give you?

or my

> So he spake, and drove with a cry his steeds into battle,

the exact points which I wish him to avoid in Cowper's

> So numerous seemed those fires the banks between,

or in Pope's

> Unhappy coursers of immortal strain,

or in Mr. Newman's

> He spake, and yelling, held a-front his single-hoofed
> horses.

At the same time there may be innumerable points in mine which he ought to avoid also. Of the merit of his own compositions no composer can be admitted the judge.

But thus humbly useful to the future translator I still hope my hexameters may prove; and he it is, above all, whom one has to regard. The general public carries away little from discussions of this kind, except some vague notion that one advocates English hexameters, or that one has attacked Mr. Newman. On the mind of an adversary one never makes the faintest impression. Mr. Newman reads all one can say about diction, and his last word on the subject is, that he 'regards it as a question about to open hereafter, whether a translator of Homer ought not to adopt the old dissyllabic *landis*, *houndis*, *hartis*' (for lands, hounds, harts), and also 'the final *en* of the plural of verbs (we *dancen*, they *singen*, etc.),' which 'still subsists in Lancashire'. A certain critic reads all one can say about style, and at the end of it arrives at the inference that, 'after all, there is some style grander than the grand style itself, since Shakespeare has not the grand manner, and yet has the supremacy over Miltion'; another critic reads all one can say about rhythm, and the result is, that he thinks Scott's rhythm, in the description of the death of Marmion, all the better for being *saccadé*, because the dying ejaculations of Marmion were likely to be 'jerky'. How vain to rise up early, and to take rest late, from any zeal for proving to Mr. Newman that he must not, in translating Homer, say *houndis* and *dancen*; or to the first of the two critics above quoted, that one poet may be a greater poetical force than another, and yet have a more unequal style; or to the second, that the best art, having to represent the death of a hero, does not set about imitating his dying noises! Such critics, however, provide for an opponent's vivacity the charming excuse offered by Rivarol for his, when he was reproached with giving offence by it: 'Ah!' he exclaimed, 'no one considers how much pain every man of taste has had to *suffer*, before he ever inflicts any'.

It is for the future translator that one must work. The successful translator of Homer will have (or he cannot succeed) that true sense for his subject, and that disinterested love of it, which are, both of them, so rare in literature, and so precious; he will not be led off by any false scent; he will have an eye for the real matter, and, where he thinks he may find any indication of this, no hint will be too slight for him, no shade will be too fine, no imperfections will turn him aside,—he will go before his adviser's thought, and help it out with his own. This is the sort of student that a critic of Homer should always have in his thoughts; but students of this sort are indeed rare.

And how, then, can I help being reminded what a student of this sort we have just lost in Mr. Clough, whose name I have already mentioned in these lectures? He, too, was busy with Homer; but it is not on that account that I now speak of him. Nor do I speak of him in order to call attention to his qualities and powers in general, admirable as these were. I mention him because, in so eminent a degree, he possessed these two invaluable literary qualities,—a true sense for his object of study, and a single-hearted care for it. He had both; but he had the second even more eminently than the first. He greatly developed the first through means of the second. In the study of art, poetry, or philosophy, he had the most undivided and disinterested love for his object in itself, the greatest aversion to mixing up with it anything accidental or personal. His interest was in literature itself; and it was this which gave so rare a stamp to his character, which kept him so free from all taint of littleness. In the saturnalia of ignoble personal passions, of which the struggle for literary success, in old and crowded communities, offers so sad a spectacle, he never mingled. He had not yet traduced his friends, nor flattered his enemies, nor disparaged what he admired, nor praised what he despised. Those who knew him well had the conviction that, even with time, these literary arts would never be his. His poem, of which I before spoke, has some admirable Homeric qualities;—out-of-doors freshness, life, naturalness, buoyant rapidity. Some of the expressions in that poem,—'*Dangerous Corrievreckan... Where roads are unknown to Loch Nevish*',—come back now to my ear with the true Homeric ring. But that in him of which I think oftenest is the Homeric simplicity of his literary life.

NOTES

1. *Iliad*, iii. 243.
2. *Briefwechsel zwischen Schiller und Goethe*, vi. 230.
3. *Iliad*, xix. 420.
4. *Ibid.*, xii. 324.
5. These are the words on which Lord Granville 'dwelled with particular emphasis'.
6. Robert Wood, *Essay on the Original Genius and Writings of Homer*, London, 1775, p. vii.
7. *Iliad*, viii. 560.
8. *Ibid.*, xvii. 443.
9. *Ibid.*, vi. 444.
10. *Ibid.*, vi. 344.
11. *Ibid.*, xiv. 84: From the reproachful answer of Ulysses to Agamemnon, who had proposed an abandonment of their expedition. This is one of the 'tonic' passages of the *Iliad*, so I quote it:

    Ah, unworthy king, some other inglorious army
    Should'st thou command, not rule over *us*, whose portion for ever
    Zeus hath made it, from youth right up to age, to be winding
    Skeins of grievous wars, till every soul of us perish.
12. From the ballad of *King Estmere,* in Percy's *Reliques of Ancient English Poetry*, i. 69 (edit. of 1767).
13. *Reliques*, i. 241.

14. *Iliad,* xvii. 443.
15. All the editions which I have seen have 'haste', but the right reading must certainly be 'taste'.
16. *Iliad*, xix. 419.
17. *Odyssey*, xix. 392.
18. Mr. Marsh, in his *Lectures on the English Language*, New York, 1860, 520.
19. *Marmion*, canto vi. 38.
20. *Ibid.*, canto vi. 29.
21. 'Be content, good friend, die also thou! why lamentest thou thyself on this wise? Patroclus, too, died, who was a far better than thou.' *Iliad,* xxi. 106.
22. 'From me, young man, learn nobleness of soul and true effort: learn success from others.' *Æneid* xii. 435.
23. 'I leave the gall of bitterness, and I go for the apples of sweetness promised unto me by my faithful Guide; but far as the centre it behoves me first to fall.'—*Hell*, xvi. 61.
24. *Paradise Lost*, i. 591.
25. *The Faery Queen*, Canto ii. Stanza 1.
26. *Odes*, IV. vii. 13.
27. *Odyssey* iv. 563.
28. *Odes*, III. ii. 31.
29. So short, that I quote it entire:

    Clearly the rest I behold of dark-eyed sons of Achaia;
    Known to me well are the faces of all; their names I remember;
    Two, two only remain, whom I see not among th: commanders,
    Castor fleet in the car,—Polydeukes brave with the cestus,—
    Own dear brethren of mine,—one parent loved us as infants.
    Are they not here in the host, from the shores of loved Lacedæmon,
    Or, though they came with the rest in ships that bound through the waters,
    Dare they not enter the fight or stand in the council of Heroes,
    All for fear of the shame and the taunts my crime has awakened?
    So said she;—they long since in Earth's soft arms were reposing,
    There, in their own dear land, their Fatherland, Lacedæmon.
    English Hexameter Translations; London, 1847; 242.

    I have changed Dr. Hawtrey's 'Kastor', 'Lakedaimon,' back to the familiar 'Castor', 'Lacedæmon', in obedience to my own rule that everything *odd* is to be avoided in rendering Homer, the most natural and least odd of poets. I see Mr. Newman's critic in the *National Review* urges our generation to bear with the unnatural effect of these rewritten Greek names, in the hope that by this means the effect of them may have to the next generation become natural. For my part, I feel no disposition to pass all my own life in the wilderness of pedantry, in order that a posterity which I shall never see may one day enter an orthographical Canaan; and, after all, the real question is this: whether our living apprehension of the Greek world is more checked by meeting in an English book about the Greeks, names not spelt letter for letter as in the original Greek, or by meeting names which make us rub our eyes and call out, 'How exceedingly odd!'

The Latin names of the Greek deities raise in most cases the idea of quite distinct personages from the personages whose idea is raised by the Greek names. Hera and Juno are actually, to every scholar's imagination, two different people. So in all these cases the Latin names must, at any inconvenience, be abandoned when we are dealing with the Greek world. But I think it can be in the sensitive imagination of Mr. Grote only, that 'Thucydides' raises the idea of a different man from Θουκυδίδης.

30. For instance; in a version (I believe, by the late Mr. Lockhart) of Homer's description of the parting of Hector and Andromache, there occurs, in the first five lines, but one spondee besides the necessary spondees in the sixth place; in the corresponding five lines of Homer there occur ten. See *English Hexameter Translations*, 244.

31. See, for instance, in the *Iliad*, the loose construction of ὄστε, xvii. 658; that of ἴδοιτο, xvii. 681; that of οἶτε, xviii. 209; and the elliptical construction at xix. 42, 43; also the idiomatic construction of ἐγὼν ὅδε παρασχεῖν, xix. 140. These instances are all taken within a range of a thousand lines; any one may easily multiply them for himself.

32. Our knowledge of Homer's Greek is hardly such as to enable us to pronounce quite confidently what is idiomatic in his diction, and what is not, any more than in his grammar; but I seem to myself clearly to recognize an idiomatic stamp in such expressions as τολυπεύειν πολέμους, xiv. 86; φάος ἐν νήεσσιν θήης, xvi. 94; τιν' οἴε ἀσπασίως αὐτῶν γόνυ κάμψειν, xix. 71; κλοτοπεύειν, xix. 149; and, many others. The first-quoted expression, τολυπεύειν ἀργαλέους πολέμους, seems to me to have just about the same degree of freedom as the '*jump* the life to come', or the '*shuffle off* this mortal coil', of Shakespeare.

33. It must be remembered, however, that, if we disregard quantity too much in constructing English hexameters, we also disregard accent too much in reading Greek hexameters. We read every Greek dactyl so as to make a pure dactyl of it; but, to a Greek, the accent must have hindered many dactyls from sounding as pure dactyls. When we read αἰόλος ἵππος, for instance, or ᾀίγιόχοιο, the dactyl in each of these cases is made by us as pure a dactyl as 'Tityre' or 'dignity'; but to a Greek it was not so. To him ᾀίόλος must have been nearly as impure a dactyl as 'death-destined' is to us; and ᾀίγιόχ nearly as impure as the 'dressed his own' of my text. Nor, I think, does this right mode of pronouncing the two words at all spoil the run of the line as a hexameter. The effect of αἰόλλος ἵππος (or something like that), though not *our* effect, is not

a disagreeable one. On the other hand, κορυθαιόλος as a paroxytonon, although it has the respectable authority of Liddell and Scott's *Lexicon* (following Heyne), is certainly wrong; for then the word cannot be pronounced without throwing an accent on the first syllable as well as the third, and μέγας κορρυθαιόλλος Ἕκτωρ would have been to a Greek as intolerable an ending for a hexameter line as 'accurst *orphanhood-destined* houses' would be to us. The best authorities, accordingly, accent κορυθαιόλος as a proparoxytonon.

34. Dr. Hawtrey also has translated this passage; but here, he has not, I think, been so successful as in his 'Helen on the walls of Troy'.

35. 'It is the fact, that scholars of fastidious refinement, but of a judgment which I think far more masculine than Mr. Arnold's, have passed a most encouraging sentence on large specimens of my translation. I at present count eight such names.'—'Before venturing to print, I sought to ascertain how unlearned women and children would accept my verses. I could boast how children and half-educated women have extolled them, how greedily a working man has inquired for them, without knowing who was the translator.'—Mr. Newman's Reply, 2, 12, 13.

36. 'O for the fields of Thessaly and the streams of Spercheios! O for the hills alive with the dances of the Laconian maidens, the hills of Taygetus!'—*Georgics*, ii. 486.

37. *Iliad*, xvii. 216.

38. *Purgatory*, xxiii. 124.

39. *Ibid.*, xxiii. 127.

40. 'A secure time fell to the lot neither of Peleus the son of Æacus, nor of the godlike Cadmus; howbeit these are said to have had, of all mortals, the supreme of happiness, who heard the golden-snooded Muses sing, one of them on the mountain (Pelion), the other in seven-gated Thebes.'

41. Lines such as the first of the *Odyssey*:
Ἄνδραμοι ἔννεπε, Μοῦσα, πολύτροπον, ὃς μάλα πολλὰ...

42. Substantially, however, in the question at issue between Mr. Munro and Mr. Spedding, I agree with Mr. Munro. By the italicized words in the following sentence, 'The rhythm of the Virgilian hexameter depends entirely on *cæsura*, *pause*, and a due arrangement of words', he has touched, it seems to me, in the constitution of this hexameter, the central point, which Mr. Spedding misses. The accent, or *heightened tone*, of Virgil in reading his own hexameters, was probably far from being the same thing as the accent or *stress* with which we read them. The general effect of each line, in Virgil's mouth, was probably therefore something widely different from what Mr. Spedding assumes it to have been: an ancient's accentual reading was something which allowed the metrical beat of the Latin line to be far more perceptible than our accentual reading allows it to be.

On the question as to the *real* rhythm of the ancient hexameter, Mr. Newman has in his *Reply* a page quite admirable for force and precision. Here he is in his element, and his ability and acuteness have their proper scope. But it is true that the *modern* reading of the ancient hexameter is what the modern hexameter has to imitate, and that the English reading of the Virgilian hexameter is as Mr. Spedding describes it. Why this reading has not been imitated by the English hexameter, I have tried to point out in the text.

43. Such a minor change I have attempted by occasionally shifting, in the first foot of the hexameter, the accent from the first syllable to the second. In the current English hexameter, it is on the first. Mr. Spedding, who proposes radically to subvert the constitution of this hexameter, seems not to understand that any one can propose to modify it partially; he can comprehend revolution in this metre, but not reform. Accordingly he asks me how I can bring myself to say, 'Be*twéen* that and the ships', or '*Thére* sat fifty men'; or how I can reconcile such forcing of the accent with my own rule, that 'hexameters must *read themselves*'. Presently he says that he cannot believe I do pronounce these words so, but that he thinks I leave out the accent in the first foot altogether, and thus get a hexameter with only five accents. He will pardon me: I pronounce, as I suppose he himself does, if he reads the words naturally, 'Be*twéen* that and the ships', and 'There *sàt* fifty men.' Mr. Spedding is familiar enough with this accent on the second syllable in Virgil's hexameters; in 'et *té* montosæ', or 'Ve*lóces* jaculo'. Such a change is an attempt to relieve the monotony of the current English hexameter by occasionally altering the position of one of its accents; it is not an attempt to make a wholly new English hexameter by habitually altering the position of four of them. Very likely it is an unsuccessful attempt; but at any rate it does not violate what I think is the fundamental rule for English hexameters,—that they be such as to *read themselves* without necessitating, on the reader's part, any non-natural putting-on or taking-off of accent. Hexameters like these of Mr. Longfellow,

> 'In that delightful land which is washed by the Delaware's waters',
> and,
>
> 'As if they fain would appease the Dryads, whose haunts they molested',

violate this rule; and they are very common. I think the blemish of Mr. Dart's recent meritorious version of the *Iliad* is that is contains too many of them.

44. As I welcome another more recent attempt in stanza,—Mr. Worsley's version of the *Odyssey* in Spenser's measure. Mr. Worsley does me the honour to notice some remarks of mine on this measure: I had said that its greater intricacy made it a worse measure than even the ten-syllable couplet to employ for rendering Homer. He points out, in answer, that 'the more complicated the correspondences in a poetical measure, the less obtrusive and absolute are the rhymes'. This is true, and subtly remarked; but I never denied that the single shocks of rhyme in the couplet were more *strongly felt* than those in the stanza; I said that the

more frequent recurrence of the same rhyme, in the stanza, necessarily made this measure more *intricate*. The stanza repacks Homer's matter yet more arbitrarily, and therefore, changes his movement yet more radically, than the couplet. Accordingly, I imagine a nearer approach to a perfect translation of Homer is possible in the couplet, well managed, than in the stanza, however well managed. But meanwhile Mr. Worsley,—applying the Spenserian stanza, that beautiful romantic measure, to the most romantic poem of the ancient world; making this stanza yield him, too (what it never yielded to Byron), its treasures of fluidity and sweet ease; above all, bringing to his task a truly poetical sense and skill,—has produced a version of the *Odyssey* much the most pleasing of those hitherto produced, and which is delightful to read.

For the public this may well be enough, nay, more than enough; but for the critic even this is not yet quite enough.

45. I speak of poetic genius as employing itself upon narrative or dramatic poetry,—poetry in which the poet has to go out of himself and to create. In lyrical poetry, in the direct expression of personal feeling, the most subtle genius may, under the momentary pressure of passion, express itself simply. Even here, however, the native tendency will generally be discernible.

46. 'And I have endured—the like whereof no soul upon the earth hath yet endured—to carry to my lips the hand of him who slew my child.'—*Iliad*, xxiv. 505.

47. 'Nay and thou too, old man, in times past wert, as we hear, happy.'—*Iliad*, xxiv. 543. In the original this line, for mingled pathos and dignity, is perhaps without a rival even in Homer.

48. 'For so have the gods spun our destiny to us wretched mortals,—that we should live in sorrow; but they themselves are without trouble.'—*Iliad*, xxiv. 525.

49. 'I wept not: so of stone grew I within:—*they* wept.'—*Hell*, xxxiii. 49. (Carlyle's Translation, slightly altered.)

Contributors

Suka Joshua, Department of English, Lady Doak College, Madurai, Tamil Nadu.

Mallikarjun Patil, Department of English, Gulbarga University, Karnataka.

R. Shanti, Selection Grade Lecturer, Department of English, C. Candasamy Naidu College for Women, Cuddalore, Tamil Nadu.

K. Krishnamurthy, Department of English, S.K.S.S. Arts College, Thruppomdal, Tanjore District, Tamil Nadu.

Umashankar Joshi, Former President, Sahitya Akademi, New Delhi.

Bijay Kumar Das, Reader English, Ravenshaw College, Cuttak, Orissa.

K. Ayappa Paniker, 111, Gandhinagar, Trivandrum, Kerala.

Harish Trivedi, Department of English, Delhi University, Delhi.

Basudeb Chakraborty, Reader in English, Kalyani University, West Bengal.

Anjana Tiwari, Department of English, Makhanlal Patrakarita University, Bhopal, Madhya Pradesh.

Rama Kundu, Professor of English, Burdwan University, West Bengal.

Sunil R. Sawant, Department of English, Shivaji University, Kolhapur, Maharashtra.

Mohit K. Ray, Formerly Professor of English, Burdwan University, West Bengal.

Prasenjit Chattopadhyay, Lecturer in English, Sree Chaitanya College of Commerce, West Bengal.

Subhas Sarkar, Formerly Professor of English, Rabindra Bharati University, West Bengal.

Niranjan Mohanty, Professor of English, Visva-Bharati, West Bengal.